A REALM OF DREAMS AND SHADOWS

AGGONID'S REALM

BOOK TWO

KATHY HAAN

This is a work of fiction. Names, characters, places, and incidents either are the product of the author's imagination or are used fictitiously. Any resemblance to actual persons, living or dead, events, or locales is entirely coincidental.

Copyright © 2024 by Kathy Haan

All rights reserved.

No part of this book may be reproduced in any form or by any electronic or mechanical means, including information storage and retrieval systems, without written permission from the author, except for the use of brief quotations in a book review. For more information, email info@shopkathyhaan.com.

ISBN 978-1-960256-00-3 (eBook)

ISBN 978-1-960256-06-5 (paperback)

First edition January 2024

Book cover design by Leo Burk and Kathy Haan

Published by Thousand Lives Press, LLC

Edited by Fervent Ink

To Mrs. G., who told me it was really inappropriate to write about hamsters pooping on a map in my term paper sophomore year of high school.

If you thought pooping hamsters were inappropriate, I have terrible news.

INTRODUCTION

A Realm of Fire and Ash left off with Morte being forcibly taken from her Underworld mates by the Luna goddess and sent back to the fae realm of Bedlam. However, instead of regenerating in Bedlam Penitentiary, where her last memories place her, she finds herself in the underground sanctuary of Castanea.

She must now pick up the pieces of a fractured mind, where she has to navigate a reality that feels both familiar and disconcertingly altered.

BE ADVISED

This is a **dark fantasy romance** with elements that *will* upset some readers. Please read CW/TW at kathyhaan.com/triggers.

Also, to all my readers in the medical field, or even those who paid attention in science class:

This is a book with **magic**. I'm going to need you to suspend reality for a bit in this book, particularly in chapter fifty-two, where one of your favorite shadow daddies uses blood to lubricate for … *ahem* certain backdoor activities. I've taken excessive liberties with this story, because again, it's dark fantasy, and it's full of magic. I'm fully aware the viscosity is all wrong (but to its credit, it has higher viscosity than water), and it dries really fast. But our unhinged demon fae is really special. He's got an unlimited supply of it, it's magically slippery, fae cannot get diseased, and it's just what Morte needs when getting her guts rearranged by two of her mates at the same time.

In the words of my editor after reading that scene, who said:

That's … niche.

CHAPTER ONE

MORTE

As a phoenix who has risen from the ashes far more times than I can count, I'm used to the disorientation that comes with regenerating.

But regeneration has never felt like resurrection to me—until now, as I rise under the veiled moonlight of my beloved Castanea, my senses drowning in a grief I can't place and a homecoming that feels like a betrayal.

It takes a few moments to work out why. This isn't where I'm supposed to be.

Grief robs the breath from my lungs, and tears blur my vision. The base of my treehouse—once a haven, now rendered alien—stands veiled in nocturnal hues, with shadows stretching long and eerie, like ink spilling in water. A constellation of candles flickers beneath it, flames dancing like restless spirits in the dark. Letters and keepsakes form a makeshift shrine, while bouquets of flowers lean against the rough bark, like silent mourners in a vigil I'd never asked for.

I sit up, my fingers curling into the cool, damp earth beneath me, seeking grounding where there is none.

"Impossible," I whisper, my voice barely breaking the silence that hangs heavy as fog. Why am I regenerating in Castanea?

Every part of me, every fiber of my existence, should have coalesced back into form in the dank confines of Bedlam Penitentiary, alongside Wilder. That's how the relentless cycle of death and rebirth has always worked for us. We regenerate where we perished, from the ashes of our remains. Tens of thousands of times, that's been the unyielding law.

Wilder.

The ache in my heart twists into a knot at the thought of him, tethering me to the haunting memories of a love that defied the ravages of time. A love now bound by the unyielding bars of Bedlam Penitentiary. I remember the stolen moment, the unsuppressed grief, and the unsaid words that Wilder was about to say. Secrets he never got to share.

What was he going to tell me?

All the stolen moments converge, crashing over me in an overwhelming wave, leaving me breathless. A drowning soul without an anchor.

Why? Why didn't I wake up with Wilder?

The shrine at my feet stands as a silent, accusing witness to my unanswered questions. Trembling fingers reach for one of the candles. Its flame flickers, as if caught between a greeting and a farewell. My eyes catch a name imprinted on the wax-sealed letter beneath it.

Noct.

My friend, and second-in-command of The Great Company, has been a loyal pillar in my life.

I crack the seal and unfold the parchment, taking a moment to inhale the scent of aged paper and faint traces of wax. Under the erratic dance of candlelight, I begin to read.

I'll never understand why you've left this plane, Morte. Every day without you is just as worse as the last. Wherever you ended up, I hope you're finally happy and no longer grieving for whoever 'he' is.

Miss you, pretty girl.
If not in this lifetime, then the next.

My brows furrow, confusion piling atop my roiling emotions like layers of fog. I scan through the letters addressed to me from Ronin, Sabine, Vero, Freya, Arwen, Harmony, Rainbow, Quinn, and even Crucey; the unofficial leader of our people, the Tolden. Each message echoes Noct's baffling sentiment—each one a piece in a jigsaw puzzle that refuses to make a coherent picture. Then, like a sunbeam cutting through clouds, realization dawns on me.

Noah Tackwater, the hydra fae I'd been sent to the prison to contain, had ended our lives in Bedlam Penitentiary, and one of my squad must have found a way to retrieve my ashes from the chaos. Despite the spells in place in the prison to block sifting—our method of teleportation—they must've managed to bring me back here, to Castanea, before I regenerated. It's the only explanation for my awakening in this familiar place, far from the prison's wreckage where the out-of-control convict had slain both Wilder and me.

My squadron's little memorial prank would be funny, if I weren't so lost in my grief over not getting to see Wilder when I regenerated. Of course, my squad knows nothing of him. Not even Noct knows. They couldn't have known they were wrenching me away from the man I'd spent a lifetime trying to find my way back to. The man I wanted to keep, to love.

I choke on a sob.

For two centuries, night after night, the rocky sand outside the unforgiving walls of the penitentiary had become my unwilling bed, the stars my silent companions. Each evening I lay there, a grieving heart beating with a single purpose, to feel closer to him. It was the only thing that could ease the ache in my chest.

My existence turned into a relentless campaign. Every deed, every fight was orchestrated to find a way to get him out and right the wrongs of my past.

The day of reckoning had arrived with a bitter twist of fate, and for the first time in two hundred years he'd wrapped his arms around me, as my heart swelled with hope, only to have it mercilessly ripped away when we were killed.

Now, as I awaken in the subterranean land of the Tolden that I call home, the pressure of starting anew bears heavily upon me. The prison's blueprint is now in my office, and its nooks and crannies within my mind, yet the path to his freedom seems just as convoluted as before. Even after two centuries of my never-ending pursuit, Wilder remains behind bars.

The timeliness of their letters suggests my squadron had been planning this tribute prank for a while. It wouldn't be the first time we'd waxed poetic about our minutes-long departures from this plane until we regenerated naked, grumpy, and ready for a snack and a long nap.

An emptiness sits inside me, as if I've been hollowed out and left raw. The very thought of food is alien, and I doubt I could force a morsel down, even if I tried.

As I scramble to gather the envelopes and photographs, the earth beneath me gnashes at my knees, dragging me back into reality. Dirt clings under my nails, as stubborn as the confusion and grief that has taken root within my soul.

Why did they have to do this now? Of all missions they could've chosen to pull a prank afterwards, this is the only one that has ever mattered.

Another surge of emotion wells up within me, making it hard to breathe. I belong with Wilder. Not here.

I tear my eyes away from the flickering candle, letting it dim, as if it's a fragment of a dream too agonizing to hold onto. I lift my gaze to the arboreal lattice above me—the bridges that interconnect the homes built within the canopy. The world is eerily silent, devoid of the usual nocturnal chatter that fills the spaces between trees and dwellings. As though the very cavern around me holds its breath.

The silence of the late hour wraps around me, but inside, the hurt is more intense than ever. For hundreds of years, I've carried the ache of Wilder's absence, a constant companion I'd accepted as part of my existence. But now, after our fleeting reunion, that ache has morphed into an excruciating, all-consuming agony. As I'd clung to him, the years of yearning had condensed into a single moment, heightening the loss to an unbearable degree.

And there's something more. A heaviness in my soul that I can't identify, an elusive grief that goes beyond the agony of our separation. It's as if a vital piece of my own self is missing, a piece that would explain this new level of anguish.

That's when I notice the soft, whispering breeze that stirs the foliage above me. It carries the faint, distant echo of the waterfall—a sound that once lured me to slumber in more innocent days. Tonight, however, the rushing water performs a dirge, a lamentation for a life that's fallen through the chasms of both time and place.

Under the subdued glow of the fae flies dancing above me, I'm caught in a tangle of emotional and cosmic complexity. It's a cruel joke, how expansive the universe feels when personal worlds collapse.

After turning toward my treehouse, I approach the old wooden rungs nailed to the tree trunk—each a scar in the wood, marking years of ascent and descent. I grasp the first rung, and the newly regenerated skin of my fingers is immediately sensitive to every splinter and groove. The night air brushes against my naked body, a tactile reminder that, despite everything, I'm alive. Each step up is a miniature battle. My muscles, also fresh from regeneration, feel both hardy and eerily unfamiliar.

Finally reaching the platform, I pause. My hand hovers, almost instinctively, over the door; its texture a blend of the familiar and the newly strange. It's like I'm meeting an old friend who has changed in ways I can't quite put my finger on.

Just hours ago, though it feels like a lifetime, I'd finally achieved what I'd spent two centuries yearning for: being in Wilder's arms. And now, I'm left hollow, condemned to restart a cycle that seems both inescapable and cruel.

The door before me creaks as I open it, as if unaccustomed to movement despite my having passed through it earlier today.

Odd.

This morning, I'd burst forth from this very threshold, my mind racing ahead of my body, fueled by the possibility of seeing him again. Desperate for it. We'd finally been assigned a mission at Bedlam Penitentiary, where my best friend had been wrongly imprisoned—for a crime that I'd committed.

Murder of children.

Of course, I hadn't meant to. They'd disguised themselves with a glamor. I thought I'd been fighting against grown fae.

But still.

To kill one child is unforgivable. Not when our birth rates had been near non-existent. To kill several? Not even Aggonid, the fae devil himself, could find a punishment wicked enough for the likes of a monster like me. I shudder at the thought of whatever retribution he'd have to conjure fitting enough for my crimes.

A clock hangs on the wall, its hands frozen in time, and I feel a ripple of annoyance. I never thought the runic timepiece, its gears powered by a subtle enchantment, would fail. "Must be out of energy," I mumble to myself, making a mental note to recharge it later. A quick glance out the window offers a clue to the late hour. Fae flies are out, their luminescence painting whimsical streaks amidst the canopy of trees, like constellations brought down to below The Wastelands that make up the western part of Convectus, where Castanea lies hidden from the rest of the realm.

I need rest, that much is clear. Even as I think it, the statement feels like an understatement. My soul is not just weary; it feels scraped clean, and every step toward my bed is an arduous journey. Yet, as I pull a thin chain near the headboard, activating a cleaning charm that freshens the sheets and pillows, I can't ignore the sharp jab of loneliness that comes with it. Another night in a bed too big for one, with sheets that will never know the warmth of the one I've lost.

I should take a proper shower, but I can't muster the energy. Depression has always snaked its way into my mind over the years without him, and tonight is no different. I'll allow myself to grieve tonight, and tomorrow, I'll map out a new plan.

I move to my dresser and pull out a set of silken pajamas. They're soft to the touch yet putting them on feels like a series of small betrayals, each motion a glaring confirmation of my solitude. With Wilder, I wouldn't have needed these—his arms would have been warmth enough. The thought lingers, unwanted, as I crawl into bed.

Though the cleaning charm has dispelled the physical remnants of time's passage, it's done nothing for the temporal dissonance in my heart. In a world that's moved on, I lie in bed, a timeless anomaly in my own life story. The clock may be broken, but the irony isn't lost on me; for someone seemingly out of sync with the passage of time, every second without him feels intolerably long.

I draw the covers tight around me, their false comfort a poor substitute for what I truly desire. As my eyes grow heavy, my last conscious thought is a painful acknowledgment of the incongruity between body and spirit. Though physically regenerated, my soul carries a weariness that no charm or spell can cleanse.

If our souls carry the scars of our losses, what kind of damaged, patchwork tapestry is mine?

CHAPTER TWO

WILDER

Bedlam Penitentiary

The rhythmic dripping of water in my secluded cell is disrupted by approaching footsteps. Unusual in their purposeful stride, echoing through the mixed stone and metal corridors of Bedlam Penitentiary's basement level. I stand, my curiosity piqued, as the footsteps halt outside my cell.

I set my flimsy steel supper tray on the bed and grab the rest of my sandwich in case they're moving me. They've done it half a dozen times over the years. There's no other reason I can think of that they'd come to my room outside of the standard meal schedule and exercise rotation.

Unless being without my anchor has caused the passage of time to warp even further. How long has it been since they came by? After glancing at the food in my hand, I take a bite of the pale mystery meat, trying to discern if it's fresh, or if I've had it in my cell for a while.

After all, being without our anchor, the merfae's equivalent to a soul bonded mate, causes us to go mad.

Before I can decide how long the food has been in the room, the slide of the magical lock sounds on my door. As it creaks open, I do a double-take at the person who fills it, causing the half-eaten sandwich to tumble out of my hand. I blink several times, brows furrowing. Am I seeing things?

I've officially lost it.

High King Finian Drake is a figure of ethereal presence, whose power can be felt more than seen as it spills into the cell. His ashy-blond hair frames a face marked by fae nobility. Mating bond tattoos line his exposed skin, and those eyes, luminous and piercing as the first thaw of winter, survey the cell with a measured gaze. The emblem of the moon on his uniform, a symbol of his connection to the lunar goddess, catches my cell's scant light, shimmering softly.

"Wilder Ripple." He greets me with a nod, a formality that belies the oddity of his visit.

Gods, he is really here.

"Y-your Majesty," I manage, stark shock lacing every syllable. His solitary presence, un-flanked by the royal guard, speaks volumes of his untouchable status. To challenge him is to defy the source of our magic—his mother, the lunar goddess herself. The revered High King, in my dingy cell, is a paradigm too discordant to grasp.

What in the hell is he doing *here*?

He steps forward, extending his hand to reveal a sealed envelope. "This is for you." His tone is neutral yet laden with significance.

Taking the envelope, I feel its weight, disproportionate to its physical heft. My fingers trace over the seal, recognizing the familiar script even before I see its contents.

This is her handwriting.

A flood of emotions, tightly reined in over the years of my imprisonment, threatens to surface.

"Morte," I breathe, my heart seizing at the thought of her reaching out. It must be urgent, or she's in trouble.

High King Finian gives a brief dip of his chin, his features clear to my senses despite the shrouding darkness. "She requested that I deliver this personally."

The importance of his words isn't lost on me. Morte's message, entrusted to the High King himself, must hold weight, perhaps a clue to her life beyond the walls of my prison.

"I appreciate you bringing this," I say, the envelope still unopened in my hands. The urge to break the seal and read her words is overwhelming, yet I restrain myself, aware of Finian's piercing gaze.

He observes me for a moment longer before speaking. "I must leave you now. But know that her message was important enough to warrant my personal attention."

I nod, understanding the subtext of his words.

The door closes behind the High King with a definitive click, and I'm left alone with the sealed envelope. The solitude of my cell feels more pronounced in the wake of his departure.

Turning the envelope over in my trembling hands, I hesitate. Morte's message, whatever it contains, will either break me or make me. Inmates don't get letters here. We don't even get visitors, unless you're mated, and even then, mates only get forty-two hours a month. Just two short overnights.

Gods, please let her be okay. I couldn't survive it otherwise.

In the quiet of my cell, with the soft sound of water from my personal pond as the only witness, I break the seal. The letter unfolds in my hands, a tangible piece of Morte, carrying her essence into the boundaries of my imprisonment. Her gentle scent of the sea and the faintest hint of smoke wafts up from the page, and I close my eyes, breathing it in deeply before opening them again.

As I begin to read, her voice fills the spaces of my mind; each word a balm to the soul, a reminder of a bond that time and circumstance have failed to break.

Because it can't be broken.

Dearest Wilder,

Gods, do I miss you. My heart aches to be with you once more, yet I fear we don't get forever after all. I want you to know I didn't abandon you, and if it's in my power, I'll do everything I can to make it back to you.

After I died, the devil reaped my soul, dragging me down into the abyss that is the Underworld. Claimed at last.

All the air whooshes from my lungs and I stumble over to the bed, collapsing onto the unforgiving stone as I re-read those two lines. Aggonid's Realm? She's in *hell*?

I'm here, but I'm not alone. I've made some odd acquaintances, one of which put some kind of spell on me so I can't feel the heat. This makes being here less miserable. Silver linings and all that.

One of the demons explained how my soul works. I had a tether in Bedlam that kept me coming back. Until I didn't.

At night, I lie awake wondering ... maybe that tether is you. If it is, my dying makes sense. I watched the light bleed out of your eyes; a death so much worse than my own. The agony of it stole my breath away and crippled my spirit.

My soul had nothing more to live for in that moment, so I assume I died when my heart broke. This is all speculation, but if it's true, I have some measure of comfort knowing I gave you a feather. I only wish I'd been able to leave you with more before I left.

I rise from the bed, pacing the short distance in front of my bed, my bare feet used to the constant chill down here. A fae's feather holds the power to defy death itself, to revive the fallen. This was her gift to me, a safeguard against an untimely end. But now that feather is nothing more than ash in the wind; its magic used up in restoring me to life after we both fell. And now, the gift feels more like a burden because I'm here, and she's not.

As a merfae, my own wings, though strong and sure in the aquatic realm, lack this miraculous ability to revive someone. With Morte gone, what purpose does my own continued existence serve? The prospect of enduring an eternity without her is more daunting than any death could be.

> *Someday, I'll see you again. Whether in Bedlam, or in the afterlife, I don't know. While the penitentiary kept me from you, I have a confession to make. Each night, I'd portal to the shores of Penn Island just so I could feel close to you. It eased the ache in my chest knowing you weren't far, even if I couldn't see you.*
>
> *I only wish I could do that now.*
>
> *There's an event coming up in the Underworld called the Forsaken Hunt. If I win, I get a favor from Aggonid. I've got a plan that'll hopefully bring me home. And just maybe we can be together again. Now that I know the security protocol at the prison, I think I'll be able to get in without being under their watch.*
>
> *We'll run away together.*
>
> *Whether we go to Earth, Romarie, or some other realm, wherever I'm with you, I'm home.*
>
> *Missing you like crazy,*
> *Morte*

The letter quivers in my grasp, the inked words of Morte's handwriting blurring as my vision swims with tears. Each sentence is a punch to the gut, stirring a storm of emotions inside me. I lean heavily against the frigid stone wall of my cell, the reality of her words sinking in.

Morte in the Underworld. The thought alone is a blade twisting in my heart. She speaks of demons, of spells, and of an unbearable heat she's shielded from, yet her courage burns fiercely through the page. The idea of her enduring such a hellish realm but still fighting to offer me peace is both humbling and horrifying.

Her nightly visits to Penn Island, just outside the gates of my confinement yet worlds apart, wrenches a sob from my throat. The notion of her, alone with only the sea and her thoughts of me, is a torment I can scarcely bear. How many nights did I stare at the same stars, unaware she was just a whisper away?

Had it been her presence that made my secret so bearable until recently?

I slide down the wall, letter clutched to my chest, as grief engulfs me. The Forsaken Hunt, her audacious plan to win a favor from Aggonid—the danger she's willing to face for us is terrifying. She has always been fierce, but the risk and uncertainty of it all is overwhelming.

I press the letter to my lips, closing my eyes, imagining her voice speaking the words. The intimacy of her confession is a balm and a curse. The pain of knowing our severed tether might have caused her death crushes me.

The mention of the phoenix feather, the one that allowed me to come back to life, sends a pang of guilt through me. She gave me a part of herself, an immortal lifeline, but at what cost? The thought that her death might be tied to our bond, to the despair of losing each other, is a burden too heavy to bear.

As I drag myself across the rough stone, the shackle of my magic suppressant cuff grates with a cold, metallic hiss against the ground. Each movement is a labor, drawing me nearer to the pond's edge. My tears, bitter with the sting of loss, fall and dissipate into the pond's serene coolness. Kneeling at its brink, I dip my hands into the water, seeking a trace of the comfort it once offered. The liquid's once-embracing chill now bites at my skin, an alien sensation, as if the very essence of my aquatic home rejects me. Ripples echo outward, distorting my reflection—a fractured image of the merfae I am. This pool, a mere fragment of the vast ocean, mocks me with its tranquility, widening the chasm between my world and me.

I envision her, my Morte, strong and brave, fighting demons and bargaining with devils. The courage in her words strengthens my own. I must find a way back to her, to the future we were promised, but for now all I can do is picture her face on that fateful day, 2000 years ago, and it's like I'm right back there with her.

I watch the excited uncertainty dance in Morte's blue-green eyes as the magnificence of the ocean opens up before us. Her pale yellow dress clings to her strong curves, and it's taking everything in me not to linger too long at the braid resting against her chest. Her soft hand trembles in mine, this fierce phoenix fae who has never known a world beyond the secretive bounds of Castanea's earthen embrace.

"Trust me," I murmur, guiding her into the lapping waves at the shore's edge. Her measured steps are hesitant, so different from the boldness I've come to admire. She's seen waterfalls, rivers, and lakes, but the ocean is a different beast, a living entity stretching beyond horizons she's never dared to imagine. I can hear its call roaring in her veins.

She's used to soaring in caverns, a bird with clipped wings.

I'm honored I get to be the one to show her the beauty of the place I call home.

As the water encases our ankles, I feel her pulse quicken, a rapid drumbeat against my skin.

"It's so big," she breathes as the current pushes her into me.

My hands quickly find her waist, positioning her in front of me so I can support her.

Unable to resist the temptation, I press my lips against her ear, my warm breath causing goosebumps to dance across her skin. "You haven't even laid eyes on it yet," I tease, the double entendre thick in my meaning.

Her laughter floats on the salty breeze, a sound that brings life to the air around us. She blushes, her cheeks turning a shade of pink that rivals the sunset reflecting off the water's surface.

Morte has always been quick-witted, but in moments like this, she becomes vulnerable, fumbling with her words and emotions. It's in these moments that I realize just how deeply I've fallen for her.

"Just hold on to me," I assure her, and with a nod, she tightens her grip. We wade deeper, and I watch a myriad of emotions flicker across her face—awe, fear, wonder. When the water caresses her chest, she looks at me, and I lean in encouragingly. "Ready?"

With a hesitant nod, she agrees, and together we dive. Under the water, her initial tension melts away as we glide through my domain. I show her the dance of light beneath the surface, the way it fractures into a kaleidoscope of blues and greens as a school of fish dances in its beams. Her eyes widen, and I feel her wonder echoing my own.

We emerge, and she laughs as she wipes her wet hair out of her face, the sound mingling with the symphony of the sea. "It's beautiful," she gasps, and there's a lightness in her I've never seen. In this infinite watery world, I see her—truly see her—for the first time.

All of time and space condenses into this single moment, and she's blissfully unaware of just how magnificent I find her. She wades in the water, gentle swells lapping around her chin as she grins up at me.

It compresses my lungs.

Surrounded by the embrace of the ocean, it feels like we're the only two beings in existence. The setting sun paints a halo of gold around her as it catches the crimson in her hair, and in this moment, she's not just Morte of the Tolden; she's the entirety of life's beauty in a single form.

Nothing in this realm or the next could stop me as I lean in, drawn by a force more compelling than the ocean's pull. Our lips meet, a gentle collision that sends ripples through my core. It's a kiss that seals promises whispered in the mind, a kiss that tastes of salt and spun sugar, of beginnings and becoming.

Her lips are a soft fire against the coolness of the sea, and when we part, it's with the knowledge that something has shifted. We're no longer just friends who've shared mischievous escapades; we're two souls that have tasted the depth of the ocean and of each other.

She smiles, a hint of newfound mischief in her gaze. "Wilder," she says, as though my name were a new discovery on her lips. "I never knew..."

Her words trail off, but I understand. She never knew the world could be this vast, or feelings this deep. And as we head back to the shore, hand in hand, I know I've given her more than just a glimpse of my world—I've shared with her a piece of my soul.

That had been the first day I kissed her, and even now, in the gloom of my cell 2000 years later, I still manage a weak smile. It was one of the happiest in my existence, knowing someone like her could want to be with someone like me. A fae who belongs in the sky, and a merfae fated to the sea.

As I clutch the letter, a new tenacity settles over me. I will not let her fight alone. I'll find a way out of this abyss, back to her side. Our bond, our love, is stronger than any prison, any Underworld. We belong together, and I will move the realms to make it so.

In the basement of Bedlam's most notorious penitentiary housing its most dangerous inmates, with Morte's words echoing in my heart, I vow to reunite with her. Our story isn't over; it's just beginning.

I will find a way back to you, Morte. Wait for me.

CHAPTER THREE

MORTE

The room dims and my thoughts drift away, succumbing to a tide of sleep. Without warning, I find myself standing in a clearing where the sun never quite rises or sets. It's the in-between of light and shadow, a place that logic tells me doesn't exist, but here I am. Wilder steps out from the trees, his image hazy like a figure at the edge of my vision, yet so vividly him.

The howling wind whips through his long, dark hair, causing it to dance wildly around his face. The flickering light from a nearby bonfire carves a glow on his sharp features, emphasizing the hints of grey in his piercing blue-green eyes. He has always been devastatingly handsome, but tonight he looks almost otherworldly as he stands with a black silk bed sheet tied around his waist.

He grins as he saunters towards me, and it's like the sun breaking through clouds, warming me from the inside out. I take a step forward, my heart pounding a rhythm for my feet to follow. There's no question of how or why, no sense of control—this is a dream, my mind's own creation, but it feels as real as anything I've ever wanted. Wilder reaches for me, and as our hands touch, the dream promises more, a gentle descent into the passion that's always simmered between us.

He pulls me against him, and my body melts as he runs his hands down my back. I gasp, feeling the heat from his touch and the coolness of the air around us. His lips find mine, a fiery brand that doesn't burn but feels like home. My body responds, a wave of longing crashing into the shore of desire. It's been too long since we've shared this, and the feeling is overwhelming.

Our tongues dance together, tasting each other's lips. The dream seems to amplify our senses, making everything feel more intense, more vivid. The taste of him is addictive. In this twilight world where nothing makes sense, our connection feels real once more.

His teeth graze my bottom lip gently, drawing blood that disappears almost as soon as it appears. It's a loss I feel acutely, yearning for just one drop to remain to prove he's here with me. Yet despite my grief and hunger for him, I savor every moment of this fantasy—our embrace fueling something deep within me that refuses to die.

We make our way to the soft green grass beneath us, and he spreads me before him. Where my clothes went, I don't know, nor do I care. Maybe I never had any.

The intricate wave tattoo across his chiseled torso surges and dips with each movement of his defined abs, inviting me to trace my nails along its curves. The muscles beneath my fingers ripple and tense as I explore the contours of his body, tracing every line with a reverence reserved for sacred art. His skin is warm beneath my touch, radiating a magnetism that draws me closer to him.

"I love this tattoo," I whisper.

His palm trails a fire down my side, his calloused hand causing a delicious contrast against the softness of my skin. "I love you under me," he groans. Eyes darkening with desire, he smirks down at me, the canines of his fae form peeking between his lips. With a quick, deft movement, he rolls me over onto my stomach and kneels behind me.

"Are you ready?" His panting voice is gravelly in the silence, roughened by the same arousal that's coursing through my own veins.

What he's asking, I don't know. But I want whatever he's offering.

I push back against him to answer, anticipation making every nerve ending in my body sing. The cool grass tickles my exposed belly as I brace myself, pressing my chest to the ground. His strong hands grip my hips, pulling me closer until I can feel the hardness of his arousal pressing against me. "Yes," I whisper, enhancing the invitation inherent in our tangled bodies.

The forest is filled with my panting breaths as I arch against him, begging to be filled. A steady breeze dances upon my exposed skin, carrying with it his scent; salty seas and fresh-picked mint. His fingers whisper against my flesh as they skillfully entwine the silk bedsheet, binding my wrists together in front of me before connecting them to my spread thighs.

I'm trussed up, legs wide and unable to move as the rough texture of his hands presses against my exposed flesh.

"Perfect," he whispers.

Immobilized and vulnerable, I still feel safe, always safe with him.

I inhale as his warm breath fans across my ass, and I let out a laugh as his fangs graze my cheeks. He nibbles on my skin lightly, causing goosebumps to rise on my flesh, and an involuntary shiver works its way through my body.

"You're mine," he growls, the words hot against my sensitive skin. "You've always been mine."

With every fiber of my being, I breathe, "Always," but the words are cut short by a sudden jolt as he heaves me up and over his shoulder. My view bounces and sways with each powerful stride he takes towards the edge of the looming forest and away from the fire.

With a confident flick of his wrist, he expertly lassos the bedsheet over a sturdy tree branch above us. Using it as a makeshift swing, he hoists me up and crouches in front of me, a mischievous smile playing on his lips. Strands of his dark hair escape their tie and fall into his eyes, making them look even more alluring. My fingers itch to reach out and brush the strands away, revealing his captivating ocean eyes.

His lips press to mine, but before I can deepen it, he murmurs, "Do you remember what it feels like?"

My brain is so lust raddled I can hardly form a coherent thought. It takes a moment for his words to catch up. "What *what* feels like?"

"Being worked over by more than one person."

A dark chuckle sounds from beside him, but before my eyesight can track who laughed, Wilder spins me so I'm facing away. He trails kisses along my shoulder blade, breath hot along my nape before his warmth recedes and I feel his hands caressing over my hips.

As I hover in the air, my gaze fixated on the swaying blades of grass below, I catch sight of not just two sets of feet, but several. My curiosity's piqued. Who are the figures behind me and why are they here during such an intimate time? Who could they be? My pulse quickens with uncertainty and apprehension as I continue to observe from my suspended position.

Slowly, Wilder kneels behind me and slides his fingers along my wetness, teasing and probing until I bite back a moan. The heat of his touch ignites a fire between my thighs, anticipating his presence even with others watching. I can see the muscles in his legs flex as he rises, his hands gently guiding me back into position.

I'm watching him upside down, his body glistening with sweat as his hand moves slowly, stroking his length as my eyes greedily track his every movement. He teases me first, running the tip of himself along my entrance, slick and pearly in the light-robbed dusk.

I squirm impatiently, drawing a chuckle from his throat that vibrates through me. With one swift thrust, he fills me completely, claiming my body in a way that robs the air from my lungs.

"She looks so beautiful being split in two." Someone chuckles.

I startle, stretching my neck to look behind me, my muscles straining with the effort. But no matter how far I twist and contort, I can't quite catch a glimpse of their faces. Their voice is so familiar. The shadows cling to their legs like tendrils, stretching out over the grass and forming dark puddles on the ground.

There is no fear, only a feeling of absolute rightness. That I belong here. That *they* belong here.

Another voice joins in, filled with lust and desire. "She'd look even better with my cock in her mouth."

They groan. A chorus of agreement follows, goading and urging them forward.

My mouth opens to ask questions, to say something, but Wilder's pace quickens, and my thoughts scatter to the wind.

A small shadow leaves the ground, moving with a serpentine-like grace as it rises to meet me before slithering over my eyes, obscuring my vision. I see the faint outline of a figure standing in front of me, their shape blurred and distorted. Their fingers cup my jaw, their thumb tracing a teasing path over my lips.

My tongue darts out to meet it, and I capture the digit, hollowing out my cheeks as I suck.

"Open that pretty little mouth," they purr, and I comply. I obey because there isn't a bone in my body that could deny their request.

Something smooth breaches my lips, gliding down my tongue. I groan at the intrusion, the sweet and salty taste just as familiar as their voice, but I can't place it.

As Wilder's pace quickens, he reaches around and dips his fingers into my eager heat. His skilled fingers find the sweet nub at its apex and begin to coax it gently but insistently, matching each thrust with precise strokes designed to drive me over the edge.

Reduced to a primal state, all I can do is moan around the cock in my mouth, losing myself to the overwhelming sensations coursing through my body. With Wilder still behind me, another person in front of me, and a third joining in, their tongue combines with Wilder's hands on my clit.

Each roll of his fingers, each thrust on either end of me, each flick of the tongue brings me closer to the edge. My body trembles and arches, the shadows of my lovers clinging to my skin as I detonate.

A powerful wave of release surges through every nerve ending, spreading like wildfire throughout my body. I'm overcome with the desire to hold on, to grasp onto something or someone, but all I can do is let out a guttural moan around the hard length in my mouth.

"That's our girl," Wilder groans.

My cries resonate through our little slice of twilight forest as I give in to the ecstasy coursing through me. They follow my lead, their low growls a complement to my high-pitched climax, and I swallow greedily.

As the aftershocks of our lovemaking subside, a new voice speaks up. "I believe it's my turn now."

A deep chuckle answers, and it's another familiar-but-new voice I can't place. "After you've all had your fun, she's mine. I need to feed."

CHAPTER FOUR

MORTE

Dawn breaks in Castanea not with the rise of a sun, but with a subtle shift in the luminescence of the cavernous sky above. Crystals embedded in the ceiling of this subterranean sanctuary begin to pulse, their glow metamorphosing from the soft blues and purples of night into the golden hues of day. They mimic the sun so convincingly that even the fauna respond. Birds nestled in the boughs of towering trees awaken to herald the morning with their songs.

I open my eyes, half-expecting to see the steel bars and concrete walls of Bedlam Penitentiary. Instead, my gaze meets the timeworn trappings of my treehouse—still inexplicably coated in a patina of neglect that confuses and unsettles me. Last night's bewilderment resurfaces, tangling itself with fresh waves of grief and yearning for Wilder.

I'm drenched in sweat, and there's a delicious, dull throb between my thighs. Wilder has starred in every one of my elicit dreams for thousands of years, but this is the first time any other has played a starring role alongside him, let alone multiple men.

Their faces were obscured, and while I vaguely recognized voices, even now I'm awake I can't place any of them. The thought of being shared by anyone other than the man I've pined for almost my entire life is a little unsettling. Not because it feels wrong, but because they feel so *right*.

That might be the most troubling bit of it all. Who the hell are they?

Flopping onto my back, I stretch, my muscles feeling thoroughly used up. It's as though I haven't slept on this same mattress night-after-night for at least a decade now. Maybe it's time to get a new one.

I quickly shut that thought down, remembering Wilder's stone bed in his cell. The very stone bed I should've been sleeping on for two hundred years.

I hope when my team collected my remains from Wilder's cell that they didn't make the connection I have with him.

Rubbing sleep from my eyes, I sit up and swing my legs over the edge of the bed. It takes a monumental effort, as if my very soul has grown heavy, burdened by sorrow and questions left unanswered. Still, I rise, threading my way through the haze of emotions that clings to me like cobwebs.

As I cross to the window, I again notice the clock on the wall. It remains frozen in time, but I'd just reset it last week. It's powered by enchanted crystals that just need topping up every couple of years. A glance outside confirms it's morning, though; the fae flies have retreated, and now only the dappled glow of the ceiling crystals lights the foliage. People make their way across the footbridges to get wherever they're headed to for the day. Now that the Tolden are no longer kept secret from the rest of Bedlam, some have moved out and started whole new lives on the surface, while others, like me, have found a way to have both.

I wonder if the royal guard will have us on cleanup duty at the penitentiary today. It's unlikely, but one can hope. Who even knows whether my team caught the hydra and what came of it. We aren't usually privy to those details.

Our jobs are always to get in, get the job done, then get out.

Dressed in my usual training attire, I exit my treehouse. The canopy walkways of Castanea stretch out like veins, connecting home

A REALM OF DREAMS AND SHADOWS

to home, heart to heart. I navigate these familiar paths, heading toward the central command, my thoughts a jumble of Wilder's last moments, the feel of his skin against mine, who the hell he dream-shared me with, and the disorienting feeling niggling at my soul. Each footstep echoes with memories and unsettled questions, and my heart tightens with each beat.

Yesterday, I saw many inmates at the penitentiary, heard their jeers, their shouts. None match the voices in my dream. So it's not my subconscious cobbling together remnants of an errant memory.

Or is it? I shake my head at that thought. For all I know, it could've been four more Wilders, each with a distinctive voice. I chuckle to myself, not minding that idea one bit.

As the ornately carved doors swing open, I step into the training room—a vast hall that spans nearly the length of a Spar Games field, built deep into the bedrock. The high ceilings arch above, usually echoing with the clash of swords and the grunts of exertion. But now, a hush pervades the space, as profound and enveloping as the depths of the sea.

My grin falls.

Seven faces that should bear smiles or at least casual neutrality are masks of open shock, eyes widened in disbelief, mouths agape. It's as if they're looking at a ghost, and in that unnerving stillness, I wonder if that's exactly what I've become.

"How come everyone's here so early?" I try to jest, my voice echoing in the room unnaturally loud against the heavy quiet, though my tone lacks its usual lightness. I'm always the first one here. Work doesn't officially start for another hour. I glance down, checking to make sure I don't have any dirt on me. "Did I miss a memo?"

Or worse, did we fail our mission at the penitentiary? A nervous tremble makes its way through me, but then I remember their prank.

"Ha, ha. So funny, carry on," I jest, my legs eating up the distance to the conference table along the far cavern wall where they're all seated.

But even as the words escape my lips, I'm hit by the uneasy realization that this silence, these reactions, go far beyond a mere squad prank. This is something else, something that rattles me to my core and leaves me grappling for understanding.

And in the eyes of those who are closest to me, I see it—disbelief, anger, and underneath it all, a flicker of pain, as if my very appearance twists a knife in old wounds.

Noct's eyes, usually bright and piercing, darken to an impenetrable silver. The dimples that normally puncture her cheeks are nowhere to be seen, and her maroon hair has seen better days. Something went terribly wrong yesterday.

Then, with startling clarity, it hits me.

She knows. They *all* know.

"This isn't funny." Her voice starts as a whisper but crescendos into a shriek. She jumps to her feet where she'd been sitting in my seat at the head of the long, map-strewn table. She crosses over to me, shoving me.

I stumble backwards, confusion and a hint of real fear gripping my insides.

"You think this is a joke? Tricking us?" With a flick of her wrist, she casts a containment spell that seals the room, preventing anyone from leaving—or entering. Her next gesture has me bound in magical restraints, lifting me off the floor.

"Morte is dead! We mourned her!" Noct screams, her voice echoing around the chamber, bouncing off the walls as if trying to find a way to escape the agony that fills it. "And you dare to pretend to be her in some sick parlor trick? I'll kill you for this. Now, who. the. fuck. are. you?" She punctuates each word, fury and misery holding equal measure in the cadence of her shrieks.

Around her, the faces of my squad, my family, are twisted masks of grief and outrage. Sabine's mossy green eyes glisten with tears she refuses to shed, her hands glowing with the onset of a spell she's dangerously close to casting. Vero, usually so fleet and carefree, looks like she's been punched in the gut, her face pale and her stance staggered. Freya, radiant Freya, looks as if she's carrying the weight of the world, her eyes meeting mine with a wounded intensity.

Arwen and Harmony, usually the calmest among us, are almost unrecognizable. Arwen's lips are pulled back in a snarl, her brilliant orange wings flaring out defensively. Harmony's stormy gray eyes, always so gentle, are dark clouds of wrath. Her aura, usually soothing, now feels like a brewing nightmare. And Bow, colorful, effervescent Bow, is a subdued palette, her multicolored locks seemingly drained of their vibrancy.

Confusion is my only companion right now as thoughts race through my head, trying to piece together what the hell is going on. They *don't* know. So what the fuck is this all about?

The room is a tinderbox, the air thick with the combustible mix of anguish and rage, ready to ignite at any moment.

"Who are you, and why are you doing this?" Noct demands, her voice cracking, her eyes shimmering with tears. Her hand starts to glow, and the space around her pulses with the beginnings of a lethal spell. One that'll hurt a whole hell of a lot if cast on me. "A Visage Veil isn't just illegal, it's unforgivable!"

My eyes widen at her accusation. Visage Veil—a complex charm designed to replicate another's appearance, down to the finest detail—is a dangerous weapon in the wrong hands. In this context, it's unbelievably cruel, mocking a camaraderie and trust that took years to build.

"This isn't funny anymore, guys," I blurt out, my own voice tinged with bewilderment. "You've had your fun, enough!"

Never in all my years have they ever played a prank as evil as this one. They're taking things way too far.

"Enough?" Noct's voice is a dangerous whisper. "You have no idea what 'enough' is." The glow intensifies around her hand, poised to release a spell that would certainly end me and cause my regeneration to be just as equally as painful.

What the fuck is going on?

"In the Waning Woods, during our mission to reroute the Caspari," I shout, locking eyes with her. "You told me that the stars that night weren't just stars, they were the souls of fallen warriors, watching over us. You said you felt your mother's presence among them. No one else knows that. It's me, Noct, it's really me." My voice is high-pitched and tinny. Real fear courses through it.

The glow from Noct's hand falters, flickers, and then disappears. She stares at me, her eyes searching my face, her expression shifting from grief-tinged rage to disbelief to a glimmer of burgeoning hope.

"Do you think a mere imposter could know that?" I press.

She sways on her feet, as if grappling with the very fabric of reality. For a moment, silence hangs heavy in the room, everyone holding their breath. Finally, her eyes meet mine, and she whispers, "Morte?"

"It's me," I insist, feeling a sudden surge of urgency. "Why is everyone acting like I'm some sort of ghost? Can someone please tell me what the everloving fuck is going on?"

The room remains taut with tension, but it's as if my words have opened a fissure, allowing a stream of complex emotions—relief, sorrow, and lingering doubt—to flood through. And as I look around at the faces of those who are my closest companions, I start to grasp the depth of the chasm that has opened up between us—a chasm I don't yet understand.

Noct's eyes meet mine again, doubt and hope tangling in her gaze. She flicks her wrist, and the magical restraints around me dissolve, letting my feet touch the floor. I almost stagger, my legs quivering, burdened by the gravity of the moment.

"So, no one is going to fill me in?" My voice is steadier than I feel, edged with a rising impatience and desperate need for clarity. I've never pulled rank on them before, but in this moment, I deserve answers.

Arwen opens her mouth as if to speak, hesitates, and closes it again, unable to find the words. It's Freya who finally steps forward, her posture one of resigned acceptance.

"You were gone, Morte. Not missing, not taken. Gone." Her timbre is soft but unwavering, as though she's delivering a verdict. "We held a memorial. We said our goodbyes. We scattered your ashes in the Whispering Glade."

Ashes. Memorial. Their implications splinter through me, each word a death knell widening the chasm of lost time and altering memories. I open my mouth to speak but words escape me, replaced by a heavy, incomprehensible silence.

And then it strikes me. The most fundamental, chilling question. "How long?" I manage to force the words out, each syllable punctuated by my struggle to comprehend the reality that is taking form around me.

Vero, who had been standing near the wall, eyes wide and brimming with tears, steps forward. Her voice trembles as she speaks, imbuing the room with a finality that leaves no room for doubt.

"Two years."

The chamber seems to contract around me, those two words echoing in the close space like a coup de grâce. Two years—transforming the fissure into an abyss, an unfathomable void that engulfs not just time but also experiences, relationships, life itself. As I look at the faces around me, it's as if I'm seeing them through a veil of years, a distorted lens that turns even the most familiar into the barely recognizable.

"You don't remember where you've been for the last two years?" Noct breathes, pacing towards me, but I can barely register her words.

The enormity of it all settles on me, a weight too colossal to measure. Two years. Long enough for grief to turn into acceptance, for life to move forward, for the world to turn pages I can never read.

And as I stand there, encircled by faces marked with both the traces of years and the freshly kindled flame of hope, I can't help but wonder: how does one begin to bridge a gap that vast? Where do I even start? Where the fuck did I go?

And if I've been dead for two years, what of Wilder's fate?

CHAPTER FIVE

AZAZEL

I stand amidst the ebbing shadows of Aggonid and Caius' bedroom, a churning storm of betrayal and fury unleashed within me. Even in the Underworld, trust is a blade that cuts deep. Aggonid, the fae devil himself, god among the damned and sovereign of deceit, stands before me. His face is a canvas of devastation, the mask of an actor who has forgotten his lines.

The room, once a bastion of regal decorum, is now a chaos-strewn wasteland in the wake of the portal's fury. The marble floors, reflective and smooth, are marred by debris and the scatters of a violent gale. Velvet drapes, ripped from their holds, lie crumpled and forlorn against the pillars, their heavy fabric twisted and soaked with the dust of the Underworld.

"What have you done?" My words come out laced with a venomous edge, a whisper threatening to become a storm. I can feel the surge of my power. Lightning crackles in my core, a primal call to the metals that dance at the edge of my will.

Gone is the pristine order of the bedchamber. The glass in the large window is still vibrating, a lingering tremor from the otherworldly squall caused by the gateway to the other side. The golden silk sheets, once meticulously draped across the grand bed, are now strewn about, and the luxurious pillows, once plump with down, are slashed open, their innards spilling out onto the floor.

The air, charged with the remnants of the portal's energy, crackles with unseen forces. It smells of ozone and carries the biting tang of displaced elements. Outside, the skies of Aggonid's realm are a roiling canvas. Winged beasts struggle against the tempest's residue, their cries a cacophonous symphony to the unrest below. The horizon, once a clear delineation of the Underworld's fiery brim, now smudges into the ashy air, the boundaries blurred.

I stride towards Aggonid. His red eyes are muted, like they've been snuffed out. The ruler of demons, despite his power, despite his might, seems lesser now. As though he's a god mourning his own divinity, but this is his doing.

His fault.

He raises a hand, not in defense but in defeat. "I didn't think it would happen," he begins, his voice a tremor shaking the foundations of our dark realm. "Morte wanted to go home. Back to Castanea. I tried to grant her that, hoping Luna would agree ... until I didn't. And by then it was too late."

A pact made at the behest of Morte before she mated us. Before she knew she loved us. A wish granted that none desired in the end. My heart, a blackened thing of shadows and sorrow, sinks. Aggonid's despair is a mirror of my own, a shared agony that does nothing to cool the searing heat of my wrath.

"I didn't know if Luna would agree. It had been months. By the time we mated, it was beyond my control," Aggonid continues, the bulk of eternity pressing down upon his words. "I didn't ... I didn't want her to go."

Caius and Emeric stand frozen, their faces etched with shell-shocked horror, yet I barely spare them a glance as they both crash to their knees as though choreographed. My focus is on the ruler of this Underworld, on the shattered bonds of what was meant to be an eternal union between us all and Morte.

"Weak." I spit the word out like a curse, because in hell, weakness is the greatest insult. My power is restless, the metal at my core pulsing with a life of its own, resonating with the truth of Aggonid's confession. "We have to get her back," I assert, my command a crash of thunder in the silence.

The shadows listen, and somewhere in the twisted reality of this place, I sense Morte's absence like a void that swallows light.

Morte rarely woke whenever she slept in my embrace, but those moments were the highlight of my miserable life. As she'd stirred for the first time, a dreamy warmth had spread through my body and I desperately wished that our circumstances were different, that I could prolong that feeling for just a little while longer. It was the first time I'd entertained the thought of taking a different path, and I wrench myself back to that moment, picturing every detail, despite knowing the pain it will cost me.

Dawn breaks with a reluctant murmur, splashing pale light that barely softens the darkness of the Underworld. I'm awake before Morte, the quiet of the morning a welcome reprieve from last night's chaos.

Her leg is slung over my hip; her face a perfect blend of sleep and peacefulness. In this moment, I feel like I'm holding the world in my arms, and I can't help but run my fingers through her hair, smoothing it back from her forehead.

Selfishly, I've enchanted her to sleep longer, to feel the press of her body against mine for another couple of hours. I've never had this. The softness of a female embrace. My mother was killed long before I could remember her, and I was raised with a cruel hand.

It's late morning by the time the enchantment wears off, and as Morte emerges from sleep, her crimson tresses, fiery even in the weak light, spills down her back in a wild tangle. Her blue-green eyes, smoldering with a resilience that's become as familiar to me as my own reflection, meet mine. There's a fight in her that even the Underworld hasn't managed to snuff out.

Resilience isn't born from the absence of scars; it's the light that burns defiantly, unextinguished, in the darkest of places.

"Morning," I offer, digging in my satchel as the side of her bed before I pass her one of the safer fruits I carry. "Eat up. We've got a busy day ahead."

She takes it, a sleepy smirk playing on her lips. "Planning on poisoning me with breakfast?"

The corner of my mouth twitches up in amusement. "Why would I kill you when I plan on feeding on you?"

She laughs, and the sound echoes against the metal walls I put up yesterday—a sound so rare in this realm that it feels like a victory. We eat in silence, but it's not uncomfortable. She has her head propped in her hand as she lays on her side, and I'm braced against the wall. The mutual understanding of the bond we're forming fills the room, unspoken. We're both of little words.

When she's finished, I stand and stretch out the stiffness from a night spent on the tiny, unforgiving cot. "Let's take a walk. You need to know what won't kill you out here."

She follows me out into the forest, the twisted trees standing sentinel around us. It's a strange sort of beauty here, one you must look closely to find. I point to a plant with a deep, maroon hue. "This one dulls pain," I explain. "Useful, but too much and you'll miss a century or two."

She grins. "Might be the best century I've ever had."

We walk further, and I show her a bush with glowing berries. "These are good for a quick burst of energy. But don't get greedy. Everything here has a price."

She plucks a berry and eats it without hesitation. It's an act of trust that doesn't go unnoticed. "You're brave," I say, half-admiring, half-wary. "Or foolish."

She locks eyes with me, her gaze intense and unflinching. "I trust you, Az."

It's a statement that should please me, but instead, a coil of unease tightens in my gut. "You shouldn't trust anyone here. Not even me."

But she just smiles, reaching up to trace a lazy circle around one of the few piercings that decorate my ear. Her touch is light, but it carves a path of warmth across my flesh. "Yet, here I am."

I capture her hand gently, lowering it from my face. "Then I'll do my best to be worthy of it."

And gods, do I wish I could be worthy of her. I don't know if she's ever going to forgive me when she learns what I've done. Who I am.

We resume our walk, the easy banter a thin veneer over the danger that lurks just out of sight. I'm teaching her how to survive in the Underworld, but with every word, every shared smile, I'm the one learning the most. She's teaching me about hope, about finding light in the darkness. And for a moment, I let myself believe that maybe, just maybe, there's a chance for something more than survival.

Yanking me mercilessly out of my reverie and back into the present, Aggonid nods, his eyes meeting mine, an inferno of agreement kindling in the depths of despair.

"I swear it," he decrees, and for the first time since this ordeal began, our purposes align with the sharp clarity of steel forged in fire. I never thought I'd see the day I'd align with this asshole.

We are denizens of the Underworld, but even among demons, there are ties that bind tighter than any chain—a mate's call, a heart's echo, a promise that not even gods can break without consequence.

The mood is a brewing thunderstorm. Charged and waiting to be unleashed. The walls themselves, wrought from obsidian and bones, seem to absorb the tension, as dark whispers slip into their cracks.

Aggonid, with his sharp tongue and commanding presence, stands as a broken god among us, his thousand-yard stare ringing hollow as he collapses onto his bed. It's a visage that chills the marrow, the usually fierce deity unraveled by unforeseen events. The depth of his gaze suggests a battlefield within, where he fights against the reality of his own making—a deal gone awry, a mate lost, and the control he so effortlessly wielded now slipping like sand through clenched fingers.

Even I, who has unshackled the chains of servitude thanks to my mate's selfless victory in the Forsaken Hunt, cannot help but feel his overwhelming despair. It's crushing.

Caius, wild and unpredictable—you'd have to be to be willingly mated to the fucking devil for millennia—moves with a predator's grace as he climbs to his feet and stalks towards the bed, his loyalty to

Aggonid as firm as it is to Morte. His laughter has long since fled, replaced by the serrated edge of vengeance. "We don't need the veil's mercy or hell's might," he hisses, a viper coiled. "We'll bend the universe to our will, Ag. Kill them all if we must."

Aggonid's response is a silent nod, but his eyes burn with regret and fury now. He's the ruler here, and his word is the law—yet now he's the most vulnerable I've ever seen him.

Emeric now prowls at the fringes, an outsider among mates. His eyes, the color of permafrost, betray nothing but the barest flicker of his own longing, one hand gripping the short curls against his scalp. He and Morte would've mated if it weren't for Aggonid barreling his way in. But I know him better than anyone else in hell, and he's hurting. It's in the faintest whimper his beast unleashes when he wrests control. It's clear he misses her deeply, and he has as many regrets as we do.

That's all this fucking devil does. He takes and he takes.

As for me, I linger in the shadows where comfort lies. "We need a plan," I finally say, stepping forward, my voice as steady as the mantle's core. I loathe this monster even more now, but I'll do whatever it takes to get her back. "One that doesn't end with us at war with Bedlam or tearing down the veils beyond. She'd never forgive us."

She'd told me about Wilder, and how she's responsible for his incarceration. If we went to war on her behalf, countless lives would be lost, and she'd feel the guilt of each one.

And I have enough to atone for, especially when she finds out who I am. What I've done.

How I've lied to her.

I should've told her when I had the opportunity, given us a fighting chance.

Caius turns, his pale eyes fixing on me with a fervor that could rival any storm I've conjured. "Then let's hear it, Tin Man. Craft us a strategy." His words suggest vitriol, but the venom is absent in his voice. Instead, desperation clings to every syllable. He's hurting just as bad as I am.

I narrow my eyes at him and raise a brow but choose diplomacy over giving into his unhinged whims.

"We reach out to the High King Finian of the fae," I propose. "We assert our claim and ask for her back."

In the shadows, I'm both observer and orchestrator. The plan I propose must not only ensure Morte's return but also safeguard the realms from the cataclysm that her absence has begun to stir.

"We proceed with caution," I continue, measured against the brewing storm of their reactions. "The High King is fair and just, and prizes balance above all. If we demonstrate that Morte's absence threatens that balance, we make a compelling case for her return."

Emeric steps closer, his gaze like ice shards cutting through the gloom. "Balance," he muses, "because we'd go to war if she isn't returned. But what of her choice? If she's found solace with this Wilder she pines after, won't that sway their ruler?"

A pang of something I refuse to name tightens in my chest. "The High King must see beyond that—"

Aggonid interrupts me as his stare hardens. "Morte is a fulcrum upon which multiple realms balance," he spits. "Her place is here, restoring the equilibrium, not just for our sake, but for all. He won't want me even more maddened than I already am. I'll level it all!"

Caius grins, a predator sensing victory. "So, we play the game of kings and courts," he sing-songs. "We don't ask; we demand under the laws that govern us all."

I meet his stare unflinching. "Not demand; appeal," I correct him, years of royal tutelage under my belt. "We show that our intent aligns with the greater good. The High King will listen to reason if it speaks in the tongue of universal stability."

Aggonid leans forward. His decision weighs heavily, like the crown he bears when he's on his dais. "If their king agrees, it's Morte who must choose. She must return of her own will, or not at all."

Before they'd solidified their soul bond, he would've already ripped her from whatever tethers her to Bedlam. Things are different now.

For all of us.

We'd all do whatever it takes to make her happy, even if that means she doesn't want us.

Aggonid's words carry the gravity of his station, and I know this is the only path forward. "Then you should present our case with the truth, not as lord of chaos, but as a being of purpose."

Caius scoffs but eventually nods in concession. Emeric, though unreadable, gives a curt inclination of his head before pausing mid-gesture.

"And if she wants to stay with Wilder?" Emeric asks, the question once again directed at me.

I let out a breath as his words carve me up inside. "Then we abide by her choice," I state, knowing full well the cost. "Even in the Underworld, love must be free, or it's nothing at all." The words taste like ash on my tongue, and I'm not certain they hold any conviction. "But he's in prison." I hesitate, my mind catching on the words she shared with me in her little hut all those moons ago. "She's been trying to get him out for two hundred years. Maybe if we find a way to get him released, she'd be more interested in coming back."

The room settles into a somber accord as we mull over what we should do next. We may not all get along, our truce is tenuous at best, and the way forward is fraught with uncertainty, but the conviction that binds us in this moment is as strong as the metals I've forged with my magic.

Morte's fate, and perhaps the fate of all realms, hangs in the balance. It's a gambit, but one we must take. For her. For us. For the very fabric of existence that trembles at the absence of its keystone.

There's nothing I wouldn't do to be with her again if she's willing. And if the High King won't let her come back, maybe we can entice her to join us again. One way or another.

"I could kill him ..." Caius grumbles, more to himself than anyone else. "Isn't the saying if you give a man a fish, he'll catch a bird, too?" He glances out the window. "Or do you catch two birds with one fish?"

"Give a man a fish, he'll be hungry tomorrow. Teach him to fish and he'll leave you the fuck alone, I do believe it goes," Aggonid smirks at his mate, his red eyes flashing.

"No, I've got it." Caius turns away from the window. "Fill his pockets with stones, and he'll swim with the fishes, and leave our bird alone!"

Aggonid shakes his head, looking back through the chapters of the book in his hand. "I don't think that's right, either. Wilder is merfae and can't drown."

Emeric and I exchange a quick, bewildered glance, our expressions mirroring the same thought: how the *fuck* did Morte tie herself to someone like them? And now we're stuck with the two of them.

I leave Caius to his unhinged spoken thoughts as I turn back to sorting through the pile of tomes in front of me.

Aggonid rifles through a drawer before taking a seat and making quick scratches across a piece of paper. He's reaching out to the High King of Bedlam, a message of urgency and unity.

A messenger comes and goes, taking with them a missive that Aggonid needs to meet with a Bedlam delegate as soon as possible, and meanwhile, we're strewn across the bedroom, consulting various books and ancient scrolls, looking for some way to bring her here or to undo the luna goddesses' work.

We'd considered time travel, but Luna has made it so no one can ever do it again. Not after the trouble it caused her daughter-in-law and grandchildren.

Breaking the stillness, Aggonid emerges from his crouched position in front of the disheveled stack of books that had tumbled during the violent portal storm. He holds a dusty tome in his hand as he stands.

"I've got it," he says, and we all stop to look at him as his fingers fly across the page. "We'll build her a dreamscape."

The idea is bold, unexpected from someone like him, known for his iron grip on reality.

Caius's reaction is instant, a smirk spreading across his face. "She already stars in every one of my dreams," he croons, tucking his feet under him on the floor as he pulls more piles of books closer to him.

"Oh, the fun we could weave into that." He chuckles, his mind already running wild with the possibilities.

"It's for Morte, not your gods damned playhouse," I snap back, keeping him in check with a look.

Emeric inclines his head, the practical peacekeeper as always. "We'll need rules. Boundaries that don't change. Dreamweaving alters the mind, and if we're not careful, it can hurt her."

That sobers Caius, his smirk falling.

"You're right." Aggonid gives a small, rare smile. "We'll tailor it to her," he assures, the fae devil everyone fears showing a hint of the soul-bonded mate he is. "Make her feel comfortable. Safe."

Gods know he never showed her an ounce of that when he had a chance.

Caius shoves a book on a lower shelf, considering. "Fine. But let's not make it boring." His eyes gleam as he looks back at us. "I don't want her falling asleep in her dream when I could be spending time with her. Loving her."

"We balance it," I suggest. "Enough of our world to feel like home, enough of her world to feel like hope."

Emeric claps his hands together, decisive. "Let's go see our girl."

No one calls him on it, because the others know just as well as I do that, she's as much his as she is ours.

As the smartest of the bunch, he starts divvying out tasks for each of us. Meanwhile, he needs Aggonid to round up some supplies you can't easily get in the Underworld.

And just like that, we're a unit, focused on a single goal: a dreamscape to bridge the gap between us and her. We each know what we bring to the table, and now it's time to put it all together—for Morte.

CHAPTER SIX

EMERIC

After I leave the others and make my way home alone, the darkness of the Underworld envelops me like a blanket, its shadows weaving in and out as the torches that line the walls flicker and dance. I'm a hellhound, a creature born of fire and shadow, and I'm supposed to be one of the most feared demons in all of the Underworld, but I don't feel that way. Not now.s

Hellhounds hold their own in any fight, but they fear us because of our light.

Once back in the echoing silence of my quarters, my thoughts turn back to her. The phoenix fae whose absence gnaws at my very being. I've been slayed by a stunning little bird with hair like crimson fire.

She's out there, beyond the veil that separates our worlds, and the yearning to reach her is a persistent ache. I move through my home, my steps deliberate, my mind weaving through the possibilities of bridging the chasm between us.

The concept of dream walking, a skill I've honed over centuries, whispers to me like an old friend. It's a subtle art, a way to tread the ethereal pathways of the subconscious. If I can maneuver this delicate magic correctly, I might be able to reach her in her dreams, to speak to her, to feel her presence once more.

Around me, my lair reflects the duality of my nature. The walls, a rough and foreboding shade of obsidian, stand guard over the ancient texts and artifacts that line them. Each item holds a secret of the arcane, carefully preserved for my use. In the center of the room stands a massive circular table, crafted from the same dark stone as the walls. Its surface is cluttered with scrolls, crystals, and a myriad of components essential to my work. The air is heavy with the scent of incense and magic, creating an otherworldly atmosphere within these dark walls.

With steady hands, I begin the intricate preparations, following the ancient rituals passed down through generations. My fingers trace delicate symbols of connection and communion in the air, each one glowing a luminescent blue before fading into the ether. The very atmosphere shivers with the magnitude of power being summoned, as if the essence of the Underworld itself is bending to my will. Every movement feels charged with energy, and I can sense the presence of otherworldly beings gathering around me, drawn by my spell. They can't enter my dwelling, but they feel it.

How had Morte managed to stir something deep within me, something I thought long dead? I long for her, not just for the physicality that was denied but for the connection, the understanding that sparked between us.

I draw a deep breath, centering myself, and reach for the pendant around my neck. It's a talisman of old, a relic imbued with the power to traverse dreamscapes. The metal is cool against my skin, so different from the warmth that thoughts of her evoke.

I close my eyes, allowing my consciousness to slip from the physical realm, to enter the realm of dreams and possibilities. My very being dissolves into shadows, merging with the fabric of the dream world as though we were always meant to be one. The transition is smooth, proof of my years of mastery over this plane.

Here, I'm a hunter of a different kind—not for flesh and blood, but for the elusive threads of dreams. In this swirling mists of slumber, every dreamer leaves behind a magical signature, a unique essence that lingers in the air like a haunting melody. And having been somewhat intimate with Morte, her signature should stand out amongst the others, like a lighthouse, signaling the way in the darkness.

Once I've found the thread, it'll be easier to tie it to a dreamscape built by my own mind, rather than one the dreamer has conjured. Though there's nothing easy about infiltrating dreams across realms.

The dream realm is a mosaic of thoughts and fears, hopes and desires. I move through it with purpose, each step a careful maneuver, each breath a silent invocation.

As I navigate this surreal landscape, the longing for her intensifies. The thought of her, lost and alone in a world away from us, fuels my fire. I will find her here, in the one place where barriers are thin, and hearts speak louder than words.

The process is taxing, a drain on my energies, but I push forward. The thought of her face, her voice, is a balm to the weariness that creeps into my bones.

And then, a flicker. A whisper in the dream's fabric that feels familiar. It's faint, elusive, but unmistakably hers. I move towards it, my heart racing, my soul aching for the connection.

As I draw closer, the dream begins to take shape, to form into something tangible. It's a reflection of her mind, a garden born of her memories. I tread carefully, mindful not to disturb the delicate balance of her subconscious.

But before I can reach her, a jolt hits me. A barrier, unseen but potent, a safeguard against intruders. Her mind, resilient even in sleep, pushes back against my presence. I'm thrust out of the dream realm, back into my body with a force that leaves me gasping for air.

I open my eyes, the flickering torches forming long shadows across my room. The attempt was unsuccessful, but not futile. I've touched the edge of her world, felt the protective barriers of her mind, and next time, she'll be easier to find.

Though it won't necessarily be easier to penetrate her subconscious.

A plan settles within me, a promise to try again, to find a way to reach her. The pendant around my neck pulses with a faint light, proof of the connection that almost was.

For now, I must rest, gather my strength for the next attempt. But I won't give up. Morte is out there in a world away from her mates, and I will find a way to bridge that distance, to speak to her, even if only in dreams.

I miss her.

As the Underworld's eternal night envelops me, I close my eyes, and images of Morte flicker behind my eyelids. She's a flame in the darkness, a flicker of hope in a realm bereft of light. Her beauty, her bravery, they're etched into my very soul.

She's not mine in any technical sense, but she should be. The gods willing, she will be, as soon as I'm able. I let her get away, and that's not a mistake I'll ever make again.

The sheets are cool and unwelcoming against my heated skin as I lay in bed. I let my thoughts wander. The dream realm is enormous, a universe of its own, and finding her there is akin to seeking a single star in an endless night sky. This doesn't deter me. The challenge only gets easier each time.

In my mind, I rehearse the plan for the next attempt. I need to refine my approach, to find a way past the natural defenses of her subconscious. It's a delicate balance, navigating the dreams of another without causing harm or alarm. I ponder the symbols I traced, the incantations I whispered. There's a key, a method to this madness, and I'll find it.

The Underworld around me is frenzied, almost bacchanalian, its inhabitants lost in their own pursuits of pleasure and power. But here, in my quarters, there's a different kind of quest unfolding. A pursuit of the heart, a journey through the unseen.

My thoughts drift to the pendant again, its magic a link between worlds. It's an ancient artifact, its origins lost to time, but its power is undeniable. I consider its potential, the ways I might harness it more effectively. There's old magic here, deep and primal, and it resonates with the untamed part of my soul.

I need a conduit of sorts. A way to harness more energy, more magic.

Unable to find rest, I rise and move towards the barred window.

The view outside is one of eternal night, a landscape of shadows and fire, a world alive with its own dark beauty. Creatures tear across the forest, seeking their next prey. I watch, mesmerized, as a pack of night stalkers takes down a wayward denizen of hell. They must've been new here. No one with half a brain stays out after midnight. Their screams echo through the trees, haunting and agonized before abruptly cutting off. In the distance, the eerie cries of wisp wraiths slice through the quiet, a ghostly chorus that echoes with longing and loss.

As a hellhound, I'm a creature of tracking and secrets. The more I know about her, the easier it'll be to secure our connection.

I turn away from the window, my gaze falling on the assortment of tools and artifacts on my table. Each one is a piece of the puzzle, a tool in the intricate craft of dream walking. I'll need to prepare, to gather my resources and investigate deeper into the ancient texts that line my bookshelves.

Knowledge is power, and in this hunt, it's my greatest ally.

They say hellhounds are nothing but monsters, driven by instinct and bloodlust—the greatest trackers in all the realms. But they don't understand us, or the complexity of our minds and the depths of our emotions. They see easy smiles and ruthless violence in battle, but they don't know it's all a calculation. A manipulation.

I am no mere monster. I'm a seeker, a solver of riddles, a master of the arcane, a demon fae; a creature of intellect and cunning. I pull out my leather-bound book from its secret cove behind a set of tomes and tuck it under my arm as I cross to the couch.

I settle at the short table, and the flickering light of the torches create dancing shadows across the pages of my most prized possession. The text is cryptic, written in a language long forgotten by most, but to me, it's as familiar as the beating of my heart.

The night stretches on, and I lose myself in study and planning. Worn, yellowed pages fill my vision as a single candle gutters out, and my eyesight adjusts to meld with the darkness. The dream realm won't yield its secrets easily, but I'm patient, and I'm driven. Morte's face, her voice, they're a constant presence in my mind as I shut my eyes and whisper another incantation.

I embrace it, pushing past the darkness until I find the faintest glimmer of light. Studying it, I realize that it's the beginning of a new trail, one that leads straight to the heart of Bedlam. My heart flutters with excitement, having found an easier, steadier path to follow to her dreams. But just as I begin to map out my route, a sinister presence creeps into my mind, sending a tremble down my spine. It's like a cold hand over my heart, squeezing the air from my lungs. My eyes snap open as adrenaline pumps through my veins.

Something is wrong.

Wrenching myself out of the dreamscape, I jump up from the table, still clutching the book. The hairs on the back of my neck stand on end as I try to pinpoint the source of the sinister feeling. It's familiar, yet foreign at the same time. I've felt it before, but never this strong.

A low growl escapes me, and I slam the book shut. The sound echoes through the empty room, and for a moment, I'm frozen, listening to the silence that follows. Then I hear it. The faintest whisper, like a breeze through the trees, or the rustling of leaves as it—whatever it is—makes its retreat. And just as suddenly as it appears, it's gone, leaving behind a metallic taste on my tongue.

I take a deep breath, trying to clear my head. That whisper, that feeling, it's not something that I can ignore. It's a warning. Of what, I don't know. I make to take my seat again, intending to continue my research, but pause mid-way. My gut tells me I need to investigate this further, that there's something important that I'm missing, and I should increase the power behind my magic before I ever try this again. With a sigh, I return the book to its hiding place and make my way towards my bedroom.

I'll find a way to reach her, to bridge the gap that separates us. In dreams, in shadows, in the secret places where the heart speaks its truth, I will find her. And when I do, I'll be ready to guide her back to the world she belongs to. A world where we can be together, even if only in the ethereal embrace of slumber.

As dawn approaches, the first hints of light begin to seep into my room, a false dawn in a realm where the sun never fully rises. It hovers near the tree line. I finally allow myself a moment of rest, my body weary but my spirit undeterred.

In the rebellion before the Underworld quiets down, I close my eyes, Morte's image etched into my mind, her absence a hollow ache in my chest. But it's an ache filled with purpose, with the promise of a reunion that spans realms and defies the boundaries of death and dream.

As long as I can keep whatever that intruder was away.

CHAPTER SEVEN

AZAZEL

It's late evening when I retreat to my home, an anomaly of refinement amidst the pandemonium of the Underworld. It's deep in the core of its largest forest, not far from where Morte briefly dwelled in a ramshackle hut. The door creaks open, the sound a harsh reminder of the silence within—no generous greetings, no warmth of a companion's presence. Just the echo of my own footsteps.

In the quiet, a thought unfurls: I should've taken her in the moment our paths crossed. And now, I don't know if I'll ever see her again.

I should've laid claim to her right away; given her a reason to stay. She should've been the heart of my home. My queen. I should've gotten down on both knees and worshipped her.

But now, my house has lost its luster.

Here, the interior is understated, purposeful. Every object has been forged by my own hands, evidence of skill rather than status. The walls are adorned with intricate metalwork, less ostentatious than what one might find in a castle, but each piece is imbued with a significance known only to me.

I bypass the comforts of the living space, drawn instead to the heart of my domain: the workshop. It's here, among the embers and iron, that the soul of my craft—and now, the conduit for our dreamscape—will take shape. The tools of my trade lie ready, the designs for the conduit etched not just on parchment but in my mind, as clear as if Morte herself were guiding my hand.

I light the forge, and its familiar roar is a welcome sound as the heat embraces me like an old friend. Tonight, I start the delicate task of crafting the dreamscape's amplifier, a device of my own invention that will bridge realms and consciousness. The metal awaits, a rare blend of sanguimetal and star silver. Materials that respond not just to heat and hammer but to intention and desire.

I'm sorry. Clang.
Forgive me. Clang.
Love me. Clang.
Come back. Clang.

The rhythm of the forge is different tonight. Each strike is precise, a step in an intricate dance of creation. The amplifier must be perfect, a convergence of metallurgy and magic, a vessel strong enough to carry our thoughts, our dreams, and our souls to where Morte lingers. I work tirelessly, and the metal yields to my will, taking on the form of a complex helix, spiraling like the very essence of our magic.

In the fire-hewn light, I pause, pondering the design's complexity. It must resonate with Morte's frequency, attuned to the echoes of her essence that still linger in my memory. I recall the feel of her energy, the fire of her spirit, and channel it into my creation. This is more than a task; it's a ritual, a silent conversation between her heart and mine across the expanse that divides us.

My purpose here has changed. It's all for her now.

My hand grazes the chalice on the table, its contents a collection of favors, each one a subtle indicator of power and influence, earned through cunning, strength, and force. These are my weapons, my armor in the unseen battles ahead.

But the favors are more complex than inanimate weapons, possessing a 'knowing' of their wielder's intensions and motivations. Once they find out what I've done, I might need them all to survive it.

I sink into the chair, and the coolness of the metal, so at odds with the heat of the forge, seeps through my attire. The screeches of the forest's creatures echo around my house. But here, in this space I've created, the plans must be drawn. If the High King of the Fae says no, I may need another avenue to be with her again. It requires more than just political maneuvering; it demands finesse, a game played in the shadows where the slightest misstep could mean ruin.

So I sit, the prince of strategy in a cottage of steel, a master of metals preparing for the most delicate work of all: weaving the future with threads of secrets of the heart, all while holding the fabric of my own identity tightly in check.

It's late by the time I drag myself from the forge, having exhausted both my body and my mind. In the solemnity of night, her image burns behind my lids, a persistent vision. Each flash of her smile or echo of her laughter nearly rends me in two.

Her spirit, as stubborn as the flames in my hearth, refuses to dim. Her red-hot defiance drew me from the shadows initially. How could it not ensnare me still, even as distance of realms holds us apart?

A quick shower cools me off before I drag my feet to my bedroom. I yank open the drawer on the side of my bed, snatching up a small vial, its glass surface reflecting a dark, murky liquid within.

It's extraordinarily difficult to get this here, as it comes from Romarie, but when you have enough favors, you can trade for just about anything with the reapers who bring back the souls.

In the distant past, I'd been addicted to this. Anything to numb the pain, to take me away, to transport me somewhere else. For most fae, *Abyssal's Embrace* kills them or causes them to confront their worst fears.

But for me? It took me away from my worst. I suspect it's because of the way my body can manipulate blood, metal, and minerals. With a childhood like mine, anyone would've become an addict. Whatever it takes to escape, if not in body, but in mind.

To the world, it's a vice; to me, it's a vessel, ferrying me away from the shores of a haunted past.

With a quick twist, I remove the minuscule cork from the jar and tilt it back, allowing the liquid within to slide down my throat, though it's thick, and comes out in tiny droplets. Each drop is an echo of solace, a silent lullaby for a soul too weary to sleep.

Instantly, a warm buzz envelops my senses, producing a tingling sensation that courses through my body. Addiction is my flawed magic, turning the discord of a scarred life into the hush of solitude, to shape my reality however I'd like.

A delicious heat races across my skin, and a smile adorns my face, unbidden, as I drop onto my mattress, still naked and slightly damp from the shower.

In the bed I forged, hands that ache to hold her now clench the cool, unwelcoming linen. Outside, midnight awakens the forest's terrors; their screeches claw at the edges of my sanctuary, drawn by the scent of a powerful creature within. Within these walls, I stifle my groan as my fingers glide down my abdomen, palming myself, the darkness becoming a theater for my own silent battle.

My eyes shutter as I picture Morte's heated stare, the way her crimson hair tumbles down her back, and the curve of her lips when she moans my name.

Her infectious laugh echoes through the room, filling it with warmth and light. My eyes snap open as I feel her crawl onto the bed, naked and settling between my spread knees. Her mischievous grin taunts me as she pouts, running her tongue along her thumb before trailing it along the head of my cock. A deep groan escapes my lips as I watch her, captivated by the way she tugs her bottom lip between her teeth, and how she leans in as though she's telling me a secret.

"Save all your come for me," she commands, her voice dripping with desire.

I can only nod in response, mesmerized by the seductive glint in her eyes. "It's all for you," I confess, completely under her spell.

With a devilish smirk, she takes me in her hand and begins to work her magic.

I let out a deep exhale as she moves in a steady rhythm, but my hand flies out to stop her, not wanting to finish so soon. "Come here." I tug her into my lap, my eyes roving over her hips before she settles on top of me.

Every bit of this feels real, from the press of her body to the softness of her skin against mine. I bury my face in the nape of her neck, inhaling her intoxicating scent as she lifts her hips to slide me into her slick heat.

A gasp escapes her, my name a prayer on her full, pouty lips. She grinds down on me, earning her a guttural moan from me.

"That's it, baby." My fingers dig into her hips as I guide her. "Ride me."

Morte doesn't hesitate to obey, rolling her hips in slow circles, grinding against me with such wanton need. Her nails digging into my chest, and her breathing becomes ragged and heavy. The room's only sounds are our mingled moans and the headboard creaking.

I sit up, flipping her onto her back before bringing her into my lap. Pulling her hair, I angle her head back to reveal her exposed neck, watching her pulse flutter faster.

"You're going to wear my mark," I growl, my voice a feral purr. "Right on this pretty little neck so the others know you belong to me just as much as I belong to you."

She arches her neck, presenting it to me like a willing sacrifice. Just as she whimpers, "Do it," she rolls her hips against mine.

I sink my teeth into her neck, and she lets out a deep moan, as though pulling from her very soul. Her blood fills my mouth, hot and thick, and so damn addictive. The blazing pleasure of her liquid fire courses through my veins, heightening my every sense and desire. I need more. I need all of her.

Her nails rake up and down my back, but I don't care. All I can focus on is the sweet taste of her blood on my tongue, and the heartbeat thumping against my lips. Her long hair brushes against my skin as her legs wrap tight around my waist, as her body writhes against me.

As I pump more of my potent venom into her, her pussy begins to squeeze my cock, and she throws her head back as she shatters. I follow, roaring out my release as I fill her, and the sound echoes in the metal bedroom. The scent of sex and blood fills the air, a primal mix that only intensifies as we reach our climax.

Withdrawing my fangs from her neck, I snarl, "You're mine. From the first day, you've always been mine." I let go of her and run my tongue over her wound, tasting my brand.

Her eyes are hazy with pleasure, and her pointy ears are tinged pink. "I know, baby." She runs her fingers through my hair.

"I miss you so damned much," I breathe, burying against her neck as I hold her tight, my arms wrapped around her back.

"Then come get me," she whispers.

"What?" I pull back to look at her, but when I do, there's no one there.

Just the faint echo of my hallucination, my release all over my lap, a sore back, and my bloodied fingertips.

"No!" I roar, scrambling to look for the vial again. My hands frantically sweep over the sheets and blankets of my bed until they finally land on the small glass container lying discarded at the foot of the mattress. With trembling fingers, I pick it up and bring it closer to my face, only to find that not a single drop remains inside.

"FUCK!" I shout, chucking the glass across the room, but it's so tiny, it doesn't shatter.

Hallucinations are a poor substitute for the real thing, but it's all I have for now. I collapse onto my pillow, my body still humming with the aftermath of pleasure, my soul aching for my mate. The night outside is still alive with the sounds of the forest, but inside my head, it's quiet. The only thing that echoes is the memory of her, and the burning desire to have her back in my arms again.

With a heavy heart, I clean myself up and curl up in the cold bed, hoping that sleep will bring me some solace, some respite from the constant ache in my chest. But as I drift off, I know that my dreams will be haunted by her image, her voice, her touch. And I welcome it, for even in my sleep, I crave her, even if it's a glimpse.

It's mere hours later when I jolt up in bed, drenched in sweat. We're not meant to be away from our mates for long. The night terrors will get worse and will begin haunting me during the day, and they'll make me emotional. Caius and Aggonid won't be as bad—as if they could get worse—because they have each other.

And Emeric? Poor Emeric has barely anyone. At least I have a mating bond to give me some reassurance, some semblance of proof that when this is all done, I have her. It's that silken thread of connection that hums through the chaos, a promise that ties our fates together even as we're apart.

It never really seemed fair to me that no matter the pitch of your soul, if you're a hellhound, you come to the Underworld when you pass. But now that I've gotten to know him, it's clear to me why. It's all about balance. His is the purest soul in all of Aggonid's Realm. The only one you can really trust, who can be a voice of reason.

Emeric, with his calm presence and consistent moral clarity, challenges the typical narrative of this place. He embodies the paradox of the Underworld, a place of contradiction, where his genuine goodness stands out amid the surrounding mayhem. In him, I sense the chance for transformation, an opportunity to challenge the ancient rules that define us. Perhaps Emeric is the catalyst we need, a sign that even in the depths, hope can take root.

His solitude in the Underworld is not a punishment, but a placement by destiny's hand, where his goodness could shine the brightest. It's a cruel kind of honor, one that burdens him with the role of a guardian amid the lost, yet it's a role he bears with silent dignity.

The memory of our first encounter will be etched in my mind forever. It was the night after the Wild Pursuit, a time when Underworld dwellers let their primal inclinations take over and engage in fights or sexual pursuits. To protect myself, I'd created an unbreakable and enchanted cage within my home. No one could enter, and I couldn't leave until the frenzy was over.

Just within reach of my cage was the communication device I'd built, which allowed me to speak with others across enormous distances. It had taken me hundreds of years to secure the parts here. I'd used the very last warp stone I had to make it. In a feral rage, I'd destroyed my invention, and spent the whole next day trying to repair it.

As I pour myself a glass of water, I allow my memories of that day to distract me, pulling me back in time as if it were yesterday.

The Underworld is always eerily subdued the day after the Wild pursuit, and this occasion was no different, the silence a harrowing reminder of the chaos unleashed the night before. I push open the door of my bedroom, the remnants of my protective spells still crackling faintly in the corners. My cage, once my salvation, now feels like a tomb for my ambitions.

Repairing it is beyond my current means because I need a warp stone. The stone is so rare it had taken me forty favors paid to the reapers, and only one managed to find one after sixty years of trying. It could very well be the last of its kind.

My heart sinks as the truth settles in, heavy like the chains around the ankles of the newly damned. I need help, and there's only one person in this godforsaken realm rumored to track the untraceable.

We both work for Aggonid, though I haven't interacted with him at all beyond a casual dip of the chin in passing. Emeric's soul is so fucking bright it's hard to look at sometimes. He's so pure, I feel guilty seeing him amongst all this sorrow, grief, deceit, and rage that permeates the denizens of the Underworld.

I stride into the market, where the air is still thick with the musk of spent adrenaline and smoldering embers. My purpose is singular as I navigate through the crowd, seeking the one known to possess a gift beyond price in this realm of fire and ash.

"Emeric." I murmur the name of the hellhound renowned for his unique talents. Though we've never conversed, his reputation precedes him, spoken in whispers by those who've long since lost hope of encountering a kind person in hell.

There, amidst the chaos of traders and thieves, I spot him, his aura permeating every vein in his body. He stands apart, a lone figure whose presence seems to command the space around him. He's not peddling wares or haggling over goods; he's observing, waiting.

Approaching him, I clear my throat. "Emeric?"

He turns, his eyes locking onto mine with an intensity that feels like he's peering into the very marrow of my being. "Azazel." He smirks, his eyes sparkling like frosted jewels. "Now he deigns to speak to me. What do you want?"

"I—" I didn't expect him to call me out for it, but he's right. But in all fairness, I rarely speak to anyone. "Apologies. You can call me Az." I offer my hand for him to shake.

My tall stature looms over him, and with my massive, ebony wings still spread behind me, I probably appear much more intimidating than I actually am. At least in his eyes.

He glances at my hand, as though judging my intent. We're all liars, cheats, and thieves here, so I understand his wariness. Emeric's hand reaches out slowly, fingers hesitantly curling around mine. His eyes flicker with uncertainty, but then lock onto mine as he firmly grips my hand.

I try to explain, "It's not personal, I just don't talk to anyone, and I didn't think you'd want to associate with someone like me."

"Someone like you?" He draws his hand back, studying me from head to toe.

I gesture dramatically at our surroundings. "Haven't you noticed we're in hell." I chuckle. "And you're—gods." I turn away, shielding my eyes from the glimpse of his aura I get. "Better than all of us combined."

He raises a brow at me. "Keep that up and I'm going to shrink you down and put you in my pocket." He strides away, and I stand there staring in his spot before my brain catches up and I trot after him. "My ego is big enough." He laughs, looking back at me over his shoulder.

"But I thought—"

He stands in my path, blocking me from moving forward. "You assumed that since I'm a hellhound and bound to hell, I would be a modest, well-behaved fae. I've heard that misconception before. If being humble was the key to entering beyond the veil, there wouldn't be any fae there."

"Oh." I furrow my brows, trying to figure him out. "Sorry for assuming."

He sighs, rolling his eyes, whispering an enchantment. Immediately, the shine of his aura is less blinding, though it's still nearly pure white, like snow-capped mountains. "This works as a deterrent to keep the thieves away. Now what do you want?"

"It's not what I want, but what I need," I admit, pushing the frustration from my voice. "I need a warp stone. I was led to believe you could track one down."

Emeric's eyes narrow a fraction. "Come with me," he ultimately decides, his tone brooking no resistance.

We weave through the alleys, and the crowd parts for Emeric as if they all know he's too good to mess with. We walk for a long time towards the woods where I reside, until we reach a small home that's far nicer than I'd expected. Before I can comment on it, he preempts my thoughts.

"People look out for me," he offers. "I help them find things, and they hook me up." He grins.

I nod. Most people must steal or earn a favor from Aggonid in order to live comfortably here, and I didn't expect Emeric would participate in the Forsaken Hunt.

He leads me inside, and I wait by the door as he gathers things from his kitchen cupboards.

His place feels like a home. Not ostentatious, nor is it bare. It's lived in, well kept, and practical.

"I need to understand what you seek before I can find it," Emeric mumbles. He retrieves a vial filled with a substance that seems to absorb the scant light in the room. "This is the essence of warp stone. It's old, nearly spent, but it might give us a lead."

He closes his eyes, inhaling the scent deeply. His brow furrows in concentration as his lips whisper incantations. The tracking ritual unfolds, and he draws invisible lines in the air, connecting the dots of his senses to form a clear picture. When he opens his eyes again, they hold a verdict I already know in my gut.

"The stone you seek doesn't exist anymore, not in this realm or the next. It might not exist at all," he says with a finality that echoes the emptiness I've been feeling since I broke my device.

So not in Aggonid's Realm, nor is it in Romarie. Perhaps it's in Bedlam or beyond.

I lean against the cool wood of his door, the reality of my situation settling in. "Well, fuck."

"Pass."

I pause, processing his words before a burst of laughter erupts from me. I reach into my pocket and toss him a small favor earned from Aggonid that holds the power to grant any wish within his abilities.

He catches it, smiling down at it before tossing it back to me. "Keep it. Sorry I couldn't find what you needed."

"Let me buy you a drink." It's the least I could do after all the trouble he went through.

He claps me on the shoulder, gesturing towards the door. "I'd like that."

We meander back through the woods, and the leaves crunch under our feet in a soothing rhythm. The conversation between us flows effortlessly, like a gentle stream winding its way through the forest.

"Are all hellhounds such great trackers?"

A playful smirk dances across his lips as he ticks off each finger on his hand. "Good trackers, undeniably attractive, unparalleled intelligence, unwavering loyalty, and we're notoriously skilled lovers."

I chuckle. "But not humble."

"No reason to be." He grins at me. "Not with two cocks."

I give him a playful shove. "Now I know you're ly—"

"They vibrate, too."

And that's how I made friends with a hellhound.

They were simpler times, back then. With a restless sigh, I rise, wiping my hand down my face and abandoning the very idea of sleep. A sliver of moon casts discerning light through the barred window, and the forest resonates with a chorus of nocturnal horrors.

I drift towards the window. The sight of one of the moon's journeys across the sky offers a perspective that I grasp at greedily. I never did find another warp stone.

But if I can use my magic and skills to build a conduit for the dreamscape, perhaps I can find a way to communicate with others. To stop the things I helped put into motion over a decade ago. Because everything is different now.

It's all for her.

Will High King Finian send her back to us? Does he understand the delicate threads that Morte's absence has frayed? A leader must stand as the custodian of balance, but what if love tips the scales? Or will I need to accelerate my timeline here to get her back?

I can't predict the moves of kings and courts, but I can ready myself for all outcomes. I turn from the window, and the metal conduit I've placed on a shelf catches the moon's gleam.

My skill, my craft, the heart that beats beneath the guise I wear, they must suffice to bridge the distances, to unravel the lies. I cross to my closet and pull out the old, broken communication device, before dragging it over to the forge.

As the night deepens, I resign myself to the workbench once more, working through my thoughts. The tools in my hands feel right, familiar. Though I can shape this with my magic, I'd grown fond of the labor of doing it by hand when I'd first arrived in the Underworld and was without magic. Metal bends and yields to my will, just as I must bend and yield to the fates that govern us. For now, the forge's warmth is my sole companion as I shape the cold metal, and I labor with singular purpose.

I'm going to test this thing before the dawn finds me. On someone whose mind I'm not bothered about shattering. Then when it's time for us to build the dreamscape for Morte, I'll be ready.

CHAPTER EIGHT

MORTE

The bonfire's crackle is the entertainment of the night, flickering through the sprawling training field where twilight is a welcome guest.

After a month back, it still doesn't feel quite like home. Not anymore. I feel out-of-step, as though I'm reading the lines to the wrong story.

Now, as I sit amongst my squadron, I look up at the crystals above us, a mimicry of a world bathed in moonlight. My rear end is sunk into the lush green grass, and I'm reclined against a sturdy log, my elbow casually propped on my bent leg. In my hand, a bottle of absinthe gleams in the firelight, the deep emerald liquid swishing gently with each movement. The buzzing hum of insects and distant chatter provide a peaceful soundtrack to my lazy evening.

"Brought the snacks," Ronin calls from across the clearing as he makes his way towards the fire. Slung over his shoulder is a duffle bag, and he tosses it towards Arsenio, Sabine's mate. The two of them catch it, digging in while I watch Ronin stalk towards Noct.

"By snacks, I hope you mean drinks," Freya singsongs, already three beers deep.

Our group chuckles, and feeling a warm buzz myself, even I

manage a smile. I've taken to drinking more nights than I care to admit since I've been back.

Ronin's towering presence commands the clearing as he approaches, his frame both athletic and imposing. The glow on his skin shimmers with an inner fire. His hair, the color of molten gold, falls in loose waves to his broad shoulders, complementing the deep amber of his eyes that sparkle with a playful yet intense light. His features are sharply defined, with a strong jawline and prominent cheekbones that speak of his fire golem heritage. As he moves, there's a fluidity to his gait, a grace that belies his powerful build. Despite his formidable appearance, his warm, inviting aura is as much a part of him as the fire he commands.

"Hey, beautiful," Ronin says with a grin that could light up the entire forest. He reaches out and wraps his arms around Noct, lifting her effortlessly off her toes. He brings his head down to rest on her shoulder, inhaling deeply as if savoring the scent of her. Gently setting her back down on the ground, he pulls her onto his lap where he sits on a fallen log.

"I'm hungry," she complains in jest.

He grabs her waist, hugging her to him as he jokes, "I've got your snack right here."

She playfully swats at him, but then her eyes light up at the sight of something in his hand. He holds out a candy bar just out of her reach, goading her on with a mischievous grin. She lunges forward and snatches the treat from his grasp before he can continue teasing her.

Gracefully, she settles back onto his lap, as if nothing had happened. She meets my gaze with mischievous eyes as she takes a large bite of the bar and begins to chew with gusto, her cheeks slightly puffing out as she tries not to laugh. Her playful grin only adds to the charm of the moment.

I love their love.

I just wish I had it, too.

For two centuries I've been a ghost of my former self, watching as my friends pair off with mates, some even having children who've grown and had children of their own.

My eyes scan the small clearing, taking in each of my squadron and the love they share with their mates, my chest compressing at the sight. It's not for them, this flutter of pain, this hollow space inside.

That void has a name—Wilder.

As I cast my gaze to the curling flames, hoping their dance can sear away the sudden wetness behind my eyes, I'm reminded that some longings are etched too deep, their grooves worn into the very fabric of our being.

Around the embers, my squadron, an assembly of the only phoenix fae in existence—that we know of—relaxes into the evening's camaraderie. We are the living, breathing heartbeat of this place, a sisterhood bound by fire and flight. Each of them is mated.

Except me.

The only person I've ever come close to considering in that way is Wilder. But he's merfae, bound by a unique sacrament where they unite with their 'anchors.' Unlike mates chosen by destiny or the mystical veil, merfae anchors are said to be determined by the very essence of the sea itself. It's a profound, elemental connection, shrouded in the mystery and depth of the ocean. A connection I've heard of, but never truly understood, remaining just another puzzle of the myriad fae cultures.

My gaze drifts across the faces illuminated by the flames, each one a story, a victory, a loss. We've witnessed a lot of death over our thousands of years.

I watch as Sabine, her hair the color of autumn's final blaze, teases Vero about her last sky-dance, and I smile. There's an ease in their banter, a history that has woven itself into the very air we breathe.

A nudge at my side pulls me back, and I turn to see Bow holding out a bottle to me, its contents chartreuse, and I blink, the ache in my chest intensifying as I reach for my absinthe.

This had been my favorite drink for as long as I can remember. So why does the sight of it nearly cleave me in two? And why the fuck have I been so emotional lately? Schooling my features, I blink rapidly, dispelling the tears collecting behind my eyes as I wrap my hand around the neck of the bottle of absinthe and bring it to my lips.

The familiar burn of the la fée verte washes over me, and I take another swig, relishing in the numbing sensation that spreads throughout my body as I drain it. As I lower the bottle, I catch Noct's eyes once more, and her expression is one of concern. She knows something is wrong but doesn't push.

It's been a month since I've been back, and I'm still no closer to any answers.

Where the hell had I been, and why can't I remember?

I feel the squadron's attention shift subtly towards me. A silent recalibration. I'm not slurring my words or stumbling over myself. I can fake happy. With a roll of my eyes, a gesture they expect, I deflect. "I'll find a way to get more, don't you worry your pretty little heads."

Absinthe is extraordinarily difficult to get here, though it's a lot easier than it used to be now that we can legally go to the surface any time we want.

The squadron laughs, and the sound carries over the bonfire's crackle, easy and unburdened. As the laughter subsides, I feel the ease of command settle around me. While they're my charges, they're my friends. My family. Yet, in the mix of warmth and light, there's a chill in my heart, a space where Wilder's memory lingers like a shadow at the edge of the fire's reach.

But it feels like more than that, I've always missed Wilder. But this emptiness? This is on another level.

The conversation ebbs and flows around me. Freya's white wings catch the light, and Arwen's laughter spills like the rush of wind through fiery orange feathers. Harmony's honey-colored hair reflects the fire's glow as she speaks with a soothing cadence.

I partake in the ritual. The banter and my laughter are genuine, but my heart is distant, as I keep my hand wrapped around the collar of this bottle, desperate to feel something other than heartrending agony inside.

So when someone tosses me a beer, I drink it fast. Anything to numb the ache.

Whatever it is. It's not just an ache. An emptiness, where Wilder should be.

And the rest.

The thought enters my mind, unbidden. What does that even mean? What else am I missing? What else is my soul craving?

For now, I let the fire's warmth keep me company amongst my friends, who I feel a heartbeat behind. I am their commander, resurrected but still adrift. As though I'm just out of step because I don't know the rules. I don't know the page they're on.

Noct steps in front of me, reaching out a hand to help me up. I take it, and she glances back at Ronin, who gives her a nod.

"She's coming home with me," I tease him, and he just gives me a playful eyeroll.

I lock my arm around Noct's, and her presence is a steady heat at my side as the laughter at the bonfire fades behind us. Our path is a meandering one, bordered by the lush underbrush that thrives in Castanea's twilight, iridescent flowers reflecting soft luminosities like earthbound stars. The muted sounds of the nighttime creatures are a quiet orchestra, a contrast to the riotous farewells of my squadron.

"You don't have to walk me back," I murmur. The bridges that connect our homes sway lightly with each step. Or is that me? The movement is familiar, a dance I've mastered over countless nights since I've been back—from wherever it is I've been.

"I know," Noct replies, her voice a smooth alto that seems to harmonize naturally with the rustling leaves. "But I want to." Her gaze is heavy with things unsaid, and with questions she's not asking.

"It's late," I say, deflecting, focusing on the verdant canopy above us, avoiding the earnestness in her eyes.

I hate these conversations with her because I don't like lying to my friends, even to protect the man I love. I've been doing it for two thousand years now, constantly redirecting and avoiding the truth. First, when I'd sneak out or smuggle him into Castanea, and then when he went to prison.

"Not too late for a stroll with a friend," she counters, her hand brushing against the wooden handrail.

We cross a bridge that spans a gentle stream, reflecting the innumerable lights above. It's beautiful here, a slice of serenity. "You've been drinking, too. Who's going to walk you home?" I point out, an attempt to keep the conversation light.

Noct chuckles. "Mostly beer. I don't even feel a buzz anymore." The teasing lilt to her words land with a weight I'm not prepared to carry.

The walk is a warren of bridges and paths that cradle the heart of our underground sanctuary. We pass by the luminescent blooms and the towering trees that have been fashioned into homes, structures that blend seamlessly with the environment. Noct is silent when we pause before the arching entrance to my treehouse, the wooden door carved with the stories of the Tolden.

"Thanks for the escort," I say, my hand hovering over the door handle.

"Anytime," she replies, and there's a hesitation in her stance. "Mind if I come in?"

I turn to her, and in the faint light, her features are soft, the hard lines of command smoothed away. "Sure."

She settles on my couch while I make a pot of tea, knowing I'm going to need to sober up for this conversation. I prepare hers with extra sugar, just the way she likes it, while I take mine with honey and lots of milk. Hers is in a pink mug with a fluffy, cloud-like saucer, while mine is in a chipped teacup with the word, POISON on the side.

After kicking off my shoes, I tuck my feet under me, focusing on the mug in my hand as I sip from it.

"Talk to me," she begs, and I meet her eyes, seeing how much I'm hurting her.

"I don't know what you want me to say, Noct, I can't tell you Wilder's name, I can't—" My cup tumbles out of my hand, the tea hot but not scalding as it spills all over my lap. It's too late. The name crossed my lips. How did that happen? A well of relief surges within me at just saying his name out loud.

Noct scrambles to help me clean up, but I grab her shoulders, stopping her. "His name is Wilder!" I cry, the words no longer holding my tongue captive.

"Who, honey?" her eyes dart back and forth between mine, and a deep groove forms between her brows.

There's always been a *him*. She just didn't know any details—such as the fact that he was on the surface, that he's my best friend, the unrequited love of my life. Where he's at now, and how he got there.

"The love of my life," I half whisper, half sob.

Her eyes widen, and I'd laugh if I wasn't about to throw up. Noct's brow furrows further, her warrior instincts on alert. "Did something happen? You never talk about him."

"He bound my tongue so I couldn't speak the truth, but then we both died. And apparently, so did the bind." I shake my head, still in shock that my tongue has finally been set free. Stubborn tears cascade down my face.

And now tonight, I'll reveal a secret that's been buried deep within me, a truth that will alter the very fabric of my relationship with Noct, the entire squadron, my whole life.

It's long overdue.

Two hundred years in the making, I'm finally able to right everything that went horribly wrong. I can hardly believe it.

She sits, her posture attentive, her gaze piercing. "What's going on? You're making me nervous."

Taking a deep breath, I stand so I can pace slowly, choosing my words carefully as I throw up a silencing charm to protect our conversation. "I'm ready to tell you everything."

I pause near the window, looking out at the network of branches and leaves, a natural tapis that feels both comforting and confining. "His name is Wilder," I repeat, my voice a mere whisper. "And I have loved him for two thousand years." Another tear tracks down my cheeks, and I could drown in my grief.

Noct leans forward, her expression a mix of concern and curiosity. "Two thousand years? But that means—"

"He's from the surface."

She gasps, and I turn to face her, the presence of the secret like a physical presence between us. Sorrow draws lines in her forehead as her brows pull together, and her eyes turn glassy. "Oh, Morte." She crosses to the window and pulls me into her arms, holding the back of my head as the tears pour down my cheeks. Her warmth is a balm to my aching soul, but it does little to ease the burden of my secret.

Tolden were hunted by werewolves seeking a cure for their affliction, and Crucey, our leader, built the underground sanctuary of Castanea to keep us safe. It was forbidden for us to breach the surface. But I did. More times than I can count over the two thousand years I'd known Wilder. It was only recently when the curse was broken for good and we no longer had to hide, and the rest of Bedlam could know about our people.

Noct's strong arms tighten around me, giving me the courage to voice my fears. I whisper haltingly, "He's a merfae, and I felt it immediately when I first saw him. It was a reckless decision, but somewhere in my soul I knew it was love. I could never deny it, no matter how dangerous it seemed."

"He doesn't feel the same way?" She pulls back, her expression softening with empathy shining in her silver eyes.

"Oh, I know he loves me," I say, trying to keep myself together, my grip on her forearms tightening with desperation. "But merfae are monogamous for life, and only sleep with their anchor." My voice breaks on the last words and I can barely bring myself to say them out loud. "And I'm not his," I whisper, letting the agony resonate through my body.

It's like a sharp blade, slicing me in two.

She scrubs furiously at her eyes, unable to stem the torrent of tears that escape. "I'm so sorry, pretty girl. I can't begin to put into words how much sorrow this brings me."

I know she's trying to put herself in my shoes, what this would be like for her if she couldn't be with Ronin. They're soul bonded mates, dictated by fate itself, much like anchors.

"I know, it's okay," I whisper, my words thick and garbled as a sob builds in my throat.

"Have you thought about bringing him here, now that we're able to have outsiders come in?"

"He can't. Because of the next secret I've been keeping. He's the reason I had my mental break two-hundred years ago." After the court handed down his sentence, I was so devastated that I had to be placed in a cryochamber for several years.

"Did he hurt you?" she thunders back with her fiery eyes blazing, her brows pulled tight in rage.

There's a lot of empathy in each of us, but fuck with one, you fuck with us all. We weren't always warriors.

"No. Quite the opposite, really." I hold her hand and guide her back into the living room and sit us down on the couch. "Till my death, or our deaths," I stumble over my words. "I was forbidden to talk about this because he used magic to bind my tongue. He's in prison because of me, and during our mission there, I'd found him."

"He was the inmate whose cell you'd been killed in," she gasps, throwing her hand up to her mouth in shock. She's always been so brilliant. Connecting the pieces where only vague hints of a shape appear.

I nod. "He was imprisoned for a crime I committed two centuries ago. He took the fall for me."

Her eyes begin to water again as her face crumples in grief. "Morte, don't—" She places her hands over my mouth, nearly crawling into my lap to do it. "Don't tell me, please, don't do this."

She's always been too smart for her own good. I shake my head, grab her hands, and hold them in my lap. "It's time, Noct."

She's full-on bawling now. "I just got you back," she begs. "Don't do this! Please!" Her voice is shrill, having connected the pieces just as quickly as I expected she would.

My heart lurches as I envision the scene as I relay to her how I'd gone to the surface and was captured by fae who were seeking immortality feathers. I'd killed them all, only to realize too late that they were glamored. I'd killed teenagers. When authorities had come for me, Wilder took the blame, even though he wasn't even on the beach yet. He bound my tongue, so I couldn't tell the truth of what happened. For hundreds of years, I tried.

Noct's sobs are the only sound in the room as I continue. "I'm finally turning myself in." I take a deep breath, trying to steady my voice. I've thought about how I would handle this for two hundred years, and now that the time is finally here, I'm not hesitating. But I'll be smart about it. Put pieces in motion.

"I'll have instructions for my things and hidden in an enchanted compartment under my bed are the letters Wilder and I would write to each other to read when we weren't together. And this," I reach for a small seashell on the coffee table and hand it to her, "is what you'll need to hold in order for the glamor on the hiding spot to disappear. Wilder will hopefully get out when I confess, and I know he will come straight here."

Her hands tremble so bad, she can barely hold on to it as she shakes her head, unable to comprehend the significance of what I'm doing.

"Please, take care of him. Wilder deserves so much more than what fate has dealt him."

As I speak, my heart feels like it's shattering into a million pieces. But this is the path I must walk. A path paved with repentance and the hope for redemption. Noct's tears, her pleas, they echo the turmoil within me, but my decision is irrevocable.

Tonight, I've laid bare the deepest root of my soul, and in doing so, I've set into motion events that will change the course of my life forever. I only wish I could've undone it all.

Noct is such a mess by the time I can get her to leave. I don't want her to, but there are so many things I have to do to make things right.

"Then I'll leave you to it. Goodnight, Morte." She kisses my cheek, squeezing me for several long seconds before she reluctantly lets go of me.

"Goodnight, Noct." I watch her turn, her figure retreating along the bridge, back into the fold of the canopy's embrace.

The door creaks softly as I push it open, stepping inside the solitude of my treehouse. I'm alone with the night and my thoughts, the echoes of our conversation lingering like the aftertaste of the absinthe, bittersweet and persistent.

I move slowly, each step heavy with the leaden weight of the grief I'm causing my friend, and my own soul-deep longing. The floorboards are cool under my bare feet as I approach the bed, an island in a sea of memories.

The room spins ever so slightly, a gentle souvenir of the night's indulgences. I reach for the steadiness of the bedpost, allowing the momentary dizziness to pass. The wooden planks beneath the bed whisper of secrets they keep, and with a steadying breath, I kneel down, my fingers tracing the edges of one board until they find the catch—a clever thing, invisible to any eye but mine, unless you've got the small seashell in your hand when you approach it.

With a press and a twist, the board lifts, revealing a small, shadowed cavity. I pause, a silent prayer on my lips, an invocation to the magic that lingers in my veins like the echo of a long-forgotten song.

"Praeservo," I breathe, the word slipping out like a lover's sigh, and my fingers tingle with the thrum of ancient power. Light, soft and blue as the twilight sky of Bedlam, dances from my fingertips, weaving over the pile of letters with the tenderness of a mother's touch on her newborn's cheek. The charm wraps around them, reinforcing the spells that keep the paper fresh, the ink vibrant, as if Wilder's hand had just swept across them moments ago.

I reach in, my hands steady now, emboldened by the presence of magic, and withdraw the stack of letters bound by a ribbon the color of the deep sea—Wilder's sea. My heart thrums in my chest, a drumbeat out of sync with the world around me.

The letters rustle as I set them down, the sound a whisper of the past, of stolen moments and laughter shared under the stars of a different sky. Wilder's script is elegant, the characters flowing like the water he called home, each word a brushstroke painting images of a time when things were simpler, or perhaps just less understood.

I unfold the first letter. The paper's now supple under the charm, and Wilder's voice seems to fill the room, a murmur carried on the currents of my memory:

Morte,

> *The surface tonight is still, a perfect mirror to the stars above. I found myself tracing constellations in the water, connecting dots of light, sketching out the shape of your eyes, the curve of your smile. It's quiet here, too quiet without the timbre of your laughter or the warmth of your hand in mine.*
>
> *You ask if I ever grow lonely, adrift in the silent depths. The truth is, I only know loneliness when I'm away from you ...*

I lean back against the bed, the letter cradled in my lap, the words blurring as tears well in my eyes. I swipe at them impatiently, refusing to let them fall. We were never more than what we were—a merfae and a Tolden, a friendship that defied conventions, tiptoeing around the edges of something more. We fooled around, and often shared a bed—for sleep—but nothing further than heavy petting. I'd respected his boundaries and the custom of merfae, who don't sleep with anyone other than their anchors, just as he had respected my virtue, yet we'd danced dangerously close to something more.

Something I would've given him a million times over, and still would if the hands of fate weren't so cruel as to not make me his anchor.

A heavy sigh escapes me, the heft of centuries settling on my shoulders. In the silence of my treehouse, surrounded by the enchanted glow of Castanea's faux night, I let myself sink into the memories. The laughter, the danger, the thrill of our secret meetings. Wilder was my secret, my solace, my ... what? Not lover, not quite, but something perilously close to it. A lover in every way except the act itself.

I whisper another spell, a simple one to dry the tears that threaten to fall. It's not the magic of Tolden, but something older, something that resonates with the sorrow in my heart. The magic does its work, and I can once again see clearly though the ache remains. I've always been an easy crier, and have used that spell more than I'd like to admit in battles.

I breathe deep, the night fresh with the scents of Castanea's eternal bloom, and I steady myself with the thought that tomorrow is another day. A day for duty, for strength, for moving forward.

But tonight, I allow myself to remember.

CHAPTER NINE

MORTE

The unforgiving light of a new day streams in through the bioluminescent foliage that veils my treehouse. I blink away the remnants of last night's absinthe and the bittersweet haze of old letters clutched to my chest. With Wilder's words still lingering on my tongue, I rise. Duty calls, even on days when the rest of Castanea slumbers in the comfort of leisure.

I want to know what happened the night Wilder and I died, because I might never get the chance again.

As I weave through the quiet treetop streets, the flora and fauna of our underground oasis are a whispering audience to my solitary march. The echoes of laughter from last night's bonfire seem to hang in the air, ghosts of joy that fade as I draw closer to the center of our command.

The door to the middle room swings open with a familiar creak, a sound I should probably oil away, but it's a part of this place as much as I am. The files, the maps, the endless stacks of reports, they all await me, as patient and unmoving as the stones that keep us hidden from the world above.

I move to my desk, a sprawling thing of aged wood and carved memories, and trail my fingers over the surface before diving into the task I've come here for. The reports from the night I died—vanished, or whatever word one would use for a two-year absence that left no trace—they must hold some clue.

Drawer after drawer, I scour through the meticulous records. General Risç's penchant for order is a blessing now, even as I curse it on busier days. His absence, a vacation to the earth realm, leaves me unwatched, free to pursue this without the burden of his scrutiny. He'll be back next week, and with him, perhaps a chance to finally discuss the gaping hole in my memory, the missing piece of my life's tapestry.

Only then can I go through with my confession. Until then, I've work to do. Staying focused is key.

Each report I read through is like a step back in time. The dry ink and crisp paper are a dramatic contrast to the warm, pulsating life of the letters from Wilder. But these hold no charm, no whispered confessions of love. They are cold, factual, and frustratingly void of any revelation.

Hours tick by, and the muted light from the crystals shifts imperceptibly. I'm so engrossed that I don't hear the hard footsteps, the approach of someone equally out of sync with the day's restful intentions.

"Hey, pretty girl, I didn't expect anyone else to be in today," comes a familiar voice, tinged with surprise. "Not after such a late night."

I glance up, blinking away the strain of reading, to find Noct standing in the doorway, dark smudges under her eyes, and the lines of grief on her brow. Her wings are neatly folded behind her, the iridescence of her feathers catching the dim light.

"Hey," I acknowledge with a sigh, my voice steady despite the churn of guilt and frustration in my gut. "I thought I'd make use of the quiet. There are answers here somewhere; there has to be."

She walks over, her movements more graceful as she reads the room. "You're looking for the night it happened, aren't you? For what we might've missed?"

I can only nod, exhaustion seeping into my bones.

Noct's hand finds its way to the stack of files I've yet to go through, her touch light. "Let's look together, then. Two pairs of eyes are better than one."

Together, we analyze the past, the missing hours of my life laid out in ink and paper, waiting to yield their secrets.

In the hushed refuge of the office, the only sounds are the soft whir of the magic that fuels this place and the rustle of pages as we sift through file after file. This isn't just about refreshing memories; it's a deep dive into the unfathomable, an investigation into a night shrouded in shadows and secrecy. How does a phoenix fae, who has died thousands of times before, die semi-permanently, and go missing for two years?

After exhausting each folder, I bring the stack to the filing cabinet and pull it out all the way. It's when I'm trying to fit the heap back into the drawer that I meet resistance. Something isn't allowing me to shove them back into place.

Setting the pile on the floor, I return to the drawer and use a lighting charm to see what's in the way. A gasp escapes me when I spot what we've been looking for. I've searched this place high and low, and now I've got it. My fingers ease it out of place before I take the statements over to the desk.

The report is official, sterile, and I'm struck by the dispassion in its language—a recollection bereft of the chaos I can scarcely remember. It's the aftermath detailed in the pages that I need, a balm for the gaps in my memory. My fingers tremble slightly as I turn to the section outlining the recovery of ... what was left.

There's a precision to the account that feels almost invasive. It narrates how the squad had found a pile of ashes, mine by the tell-tale aura they give off, the remnants of what used to be their commander. The horror of that discovery, the grief, is lost in the formal tone of the document, but I can almost hear the echoes of their cries between the lines when I didn't resurrect. They'd brought my remains to my treehouse for resurrection, as they'd been ordered to clear out of the prison.

Wilder's name is absent. Of course it is. His existence, a closely guarded secret of mine, a chapter of my life known to no one within these cavernous walls.

Until now.

The hydra fae's rampage is documented with cold clarity—its escape, the havoc it wreaked, the chase. But there's nothing of my excruciating pain of torn wings, the brief time I spent in Wilder's arms in his cell, the moment he was about to tell me his confession. And nothing of the noble sacrifice he made to try to save me.

A sob gets caught in my throat and I toss up a silencing charm on the room as I bury my head in my hands, trying to hold it all together but failing.

Warm arms wrap around me, along with soft whispers of, "we'll find answers, it's okay, you're so strong, so brave, let it all go," from my friend.

So I do. I wail, a guttural cry that echoes through the room and fills the space with my pain. Noct doesn't let go, holding me tighter as she lets me weep. My entire body shakes as I let out all my grief and guilt.

For hours, she rocks me, whispering soothing words against my red hair. When it feels like I have no more tears left in my body, I swipe at my cheeks and take a deep breath. "I'm sorry," I croak, still feeling raw.

"You needed to let it out. And you never need to apologize for being real with me," Noct says.

She leaves to get me a glass of water from our little kitchenette in the back of the room. This space is built right into the bedrock, with natural cave walls, which helps keep the place cool.

Straightening my shirt, I pick up the file detailing that night again. The omission is a glaring void where the truth should be. My death, the hydra's lethal bite—what am I missing? Does a bite from a hydra do something different to phoenixes in particular? I know they have venom in their saliva, but we've all died in unimaginable ways over our thousands of years ... and have always come back.

I need to remember. The edges of the file blur as I focus inward, attempting to coax forth the shadows of the past. But there's only darkness, a void where my memories should be. Wilder's face is clear in my mind's eye, his expression as he launched me away from danger—desperate, determined, doomed. A silent plea escapes me, for these memories to return, for the gaps to be filled.

What was different about that night? And why did I disappear for two years?

As I dwell on the possible reasons for the missing information, a new drive solidifies within me.

If the answers won't come from within, then I must seek them without.

I need to find my way back to Wilder. The connection we share, perhaps that's the key to unlocking what's been lost.

General Risç's return looms in my thoughts. With him might come answers, or perhaps more questions, but either way, this is long overdue.

"You're not alone in this." Noct rises from her seat, her gaze meeting mine across the clutter of reports scattered on the desk. "Before you confess, we should be certain we have everything we need to free Wilder. There might be something we don't know. Something huge that could help. We need to know where you've been. How do we know it isn't all connected?"

I look up from the damning report in my hand, as the worry of centuries press down on me. "But every day I wait feels like another betrayal," I admit, my voice barely above a whisper.

"Morte," she begins with a hint of firmness in her otherwise soft tone. "Wilder took the burden of your fate *willingly*. Let's ensure his sacrifice wasn't in vain. We can't predict how the court will judge him for shielding one they consider a criminal." She pauses, and a fleeting grimace crosses her face.

I offer a dismissive tilt of my head. A silent dismissal of any hurt.

"Just give us a week," she continues. "If we uncover any new evidence—any sliver of truth—it could sway the scales in Wilder's favor. It's our duty to leave no stone unturned for the both of you."

Her words, heavy with implicit understanding, hang in the air between us. "I ... I'm scared," I confess, the vulnerability in my voice new and unnerving. "What if my silence costs him more than we realize?"

"We've stood by each other for millennia," she reminds me, her hand reaching out to still my fidgeting fingers. "One more week won't break us. But it might just be the key to setting everything right."

A silent moment passes, and I nod. The belief in her eyes kindles a spark of hope within the cold dread that's settled in my heart.

"Okay," I agree. The file in my hands feels less like a sentence and more like a starting point. "One week to unearth the truth, for Wilder's sake. And then ... I'll do what must be done."

She smiles, a warrior's smile, all grit and strength. "Then let's get started. We have a truth to uncover and a friend to save."

CHAPTER TEN

AGGONID

I stalk through the clandestine corridor, a chess master on the brink of his defining move. The walls, lined with ores that pulsate with suppressed energy, seem to close in around me. I'm waiting, not merely as the feared ruler of the Underworld but as a god among beings, for an audience with one whose power almost rivals my own.

High King Finian Drake.

My blood boils as I traverse the realm of Romarie, remembering my last visit here with Morte, and King Valtorious's senseless attack. This is our standard meeting place on neutral ground for inter-realm matters. We'd needed to meet with Finian, and King Valtorious thought he could test me. He's always craved power, pushing boundaries, itching to take over more than just Romarie. He wants to ascend, become a god.

To take over as ruler of my domain.

I probably should've just killed him when I was here last, but I didn't want to deal with the paperwork, nor the rest of the god's council. Not when I had my soul bonded mate with me, whether I recognized the bond at the time or not.

Glee courses through my veins as I imagine Valtorious cowering in fear somewhere, unaware when my retribution will come. I revel in the thought of his dread, relishing the day when I get to even the score.

But not today.

Today's about necessity. To get to Bedlam from the Underworld, you've got to pass through Romarie—no way around it unless I go through the god's council and a whole lot of legalities. I may be the fae devil, but they act as though I'd ransack the realms, taking whichever souls I please. Only my reapers have the run of the place to collect souls when they're due. So, here I am, in Romarie, playing by the rules, for now. King Valtorious won't even know we're here.

He lacks the power.

Silence hangs heavy as I get closer to the meet, putting on my game face. Cold, composed—that's what I need to be. Finian's got his own agenda, sure, but he knows this dance as well as I do. We're both playing a high-stakes game, and neither of us wants to tip the board.

Finian, for all his diplomacy, knows the underlying nature of our relationship: two potentates negotiating on a knife-edge.

I place the marker in the center of the alleyway, one that's only ever carried by the gods, so Finn knows where to arrive. Sometimes he gets here before I can do that, and I have to track him down. The portal's hallway is always the same, but where it comes out depends on the crowds, and where I can find a quiet corner of the city.

He materializes from the shimmering portal, a figure both venerated and daunting. Finian's hair, white as moon-touched frost, frames a face of glaring, otherworldly beauty. All luna fae glow blue under the moons. His stature exceeds mine, not significantly, but enough to remind me that in physicality, as in power, we are closely matched.

His form is sculpted, the embodiment of fae nobility, his build suggesting a strength that need not boast, for it's understood. We stand in the muted glow of Romarie's city of metal, two immortals locked in a silent appraisal.

The alleyway is narrow and cramped with towering walls made of rusted iron that seem to close in on all sides. Each time the portal opens, it's in a new place, just in case prying eyes see what they're not supposed to. The soft light of the city filters through cracks in the walls, casting eerie shadows on the slick, rain-soaked ground. The metal is marred with scratches and scorch marks, giving the impression of a place that has seen its fair share of violence.

"Aggonid," he greets, his voice a low rumble that resonates against the metal bones of the corridor.

The city is thick with the scent of rust and decay, a reminder of its metallic underbelly. Mixed in is the pungent aroma of magic, both dark and alluring.

"Finn," I return, my voice edged with the timbre of the abyss, a subtle nod to the darkness I command.

His eyes, sharp as the first snow, do not flinch. "What brings the fae devil to broker terms in the shadows?" he inquires, his tone laced with wariness and an acknowledgment of our past dealings. "Again."

I allow myself a small smile, one that doesn't reach my eyes, a smirk befitting the infernal lord that I am. "A certain situation has become convoluted, and the equilibrium between the realms has been upset."

It's me, I'm the one that's upset.

We stand veiled in shadows, a consequence of our chosen nook's partial obscurity, our gazes locked in silent conflict. Enveloped within a silencing bubble, our words are ours alone; even whispers are turned secret confessions, imperceptible to the world beyond. A privacy cloak renders us invisible to idle eyes, a pair of phantoms in a crowd unseeing. Yet, this concealment would falter against the adept —those versed in the Sight of the Unseen—a rare enchantment that peels back cloaks of secrecy. But even this magic has its limits, requiring the wielder to know precisely where to cast their gaze.

But it doesn't stop me from glancing down the alleyway, watching as two passersby clear the entrance before turning my attention back to the High King.

Finian's eyes narrow, filled with our shared history. He knows the stakes as well as I do. Meddling rulers have threatened this balance for millennia. He doesn't have to know that it's me.

"The boon I granted, I presume," he breathes, and I incline my head. "Speak your terms."

I step closer, the power within me unfurling like the wings of a raven in the dead of night. "The phoenix fae, Morte. She is ... integral to the balance of my domain. Her return to Bedlam disrupts more than you know."

A muscle twitches in Finian's jaw, his façade of calm challenged. "And what do you offer in return for entertaining this switch ... again?" His stance is obstinate, a mountain challenging the storm.

"A new pact," I declare, my voice a purr of velvet draped over steel. "A boon of your choosing, at the time of your choosing, within reason. A favor that could tip the scales back into alignment. Perhaps I'd feel more generous should one of your little pets happens to find themselves in my domain again."

I think back to Caius and his twisted delight in tormenting the vampire Gideon, a soul unfortunate enough to fall into our realm. When creatures with souls as dark as his end up here, my mate makes it feel as though they're living a thousand years of torture in mere hours. The memory brings a dark amusement. Pity we didn't keep the vamp here, then we wouldn't be in the mess we're in now.

For a moment, there's silence, as if the realms themselves hold their breath.

Finally, he inclines his head slightly. "I'll consider it," he says. "But be warned, Aggonid, the cost will reflect the magnitude of your request. I'll see if Mother can send her back, but only if Morte wants to go, and I'll need reassurances she'll be treated well there."

I nod, the barest dip of my chin acknowledging his terms. Movement between the Underworld and the realms isn't simple. It has the power to disrupt, blur the lines of the afterlife. There's no way to do it without Luna's blessing and intervention. Finn's grave answer is so predictable.

"I haven't forgotten the war you waged to try to get your soul bonded mate back from the kings." I chuckle. He tries to be so noble. "Slaughtering thousands. Funny how so many of your alleged 'good' fae ended up in my clutches, isn't it?" I pluck an invisible speck of dust off his coat, but he doesn't flinch. Shows no emotion as he stares me down. "Should any of your precious royal court end up in my domain again, I'm happy to play chess with you to reclaim them."

He doesn't acknowledge my underlying threat, but he hears me. *Play nice, and I'll ensure that if your little friends end up in hell, I'll ensure they find their way back.*

As he retreats, the portal swallowing his form, the heavy cloak of potential outcomes settles upon my shoulders. The game continues, and the next move will define the fates of realms.

Because if I can't have her? The realms think I'm unhinged now. It'll be nothing compared to the denial of seeing my mate.

Morte must return to me. To us. The boon must be granted, and I'll wait, with the patience of eons, for the High King to grant us this. For now, the image of Morte's spirit remains emblazoned upon my mind, a promise of cataclysmic reunions to come.

As I turn away, the echo of my steps rings out like a proclamation. The deal will be struck, the balance restored, and Morte will be mine again. This I vow, with all the certainty of the dark throne I occupy.

CHAPTER ELEVEN

CAIUS

The gloom of our room is like a second skin, comfortable and familiar. In the velvety blackness, I feel rather than see Aggonid's presence beside me. His breath is a slow rhythm, the only sound in the silence that stretches around us like a physical thing.

I spent my day cutting the fingers and toes off the latest batch of souls that arrived in our domain. As soon as I'd seen the pitch of their souls, so dark as though they consumed everything around it, I'd reveled in breaking them until they were nothing but whimpering shells.

These ones have committed unspeakable acts against their own mates, a crime that even I, with my monstrous nature and dark soul, cannot condone. The bond between mates is sacred, and these beasts have defiled it beyond repair.

I made it feel like they'd been tortured for ten thousand years, all in the span of minutes. Timeweaver, some call me. But if I could really do anything more than expand and condense time, I would've traveled back to stop Aggonid from brokering a deal to let Morte go.

As I reflect on the pitch of Aggonid's soul, I'm consumed with guilt and regret. I should have taken notice sooner, should have intervened before it was too late. Should've seen the unspeakable things he did to push her away from us. I would've made him see reason. That a soul bonded mate could never be sent here to destroy him, that the fates would never be so cruel.

But now Morte has been irreparably hurt by Aggonid, and perhaps she wouldn't have wanted to leave if I had acted sooner.

I'd never speak those words out loud, because I love him. He knows how bad he fucked this up.

He's been gone to Romarie all day, meeting with the one lifeline we have to get our mate back. I don't know why we're bothering with waiting on Finian to ask Mommy Dearest for help. I say Aggonid should just go steal her back, fuck the consequences. As his soul bonded mate, the magic that powers this realm shouldn't reject her and send her back because she belongs here, especially as she's already died and been brought here once before. Just take the portal to Romarie then take the portal to the Underworld.

Aggonid shifts, and I know he's awake now, no doubt caused by my tossing and turning. His movements are a language I've come to understand, a silent conversation between two beings who have seen the millennia pass. I lie here quietly, letting the silence stretch a bit longer, respecting the communion of our shared solitude.

"You're thinking loud enough to wake the dead," he murmurs, the amusement in his tone belied by the tension I sense in his frame.

I turn to face him, seeing his outline in the dark. "If I could, I'd rouse them all to bring her back," I confess, my voice barely threading through the dark. My desire for Morte is a constant thrum beneath my skin, a longing sharpened with every night she's not here.

This is how we descend into madness.

Fae lose their minds by the absence of their mates, unraveling into psychosis. But first, it makes you emotional, irrational, desperate. Accusations of my own sanity—or the lack thereof—have never been foreign to me. I have to be to endure the work I do here. The idea that I could fray further tightens a knot of fear within the longing.

My mate is silent for a moment. "Patience. Even the dead must wait their turn."

I can almost see the smirk playing on his lips, a shadow of mirth in the obscurity as he turns over towards me.

Finally, I sigh. "Patience is a virtue I never possessed." No, my craft is the art of chaos and agony, the sweet chorus of screams that echo through these infernal depths. Gluttony, lust, greed—these are not mere indulgences; they are instruments of torture, wielded with demonic precision. In my mate's dominion, I am the dread enforcer, the hand that delivers excruciating lessons to the damned.

A low chuckle escapes him, and the sound is a flicker of light in the void of our chamber. "True, but for her, we bend. We wait."

I nod, feeling the heft of his gaze as I throw the blanket off me. "For her, I would twist the very fabric of time, if only to quicken her steps to our side." I'd never eat another bird again if it meant she'd come back. I've already sworn off ground gnomes for her sake.

Aggonid's hand finds mine in the darkness, his grip firm. "And she will walk it, in her own time. We must trust in that. And if she won't, we'll drag her back to hell if we must."

I'm not so sure he means that. We'd both do terrible things for each other, but if Aggonid wanted to be rid of me and truly meant he was going to be happy without me, I'd leave. I'd also descend further into madness and probably off myself, but I'd leave if he didn't want me. I squeeze his hand, the only concession I'll make to this helplessness that has taken root within me.

"Azazel said he tested the dreamsca—"

"He saw Morte without us?!" I sit up in bed, turning towards Aggie.

He tugs me back down to lay beside him. "No, he said he tested it on a neighbor. He created the dream, saw them, and he could hear the man, but they couldn't communicate back-and-forth. He said he needed more power."

"Then with all of our power combined, we should be fine, no?" I can't wait to see our mate. It won't be the same as getting to hold her in reality, but I need her, and I'll take her any way I can get her.

His red eyes glow bright, all the love for Morte shining in them.

"Yeah, we should be able to do it with a few more pieces Emeric is working on now."

"We should've allowed her to keep her chained to you," I say softly, releasing his hand as I lie back. "When I see her again, I'll ask her to chain herself to me. She'll never get taken away again."

Aggonid's quiet chuckle is a comfort, a reminder that in this agony without her, I'm not alone. We're bound by more than just power or dominion; we are bound by a love that even the fates have dared not to sever.

And in the quiet before the dawn, in a world that knows neither sun nor starlight, we wait. For her. For Morte. Our phoenix, our flame, our fate.

"What do you think she's doing right now?" he whispers.

I close my eyes, imagining her in Bedlam. I can almost see her fiery wings beating against the magical winds, her eyes blazing with a belief that could move mountains. "She's probably plotting her escape," I sigh. "Morte wouldn't just sit there and wait for us to rescue her. She's a warrior there, Aggie. I bet she'd find a way to us before we even figure out how to get her back." Such a smart little birdie.

"Wouldn't that be something?" I can hear his grin, and I open my eyes to get a good look at him.

The soft crimson glow emanating from his eyes is a clear indicator that his powers are building up, ready to surge at any moment. As we approach the Forsaken Hunt once again, he knows he'll have to grant another favor or risk being overwhelmed by his own power. Now that he's formally mated with Morte, it'll get worse if he can't tamp it through their bond. I can only do so much.

His touch lingers a little longer on my skin, a silent plea for comfort, for reassurance. I give it freely, knowing that he needs it just as much as I do. The absence of our missing mate is substantial, almost suffocating, but we bear it together.

The silence settles once more, a veil that cloaks the words and the heat that simmers between us. Aggonid's hand has not left me, his fingers tracing small, searing circles on my chest, igniting a fire that's all too ready to burn.

His touch is deliberate, each contact a spark that lights up the darkness. I draw a breath, letting the air fill my lungs, feeling it mix with the power that courses through our veins—a power that fuels desire as much as it does fear.

"Remember the first night I took you?" His voice is a whisper, a caress that dances down my spine. "The clash of wills, the meeting of storms?"

I chuckle, the sound resonating in the closeness between us. "How could I forget? The Underworld hadn't seen such a tempest, not before, not since." Our mating was cataclysmic. Although I may be exaggerating my role a bit. He humors me anyway.

Aggonid moves closer, his body now a line of heat against mine. "You were wild fury," he continues, his breath a tickle against my ear. "A force untamed."

"And you," I grin, my voice husky with the memories, "a god to be reckoned with. A darkness to consume my chaos."

There's a shift in the air, a charged energy that wraps around us. His lips brush against my neck, a featherlight touch that seizes my pulse, commanding it to quicken. Rarely do my shadows come out to play, but they're out now, entwined with his, a union of darkness and desire. I turn my head, seeking his mouth, and he obliges, capturing my lips in a kiss that's both savage and tender.

The taste of him is like a drug, an addiction that I can't resist. His tongue sweeps into my mouth, claiming me, possessing me. He nips at my lip, tugging it between his before he pulls back so he can press a kiss to my neck.

"I saw eternity the moment we met," Aggonid confesses, the words vibrating against my skin. "A bond that would transcend the aeons."

His mouth finds mine again, and it's like the first rain after an endless drought—eager, intense, life-affirming. Our kiss is a melding of shadows and power, a demonstration of the depths from which we've risen and the heights to which we soar when we're together.

The hand that isn't holding mine roams across my chest, each movement a word in our silent language. I respond in kind, my own hands exploring the expanse of his back, feeling the ripple of muscles, the strength of power, coiled, but at rest.

He climbs over me, his body pressing into mine, and I can feel the heat of his arousal against my thigh. His lips move to my ear, and he whispers, "Let me show you eternity, my love."

"I've been waiting an eternity for you to get on with it." I grin up at him, relishing the way his eyes flash with a promise of the punishment I will surely be getting. I can't wait.

He smiles in return, a slow and wicked smirk as he collects spit in his mouth, watching as it dribbles generously onto his cock. When I move to fist my own, his shadows strike out, lassoing my wrists so they're above my head.

After easing himself inside me and waiting for me to be ready, he then shoves himself deeper and harder, and the headboard slams against the wall. I gasp at the sudden intrusion, but soon I'm lost in the sensations. More of his shadows curl around my dick, tight and silken, while his hips drive into me with a relentless rhythm.

There's a ferocity in the way we seek each other, a fervor fueled by the absence of our mate. Morte's presence lingers in the space between us, a ghost touch that drives us to seek solace in each other's embrace.

His fingers grip my thighs, caressing me in a way that is both punishing and reverent. My breathing grows heavy as he pulls me in closer, throwing both of my legs over one of his shoulders.

"I needed this," he groans as he sinks deeper.

I don't need him to say it, because I feel it in the urgency of his touch, in the way he holds me. His lips move down the back of my thigh, leaving a trail of fire in their wake. My hands clutch at the headboard, but I can't find purchase to hang on.

The heat between us builds until it's almost unbearable, an inferno that threatens to consume us. My pulse thrums in my veins, the pressure building in me. We've needed this—to cling to each other while we're falling apart.

Our movements become more desperate, a frenzied dance of desire and longing. His eyes find mine in the dark, and they glow red, smoldering. I groan, so close to orgasm as I buck my hips to meet his.

A wicked smile plays on his lips as he pulls out of me.

The bastard is edging me!

"Hey—" I make to protest, until he settles himself between my thighs. His breath is a tease against my skin as he nips at my abdomen. I moan in pleasure when his hands travel down my body, savoring the sensations as his fingertips trace fire patterns against my skin.

He takes his time exploring every inch of me, teasing with his teeth and tongue.

I squirm under him. "Let me touch you," I beg. "Please."

He grins up at me, wickedness in his eyes. "After I've had my fill."

"Your fi—Ohh," I groan, as he takes me in his mouth. His tongue toys with the piercings on my cock, sending sparks of electricity through my body. I writhe beneath him, pleasure building with each stroke and pull.

My hands clench what little of the sheets I can grab as I buck my hips, my head thrown back as he brings me to the edge. I can feel the intensity rising, the fire within me threatening to consume me. But just before I can erupt in his warm mouth, Aggonid eases off, tsk'ing at me.

"I didn't say you can come yet, pet," he warns, his fingers tightening on my balls just as the shadows pin me tighter to the bed. "I'm going to fuck this hot little ass again."

"Please let me come," I beg.

My runes glow brightly, illuminating the sweat that drips down the broad plane of his chest and the necklace hanging around his throat. He's so fucking beautiful.

The dark, inky shadows that had been clinging to my wrists suddenly release their hold, allowing me to move freely. My hands reach for my throbbing cock, eager to relieve the tension, but before I can grasp it, the shadows flip me onto my stomach. The air is knocked out of my lungs, and I can only grin as Aggonid's voice cuts through the rough sound of my heaving breath.

"Hands on the headboard," he growls.

I quickly obey, my fingers gripping the wooden frame as Aggonid kneels behind me. His hands grip my hips, and I moan as he slides his hard length inside me, inch by inch. He moves slowly at first, but soon his thrusts become more urgent, pushing me closer and closer to the edge. Our ragged breaths and moans mix with the creaking of the bed frame as it slams against the wall.

My fingers turn white as they hold onto the wood, my body trembling as Aggonid's hands bruise my hips, hard and unyielding, and his thighs slap against mine with each thrust. The sensation of his skin against mine, the softness of the bed sheets beneath me, it all undoes me.

The tension builds again, threatening to consume me, and I cry out in pleasure as I reach the peak.

Aggonid follows me over the edge, and I collapse against the headboard, my body trembling from the intensity of the orgasm. We lay there for a few moments, reveling in the afterglow before he finally pulls out and collapses beside me.

"That was amazing," I whisper, my voice still trembling.

His lips curl into a lazy, satisfied grin and he leans down to press a soft kiss to my forehead. The warmth of his touch sends shivers down my spine, filling me with an equal sense of love and heartache. Morte should be here between us, soaked in our come. Instead, it's all over our sheets. I like leaving my scent, so by morning, Aggonid is drowning in it.

His rhythmic breathing lulls me into a peaceful slumber as we drift off together in each other's arms.

CHAPTER TWELVE

AZAZEL

In the highest chamber of the castle, where the air is thick with the potential of unleashed power, I stand before the conduit made of sanguimetal and star silver—the core of the dreamscape device that I've painstakingly assembled. I've tested it, but it wasn't strong enough. It needed more power and the components Emeric was tasked with gathering to help amplify the dreamscape: ashes of a fallen star, shattered moonstone, and a basilisk fang. It took him days to track down the fang, and a whole week for the other two ingredients. We had to have a reaper bring them in from *Nethermore*, a distant fae realm filled with ether, icy wastes, and inhospitable landscape.

"Was your reaper able to get what you needed?" I ask Aggonid, turning my attention to him.

His silver hair is braided against his scalp, and he wears an oversized silk button-up shirt over black slacks. His skin is a rich, burnished pewter, shining with a metallic sheen as if it were forged from precious metals. He wears a leather cord around his neck adorned with three fangs from some kind of beast.

The devil, wearing a smirk that doesn't reach his eyes, hands me a velvet bag. Curiosity piqued, I take it and slowly untie the drawstrings. Inside lies a dark, sandy substance resembling insect droppings.

"What the hell is this?" I squint at the strange powder.

Emeric snatches the bag from my grasp and takes a whiff before recoiling in disgust. "Gods, is that supposed to be coffee? It's foul." He gags into the collar of his shirt, shoving the satchel my way.

I step back, holding up my hands, and Aggonid takes it instead.

"That's because it's instant coffee. From the far reaches of Earth, in a seedy little market that's open all night and sells fuel for those infernal metal beasts they all have." The devil's eyes glint with mischief as he takes pleasure in our discomfort at the thought of drinking such foul-smelling coffee. "Had to bribe the blasted reaper six favors to deal with those violent little humans."

"No wonder the humans don't live very long," Caius says, haunted. "They're forced to consume things the fae wouldn't even give the Caspari."

"How exactly is this going to help the dreamscape stay open?" Skeptical of the plan, I shift my weight, crossing my arms over my chest.

"Trust me." Caius leans in and whispers with unhinged, manic glee. The runes on his translucent skin ripple with light. "I've been up for four days." He chuckles, shoving his dark blue hair behind his ears as his tail whips behind him. "It works."

Emeric steadies his hands on the table, head tilted as though he's trying to recall something he's read. "Caffeine gives a concentrated burst of energy and alertness in every granule. It's just what we need—for Morte to stay awake enough to interact with us."

I pick up the conduit, studying it. The metal glimmers under the light of the flickering torches, my heart racing with excitement to finally try to reach Morte. I check the time. "She should be asleep by now, " I offer, setting the device back on the table.

Emeric's fitted trousers cling to his muscled thighs, the black fabric stretching as he bends to reach in his satchel for the rest of his tools. The top he wears is equally dark, hugging his torso and accentuating his lean frame. He places each piece on the table next to my contraption, carefully arranging them in precise positions. The others gather around, their eyes fixed on the ingredients with a mix of curiosity and apprehension.

"This little thing will help us sleep with Morte—" Caius starts to say, but he's quickly interrupted by Emeric.

"We're infiltrating her dreams. Not fucking her," Emeric corrects him, his tone laced with annoyance.

"Well, maybe you're not." Caius smirks, making to prop himself against the rough stone wall, but forgetting there's a tapestry sitting several inches in front of it, so he startles, nearly falling.

I flash Caius a harsh look and mutter under my breath, "If Morte wants to fuck, I'm pretty sure she'd happily choose the man with two cocks."

"Oh, you do have a point," Caius muses. "Perhaps she wouldn't mind if we both—"

"Do *not* finish that sentence," Aggonid growls, his fingers tightening on the edge of the table, earning a smirk from Emeric. "My cock is more than enough for you."

"If you three would stop flirting, I'd like to see my mate," I snarl, the frustration clear in my tone.

Both Aggonid and Emeric's heads snap to me, their mouths hanging open in surprise that I'd dare to call attention to the obvious sexual tension between them. I shrug nonchalantly, indicating that it's obvious to anyone paying attention.

Caius just crosses his arms and smirks like a cat who caught the canary, his gaze drifting back and forth between his mate and the hellhound, savoring each moment of their interaction.

With a dramatic eye roll, Emeric snatches up the ingredients, his hands moving with practiced precision as he performs an incantation over the metal conduit. The air crackles with energy and a faint scent of burning herbs fills the room as he channels his magic.

Emeric drawls, his deep voice echoing off the walls of the ancient chamber. His eyes are fixed on the intricate runes he's drawing in the air above the device before him. "I believe it would be wiser if only one of us enters."

"Me." Caius rocks on his feet, his energy substantial in the air. "She'll want to see me first. She loves me the most."

"You're too hyper right now." I scowl at him. "I should be the one to go in."

Aggonid leans in closer, a hint of danger in his voice. "Let's not forget who holds dominion over this realm," he growls.

"Az is right. She trusts him," Emeric adds, and a pang of guilt hits me so fierce that it threatens to consume me.

Knowing I don't deserve her trust weighs heavily on my heart.

Emeric continues, "Aggonid, you really hurt her and haven't yet made strong enough amends to be the first person in. Azazel should go."

Caius crosses his arms like a petulant child but concedes. "Fine, but tell her I miss her."

My expression softens at his words, and I give a nod of understanding.

Emeric takes a step back, and his sharp eyes scan each of us in turn. "It's time to channel our power, gentlemen."

I'm finally going to see my girl.

CHAPTER THIRTEEN

MORTE

*L*ush greenery surrounds me, the scent of wildflowers and damp earth filling the air. The gentle sun warms my back, and the sound of a nearby stream whispers promises of eternal serenity. We're stretched out on a soft blanket, its pale blue matching the sky, and my fingers idly braid blades of grass as I feel the rise and fall of his chest beneath me. The tranquility is perfect, almost too perfect, like the prelude to a storm that's never meant to break.

The solid warmth under me feels like home, a presence both protective and familiar. It lulls me into a sense of security, a place where the past and its shadows can't reach. I nuzzle in, content, until a ripple of awareness tickles my consciousness.

I lift my head, and my breath catches. It's not Wilder's kind eyes that meet mine.

It's a stranger.

But no, not a stranger. There's something about him. Something that beckons to the deepest part of my soul.

His eyes are a tempestuous blue, deep and fathomless, and they hold me captive. His face, framed by thick black hair that spills in waves to his waist, is adorned with piercings that glint in the sunlight, a bold contrast to his golden skin. He's both terrifying and magnificent, a creature of myth made flesh, and he's got to be one of the most beautiful men I've ever seen in my life.

He doesn't speak, but his gaze is intense, searching. Something in the way he looks at me flays me wide open. His face is the epitome of beauty, with a chiseled jawline, full lips, and intense, penetrating eyes.

I push myself up, turning fully to face him. His overwhelming presence fills the space between us with an energy that's both exhilarating and unnerving. A faint scent of warm vanilla and earth surrounds him, bringing a sense of calm with it.

"Who are you?" I whisper, the words slipping out despite the tightness in my throat.

He tilts his head, humor dancing in his expression as he lets out a laugh. "Mmm, cute." He grins, cupping the back of my neck and pulling me in for a kiss.

It catches me off guard, but it doesn't feel unwelcome. No, it feels like ... home.

Like I've been waiting for this kiss my entire life. His lips are warm and soft as he teases my mouth open with his pierced tongue, and I find myself responding instinctively, my hands gripping his shirt as if my life depended on it.

The kiss is slow, sensual, and it awakens in me a hunger I didn't know I possessed. My body aches in response, every nerve ending singing with need as my heart pounds an erratic dance in my chest.

When we pull apart, I'm flustered.

"I miss you so much," he breathes, his hands, warm and strong, still cupping my cheeks. Somehow, I ended up in his lap, and I can feel the bulk of his body beneath me, the slight tension in his muscles as I lean into him.

And a very large, obvious erection between us.

I bite my lip, wincing. "I'm sorry, I—I don't know who you are."

He laughs again, the sound like music, sending shivers down my spine. "I'm quite hurt," he teases.

But when my brows remain furrowed, searching his eyes for some kind of recognition and finding none, he sits back, frowning, his perfect features clouding with confusion.

He brushes a stray lock of hair from my face with a gentle touch that belies the strength evident in his thick fingers. "It's me, Az."

I stare at him blankly, my mind racing as I try to place his face, his voice, anything about him that seems familiar. But I come up empty.

"I'm your mate."

My mental gears grind to a halt at those words, like a record player scratching to a stop. "My mate?" I repeat, as if it's a foreign concept.

He nods, concern creeping into his dark, ocean-blue eyes. "You don't remember me?" The heartbreak etched into his features sobers me, and every bit of me wants to soothe him, to protect him. I stare blankly at the man calling himself my mate, unable to place his striking yet unfamiliar features.

As he gazes at me with such raw distress in his eyes, an aching sadness blooms in my chest. Though my mind holds no memory of him, something deeper stirs, like a forgotten song.

Beneath me, his body shimmers like a mirage, wavering and flickering as if struggling to maintain its physical form. His features are twisted in panic, and fear darts from his eyes as he speaks frantically, but not to me.

"She doesn't remember who we are, or that we're her mates!" he shouts.

My gaze follows his line of sight and I notice several other men have joined us, each with their own unique features. One has skin so translucent it's almost blue, a long tail swishing behind him like a lion's; another is a man with brown skin and sharp fangs glinting in the sunlight; another has piercing red eyes and skin that gleams like polished metal. They are all strikingly handsome, yet none of them instill fear in me.

As the sky above begins to fracture and splinter into a thousand pieces, I'm jolted awake from this strange dream, sitting up with a start. It's still dark out, the false moonlight filtering in through the canopy outside. I take a few deep breaths to steady my racing heart as the vivid dream lingers in my mind.

Everything about them felt so real, as though their song is a melody I've sung a thousand times before, I've only forgotten a line.

That recent dream flickers in my mind. In it, Wilder stands tall and confident, surrounded by a group of faceless men. I'm tied with ropes of silk to a tree, my body exposed to their lustful gazes as they take turns indulging in me, some even sharing me. The vulnerability and pleasure intertwine as the unknown men ravage me. Is it them? Are these the same men from my subconscious desires?

As the memory of the dream lingers, their scents surround me, and I can still feel the whisper of Az's kiss on my tongue.

A familiar ache grows between my legs. Knowing the stress and strain awaiting me for the rest of the day, I decide to give in to the yearning and allow myself some much-needed release before I turn my world upside down. My hand travels down my body, fingertips tracing every curve and dip, until they reach my core.

With each touch, the flames of desire grow stronger within me, fueled by vivid images of Wilder and Az. My eyelids flutter closed as I surrender to the fantasy, pretending they're here in my bedroom with me. It's not me, sliding my panties off and tossing them across the room.

It's no longer my own fingers teasing my clit, but Wilder's skilled hands, sending shivers through me. And Az, his lips on my neck, his touch igniting a fire within as he massages my breasts. The room is filled with the heady scent of arousal and the sound of our ragged breaths mingling together.

Wilder's warm breath tickles my skin as he growls against the inside of my thigh. "If I'd known you tasted so good, I would've done this the day I met you." He moves higher and kisses the sensitive skin on the inside of the very top of my leg, his tongue swiping up my center as I arch my back, letting out a moan.

"What does she taste like?" Az whispers against my ear, his words giving me goosebumps. "I bet she's delicious."

Wilder's lips curl into a mischievous grin, and his fingers reach up to Az's lips before pressing gently. I can't look away as Az takes his fingers into his mouth, tracing them with his tongue until they're clean.

"Fuck, she does taste good," he groans. "Is she ready for us yet?"

The sound of a new voice, deep and velvety, cuts through the hazy air. It belongs to one of the men in my dream, his skin a rich shade of brown and his fangs flashing with an irresistible allure. I can practically feel them piercing my flesh in the most enticing way. "Oh, she's ready." He smirks, his words laced with desire and anticipation.

"Line her up, Wilder," Az says from beneath me. And then he's sliding into me, Wilder's hand guiding him in.

My best friend sits back, admiring the view before conspiring with the newcomers. The man with metallic skin and red eyes looks over their shoulders, admitting I can handle more, and that I must.

"If she can't, I'll use magic to make us fit." This comes from the one with such pretty, near-translucent skin.

"You can't possibly all fit," I protest as Wilder pushes inside of me, my words dying when his mouth closes over my nipple, his tongue teasing and biting just the right amount.

Their bodies move in perfect harmony, each thrust sending a jolt of electricity through my veins. I'm a puppet pulled by their strings, each touch a masterstroke designed to break me in all the best ways. The other trio closes in on me, their hands exploring the landscape of my flesh, their fingers seeking, reducing me to smoldering embers of bliss.

My body is no longer mine as every inch of me is ravaged by Az's deep thrusts and Wilder's unrelenting pace. My cries escape me uncontrollably, lost in the overpowering sensations that consume me. With my eyes screwed shut, I'm consumed by a powerful orgasm, my sweat-slick back arching. Their breath is hot on my skin until I'm left with a chill as I come down from my bliss and open my eyes.

And I'm alone.

My chest rises and falls rapidly as I lie there, still reeling from the intensity of the moment. But as reality seeps back into my consciousness, a cold emptiness envelops me. I reach out tentatively, hoping to touch their warm body against mine, but all I feel is the cool air brushing against my fingertips. The room feels eerily silent, almost suffocating in its emptiness. An ache washes through me like a wave, stirring up the remnants of pleasure and leaving behind a profound sense of disappointment.

I'm always fucking alone.

I push myself up, my body feeling strangely foreign to me now. The sheets beneath me are tangled, a clear reflection of the chaos that had just consumed me moments ago. As I glance around the poorly lit room, shadows mock me with their playful movements.

Tentatively, I rise from the bed and wrap a loose sheet around my trembling body. Each step feels uncertain, as though I've been hollowed out, and I'm walking through uncharted territory; my senses heightened, stumbling to the small kitchen to start my day.

With each passing second, a growing ache weighs on my heart, a gnawing hunger for connection that remains unfulfilled.

If only I really did have a mate.

Tucking the sheet in front of me, I lean against the counter, knowing I've got to snap out of my wallowing. I shouldn't be indulging or torturing myself with fantasies. I need to stay focused. Saving Wilder is what matters.

This whole time, I should've been the one in prison. But instead, my best friend is in my place, and he's been rotting away while he should've been out here, looking for his anchor.

Soon, Wilder, I whisper. *I'll make it right.*

CHAPTER FOURTEEN

AGGONID

I storm into the council of gods, my fury a living, breathing entity that consumes the air around me. Shadows curl and twist at my command, an extension of the rage boiling within my veins. This is my domain as much as theirs, and I will not be subdued or ignored.

The celestial chamber, a convergence of divine power and ethereal beauty, feels like a cage that I'm ready to shatter. The gods, usually a picture of stoic immortality, look at me with a blend of wariness and hidden fear. Good. They should fear. They should all tremble.

Luna, the moon goddess, her light a vivid counterpoint to my swirling darkness, meets my gaze. Her usual calm is a façade I'm about to tear down.

"Luna," my voice thunders across the chamber, "you've dared to tamper with her memories, with her very soul. That is not your right. It's not your decision to make."

The chamber vibrates with the power of my words, echoes of my anger reverberating off the crystalline walls. My rage is not just for show; it's a weapon, sharp and deadly, and I wield it without mercy.

"You will undo what you've done," I demand, my presence dominating the space, my shadows reaching out like dark tendrils, threatening to engulf the room. "She deserves to know her life, every bitter and sweet moment. You've robbed her of her truth."

Luna's radiance seems to flicker under the intensity of my wrath. The other gods, even Chaos with his unpredictable aura, watch silently, knowing well the depth of my power.

"You will return her memories," I continue, my voice a low growl. "Every single one. She deserves to know everything, and I will accept nothing less."

My fury electrifies the surroundings, every corner brimming with the promise of retribution. Here, in this gathering of gods, I'm more than a ruler of the Underworld; I'm a force of nature, a deity fueled by a love as relentless as my power.

My ultimatum hangs in the air, a declaration of a battle I'm more than ready to wage. For Morte, for the restoration of her memories, I'll move heaven and earth. Luna and the council now face the full might of my power.

Luna's gaze, usually an embodiment of serene authority, wavers under the gale of my demand. The council room, a realm usually resonant with harmonious energies, now shudders with the clash of our wills.

"Aggonid," she begins, her voice maintaining its ethereal quality despite the tension, "the memories of your mate were not removed lightly. Her time in the Underworld was filled with pain and suffering. I acted to spare her further torment."

Her justification falls on deaf ears. My anger doesn't abate, it simmers, a cauldron of dark rage. "Spare her?" I sneer, the idea ludicrous, insulting. "You've stripped her of her experiences. The things that molded her. That isn't mercy, Luna. That's theft."

Around us, the other gods shift uneasily, a reticent chorus to our confrontation. Even Chaos, master of the unpredictable, seems caught off-guard by the ferocity of our exchange.

Luna's eyes soften, but her words don't waver. "To restore what was taken is no simple task, Aggonid. Her memories, they were ... distilled, extracted to ensure her peace."

"Distilled?" I echo, the word a bitter taste in my mouth. "You speak as if her life were a potion to be tampered with at your whim."

A sigh escapes Luna, and she gestures to a large, ornate container on a nearby pedestal. "Within this chest are vials containing her memories. Each one, a moment, a fragment of her time in the Underworld. But be warned, the process of restoration is not without risks. The flood of returning memories can be overwhelming, even damaging."

My gaze fixates on the coffer, its contents more precious than the rarest of jewels. "I'll take that risk," I state, the shadows around me pulsating with my wrath. "Her memories belong to her, and to her alone. I'll see them restored."

Luna nods, a gesture of reluctant agreement. "Then take them. But know this: the journey she must undertake to reclaim her past will be hers alone. You cannot bear this burden for her."

With a wave of her hand, the chest opens, revealing rows of vials shimmering with an inner light, each a captured echo of Morte's past. I approach, my hand hesitating above them. These fragile containers hold the essence of my mate's lost time, the key to unlocking the truths she deserves to know.

As I gather the crate, a weight settles upon me, a responsibility far greater than any I've borne before. This is more than a mere retrieval of memories; it's a quest to restore the soul of the one I love.

As I take possession of the chest, the council chamber seems to exhale, the tension dissipating like mist in the morning sun. But for me, the real challenge is just beginning.

With the container secured, I turn to leave, the shadows swirling in my wake.

Before I step through the doors, I turn back and sneer, "If you ever fuck with my soul bonded mate again, I'll kill you. But not before I torture and slaughter Rune, the love of your life, and then your precious Finn, and everyone he loves."

A gasp is the only thing I hear before I exit the room, a whisper of fear that lingers long after I'm gone.

CHAPTER FIFTEEN

MORTE

The shores of Convectus welcome me with their familiar embrace, the gentle lap of waves against the sand a soothing backdrop to my anxious heart. It's been two years since I last set foot here. Two years since Wilder's parents have seen me. They think I'm dead. The thought of their grief, a mirror of my own, knots in my stomach. I used to come here every Sunday, seeking comfort in the traces of Wilder I found in them—Alaric's high cheekbones, sculpted like those of his son, and Elara's eyes, reminiscent of the deep-sea gaze that always felt like home.

I want them to hear it from me before they hear it from anyone else. They deserve to know their son is a good, honorable man, who gave up his life to save me eternity in prison.

I stand at the water's edge, where the sea meets the land, and wait. Here, the shore is a melody of crashing surf, seagulls crying, and the placid murmur of the tide. I shiver, the wind bristling across my skin, sending an early evening chill through my bones. The sun casts a melancholy glow, painting the scene in hues of farewell. The briny smell of sea water wafts from the waves, soothing me, and reminding me of *him*.

It's not long before two figures emerge from the depths, their elegant merfae forms cutting through the water with hurried, frantic grace. As they transition into their fae shapes upon reaching the shore, I brace myself for the moment of revelation.

Elara's reaction is instant and visceral. Her jaw drops open in shock, her hand slapping over her mouth to stifle a scream. For a fleeting moment, she stands frozen in disbelief, her features contorted with suspicion. Then, as recognition dawns, she sprints toward me, her arms wrapping around me in a fierce embrace as tears spill down her cheeks. "Morte, my dear child." She sobs, her body trembling with relief. "We thought ... we feared ..."

That I was dead.

Alaric approaches more slowly, his eyes a tumultuous sea of emotion. He lays a hand on my shoulder, a gesture heavy with tacit questions. "How? We mourned you, Morte." His voice cracks as he pulls me into his arms. "We mourned *for* you. Where did you go? The news said you'd died. That you—that you'd been killed in the line of duty."

The rawness in their voices, the tremble of Elara's embrace, it all speaks of a pain I know too well. We sink onto the sand, the sea a quiet witness to our reunion. I take a deep breath and begin to unravel the tale of my disappearance, of the two years lost somewhere beyond their reach.

Beyond anyone's reach.

"And then, I saw him," I whisper, the memory of their son in the prison cell surfacing amongst the pain. "We were together, just before ... before I died." I didn't mention their son's death because he had my feather to revive him, and I don't want to cause them any more undue grief. If it turns out I can't get him out of prison, I must at least find a way to get him another phoenix feather.

Elara's grip on my hand tightens, her green eyes, so much like Wilder's, fill with a mother's sorrow. "Tell us everything. Please." Her silver hair flows around her like a halo.

My story spills out, the words a mix of grief and longing. I describe the chaos of the prison, the hydra's attack, and how Wilder had caught me as I fell, torn and broken. "He thought only of saving me," I say, the vision of Wilder's arms, strong and desperate, vivid in my mind. "He did everything he could to keep me safe."

Our shared grief hangs in the air, a substantial thing that wraps around us like the evening mist. Elara's tears mingle with the sea breeze, and Alaric's stoic façade cracks under the reminder of his son's predicament.

Vita damnationem. Prison for eternity.

"I'm getting Wilder out," I declare.

"How?" Elara whispers, her eyes darting around to ensure no one is listening who shouldn't be. "What do you need from us? Anything, anything at all."

"I'm going to confess," I breathe, watching the shock ripple across their faces. They make to speak, but I put my hand up. "Please. You need to know that your son didn't kill a single soul. It was me," I whisper. I tell them about that night 2,000 years ago. How he was protecting me and bound my tongue so I couldn't tell the truth. "But when I died again, the spell broke."

Their grief is so potent, it nearly pummels me.

My chest tightens as I brace myself for the question. *Why didn't you regenerate?* I can't tell them Wilder died and broke my tether to the world. It would break them into even tinier pieces. A white lie. If they ask, I'll go with the hydra venom thing. That they can kill for good.

"Morte," Elara whispers, her trembling hands smoothing my hair, as though the very act could keep me safe. "Oh, my sweet girl," she cries. "You can't have known. You wouldn't have hurt those children." She turns towards Alaric, whose grief matches her own. "We've got to do something!" Her voice is shrill, desperate.

"We won't stop trying," he assures her. "Now that we know the circumstances, the truth ..." he shakes his head. "I won't lose you again."

"I'm going to give him his life back. I owe it to all of us."

Elara looks at me, her face lined with the years of worry and grief. "You're the daughter we never had, my sweet girl. Please be careful." Her grip tightens on me. "He'd never forgive himself if something happened to you."

Alaric stands, his figure tall and resolute against the star-dappled sky. "Bring him home, little flame. Bring our boy home."

I smile at the nickname. I'm average height for a fae female, but merfae are large. Next to them both, I look small.

Their farewells are a mix of hope and heartache as they disappear back into the sea, leaving me alone with the enormity of my promise. I stare at the horizon, where the sky kisses the sea, and whisper a vow into the wind.

Wilder, I'm coming for you.

With their blessing warming my soul, I turn away from the shore. The journey back to Castanea isn't just a walk across barren land; it's a march towards destiny, a chance to right all my wrongs.

The Wastelands stretch before me, a broad, desolate expanse sitting atop Castanea. In the night's darkness, the landscape is subtly illuminated by Bedlam's array of moons. Their light filters through the swirling sand, splashing an eerie, diffused glow across the barren terrain. The wind howls, kicking up a sandstorm that obscures the horizons and dances wildly across the vast emptiness.

I move forward, feeling the bite of the wind-driven sand against my cheeks. Grit finds its way into my mouth, the taste of the Wastelands, a blend of earth and arid desolation, lingering on my tongue.

Despite the multiple moons hanging in the sky, their light is not enough to fully penetrate the thick veil of sand and dust churned up by the storm. Shadows play tricks on my eyes, making the landscape seem as if it's constantly shifting and changing, a web of dunes and hollows with no end in sight. It's a harsh and unforgiving environment, one that tests the resilience of any who dare to traverse it.

To sustain our underground sanctuary, it leeches the earth of all its life, leaving this hellscape. It works as a great deterrent for anyone who'd want to get near to Castanea before the rest of Bedlam knew about us. To get to the little pond that allows entrance to our hidden refuge, we must traverse the arid desert on foot as it doesn't allow for sifting, or if you're lucky enough to have wings, you could fly. Provided there isn't a sandstorm.

Like now.

It gives me a lot of time to think while I set up my canvas tent. It's a black, two-person shelter.

I finish erecting the small refuge just as the wind begins to intensify. The sun is setting, and sand pelts the outside, peppering the fabric with a constant patter. I hunker down inside, pulling my blanket tight for warmth, as it always freezes at night. The howl of the gale is deafening.

The storm batters my haven, but this isn't my first time seeking shelter from nature's fury, so I take some deep breaths and let the deafening noise lull me to sleep as my teeth chatter.

Suddenly, the zipper on my tent is pulled open, and a figure steps inside. My heart jumps in surprise, but as I recognize Az's face in the pale moonlight, I relax. "What are you doing here?" I ask, my voice quivering with both confusion and relief as I scoot over to make room.

He shrugs, laughing as he looks around the cramped space. "It's your dreamscape."

"While this is certainly a very nice view, I'm getting sand in my netherbits. Would be a pity to chafe." A new, aristocratic voice sounds from behind Az.

As Az enters the tent, I take in his dark hair, disheveled from the wind; his face streaked with dirt and sand. The other man leans against the tent door, his face hidden behind a curtain of long, dark-blue hair. When he glances up at me, his hair parts, revealing a warm and inviting smile, and I recognize him as one of the other men from my dream.

"Little Bird," he breathes before he closes the tent, crawling over to me and pulling me into his arms, and he's so warm. "I've missed you so much." The familiar scent of his cologne lingers in my nose as he pulls back to gaze at me, his eyes tracing every curve and contour of my face with deep adoration.

Wilder calls me Little Bird. But this man isn't my best friend.

"I don't know your name," I whisper, biting my lip. "I probably should've asked that before letting you all have your way with me ..." I trail off, laughing nervously to cover up my discomfort.

A deep, rumbling chuckle escapes him, filling the air with a warm, velvety sound. "Well, I'm certainly wearing more clothes than I usually tend to when in your presence." He pauses, his piercing gaze considering my words before a mischievous smile spreads across his features. "Did you say you want me to have my way with you?"

"That's not what she said, Caius," Az growls protectively. The name rolls off his tongue like a warning.

Caius.

"She—"

The seductive fae leans back, his full lips curling into a devilish grin as he turns his attention fully on me. His bright eyes glitter with amusement and something more primal. "Are you saying you dreamed about us sleeping together?" he asks, his voice laced with seduction, his expression full of wicked delight. "Tell me all about it."

I cast a nervous glance at Az, and he just holds up his hands, a bemused look on his face as though to say, *that's all on you, though I'm interested in hearing all about this.*

I struggle to form words, my mouth opening and closing like a fish out of water. But before I can even muster a response, Caius interjects with a sly suggestion. "Or," he begins, his grin lighting up his entire face even in the darkness, "we could re-enact it?" His mischievous tone hints at a devilish plan forming in his mind.

"Caius." I say his name, and he lets out a full-body shudder. The runes on his skin pulse with the movement. "Who are you?"

He leans in close, nose-to-nose, his eyes a haunting shade of glacial blue, almost translucent in their intensity. "We're mates. Do you know what mates do when they're in love?" His tail, long and sleek like a whip, wraps around my leg and caresses it gently. It's as if every movement of his body is meant to draw me closer to him, to claim me as his own. Heat radiates off of him, and the electric pull between us grows stronger with each passing second.

"How about you give her a little space?" Az scoots over, patting the ground between us.

I reluctantly slide out of Caius' lap, much to his vocal objection. The three of us now huddle closely together, our forms pressing against each other in the small shelter. The warmth from their bodies radiates onto mine, creating a cocoon of comfort and protection.

"I can't wait until you have your memories back." He scowls as I glance at him.

"Wait, my memories?" I gasp. "You guys know where I've been the last two years?"

Caius lounges on the makeshift bed, his sleek body stretched out and relaxed. His long tail swishes back and forth rhythmically as he locks eyes with me. "Of course we know where you've been. Warming my bed," he purrs, a playful smirk on his lips.

The heat in my cheeks intensifies as I try not to let his words affect me.

"Having lots of orgasms," he continues.

Embarrassment floods through me, heating up my cheeks further and making me look away from Caius to Az. He meets my gaze with a knowing look, tucking his lips between his teeth in amusement before nodding his head in confirmation.

"We're working on getting your memories back in the safest way," Az explains. "We don't want to cause any lasting damage by giving them to you all at once, so Emeric is doing some research."

"Emeric?"

"He has two cocks?" Caius offers.

"Two?" His statement catches me off guard and I do a double-take, my eyes widening in disbelief. My mind races with questions and curiosity, trying to imagine the logistics of such a situation. The shock and novelty of it all leaves me speechless for a moment.

"Yes, but you can technically count my tail as another cock, as it's just as prehensile as both of his are," he offers. "You never once complained about my ability to make you orgasm. And I'm pierced."

His words are brazen and provocative, causing my cheeks to flush with more heat. But his nostrils flare, and his eyes go hooded as he notices my arousal.

A small gasp escapes my lips as I try to regain control of myself. But it's no use, he knows exactly which of my buttons to push and is enjoying every second of it. "You're thinking about it, aren't you?" he taunts, a smug smile playing on his lips.

"You don't have to answer that, Morte," Az says. Shadowy smoke curls from his nostrils as the low murmur of his voice carries through the air like a soothing melody. "How about we lay down and talk?"

"Oh yes, good idea. Let's all lay down together," Caius chimes in, the sound light and carefree.

Everyone shuffles around, trying to find a comfortable position in the limited space. Az settles first, lying on his back with his arms folded behind his head. Caius mirrors him on my other side, a self-satisfied smirk playing at his lips.

"He's just trying to provoke you," Az warns me.

A surge of unfamiliar warmth spreads through me as I realize that it's nice to feel wanted for once. There's someone who desires and craves my presence, unashamed and unrestricted in their love for me.

"It's okay," I whisper softly, the words carrying weight as they leave my lips. My heart swells with gratitude at this unexpected intimacy, and I can't help but revel in the sheer bliss of being wanted so deeply and completely.

"Deep down, she knows she's safe with us," Caius says. "The little beastie inside of her would never forget we're mates."

A beat of silence fills the tent. Caius chuckles, a low and throaty sound that does funny things to my insides. "Your phoenix." He smirks, his voice dripping with confidence. "She loves me." He moves closer to me, his body radiating heat against my skin as his hands gently cup my stomach, claiming it as his own. "Though calling her *the beast inside you* just made me imagine you as pregnant. I do love the idea of filling your womb, watching your belly swell with my offspring." Gently, he presses a kiss to my flat stomach, tilting his face up to meet my gaze. "And even if you don't want children, we can play pretend as you take my seed," he whispers, his breath tickling my skin. "It'd be a lot of fun to breed you."

I sputter, choking on my spit. "Is he ... is he always like this?" I laugh, glancing nervously at Az.

"Unfortunately so," he drawls in that familiar tone of his, his expression nonchalant as he gazes down at the fae now lying at our feet. "But he has a way of growing on you." A smirk tugs at the corner of his lips before fading into a slight frown.

Caius' mouth drops open. "I love you, too, big guy!" he gushes.

"I didn't say—oof." Caius tackles Az in a hug, causing the tent to tilt precariously.

"All right, all right," Az grumbles, nudging Caius away. "Space, man. You know the rules." But a reluctant smile hides at the corner of his mouth.

In the midst of my laughter and all the scuffling, a warmth spreads within me. *This isn't so bad*, I think. A small sense of belonging and contentment settles around my heart. A place where there is playful banter, involuntary trust, and a hint of love.

Caius releases Az from the hug, settling back on my other side, pulling me close to him then covering us with the blanket.

"Tell me about your dream," he whispers into my ear, his breath tickling my skin and sending goosebumps along my flesh. I can feel the warmth of his body next to mine, radiating through the blanket.

Az clears his throat. "I wouldn't mind hearing that, either."

"The first or second dream?" I cover my face, embarrassed.

"Okay, now I really need to hear this," Az groans.

"The first dream I was tied up in a tree and you all had your way with me, and the second ... well, that was technically a fantasy, because I was awake, but I wanted to, erm ... continue with the dream experience. I was in my treehouse, and one of you kept trying to tell me you'd all fit, even though I definitely only have three holes." I laugh.

Both men groan, biting their fists.

When Caius' tail slithers up my leg under the blanket, tentative and probing, my eyes find Caius', but I don't say a word. My breath hitches as his hand comes up to thread through my hair, pulling my face closer to his.

Next to me, I hear Az's breathing stall, and the tent stills, as though every second boils down to this very moment.

Caius presses his lips to mine, consuming and devouring me.

I let my eyes flutter shut, surrendering myself to the sensation. His lips are warm, encouraging as they move against mine and coax a sigh from my lips. His tail continues its exploring journey, a perverse sensation that adds another layer of intensity to the moment.

Az groans again, this time more strained, more urgent, as though a dam within him is ready to burst. His voice shatters the silence that has fallen across the tent. "Shit," he whispers, the syllable a prayer on his lips.

Caius releases me with a gentle tug, and although I want nothing more than to hold onto him, I resist the urge and instead lean forward to capture his lips once again. He responds eagerly, nipping at my lower lip before pulling away again. His large hands cup my face, lightly tracing the contours of my cheeks as he turns my head towards Az, who captures my chin, dragging me closer to him.

Az's fingers are rough, calloused, yet they trace the line of my jaw with a gentleness that contradicts their appearance. His gaze is intent, a deep well of sapphire blue that seems to hold every star that's ever shone in all the realms.

His lips crash to mine with a fervor that rivals Caius's. A shockwave of heat sears through me, taking me by surprise. He tastes like a summer storm, wild and unpredictable yet intoxicating all the same. A tongue ring teases against mine, a cool metallic sensation that makes me gasp. He takes advantage of my surprise, plunging deeper and drawing a moan from me. His grip tightens on my chin, tilting it to give him better access. His other hand snakes around my waist, firmly holding me against the hard planes of his body. He's a furnace, radiating a luxurious warmth that seeps into me, stirring an insatiable hunger deep within.

"Can I take these off?" Caius' voice tickles my ear.

I pull back, gasping as Az's lips trail down my neck, leaving a path of scalding kisses that feel like molten fire on my skin. I can only nod at Caius, unable to voice my consent as Az nips lightly at the base of my throat. His teeth scrape against the delicate skin there, sending a shiver down my spine, a delightful shudder.

Caius undresses me with a reverent gentleness; each piece of clothing shed revealing more of my skin to the two men whose gazes are sinfully hungry. His fingers dance lightly upon my bare flesh, tracing the line of my collarbone, down to the shallow dip of my belly. He is a sculptor appreciating a precious work of art, worshipping me as if I were made of the finest marble.

A deep rumbling shakes the ground beneath me, causing the walls of the tent to shudder. My heart races as I sit up, a surge of panic jolting through me as the men in front of me start flickering out of existence.

"What's going on?" I cry out, my voice trembling with fear.

"The dreamscape is collapsing," Az answers grimly.

"Fuck!" Caius roars, his face twisted in anguish. "I love you, baby bir—"

Fear shoots through me, and my eyes snap open to the sound of my own gasping breaths. The oppressive heat of the sun beats down on the tent, causing sweat to pour from every pore of my body and trickle down my back, pooling in the creases of my skin. How long was I sleeping? It must have been hours, judging by the scorching rays that pierce through the canvas walls.

My body aches as I gather my things and take down the tent, frustrated my dream ended just before it got to the good part.

But as I cross the barren land, my steps are a little lighter, both from the dream and knowing I'm one day closer to setting Wilder free.

Sweat beads on my forehead, and my heart constricts at the thought of his reaction when it's all said and done. I take a deep breath, a silent prayer to the gods for courage, and just hope he won't hate me for what I'll have to do.

CHAPTER SIXTEEN

MORTE

The long weekend following my arrival back home from the Wastelands brings a rare stillness to the buzzing Castanea, but for me, it's the perfect opportunity to tackle an ambitious project. My goal is clear: to construct a hidden passageway from my treehouse, nestled high in the canopy, all the way down to the river below. It's a challenging undertaking, combining detailed spells with precise engineering techniques.

Wilder deserves to always have easy access to the water. The tiny little pool in his prison cell isn't enough, and I want this to feel like his place whenever he visits, which I know he will, even though I'll no longer be here.

Standing in the living room of my treehouse, I survey the room. It's a cozy haven, built with precision and care, and it's far bigger on the inside than the outside. The wooden walls are adorned with intricately carved designs, and the furniture is crafted from the same sturdy material. In the center of the main room stands a massive tree trunk, the natural support of the entire structure. My gaze follows the trunk upwards, marveling at how it seamlessly blends with the branches of the tree above.

A creaky, spiral staircase winds its way up to the next level, beckoning with each step. I rarely venture upstairs, as it's mainly used as a storage space for my cluttered belongings. The stairs groan under my weight, and the musty smell of old books and forgotten treasures fills my nose. Silver cobwebs cling to the walls and ceiling, as if they too are trying to escape from this neglected space. But despite its neglect, there's a certain charm to this hidden area of my home.

I should tidy up, but I'll get to that later.

Maybe.

The wooden floor beneath my bare feet is smooth and cool. As I run my hand over the tree trunk, I can feel the rough texture of the bark beneath my fingers, proof of the tree's age and strength.

I start by casting a detection charm, a pulse of magic that maps out the intricate network of roots and branches, revealing the safest path to burrow through. The charm paints a glowing trail along the trunk, a guideline I'll meticulously follow.

Gently, I lay my hands on the bark, feeling its course surface against my skin. Closing my eyes, I focus on the delicate balance of my task: to tunnel through without harming the tree. I summon my magic, not the fierce blaze of fire but a more subtle, controlled warmth, like the sun coaxing a seed to sprout.

The bark responds, fibers slowly parting under the coaxing touch of my power. It's a dance of respect between the conjurer and the nature, an understanding that I'm not here to harm but to coexist. The wood curls away, forming the beginning of a passage, spiraling down through the heart of the tree.

The work is slow, demanding both concentration and patience. I move with care, ensuring that each layer of wood and each ring of growth is respected, the tunnel taking shape in a slow descent. My magic, usually so bold and fiery, is a gentle whisper here, a nurturing force that guides rather than seizes.

By nightfall, I've made substantial progress, the tunnel now a spiraling path hidden within the tree's embrace. My muscles ache from the strain, evidence of the day's labor. I retreat to rest, knowing the next day demands more: reinforcing the tunnel, smoothing its edges, and ensuring its secrecy.

It's all for him.

For Wilder.

The tunnel, once complete, will be more than just a path. It's a symbol, a silent vow, its true significance known only to me. And as I drift to sleep, surrounded by the whispers of the forest, I hold onto that secret, a hidden truth cradled in the heart of the tree.

CHAPTER SEVENTEEN

CAIUS

My body aches with desire, my erection straining against the tightness of my pants. Aggonid's heated gaze burns me from across the table holding our dreamscape device.

"I see you've made progress," he teases, his words low and sultry as he stalks around the table to approach me.

"It didn't last long enough," I growl in frustration, watching as Az paces near the window, shadows pouring off him in frustration.

"That sounds like a personal problem." Emeric raises a brow, glancing down at my erection.

I release a low, dark chuckle, locking gazes with the wicked hellhound before me. "You couldn't handle what I offer." It's the first time I'm noticing how similar our eyes are, as though our mothers left us in the cold too long, and the first thing to freeze was our irises. Where I'm pale, he's dark. Total opposites in every other way.

"You're not offering anything," Aggonid snarls, his red eyes flashing as he pulls me in possessively.

As I press my lips to his, he tugs at my bottom lip with a gentle fierceness, drawing blood. The metallic tang lingers on my tongue as he licks the wound, and I can't help but feel a rush of excitement. He gazes at me with smug satisfaction. I love when he gets all possessive and stabby over me.

"I think she's ready to meet you," I say, smoothing my fingers through his hair, admiring the soft strands of silver as it slides between my fingertips. "She's receptive to us, even without all her memories back. It's very clear her soul knows who we are, even if her mind doesn't. I don't think you'll frighten her."

"You're certain?" His tone lacks all the bite in it he had only moments ago. It's been a long time since I've seen him so vulnerable. "Maybe you should give her the memories of me first, and then she can decide if she wants to see me again. I don't think I can stand to see her rejection."

"The least she deserves is the truth, straight from her soul bonded mate," Az replies sharply, his deep blue eyes burning with a mixture of defiance and something more profound, a hidden pain. "She ought to look you in the eye when she regains the full scope of what's been done to her."

"You're right," Aggonid murmurs, the fire in his crimson eyes flickering, replaced with a veil of dread. He withdraws from me, moving to the door. "I'll wait for you in bed," he calls, his voice melancholy as he slips out of the room.

"I thought tact and diplomacy were your strong suit." Emeric nudges Az with his elbow. "Might not be the best idea to poke the big, bad devil?"

Glaring at Az as I trail after my mate, I hiss, "Leave the poking to me."

I find Aggonid tucked in gold sheets, his metallic skin gleaming against the muted glow of a candle on the nightstand. His eyes are closed, and his scarred chest rises and falls with a calm rhythm that belies the storm I know is brewing within him. Each muscle is taut beneath his skin, tension rippling through him, the power rolling off him in waves so thick it chokes the air in the room.

Tomorrow is the Forsaken Hunt, and not long after it'll be the Wild Pursuit, but for the first time in a long time, we're not participating in either. I've delegated oversight of the competition to another demon. And the Wild Pursuit just won't feel the same without our mate.

Between Aggonid's growing power, our grief over Morte, and the emotional toll just being away from her takes, he's struggling.

I crawl in next to him, knowing he doesn't need my words right now. He just needs my touch, to know that no matter how bad he fucks up, I am the one constant he can count on. That I'll never, ever leave him.

My lips press against his chest, and I feel his tension ease as I pull him under my arm. Because sometimes, big, bad devils just need to be held by their ridiculously good-looking mates.

CHAPTER EIGHTEEN

MORTE

The afternoon in Castanea unfolds with its usual tranquil cadence, the lush flora of our underground haven basking in the gentle glow of our magical sky. I'm perched in my treehouse, paperwork sprawled across my desk. It's my day off, meant for peace, yet my mind is anything but still. With every tick of the clock, I'm reminded that this is one of my last afternoons of freedom. Somewhere, in a cell that echoes with despair, Wilder might be counting his final moments in unjust confinement.

The thought haunts me, forming a shadow over the room that no spell can brighten. With a resigned sigh, I scan the letter in front of me, its lines blurring into irrelevance. Wilder's sacrifice is a constant whisper in my ear, that our fates are intertwined in a web of sorrow and grief.

My hand hovers over the documents, the pen idle, as a knock at the door jars me from my focus. The sound is unexpected, a rarity in the quiet routine of my day off.

I rise, smoothing out the front of my shirt, curiosity piquing as I make my way to the door. When I swing it open, the sight that greets me is as surprising as the knock itself. Standing before me is Bellamy Nightblade, a high-ranking member of the royal guard, and his presence here in Castanea feels like a giant ripple in a still pond. He's the guard member courting our High Queen.

So why is he here?

At my door?

Bellamy stands tall and confident, the epitome of royal guard allure with his sun-bronzed skin and deep-set dimples. His blond hair, longer than that of most males in the guard, frames his face, dusting his cheekbones and accentuating his pointy ears. His attire, standard-issue for the guard, save for the royal emblem above the breast pocket, clings to his muscular form, leaving little to the imagination about how he spends his free time. The lazy grin he offers is disarmingly cocky, and his lilac eyes hold a spark of mischief.

He's a well-respected and formidable soldier. Easy on the eyes, too, if I were being objective. Not my type. I prefer them a little rougher around the edges.

He briefly worked at the prison, though he hasn't been there in a while. Not since the war. I want to shake him, ask him if he knows Wilder, but I can't give up my ruse yet. I'm not finished putting things into place.

"Commander Incendara," he greets me, his deep voice filling the space between us. People rarely ever address me by my last name. Not even General Risç. He reaches into his pocket, producing an envelope sealed with wax. The seal itself sends a jolt through me—a moon, the unmistakable symbol of High King Finian Drake.

I swallow hard, my mind racing. Why would the High King be sending me a letter? My hands feel uncharacteristically shaky as I take the envelope from him, my eyes not leaving the seal.

"Is everything alright?" Bellamy asks, noting my hesitation. The scent of coconut wafts toward me as he leans a bit closer, concern etching his features.

I manage a nod, unable to find my voice for a moment. "Yes, just wasn't expecting ... this." I gesture towards the letter.

He snaps his fingers, conjuring a small spray of water that dances between his fingers, a casual display of his control over the element. If I remember correctly, he's of the dragon order. His lax demeanor eases my nerves, but only a little. "I can only deliver it. The contents are beyond my purview. Though if you were in any kind of trouble, they would've sent a few more of us to handle any fallout. You're probably okay." He grins.

Easy for him to say. He's part of the royal's inner circle and has been for a long time now. He's cousin of the former king of Draconum.

The envelope feels heavy in my hands, heavier than paper and wax have any right to be. It's the burden of uncertainty, a thousand possibilities that this letter could represent.

He watches me, his expression a mix of curiosity and professionalism. "If there's nothing else, Commander, I'll take my leave. He expects your answer within a fortnight."

I blink, returning to the present. "Of course, thank you, Bellamy." I find my manners, though my mind is still wrapped around the letter in my hands. I probably shouldn't be calling him by his first name, and should instead use his title, but I'm too shocked to think beyond the significance of the envelope.

With a nod, a small salute, and another of his signature grins, Bellamy turns, disappearing into the foliage of the canopy, leaving me alone with the sealed message from the High King.

The stillness of my treehouse feels more pronounced now, the air thick with unanswered questions. I stand there for a moment longer, gathering my thoughts, before I make my way back to my desk. The letter sits before me, an invitation and a mystery all at once.

My fingers trace the edges of the seal, the imprint of the moon a sharp reminder of the power and authority behind this message. All our magic comes from his mother, the Luna goddess. Taking a deep breath, I break the seal, the wax giving way under my touch. The letter unfolds, and I brace myself for whatever words await me.

The High King and the High Queen and I are on friendly terms, though it would be a stretch to call us good friends. Why would he send a member of the royal guard with a message for me?

Oh gods.

What if they've found out about my connection with Wilder, and as my friend, Finn is sending me a warning beforehand? If they find out about my connection too soon, it'll screw up everything I've set into motion. My hands tremble so violently, I drop the page three times before I'm able to steady myself enough to comprehend its contents.

I read it once, then twice, trying to make sense of what's on the parchment.

The script is clear and concise, each word seeming to ricochet with the influence of the authority behind them. My eyes scan the message, and with each line, a cold sense of disbelief begins to coil in my stomach.

Morte,

Aggonid asked that you be returned to the Underworld. The choice is yours.

Do let me know post haste.

Best,

Finn

The letter slips from my trembling fingers, fluttering like a wounded bird before landing with a soft thud on the desk. My heart pounds against my ribcage, a frantic rhythm that seems to echo in the stillness of the room. The Underworld—a chilling thought that grips me like icy claws, causing every hair on my body to stand on end.

Hell.

The place of damnation and eternal suffering, and I was there? But how? Why?

Memories scramble at the edges of my consciousness, desperate and fleeting, like trying to catch smoke with bare hands. There's nothing, just a gaping void where two years of my life should be. And now, the High King of the Fae, Finn, tells me the devil himself wants me back.

I press a hand to my chest, feeling the galloping beat of my heart, the only sign of life in a moment that feels surreal. My mind races with questions, each more unsettling than the last. How did I end up there? How'd I get back home? And why, why would the devil want me back?

Did I claw my way to Bedlam, escaping the inescapable? As far as I know, only one fae has ever left the Underworld. Gideon Cathal, one of the High Queen's mates. How did I get away? Did I have help? If so ... who?

My breath comes in short gasps, and the walls of the treehouse suddenly feel too close, too confining. I stand up abruptly, needing to move, to breathe, to flee the crushing weight of this revelation.

The idea of having spent time in hell, a place of legend and fear, sends a tremble down my spine. I've heard the stories, the tales whispered in the shadows of Bedlam. But they were just that. Stories. Now, the possibility that I might have lived them, breathed that air of fire and brimstone, is too much to comprehend.

The question echoes in my mind, a haunting refrain that refuses to be silenced: Is the weight of my crimes enough for hell? I've always known there was a distinct possibility, given the shadows that skirt the edges of my life, the hauntings of my past deeds. But considering it as a mere possibility and knowing it as a cold, hard truth are two edges of a blade I never wanted to feel pressed against my skin.

Panic rises like bile in my throat, and I stagger to the window, pushing it open to let in the night air of our underground sanctuary. The bioluminescent foliage glows softly outside, a striking contrast to the chaos raging within me. Out there, it's all beauty and color, and inside, I'm a desolate landscape, barren and bleak. The gentle hum of life in our haven does little to soothe my frayed nerves.

I lean against the window frame, my eyes scanning the horizon, seeking something, anything, to anchor me in this storm of emotions. But there's no comfort in the familiar sights, no solace in the magical lights that twinkle like distant star-like gemstones illuminating the cavern. I'm untethered.

A shudder courses through me as I grapple with the enormity of what this implies. My past, the parts I remember and the parts I don't, all seem to converge in this singular, terrifying moment of revelation. The Underworld, a realm of eternal damnation, a place for the condemned and the damned—could I really belong there?

The thought is a bitter pill, a jagged shard of reality that cuts deep into the fabric of my identity. I've always prided myself on walking the fine line between righteousness and necessity, doing what must be done for the greater good. Yes, I murdered innocents, but it was an accident.

I didn't know they were children.

But if I've been to hell and back, literally, what does that say about me? Have the sins I committed weighed so heavily on my soul? Do I dare to seek out the truth of my time in the Underworld, to uncover the secrets that my own mind has hidden from me? Or do I bury it deeper, let sleeping demons lie, and continue on the path I've carved in this realm?

The idea that I could choose to go back to that unknown hell is unfathomable. But the even more terrifying thought is the unknown itself—what happened to me there? Was it so horrific, that even I found a way to do what has only ever been done once before? Was my time there so awful that my mind literally built a wall around those memories, seeking to preserve what little peace I have in my mind?

Tears well up in my eyes, spilling over and tracing hot paths down my cheeks. I'm lost in a sea of confusion and fear, a ship without a rudder in the stormy waters of my own fragmented history.

I need to talk to someone, to make sense of this chaos. But who? Everyone here knows me as the commander, the resilient leader of the phoenix fae. To show them this vulnerability, this fear, feels like exposing a wound to the world.

With a shaky breath, I decide to seek counsel from the only person who might understand the depths of my unrest.

Noct.

For now, though, I'm alone with this letter, this choice, and the haunting absence of my own memories. Hell is calling for me, and I don't know why. But I'm determined to find out, even if the truth is as terrifying as the realm itself.

The night stretches on, and I am lost in a tangle of dread and confusion, the subtle wind outside my window a hushed witness to my secret agony.

JUST BEFORE MIDNIGHT, I tread the familiar path to Noct's dwelling, my heart pounding a frenetic rhythm that echoes the tumult within me. The Castanean night, usually a comfort, now feels oppressive.

Noct's home, nestled among the lush foliage fifteen treehouses away from mine, greets me with its usual warmth, but tonight it feels like an asylum. Only she can keep me safe right now, safe from myself, from the ghosts of my past that have come knocking.

I knock, each rap a plea, for an anchor in this chaos inside my head.

The door opens, and Noct stands there, steaming mug in one hand and two thick slices of toast filled with creamy peanut butter sandwiching half a banana in her other. The scent of lavender and chamomile wafts from the face mask lathered across her cheeks and forehead. Her eyes widen when she sees me, taking in my disheveled appearance and tear-streaked face.

Her mate Ronin patrols each weeknight on the surface, leaving her alone, which feels like a mercy now. Without a word, she steps aside.

"Noct," I stammer, my voice barely a whisper as she ushers me in, "I need ... I need your help."

Her eyes scan my face, reading the distress etched into my features as she sets her things on the coffee table. "What's happened?" she asks, concern lacing her tone. "You're scaring me."

In the safety of her living room, I hand her the letter and tuck my hands under my elbows, hugging my stomach. As she reads, her silver eyes widen, and a frown mars her usually serene face, cracking lines in the grey film on her skin, little flecks of her mask flaking off as she sinks to the black couch beneath her. The fire pops and sputters in the hearth.

"You were in the Underworld this entire time? Is that what this means?" Noct slumps back, disbelief and worry mingling in her pitch. "Why?"

Her reaction mirrors my own terror. "I'm scared, Noct," I confess, the words tumbling out in a rush. "What if he forces me back? I don't want to go!"

Her expression softens as she takes my hands in hers, grounding me as she pulls me down with her. "You're a good person." *I'm not.* "Strong and brave." *Maybe.* "We won't let that happen."

Her words are meant to reassure, but they stir a beast in my soul. I'm not a good person. "But what if saying no isn't enough? He's the devil, Noct. I can't fight the devil!"

"You wouldn't be fighting him alone," she growls, her mettle unshaken and far more confident than I am. "No one fucks with my friends. We'll talk to General Risç when he gets back from Earth, and we'll figure this out together."

"Thank you," I whisper, feeling a sliver of hope among the soul-rending dread. "I just can't shake this feeling of being ... hunted." A chill sneaks its way up my spine, unbidden.

My friend pulls me into a hug, her presence a bastion against my spiraling thoughts. "You're safe here. With us. And we'll do everything to keep it that way, okay?"

I cling to her, drawing strength from her. In her embrace, the terror doesn't recede, but it becomes bearable. For now, that has to be enough. I've got to right the wrongs of my past before it catches up with me.

"We'll stand by you," Noct murmurs, her tone taking on a bit of sass. "Whatever it takes. If I have to fight the devil myself, I will!"

She spends the next several hours comforting me, her touch and her words soothing the raw edges of my fear. In her presence, I find a fragment of peace, a respite from the chaos of my own thoughts.

As the night wears on, exhaustion seeps into my bones, and I lean my head against Noct's shoulder, my eyes heavy with weariness. "I should go," I say, my voice a hoarse whisper. It's the middle of the night, and I've already monopolized what I'm sure she thought was going to be a quiet evening.

Noct nods, her hand still resting on my back. "Sleep well. We'll get through this."

With a last, grateful squeeze of her hand, I leave her house, the burden of the letter still heavy in my pocket. But now, with Noct's strength at my back, a tiny glimmer of hope sits among the darkness. A hope that, together, we might be able to face whatever the devil has in store for us. Facing life imprisonment is terrifying, but I know what I'm getting. Being plucked into hell for all eternity by the devil is surely the greater of two evils.

Though it's nearly three in the morning, the night no longer feels quite as menacing. Noct's words echo in my mind, a mantra against the darkness. I won't let fear dictate my life. I am Morte, commander of the Phoenix fae, and I will face whatever comes.

But as I walk back to my treehouse, the shadows seem to whisper, and I can't help but glance over my shoulder, half-expecting to see the devil himself in pursuit.

CHAPTER NINETEEN

MORTE

A restless night gives way to a dawn I greet begrudgingly. I lie in my bed, nestled high in the canopy of my treehouse, the lingering echoes of a dream tugging at the edges of my consciousness. It had started pleasantly enough, a serene landscape that felt both familiar and otherworldly, but then ...

The memory sends a quake down my spine. I recall walking through a forest that seemed to glow with an ethereal light, the leaves shimmering in hues of amethyst and sapphire. A calmness enveloped me, a sense of being connected to something vast and comforting. Yet, as the dream progressed, something shifted. The air grew colder, the light dimmed, and a sense of foreboding crept over me.

I'd looked around, searching for the source of this unease. The forest, once alive with the whispers of leaves and the gentle hum of magical creatures, fell silent. It was as though the very essence of the dream was holding its breath, waiting.

Choking without any intake of air.

The sensation was indescribable—an oppressive weight that seemed to press down on my chest, making it difficult to breathe. I couldn't see anything, but I could feel it. A presence, dark and menacing, lurking just beyond my sight. It was like a shadow in the corner of my eye, a whisper in the back of my mind.

I tried to call out, to demand this unseen entity reveal itself, but my voice caught in my throat. Fear gripped me, a primal, instinctive fear that seemed to seep into my bones. The peaceful dream had turned into a nightmare, and I was trapped within it.

Suddenly, I felt a rush of wind, a movement that seemed to come from all directions at once. The trees swayed violently, their leaves rustling in a chorus of alarm. Then, as abruptly as it had appeared, the presence was gone, leaving behind a chilling emptiness.

I woke with a start, my heart pounding in my chest. The safety of my room did little to calm my nerves. The dream had been too real, too vivid. And that presence ... it felt familiar, but not in a comforting way. It was as if something—or someone—from my past had found its way into my dreams.

I sit up, pushing the tangled sheets away from me. The room is bathed in the soft light of the bioluminescent plants that adorn my treehouse, their gentle glow a welcome contrast to the darkness that lingers in my mind.

Could it be Aggonid infiltrating my dreams? Or is it just a nightmare, spurned by earlier revelations of my whereabouts for the last two years?

I need to shake off this feeling, to find some semblance of normalcy. Perhaps a walk through the lush pathways will clear my head. I dress quickly, choosing comfortable clothing that allows for ease of movement. As I step outside, the fresh air of our underground sanctuary fills my lungs, a welcome reprieve from the stifling atmosphere of my room.

The winding paths are still and serene in the early morning light, the only audible sounds coming from the distant murmur of the nearby waterfall and the occasional chirp of a tree minx.

The dense foliage that engulfs me is a mesmerizing display of colors, each leaf and flower radiating with its own enchanting magic. The vibrant shades of emerald, sapphire, and ruby dance in the gentle breeze, a masterpiece of hues that usually brings me a sense of tranquility. But today, it feels like a fragile front masking something more ominous lurking beneath its surface.

As I walk, fragments of the dream swirl in my mind. What could it signify? A mere trick of the subconscious or something more? The memory of that sinister presence persists, an unsolved puzzle.

Ahead, the path brings me to the waterfall. Here, water tumbles into a crystal-clear pool below, its melody typically a balm for my restlessness. Today, however, the comforting sounds are drowned out by the remaining echoes of my nightmare.

I sit by the water's edge, my gaze lingering on the reflections of light, shimmering and skimming across the surface. The tranquility here belies the inner mayhem I'm grappling with. Drawing a deep breath, I close my eyes, attempting to anchor myself among internal chaos.

But even here, in this place of beauty and serenity, the shadows linger, a reminder of a fear I can't quite escape. I see flashes of fire and brimstone, nightmares my mind conjures of my time in the Underworld.

And in that moment, I realize.

Whatever it was that invaded my dream, it's not done with me yet. It's a thought that sends another shudder down my spine, a premonition of challenges yet to come. But I am Morte, a phoenix fae, a creature of fire and resilience. Whatever this is, I will face it head-on, as I always have.

I hurl a stone across the water, watching it plunge out of sight. Energized, I get up from my spot by the waterfall. The day calls, filled with mysteries to solve. Talking to Noct again seems like the right place to begin.

As I draw closer to her home, the delicate fragrance of wildflowers mixed with the earthy scent of ancient bark fills the air, invigorating my senses.

I pause for a moment at the base of the tree, looking up at the sprawling structure above. It's a formidable climb, but one I've made countless times before, often after a boozy brunch at the Braised Wolf. It's much easier to get here from the canopy, as I can use the foot bridges, rather than the rickety stairs built into the tree's side. I tried flying up here once, but my wings got caught in the long willow branches.

I think this was all part of Crucey's defenses for us—she planted so many trees when she took our people underground.

Taking a moment to steady myself, I reach for the rugged bark, feeling its texture beneath my fingertips. I start my climb, ascending the spiraling wooden staircase that wraps around the ancient trunk like a giant's coil. Each step creaks slightly under my weight, a familiar melody in the stillness of dawn.

After reaching the top, I stand before Noct's door, hesitating for just a moment. The crisp scent of morning dew and the faint chorus of waking birds fills the air around me. Raising my hand, I rap on the wood, the sound echoing more loudly than I intended, a painful interruption to the dawn's peaceful lull.

The door promptly opens, and Noct appears, clad in her typical attire of practicality and readiness. Her eyes, a striking silver akin to moonlight on water, flicker with an alert sharpness as she surveys me. A trace of toast crumbs sits at the corner of her mouth, which she brushes away with a quick, efficient motion.

"Everything okay?" she asks, her tone laced with concern as she steps back to allow me entry. Her gaze lingers on me, scrutinizing, as if trying to read the fear etched into my expression.

I step inside, the familiarity of her home wrapping around me like a warm embrace. "I had a nightmare, Noct. A disturbing one. It felt ... different. I need to talk about it. It felt less like a bad dream and more like it was actually happening."

She motions towards a chair, and I move to sit down. Around me, Noct's living space unfolds like a gallery of her life's journey—a continuous blend of functionality and personal history. The walls are adorned with an array of weapons, each telling its own tale of battles fought and victories won. Interspersed among these tools of war are mementos, each holding a story, a fragment of time captured and cherished.

My eyes are drawn to the large, prominently displayed frames.

They house photographs, vibrant and full of life, chronicling key moments. One picture captures Noct and Ronin in the stands at their first Spar Games, their faces alight with the thrill of being on the surface for the first time. Another frame holds the memory of their pinning ceremony, a moment of mutual respect and achievement, where they proudly pinned each other, marking a significant milestone in their warrior's path.

Each image is a window into Noct's world, a world where the lines between the soldier and my friend blur, creating a mosaic rich with experience and emotion. The room breathes with the essence of who she is—strong, dedicated, and deeply connected to those she holds dear.

I'm going to miss her so fucking much.

As I sink into a chair, Ronin strides into the room, his presence bringing a comforting sense of solidity to the space. He greets me with a friendly nod, his eyes briefly meeting mine in a silent acknowledgment. Approaching Noct, he leans down and plants a tender kiss on her forehead, a simple gesture that speaks volumes of their deep connection.

"Morning," he says, his voice warm. "Need anything while I'm out?"

Noct shakes her head, a small smile playing on her lips. "Don't forget sorrow's root and moon orb dust."

He nods before he turns to me, his gaze inquiring. "Anything I can pick up for you?"

I offer him a grateful smile, shaking my head. "No, thank you. We'll just be having a chat."

"Alright then." The corners of Ronin's mouth lift slightly. He gives Noct another quick glance, full of tacit communication, before heading towards the door. "I'll be back in a bit. Take your time."

His departure leaves a quieter space, filled only with the subtle sounds of the treehouse and the distant hum of life outside.

Noct sits opposite me, her posture relaxed yet alert. "Now tell me about the dream," she prompts as she fills a mug with coffee and slides it my way.

Gripping the warm stoneware, I describe the dream in detail. The ethereal forest, the oppressive presence, the sudden shift from peace to terror. As I speak, she listens intently, her eyes never leaving mine.

"It sounds like more than just a nightmare," she muses once I finish. "Dreams can be windows to deeper truths, especially for those with our kind of magic." She pauses before leaning in, and speaking in a hushed whisper, "Do you think it was Aggonid?"

I nod, feeling a mixture of fear and anxiety at her words. "It felt real, Noct. Like a warning or ... a message."

She leans in further, her expression fearful. "Dreams can be influenced by many things—our fears, our desires, even external forces. Considering everything you've been through, it's not surprising your subconscious is trying to process it all. But if you feel there's more to it, we should look into it."

My breath wheezes out of me. I'm used to going into suicide missions, facing the scariest that our realm has to offer ... but if Aggonid, the most feared god in all the realms is after me? Panic seizes my chest. "I don't ..." I stumble over my words. "D-don't even know where to start."

"We'll figure it out together," she assures me. "For now, try to focus on the present. Ground yourself in what you know is real. General Risç comes back tomorrow."

I exhale, my cheeks puffing out as I do so. "Thanks," I say with a genuine smile. This is exactly what I needed." But even as the thought registers, fear strikes me again. It won't be long before he knows that the woman he trusted to keep the realm safe is nothing but a fraud who's being put away where she belongs.

The questions are sobering, and a slight tremble starts in my hands and works its way to my chest.

She returns the smile, as she scoots back from her chair. "What you need is a little normalcy. How about we get some breakfast?" She grins at me, knowing I just walked in on her eating toast, but I'm not going to mention it. "Let's head to the Braised Wolf!"

For generations, werewolves were the sworn enemies of the Tolden. They hunted us relentlessly, driven by the belief that consuming a Tolden heart could transform them into wolf fae. This dark and violent period in our history is now remembered by the name of our most popular establishment. Its menu, with each dish recalling different aspects of our tumultuous past, serves not just as a grim nod to our history with the werewolves, but also as a reminder of the Tolden's enduring strength and the harrowing trials we've overcome. The High Queen of the Fae cured their affliction, which meant we no longer had to hide our people from the rest of Bedlam.

As we leave her home, the crystalline sky brightens, projecting shimmering patterns on the forest floor. Despite the lingering unease from the dream, I feel a sense of belonging here, among my people, my friends.

Together, we walk toward the restaurant, the hub of Castanea's daily life. The chatter and laughter of our people rises to greet us, proof that life goes on, resilient and enduring, even if you're not ready for it to. None of these people know the secret of my whereabouts the past two years.

No one comes back from the Underworld. Well, no one like us. I'm not mated to the High Queen like Gideon was. Nor am I special. So, why me?

Noct and I weave through the increasingly busy pathways, the early risers of our community moving with purpose. The ground beneath our feet is soft and damp, the grass and leaves cushioning our steps. The breeze picks up, stirring the air around me. It's filled with the subtle movements of the crowd—a feather drifting down from a fae's wing as it soars through the sky, a faint rustle of fur from a shapeshifter brushing past.

As we walk towards the restaurant, the open space comes into view, bustling with activity. Tolden of all ages go about their morning routines, some sitting at tables and sharing meals, others engaged in lively conversations. The vibrant colors of their clothes and the diverse mix of species create a mosaic of daily life in our little refuge.

I'm really going to miss this.

A delightful mix of aromas fill the air. Freshly baked bread, sizzling dusk hare, and brewing coffee. The comforting scent of home and family.

We find a spot among our peers, and the warm murmur of conversations envelopes us. Noct fills our plates with an assortment of fruits, bread, and a warm, savory porridge that's a staple in our diet. The simple act of eating, of participating in this daily ritual, grounds me.

"So, what's the plan?" She breaks a piece of bread and dunks it in an oil sprinkled with shredded cheese.

"I'm not sure yet," I admit, stirring the porridge. "But I can't shake the feeling that this dream is important. It was so damned invasive. It felt sinister."

She nods thoughtfully, chewing on her food. "Maybe you need someone to sleep next to you, keep outside forces away."

"Outside forces?" I pause, the spoon halfway to my mouth. "Like you-know-who?"

She leans in, lowering her voice despite the sound bubble we put up when we first sat down. "Maybe. There are entities, beings with the power to influence dreams. But it's rare. *Dreamwalkers* I think they're called, and it usually requires a connection of some kind."

A chill runs down my spine at the thought. The Underworld, my unaccounted two years, the dreams ... all signs point to it being connected.

"We need to be careful," Noct continues, her tone laced with concern. "If someone or something is trying to reach you through your dreams, whoever it is, it's not to be taken lightly."

A knot of unease forms in my stomach as I hug my middle. "Damn. Maybe I should look into some protective charms, just in case."

She nods in agreement, her eyes reflecting her earnestness. "That's a good idea. And remember, we're always here for you, whatever you need. I'd be eager to see how I'd fare against the devil," her last words are more of an inner thought spoken out loud than something she meant for me to hear. "I bet I could last two, maybe three seconds if I can use a sword."

Mirth dances in her gaze as she snags a piece of bread from the basket in front of me.

"As long as those charms and swords don't keep me from having sexy dreams about multiple men ravaging me at the same time." I grin at her, trying to keep the mood light.

Noct's eyes widen. "What about Wilder?"

"That's the thing!" I whisper. "He was there for my first dream, sharing me with the other guys. Maybe if I can't have him in real life, at least he can be there waiting for me in my dreams."

I can tell Noct isn't sure whether she should laugh or feel sorry for me. Instead, she shoves a giant spoonful of food in her mouth, and I chuckle. "I'm serious! Maybe ... my mind knew how badly I've pined for the same man for thousands of years, so now it's not only giving me him, but more." I sigh, thinking back to the fun in the tent. "They said they were my mates. And now all I want to do is sleep, in hopes I run into them all in my dreams, to feel wanted. I crave that so badly," I whisper. "I think that's what I've been missing from my life."

Her eyes go glassy as she grabs my hand. "If Wilder wasn't so noble, sparing you from an eternity in prison, I'd want to punch him for not taking you as an anchor. To hell with tradition."

I shake my head. "If the sea doesn't recognize me as his anchor, he never ... we never could consummate our mating. The tools." I cough. "They wouldn't work."

She gasps. "No."

I nod, wincing. "That's how we knew I wasn't his. No matter how much heavy petting we did, it just wouldn't work as nature intends. That's how all merfae work."

"Gods ..." She covers her mouth with her hand. "Poor guy."

"I know."

Though if I were his anchor, I'd feel a possessive kind of pride knowing I'm the only one he could ever be with.

But I'm in love with a man who's moved on, all while I sat still. But grief is love's receipt, and it chokes me, drowning me in it. Whoever Wilder's anchor is, they are the luckiest fae to ever exist.

Noct squeezes my hand, her touch warm and genuine, and I blink away the moisture that's gathered in my eyes. With friends like her, I'm not alone in this. Guilt eats at me, because when everything is said and done, I know I'll break her heart, too. I taint everything I touch. I know she's worked so hard to not show her grief, knowing I'm going to prison, but I see it in the way her eyes linger on me a little longer, her touch, too. I'm slipping through her fingers and there's nothing in this life or the next that can stop it.

Breakfast continues with lighter topics, but the undercurrent of my grief lingers, a shadow at the edge of my consciousness. As we finish our meal, I feel a renewed sense of what I need to do.

"I should get started on those protective charms," I say, rising from the table.

Noct stands with me, clapping a hand on my shoulder just like her mate does. "Want me to send Ronin by?"

He's a master at protection spells. I've never really found the need for them, so I'm rusty at best. When you're a phoenix who literally comes back to life, you take big risks, a daredevil. I normally have no need for protection ... from literally anything. They protect people from me.

"Couldn't hurt, I guess," I grumble.

My nerves quicken as I arrange the pillows on the couch and turn to see Ronin walking towards me. His long legs eat up the path, and his golden hair, catching the simulated sunlight, adds a radiant aura to his strong, fire golem features.

"Hey, Trouble." He meets me as I open the door to greet him. "Heard you needed some help with protection charms."

"Yeah, thanks for coming on such short notice," I sigh, motioning for him to come inside. "I know you're probably getting ready for bed." He usually works nights, so this is when he's typically asleep.

He steps into the treehouse, looking around with an appreciative nod. "I like what you've done with the place." His fingers trail over the wooden beams and the various crystals that adorn the space. "Cozy."

When I woke up after two years of being in the Underworld, I redecorated the place, made it less cheery, and more a reflection of how I feel on the inside. It's darker, more woods and metals than ever before. My eyes follow his, and I wince. So maybe there's more than a little metal.

Why did I add so much?

Smiling awkwardly, I mumble, "Thanks, it's been a work in progress." I snatch a little metal figurine and put it behind a picture frame on the mantle of the fireplace.

I lead him to the table where I've laid out all the materials we'll need, including various herbs, crystals, and candles. He takes a seat across from me, his eyes focused on the items in from of him.

"So. Protection charms. What exactly are we protecting against? Noct said it wasn't her place to say."

I hesitate, unsure how much to divulge. "Bad dreams," I say finally. "Last night I had one that felt ... invasive. Ominous, even. Less like I was being watched and more like I was being hunted."

Ronin frowns, his playful demeanor slipping away. "Hunted?"

I take a deep breath, trying to steady my nerves. "Yes," I begin, recounting the details of what had me nearly falling out of bed in the middle of the night as I scrambled to get away from something, someone. "I'm not entirely sure what it means, but I have a feeling that something is after me."

His expression darkens, his eyes flashing with a protective instinct. "Okay, we'll start with a basic warding spell," he says, reaching for the herbs. "We need to create a barrier around you, one that will keep any unwanted entities at bay."

As he works, I watch him with a mix of fascination and awe. He's always had my back, even when I don't deserve it. The muscles in his forearms coil and release as he grinds the herbs together, muttering under his breath as he concentrates on the small, crystalline bowl.

He adds a few drops of his own blood, which I know is a powerful ingredient in any type of warding spell, and then lights a white pillar candle. As he's a fire golem, it'll take a lot for this flame to go out.

"First, we'll set up a basic warding circle," he explains, arranging the crystals in a precise pattern around the candle. "This will create a barrier against any unwanted intrusions."

I watch him work, his movements precise and confident. There's a rhythm to his actions, a dance of magic and intent that's fascinating to observe.

As he chants softly, the air within the circle begins to shimmer, a visible sign of the magic at work. The energy is substantial, a gentle hum that resonates through the room.

"Next, we infuse the barrier with specific intentions," he continues, selecting a vial and uncorking it. "This is where you come in. You need to focus on what you want to keep out."

I close my eyes, concentrating on the feeling of the invasive presence from my dream. The darkness, the oppression, the fear—it all comes flooding back. I push those emotions into the circle, imagining them being repelled by the barrier.

Ronin's presence is a quiet constant beside me. Even with my eyes closed, I feel him shifting to action. "Good, keep focusing on that. I'll reinforce the barrier," he states.

He begins to chant again, his voice rising and falling in a hypnotic rhythm. The air in the circle thickens, the shimmer growing stronger until it's almost blinding, even with my eyes squeezed shut.

After a few moments, he stops, and the light dims to a comfortable glow. "There, that should do it. This barrier will protect you from any intent to harm while you're at your most vulnerable."

I open my eyes, feeling a sense of relief wash over me. "Thanks, Roe. I really appreciate this."

He shrugs, a hint of his usual cockiness returning. "If it helps my mate sleep at night, knowing you're safe? Worth it." He grins, reclining on the couch as he stretches out his legs. "Just don't let this flame go out, otherwise you won't be protected."

I nod, my mind still processing the intense magic that just took place. "Got it. So, what now?"

He leans forward, his eyes serious. "Now, we need to figure out what's after you. You said you had a feeling, right? Maybe we can try to track it down."

I hesitate, unsure if I want to involve him any further. "I don't know, Roe. It could be dangerous. I don't want to put anyone in harm's way."

He scoffs, a playful roll of his eyes accompanying his words, "I can handle myself. You know that. Besides," he adds with a reassuring tone, "we're not going to let you face this alone."

Their solidarity warms me, yet guilt lingers, an uninvited shadow. "I appreciate it, really, but the thought of dragging you into this mess," I confess, a troubled sigh escaping me, "and if anything were to happen to you or Noct ... I couldn't bear that guilt."

He reaches out and takes my hand, his grip firm and reassuring. "You're not dragging us into anything. I'm here because I want to be. When you died and didn't come back, everyone was wrecked. Noct was inconsolable. Every phoenix was. And suddenly, all of us mates had a whole new fear unlocked: phoenixes can stay dead. You don't think any one of us would do anything to keep you all safe? We're family."

I feel my cheeks heat up at his words, and I look away, unable to meet his gaze. "You can't put yourselves in harm's way—"

"Can't we make that decision ourselves?" he interrupts.

"Yes, but I'm the only unmated phoenix, and if something happened to me, it's okay. If something happens to any of you, it hurts more than one person," I whisper. "This is what it means to be Commander. I bear the brunt of the risk, and I'm okay with that."

I can never be with Wilder. I'll spend the rest of my days pining for someone who can never love me back. Not in the same sense, anyway.

Ronin sighs, but not in a way that suggests he's angry. It's more of a respectful disentangling, a resignation of fate. I finally meet his eyes, and I'm relieved to find him not upset, but at peace.

He squeezes my hand gently, his voice soft. "I just want you to know that we're here for you. Anything you need. Especially if it involves bashing in some heads, or taking out a rogue asset," he grins.

I can't help but smile at his words, feeling the warmth of his platonic affection envelop me. "Thank you. I appreciate that more than you know." *More than I deserve.* I shake my head, feeling a sense of dread creeping in. "I think we've figured out where I was the last two years."

Noct said she wouldn't tell a soul, and I know that means she wouldn't even tell her mate. But I can't ask her to keep secrets from him.

"Really? Where?"

"In the Underworld," I say, my voice just shy of a whisper, as though the devil himself is listening. "I don't remember a thing, but I suspect that's where I've been."

His eyes widen, the playful glint fading. "The Underworld? Do you think it's connected to whatever's after you now?"

"I don't know," I admit. "But I can't shake the feeling that it's Aggonid. He's the only one I can think of that would have a reason to come after me."

He pales and his jaw tightens at the mention of Aggonid's name. "Why would the devil be after you?"

"Because of this." I cross the room to my end table and pull the folded letter out of my drawer and hand it to him.

"Gods," he whispers as his eyes race across the parchment. "Do you think maybe you weren't supposed to leave the Underworld, and that's why he's demanding you be sent back?"

Fear snakes its way up my spine at the thought and I sink to the couch next to him and hug my middle. "Who knows," I grumble. "If it is, it might be him hunting me in my dream. I'm going to feel really stupid if this is all a standard-issue nightmare and I'm blowing this way out of proportion."

He shakes his head. "They didn't make you commander because you ignored your instincts against your better judgment." He pauses, his expression thoughtful. "We nee—"

"It doesn't freak you out that I was sent to hell?" I wince. "That I've committed horrible enough deeds to be sent there?"

Ronin rests his hand on my forearm. "I don't pretend to think these suicide missions you get sent on are always on the noble side of things. Lawful, usually, but morally? You take orders. Fulfill them. It's not your job to ask questions. I can't fault you, Noct, or any of the other Great Company for that."

I exhale a deep breath, letting his words sink in. He's right. I follow orders without question. But I guarantee that isn't why I was sent there.

He hands me a rose quartz from in front of him, and I take it, holding it in my palm. "I can see your mind warring with itself. I know you, and I'm sure whatever it is that's troubling you or causing you to question the good in you isn't something a bad person would think twice about. You've got to know that, right?"

Does a psychopath question whether he's a psychopath?

I offer him a small smile, grateful for his help but mindful of keeping him too long. "What do I owe you for this?" I rise to my feet, the universal sign of 'things-are-getting-too-deep-so-I-need-to-shut-this-down.'

He stands with me, adjusting the straps on his satchel. "Nothing, Trouble. You don't owe me anything. I just want to help you."

I nod, appreciative of his sentiment. "Thanks, Roe. I'll repay the favor somehow."

He smiles, but it doesn't reach his eyes. It's a sad smile, the kind that tells me he knows exactly what I'm doing. "You don't have to repay anything. I'm doing this because I want to. Because we care about you," he leans in to press a quick peck to my cheek in goodbye. "Let me know how this charm works tonight?"

"Okay," I murmur as he gathers his things.

As he leaves, I'm left alone with the newly erected barrier and my thoughts. The idea of being protected brings a sense of security, but it's tinged with the knowledge that such measures are necessary. The nightmare, the letter from Finn, the fear of Aggonid's reach—it's all so much.

The prison is impenetrable. I know because I've tried for hundreds of years. It's forged with sanguimetal, the toughest metal in all the realms, and it's imbued with its own inherent magic that isn't reliant on the moon. It makes it extremely difficult to manipulate.

Getting to the prison, out of Aggonid's reach, suddenly can't come fast enough.

CHAPTER TWENTY

WILDER

Under the unforgiving gaze of the penitentiary's watchful eyes, I've found an unlikely friend in Corwin, the mouse shifter guard whose size contradicts his significance. In the hidden corners of the prison yard, a realm where whispers are a form of currency, he leans in, his glance furtive, that of someone who understands the power of words.

"Corwin," I murmur, the clank of chains a dull soundtrack to our covert meeting, "Who do the guards fear the most out of all inmates in the prison?"

The mouse shifter glances around before answering, his voice a hushed tone that barely rises above the din of the yard. "Lucius," he confesses, "a soul so vile that his cell reeks of the dread he conjures. He's the one who made a game of torment—"

I hold up a hand to halt his words, feeling the chill of his name settle into my bones. I only need to know his name and what he's done. "Enough," I say, the suppressant bracelet on my wrist a cold reminder of my inability to retaliate against such evil. But if I had it off? I could drown him in his own fluids. "What did he do?"

Corwin's nose twitches, and though he's in his fae form, I can picture his whiskers there, and he looks away, a gesture of discomfort. "It's not just what he did. It's what he delights in, the chaos he still tries to sow even from within these walls. He's constantly in and out of solitary for tormenting other inmates. And if it isn't him, it's one of his little pets doing his bidding."

I nod, the cogs of my mind turning with a plan that's forming, as delicate and dangerous as the threads of a spider's web. "I need a favor, a way to make right what's been wronged."

The fae's beady eyes meet mine, understanding dawning in their depths. "You're planning something," he states, not a question but a realization.

"Justice," I correct him, conviction sharpening my tone. "If Bed Penn is the end of the line, then let's ensure it's just that for those who deserve it."

Corwin's hands rest on the hilt of his magical weapons, a gesture of solidarity. "I'm with you. Just tell me what you need."

I draw in a breath, steeling myself for the path I'm about to tread. There is no turning back. "Information, access, and your silence. Can you do that?"

He nods eagerly as I whisper what I need him to do, and I feel the swell of gratitude for this small fae with the heart of a lion. "I'll do what I can," he assures me, and I know that in this place of despair, I've found a flicker of hope, not just for justice, but for a one-way ticket straight to hell.

Right into her arms.

We make plans for me to have a change in schedule so I can be in the prison yard at the same time as Lucius and his crew. I learn more about the heinous things they've done. Raped a bonded prisoner in front of her mate, while the others held him back so he could do nothing, tricked a new inmate into provoking a berserker in the yard, and fed poison to a rat so that when an eagle shifter was expelling his magic, he'd swallowed the rodent, dying. And those are just things they've done this month.

They deserve every punishment that comes their way. Their

names are whispered in fear and disgust among the other guards, their actions painting a shadow over the entire facility. It's a constant reminder of how far people can fall and how twisted the fae psyche can become, and why so many of them deserve exactly what they're going to get when they leave this realm.

They're monsters.

And I've got to become just like them.

In the dark, murky boundaries of my cramped cell, beneath the ever-watchful eyes of the prison guards, a plan begins to take shape. The walls of the penitentiary, steeped in despair and monotony, become the canvas on which I plot my escape. Every day, every mundane interaction with the guards and other inmates, I'm searching, calculating, hoarding.

Biding my time until the schedule shift.

The first piece I secure is a small, jagged shard of metal, a discarded remnant from a meal tray that had seen better days. The sharp edges glint as I conceal it within the lining of my threadbare mattress during the daily cell inspections. My heart hammers against my ribs with each passing second, daring the guards to discover my secret and crush my hopes of freedom. The stale air weighs heavily on my skin, but I must break free from this suffocating prison and find my way back to her.

By any means necessary.

I spend hours observing the guards, learning their patterns, their weaknesses. Each shift change, every distracted moment, I commit to memory. In the prison library, I feign interest in mundane books while actually studying the layout of the prison, piecing together a mental map of its corridors and exits. In case my plan goes awry, and I need to find a way to hell another way. And I won't know which tools I need to enact my plan until I've met Lucius and his crew, so I hoard anything I can.

With furtive glances over my shoulder, I carefully pluck a sturdy length of wire from the discarded remnants of an old gym machine in the recreational area. The guards' eyes dart around, ever watching for any signs of disturbance, but necessity breeds boldness within me. I wrap the cool metal around my torso, feeling its reassuring weight press against me beneath my uniform.

The small pond in my cell, a tiny oasis in this barren prison, serves as a lifeline to the world I once knew. With trembling hands, I gather my makeshift tools and carefully conceal them in a waterproof pouch made from scraps of fabric. The surface of the water remains undisturbed, hiding my only means of escape from prying eyes. The faint shuffle of the guard's boots outside my cell remind me of the perils that lurk just beyond my door. If I'm caught and I get sent to solitary, it'll be so much harder to kill the inmates I need in order to get sent to the Underworld.

But for now, my secret stash remains safe beneath the calm waters of the pond, ready for when the time comes to break free.

In the middle of the night, when shadows cloak the prison and only the distant echo of a guard's footsteps breaks the silence, I practice. Each silent step on the cold stone, each careful, measured movement, is a rehearsal for my final act of liberation. Every night, the plan becomes clearer, a doorway to a different kind of freedom, one that promises an end to the endless cycle of captivity and will deliver me right to where I belong.

Not only will I get to be with Morte, but I'll be able to take out the evil permeating these walls. When I end the lives of the worst of them, the guards will happily take me out, and I'll finally be free to be with her.

I'll make my death count.

In the seclusion of my cell, with Morte's letter hidden away, a flame of hope flickers within me. I won't be caged forever. For her, for the love that binds us, I will reclaim the freedom that was stolen from us. The darkness of Bedlam Penitentiary will not hold me; I will find my way back to her, back to the life we were meant to share.

It's unfortunate it'll be in the Underworld, but she is my home, so I'll go wherever I need to.

Each night, I painstakingly collect and conceal small, seemingly insignificant objects within the borders of my small pond. A sharp fragment of a stone from the wall, a stiff wire taken from the bed frame. With each hidden item, I feel both exhilaration and fear, knowing that my plan could either lead to freedom or ultimate destruction. Probably both. My hands tremble as I carefully arrange and conceal the pieces, hoping they'll be enough to secure my escape if Plan A doesn't work.

Whatever it takes.

THE DAYS BLEND TOGETHER in a monotonous haze, each one a prisoner in itself. Bedlam Penitentiary remains for now, my inescapable reality, its iron grip suffocating my very spirit. But within the depths of this despair, a flicker of opportunity presents itself—my prison yard shift change finally came through.

Weeks of waiting, all the pieces are in place, and I'm just waiting for them to fall. To take out the one whose acts are so vile, even the guards fear him, and stories of his crimes keep the rest of the shift in line. But those tales hold no sway over me. In this place, where monsters roam unrestrained, it takes one to know one.

And for her, I'd be the worst monster of all.

I'll bathe in their blood, wearing a smile as I do it, knowing I'm going to finally have her in my arms again.

Over the past few days, Lucius has been observing me with a sinister smirk, his cold eyes assessing my every move. The other inmates cower in his presence, like loyal subjects bound to their sadistic king.

To him, I'm fresh meat. But I refuse to be just another pawn in his twisted game. I'll flip the board, take out his subjects, and not regret a second of it.

I've watched him closely during our shared recreation time in the courtyard, studying his routine, his weaknesses. He's Machiavellian, always surrounded by a pack of loyal followers who do his bidding without question. These inmates, like him, are marked by darkness, their souls tainted by the atrocities they've committed.

They're the ones who deserve to meet their end at the tip of my blade.

Despite their cunning ways, I've found cracks in their armor that give me hope.

During my clandestine practices after most of the prison have gone to sleep, I've honed my skills, sharpening my instincts and perfecting my movements. Each step is one of calculated precision, my body becoming an extension of the malevolent energy that surrounds me, and it feels good to finally carve out a place for myself here. Albeit temporary.

As I make my way to the courtyard for my daily rec time, I focus my mind on my concealed weapon. I enter, eyes searching for the blond-haired little asshole terrorizing inmates. Lucius and his pack revel in their power, taunting and brutalizing weaker inmates with sadistic pleasure. It sickens me to witness their cruelty, but it also fuels the fire burning within me—the fire of vengeance. I have longed for justice, for a reckoning against those who have taken so much from innocent lives, and now I've got a reason to do it. With Lucius and his minions in my sights, that longing transforms into purpose.

Guards don't get involved unless someone is dying. And that's a weakness I'm betting on today.

I watch as Lucius circles his prey, a scrawny fae with fragile wings and terror in his eyes. The pack, brimming with brute strength and primal instincts, encircles the helpless inmate. Their cruel laughter reverberates through the stale air of the prison yard, while other inmates shrink back to the outskirts, knowing better than to interfere. But today will be different. Today, they will face their reckoning.

The time has come to put my weapons to use.

With a steady hand and a heart heavy with purpose, I grip the sharpened metal I hid away in my cell. Its jagged edges flash in the sunlight, a reflection of the darkness that resides within me. As I approach the scene, my steps fall silent, my movements fluid and calculated. Lucius is too consumed with his sadistic amusement to notice my presence until it's too late.

The fae's eyes widen as he catches sight of me, a glimmer of hope replacing the fear that once clouded his gaze. I nod at him, a silent reassurance that help has arrived.

Lucius and his pack turn their attention toward me, their twisted grins faltering for a split second before being replaced with a mask of arrogance.

"Who do we have here?" Lucius sneers, his voice dripping with disdain. "A pathetic inmate trying to challenge our authority? I'll give you one chance to get the fuck away before you're our target for the day."

I don't respond. Instead, I let my actions speak for me.

With a rapid and precise movement, I plunge the sharpened metal into the nearest assailant—a hulking brute with a rugged face marred by scars. The metallic clang echoes through the courtyard as his body slumps to the ground, leaving behind a pool of crimson blood staining the dull grey concrete. The scene now falls into a stunned silence, the air thick with disbelief and fear. The remaining members of Lucius' pack hesitate, their eyes flickering back and forth between their fallen comrade and me, their previously confident expressions now trembling with uncertainty.

But I don't give them a chance to recover. Like a harsh storm, I unleash with deadly precision, striking each one down before they can even raise a weapon. The sound of my attacks fills the air, punctuated by the thudding collapse of their bodies like marionettes with severed strings. With every strike, their cries come to an abrupt end, leaving only the eerie silence of their defeat in its wake.

Because while they have their magic suppression cuffs on, mine only look as though they're secured. Thanks to a little help from Corwin, I'm faster, stronger, deadlier.

The shrill alarms blare, piercing the air with their insistency. A red light bathes the courtyard, painting an eerie glow on the frantic guards as they clamor to reach me. The sound of footsteps and shouts take up the space, creating just the chaos I want.

Lucius, the self-proclaimed king of this twisted prison, is left standing, his expression shifting from arrogance to genuine surprise and a healthy dose of fear. I've been the perfect inmate here. Kept my head down. Didn't stir trouble.

He never saw this coming. He takes a step back, his hand trembling as it reaches for the concealed shank I know he keeps at his side. But I'm faster. In one swift motion, I disarm him and press the blade against his throat.

With gritted teeth and a primal growl, I plunge my weapon deep into his flesh. The sound of tearing muscle fills the air as I yank it out, triumphantly holding up his severed head for all to see, a maniacal grin on my face as I spin around, brandishing his head. His lifeless body slumps to the ground, a token of my victory. The metallic scent of blood lingers in the courtyard, mixing with the adrenaline and rage coursing through my veins. This is the end of his reign, and the beginning of mine.

Never again will he torment another soul.

The guards unleash their powerful magic at me, a searing light that rends me in the air and sends me spiraling towards the ground. My body slams against the hard concrete, every bone and muscle aching with the impact, but I refuse to give up. The fire within me blazes fiercely, driving me forward despite the pain and chaos around me. My vision is cloudy and blurred, darkness crowding in.

With a mix of fear and awe, the guards cautiously approach, their eyes wide with disbelief. Slowly and deliberately, I rise to my feet, blood dripping from my wounds and staining the cement below. They form a tight circle around me, weapons drawn and ready for any sudden movements. But I stand tall, refusing to let them intimidate or control me any longer. The pent-up fury within has reached its boiling point and nothing will stop me from unleashing it now.

"I've done what you all were too afraid to do." My tone is steady despite the pain coursing through my body. With my hands raised in the air, I shout so all can hear me over the blare of the alarm. "I've rid this prison of its darkest plague."

The world buzzes with tension as their eyes dart between the mangled corpses littering the ground and my swerving stance. Agony sears me, making me unstable on my feet, and my chest heaves, adrenaline fueling me. An unmistakable uncertainty hangs in the air, a question of whether I'm a savior or a twisted abomination. But it's inconsequential. Their thoughts hold no sway over me—they are mere pawns following orders, and they silence me with a brutal blow to the skull.

I'm coming for you, Morte.

CHAPTER TWENTY-ONE

AGGONID

The room is still as I center myself, trying to focus and contain my excitement. The others have said Morte would be ready to meet me now, and as a team we've worked hard over the past week to make sure the dreamscape is strong enough. The sanguimetal conduits hum with latent energy. I close my eyes, the darkness behind my lids soon giving way to the unfolding dreamscape—a lush, ethereal meadow under a twilight sky. I stand alone, the air rich with the scent of jasmine and a cool breeze that carries the promise of a meeting long-awaited.

I wait, anticipation coiling tight within me, each moment stretched thin by the silence of her absence. The landscape, once vibrant, seems to hold its breath, the colors dimming to hues of anticipation and worry. Morte's presence is near, I can feel it—a gentle touch upon the veil that separates us.

So where is she?

As the time slips by, the atmosphere shifts, the warmth leeching from the air replaced by a creeping chill that whispers of something sinister drawing near. The meadow's once soft grass bristles like quills, and the sky darkens as the breeze turns into a howling gale that speaks not of tranquility, but of warnings unheeded.

An unease settles over me, a dread that clenches my gut. I cast my senses wide, searching for the source of this malice that dares to taint our sacred space. The dreamscape quivers, a shiver running through its very essence as if the land itself is afraid.

Few have the balls to challenge me.

A shadow emerges, not of Morte's gentle night but a darkness so profound it seems to devour the light around it. The putrid scent of tainted blood fills my senses. The air pulses with malevolence, a malignant force that has no place in this sanctuary of slumber and secrets. It moves with purpose, its presence a blight upon the dream woven of hope and delicate threads of connection.

I stand firm, my might as defiant as the ancient magic that fuels my being. This evil will not go unchallenged. The very fabric of the dreamscape shudders under the might of my fury, the power at my command rising like a storm within, ready to break upon this intruder.

Yet, it halts, the darkness pausing at the edge of my wrath as if savoring the fear it seeks to instill. A silent battle of wills ensues, neither yielding, the dreamscape a battlefield marked not by blood, but by the struggle of light against the encroaching void.

The presence recoils, the darkness ebbing as if biding its time, a serpent slithering back into the obscurity from whence it came. But the threat remains, a looming specter on the horizon of our shared dreams.

The dreamscape steadies, and the evil presence retreats but leaves behind a residue of fear. Our sanctuary remains intact, but the echoes of its intrusion linger.

"Fuck!" I shout, causing the dreamscape's birds to take flight from the trees.

My shadows seem to multiply and consume the space around me as I frantically pull away from the dream. My fingers dig into the table, leaving deep indentations in the wood as I try to ground myself.

The others crowd around me, their words laced with concern and fear as they ask what's wrong. My breaths come in ragged gasps, each one a struggle to regain control of my racing heart and swirling thoughts.

"Something's wrong," I breathe, the sound only loud enough to hear if you strain to listen. "The dreamscape ..." I trail off, closing my eyes as I try to sense what had changed in the delicate balance of our sanctuary.

"Is Morte okay?" Caius places a hand on mine, real fear in his eyes as I meet them.

My lungs feel thick as panic grips me, almost suffocating. "I don't—I don't know. She wasn't there." The familiar scent of the dreamscape was tainted with a metallic tang, like blood coating my tongue, as if it knows something is wrong.

"What the fuck do you mean, she wasn't there?" Az stalks towards me.

"The dreamscape started out as it always does, but then there was this presence, some shadowy entity that didn't belong. I felt its sinister intent."

"What else did you see? Feel? This could help us pinpoint who, or what, it was." Emeric drags an ancient tome off the shelf and brings it over to the table, flipping through the pages as though he knows exactly what he's looking for.

"There was an overwhelming scent of blood magic. Metallic, and—"

"Wait. Blood magic?" Emeric interrupts, meeting my eyes, his hands stilling on the pages.

Caius paces back and forth, his fists clenched. "Valtorious," he hisses, the name slicing through the stillness. "It reeks of his kind of treachery."

I lean against the stone wall, my arms folded, my gaze dark with thought. The idea of King Valtorious meddling in our affairs isn't far-fetched. His hunger for power is a ravenous beast, always seeking to devour more than it's due.

Emeric, usually the voice of calm, lets out a frustrated sigh, his brow furrowed deeply. "If he's behind this, it's not just Morte at risk—it's the fragile balance we've fought so hard to maintain," he finishes, the white light in his eyes flashing with a rare intensity. He can usually tamp his blinding aura, but not right now.

Az shifts uncomfortably, his discomfort as evident as the tension in his shoulders. "We need to consider every possibility," he mutters, avoiding our gazes. His nerves, usually steel and fire, now resemble the surface of a disturbed pool, betraying ripples of something deeper.

I scrutinize him, the pieces of an unsolved puzzle gnawing at my mind. "Az, you've been unusually tense since we felt that presence. Anything you want to share?" The question is a barbed hook, aimed and ready to catch the secrets he might be hiding.

Caius stops pacing and turns to look at Az, his eyes narrowing. "Yes, out with it. We can't have secrets between us. Not when Morte's safety is at stake."

Az looks between us, the lines of his face etched with conflict. "I just ... hate the thought of him having any power over her. Or us." His voice is a low growl, barely contained fury simmering beneath the surface.

Emeric places a hand on Az's shoulder, a silent show of support. "We'll make sure she's safe," he says firmly. "Whatever it is, we can handle it. But we need to trust each other completely."

I nod, my gaze still fixed on Az. "Valtorious may be a serpent lurking in the grass, but we're not without our own fangs and venom. We'll strike back with everything we have if he dares cross into our dreamscape again."

I should've killed him when I had the chance. Fuck what the god's council says.

Az takes a deep breath, shadowy smoke pouring off him and filling the room. "He can't have her."

Emeric's expression softens, but the steel in his tone is unmistakable. "Then we need to focus on getting her back." He glances at me. "Have you heard anything back from High King Finian about Morte?"

I shake my head. "Not yet." An intrusive thought keeps whirring around inside me; one I don't want to acknowledge myself, let alone voice out loud to the others.

Morte's very soul recognizes her mates. We know that much,

otherwise she'd never allow herself to get so close to Az and Caius, even in a dream. It should be enough for her to yearn for us all. Enough for her heart to skip when she gets my note calling her home to where she belongs, even without her knowing the full picture. Enough for her to yes.

But what if she doesn't?

"We need to be proactive, not just reactive." Emeric says.

Caius, still not fully appeased, adds, "Let's kill Valtorious anyway. He's like an annoying fly, always popping up at the most inopportune times."

"We need to strengthen our wards, reinforce our defenses," I state, "and perhaps it's time to dig into some of the older, more ... potent forms of protection. If Morte wants to come back and Bedlam's king won't let her come, it'll be a war of the gods once I attack Luna's precious son."

High King Finian has a spine of steel, and I grudgingly admire him for it. But if he'd go to war for his soul bonded mate and deigns to keep me from mine? He's got to know I'd do worse if he kept me from her. Even if it means slaughtering his whole family.

CHAPTER TWENTY-TWO

WILDER

I come to with a gasp, the echo of my heartbeat loud in my ears. The guards' fists are a recent memory, their cruelty a fresh wound on my spirit. I'm alive. Alive and still here, in a place that's far from the fiery embrace of the Underworld I long for.

Grief is a blade that cuts deep. My head throbs with a persistent, dull ache, and a sticky warmth clings to my face—blood, no doubt, from injuries not yet tended to.

The room tilts as I force my eyes open, the stark whiteness of the hospital walls a cold comfort. The scent of iron from my own blood mixes with the sterile sting of antiseptic, unwelcome proof of where I am. I try to lift my head, only to be met with the sharp pull of restraints at my wrists—chains of cold steel and colder magic, glowing with the intent to keep me in place.

The realization hits me, a crushing wave of despair. Freedom is nothing but a cruel illusion in this place. I'm trapped, body and soul, in a world that refuses to let me slip away.

I just need to be with her.

The room is filled with an odd blend of modern medical equipment and arcane instruments, proof of the prison's reliance on both science and sorcery.

A soft humming sound fills the air, emanating from a device at my bedside. It's not just monitoring my physical state; it's scanning for magical injuries as well. In a place like this, where magic can heal but also harm, they need to be cautious. They can't heal what they haven't diagnosed, and some wounds, particularly those inflicted by magic, require precise and careful treatment.

I lie here, a prisoner not just to the bars and walls, but also to my own battered body, waiting for the healers to decipher the scans, to untangle the complex web of physical and magical trauma before they dare to weave their spells of healing. Until then, I'm left in limbo, suspended between pain and the hope of relief.

I'm supposed to be in the Underworld with Morte. Not still in this prison.

Why couldn't they just let me fucking die?

A roar escapes me as I try to pull from my manacles, slamming against the guardrails of the bed. The metal creaks under the force of my rage, but it holds. Suddenly, the door creaks open, and a figure steps inside. A short woman with sleek grey hair spilling down her back, her eyes gleaming with a mix of curiosity and concern. The wrinkles marring her face tell me she's a witch, rather than fae. She wears the uniform of the prison healers, a pristine white robe embroidered with intricate sigils and symbols of healing magic.

"Mr. Ripple," she says in a calm voice, her tone carrying an air of authority that demands attention. "You need to remain still. Your injuries are severe, both physical and magical. We need to assess the damage before we can proceed."

Her radiant hands, pulsing with energy, reach out towards me in a gesture of assistance. But as she draws near, I spring forward and lunge towards her, my voice erupting in a loud cry. In my blind panic, I failed to see the guard lurking behind her, who swiftly strikes me with magic until I'm rendered unconscious. Darkness engulfs me as I fall into a deep slumber, unaware of what will come next.

A REALM OF DREAMS AND SHADOWS

Despite the enormity of my crime, there was surprisingly little reprisal for taking the lives of several inmates. They said I'm stripped of any recreation privileges; everything goes back to normal within the prison walls not long after. The monotony of daily life gave me ample time to reflect on what comes next. My future, my choices, and the consequences of my actions.

I should feel bad for taking lives, but I don't. They were horrible people who deserved every bit of it. My only regret is not having the time to make it hurt. Their ends were too swift for their crimes.

As I gaze out at the barren yard and watch the other inmates continue their daily routines, I consider my own fate in this place. The silence is deafening, broken only by the occasional distant shout or clang of metal against metal as the gates open and close. It's in this eerie stillness that I confront my own thoughts and make sense of the chaos that surrounds me.

My new plan is simple: I shouldn't have been trying to get the guards to kill me. I need to take matters into my own hands and do it myself if I ever want to reunite with Morte in the Underworld.

It's the only way.

As the prison falls into the deep embrace of night, cloaked in shadow, I make my move. It's a meticulously chosen moment, synchronized with the guard's shift change, when their attention is momentarily diverted. I glide into the small pond of my cell, which though confined, feels like a fragment of the vast ocean, a distant echo of my merfae heritage. Underneath the surface, the water is clearer to my eyes than to any other being; it's a world where I can navigate with little effort. My merfae abilities afford me a unique perception, an echolocation that guides me through the dark, murky depths. I move with precision, the fluid grace of my kind, causing barely a ripple on the surface, proof of the years spent honing my skills in the water, even after two hundred years away from the source.

The cool water envelopes my hand as I sift through, feeling for the familiar shape of a small, sharp object that I've specifically chosen for tonight.

The pond's water whispers secrets, its gentle currents conspiring with me, hiding my movements from the unsuspecting world above. I retrieve the concealed item, its metallic surface cold and reassuring against my palm.

Once back in my bed, my thoughts a tumultuous sea, as I wait for the right moment to enact the plan that has been carefully crafted in the depths of despair and grief. The night stretches on, a canvas of darkness and possibility, as I brace myself for what's to come.

With a creak of metal, the new guard lifts the heavy flap on my cell door. His sharp eyes sweep over me, searching for any signs of movement or deception, as I force myself to inhale and exhale in slow, measured breaths. The air is thick with tension and the smell of stale sweat and despair. I keep my eyes squeezed shut, pretending to sleep, but my nerves buzz with fear and anticipation. Just a little longer, and I'll get to see her.

The guard's footsteps echo down the hallway, leaving me alone once again with only the dull hum of the magical lights in the hallway for company.

Gripping the sharp edge in my hand, I dig it into my skin above the cursed manacle that suppresses my powers and drag it. As the blade cuts through flesh and muscle, I gasp at the searing pain that shoots through my arm. Just a little more and I can be with her again.

Numbness quickly follows as I sever important nerves and arteries, but I push through it, needing this to work. Blood trickles down my hand and splatters onto the cold stone floor. It's a macabre scene, but it's just the beginning.

My fingers tremble as I now take the makeshift blade to my femoral artery, my heart pounding in my ears as I press it against the pulsing vein, feeling the resistance before it finally pierces through, sending a surge of agony through my entire body. The pain intensifies, but I steel myself against it, knowing that this sacrifice is necessary for my escape.

With a deep breath through gritted teeth, I push the blade forward, slicing through the delicate layers of skin and muscle. A rush of warm crimson spurts up, painting the ceiling in short bursts as I begin to feel faint. It's a terrifying sight, even to my own eyes, but I focus on the end goal. Reuniting with Morte in the realm beyond.

I cannot waver now. I refuse to spend another moment trapped within these desolate walls.

As the blood continues to spurt, my vision begins to blur, and darkness encroaches from the edges. Time seems distorted, reality slipping away like water through my fingers. And in that moment of surrender to oblivion, a glimmer of joy flickers within me. Finally.

Finally.

CHAPTER TWENTY-THREE

MORTE

Steam dances around me, a serpentine waltz of heat and mist, as I stand beneath the cascade of water in my shower, trying to wash off my growing fears of the future and the worries of the day. The support of Noct and Ronin took the edge off, but I still have Risç to face.

I'm lathering my body when white-hot agony blooms in my chest, slicing through the warmth with a scalpel's precision. I press my palms against the wooden walls of the shower, the grain of the timber grounding me, trying to anchor me against the sudden onslaught of pain. It's a storm within my soul, a gale that I can't see but feel tearing through me. I gasp, the sound lost in the rush of water as my legs buckle, betraying me.

Then as quickly as it arrived, the torment recedes. The relief is so abrupt, it leaves me hollow, gasping for air that suddenly feels too thin. I slump to the floor of the shower, the water a comforting embrace as I try to make sense of the torture that gripped me.

With shaking hands, I turn off the faucet, the silence deafening in the wake of my cry.

I curl into myself, the cool tile beneath me grounding, yet offering no comfort. The echo of the pain is a refrain that lingers in the steam, still throbbing faintly in my chest.

What the fuck was that?

CHAPTER TWENTY-FOUR

WILDER

Consciousness creeps back to me, not with the gentle touch of a lover, but with the harsh, rigid grip of reality. The first thing that registers in my senses is the clinical sterility of the infirmary, a room draped in blinding white, each corner echoing with the coldness of my continued imprisonment. The air here is thick, heavy with antiseptic and reprimands, a far cry from the freedom of the ash-filled realm I long for.

The guards stationed around me have eyes like eagle shifters. Sharp. Scrutinizing. I can feel the burden of their judgment pressing down on me, an invisible but real force that reminds me of what I am here: a prisoner, a would-be escapee, a failed soul.

Failure clings to me like a second skin, suffocating in its embrace. I attempted the unthinkable, a desperate bid to escape this reality, to find comfort in the Underworld where I hoped to reunite with Morte. But fate, it seems, is a cruel mistress. The realization that I'm still here, that my attempt to traverse the realms was all for naught, sends waves of despair crashing over me.

Lying in this bed, surrounded by the barren walls of the infirmary, I close my eyes, wishing for a reprieve, a momentary escape from my crushing reality. But even in the darkness behind my lids, there is no escape, no relief. There is only the acute awareness of my existence, of the life I'm forced to endure without her. The infirmary, with its promise of healing and life, has become my purgatory, a place where hope comes to wither and die.

My purgatory should've been in hell.

In the aftermath, I'm returned to my cell, but not the same one. This time, it's solitary confinement. A small, windowless box where the light of day never reaches. Here, in this new level of isolation, the truth of my situation settles in with a chilling clarity.

The days blend into each other, indistinguishable in their tedium and despair. My thoughts are a whirlpool, constantly circling back to Morte. The pain of our separation is a constant ache, a wound that refuses to heal, and I'm slowly losing my fucking mind.

I need her to know the truth.

CHAPTER TWENTY-FIVE

MORTE

The soft rustling of luciferin leaves filters through my office window, a soothing balm that belies the unrest within me. Amongst this tranquility, my mind is chaos, whirling with the impending arrival of my boss and the unnerving proposition from Finn. The office around me reflects the dichotomy of my life: functional yet personal, a space of both command and comfort.

The walls are adorned with intricate carvings, depicting scenes of Tolden history and fae folklore, so we never forget how far we've come, and how easily tyrants can topple it all. In one corner stands a tall, ornate bookshelf, its shelves laden with ancient texts and scrolls, each one a repository of knowledge and lore.

My desk, a large, solid piece of dark wood, sits in the center of the room, its surface cluttered with maps, reports, and various artifacts of my command. The chair behind it is high-backed and imposing, upholstered in deep blue fabric that matches the hues of the underground sanctuary outside.

The room is equipped with a variety of magical instruments and devices, each serving a specific purpose in the management and protection of our community. A large, interactive map of Castanea and the surrounding areas is mounted on one wall, glowing softly with magical energy. Next to it are models of castles and strongholds throughout the realm, as well as various collections of artifacts from other realms, such as VHS tapes and players from Earth.

As I take in my surroundings, I feel a sense of pride mixed with the heavy burden of leadership. This office is a reflection of who I am as a commander and as an individual—someone who must balance the needs of her people with her own inner struggles and desires.

I wasn't always a warrior. I prefer the quiet moments of solitude over the clash of battles, but I've always been a bit of a rebel. It's what got me into this entire mess in the first place.

The door opens, and General Risç steps in, his silvering hair cut close to his scalp and eyes that have seen decades of service. He stands with an unyielding military posture. "They said you'd found your way back to us, but I didn't believe it until I saw it with my own eyes." His voice is gruff with emotion, softening the lines etched by stern command.

"General." I stand from my seat behind the desk and approach him, steeling myself for the conversation. "It's good to see you again," I say, trying to keep my emotions in check. I give him a small smile, trying to ignore the discomfort of being addressed as if I'd been missing from my post, rather than being dead for two long years. It seems I've forgotten my formality, too.

He closes the door and strides forward, his boots echoing softly on the polished floor. "Your absence was ... heartbreaking. You're my best warrior."

I don't really know about that. I can put on a mask of indifference like any warrior, but at night, long after the battle is over, grief eats at me.

His voice carries a note of professional restraint, tinged with personal concern. "Rumors about where you've been are rampant."

I take a deep breath, the burden of the sealed letter from Finn heavy in my mind. "I was in the Underworld, General. I don't remember how or why, but I know that much. The last two years of my life are a blank slate, sir."

Risç's eyebrows knit together, his military demeanor momentarily wavering. "Aggonid's Realm," he muses, as if considering the gravity of this revelation. "This raises serious questions, Morte, about allegiances, about consequences."

"My allegiance has always been to Bedlam, to our people," I reply, the certainty in my voice belying the chaos of my thoughts. Wilder's face flashes in my mind, a reminder of my deepest loyalties.

He nods, though his expression remains guarded. "Your return is timely. We have much to address, and your leadership has been missed. However, we must also consider the impact of these ... revelations."

"I'm ready to face whatever comes," I assert, though a part of me trembles at the thought of confronting the shadows of a past I can't remember.

"Officer Nightblade tells me High King Finian sent him to deliver a message as well," Risç adds, watching me closely. "He mentioned something about a choice you have to make? I don't need details—"

The letter. Finn's words echo in my head, a choice that feels like no choice at all. Either answer I give will have fallout I'm not prepared to deal with. "Yes, there's a request for me to return to the Underworld. A request I'm still processing."

Risç's eyes narrow slightly. "That's a significant request. Your decision will have repercussions, Morte. We must tread carefully."

"I know," I reply, feeling the burden of a decision that will unravel the threads of my life. Taking a deep breath, I meet his eyes. "There's something I need to tell you."

Risç studies me for a moment longer before nodding. "Alright. Let's have a seat." He gestures towards the table on the other side of my office.

With tentative steps, we make our way to the seating area. My hands tremble and I struggle to still them, tucking them under my thighs as I try to steady myself. The atmosphere is heavy with tension, and I can feel my heart racing in my chest. "I wanted you to hear it from me first," I finally manage to say, my voice shaking slightly. "Later this week, I'm confessing to a crime I committed two hundred years ago, one that sent an innocent merfae to prison, *vita damnationem*."

He startles at the news, losing his careful composure. "What?"

"I took the lives of several teenagers," I say grimly, my heart heavy with guilt. "And my best friend took the fall, using powerful magic to bind my tongue so I couldn't speak the truth. But now, after all these years, the bind has broken, and I can no longer keep this secret." My confession hangs heavily in the air between us as we sit in silence, like the aftermath of a bomb, when all stills.

"This isn't funny, Commander."

"It's not a joke, sir."

He releases an anguished sigh, visibly shaken. "I don't believe you'd do something like—"

"Sir, with all due respect," I cut in. "The inmate whose cell I died in two years ago is my best friend. I refuse to tarnish his sacrifice by denying my sins now."

His expression hardens, the façade of a soldier returning. "Tell me it was an accident."

"I meant to kill them. What I didn't mean for was to kill children."

"You didn't know?" He studies me with a sharp, assessing gaze.

"They were glamored, sir."

"What now?" he asks, unable to mask the sorrow in his words.

"Now I right the wrongs of my past and let an innocent man go free. I've been working to regain my memories before confessing, but I don't think that's in the cards. I have no right to ask, but I'm going to do it anyway, because it means everything to me."

He leans back, running his fingers through his perfectly groomed hair. "If it's within my power, Morte, I'll do it."

"I need you to make sure he goes free when I confess to my crimes. He's already served two hundred years. That's more than enough for lying."

His face fills with sadness as he nods slowly. "I'll do what I can."

CHAPTER TWENTY-SIX

AGGONID

*I*n the hushed, shadowed streets of Romarie, I tread with a predator's grace. The city, a stronghold of metal and machinations, hums with the undercurrents of oppression and rebellion. Here, in King Valtorious's domain, every gesture is a play of power, every conversation a veiled dance. I wish there was a way to reach Bedlam without having to cross through this realm. It only serves as an obstacle between us. I do, however, take great pleasure in knowing Valtorious can feel my presence here—the oppressive, ominous aura that lingers in my wake now that I'm no longer tamping it down. I want him to know I'm coming. Biding my time, letting him stew in fear while I put several moving pieces into place. There is a shadow that looms over him and his kingdom. And beneath it lies the promise that you do not threaten the devil, because he is always lying in wait to strike when you least expect it.

If he's going to fuck with my soul bonded mate, haunting her dreams, I will become his nightmare. And once he's dead, I will take great delight in spending the rest of eternity torturing him.

After I put his head on a spike, I'll carry it around with me while I dance through the halls of his castle, so he'll be forced to watch as I desecrate his beloved throne.

A smirk adorns my face as I stalk through the city. The night air, sharp with the tang of iron and distant forges, carries the muted sounds of a city both vibrant and oppressed. It's mostly lawless here, which is why we see far more fae and other supernatural orders in the Underworld from Romarie than any other realm combined.

The sky, a sprawling blanket of stars and galaxies of light, is obscured by the city's metallic rooftops. It's all sharp edges and spires with the occasional building jutting above the rest. The lamps here burn with a bluish light.

Ancient cobblestone streets are worn smooth and rounded from centuries of use. The buildings, great structures of steel and iron, have seen better days. Some are so rusted, they look like they're made of red clay, their once brilliant dyes faded to earthy tones of terracotta and brown.

The city of iron and stone is thick with the scents of life and death. Lurking subtly beneath these dominant aromas, if one pays close enough attention, are the elusive scents of the ocean. A hint of fish, brine and an almost forgotten taste of freedom for those who call the sea their home.

My destination is a nondescript tavern, 'The Gilded Anvil,' hidden in a quieter part of Romarie's capital, Ironhaven. Its sign creaks gently in the breeze, a whisper among the clang of the city. Inside, the atmosphere is dense with the aroma of ale and the low, careful cadence of conversations. The patrons, a blend of wary locals and travelers, stick to their huddled groups, a sign of the times under Valtorious's rule.

Choosing a secluded, but sticky, table at the back, I survey the room. The patrons' guarded exchanges and furtive glances speak volumes of life under a tyrant's thumb.

A brown sign hangs on the ground floor of the tavern, barely visible behind the iron grate. The windows are stained with brown from decades of smoke. Inside, the windows are boarded up, leaving the tavern almost completely in the dark. The light comes from several lamps hung from the ceiling. The smoke is pungent, a mix of hardy pipe tobacco and a sweet scent of dried berries.

The door creaks open, admitting a cloaked figure who scans the room with a practiced eye. They're disguised, wearing hooded, grey-washed leathers and soft boots, and a well-worn satchel is slung over their shoulder. It obscures the crest of the moon on their breast. The delegate from Bedlam. They make their way to me, their movements a careful choreography of caution.

"Well met," they greet, their voice a balance of respect, wariness, and a tinge of fear. Exactly as it should be.

My lips curve into a grin, relishing the subtle undercurrents of power at play. A sealed envelope, emblazoned with High King Finian's distinct seal, slides across the table towards me.

Taking the letter, I sense its profound significance. "You've traveled far for this," I observe, my gaze lingering on the parchment.

"The High King stressed utmost secrecy," the delegate responds, their eyes flickering with unease across the room. "An immediate reply isn't necessary."

I acknowledge this with a nod, fully aware of the sensitive nature of this clandestine meeting. Finn's decision to engage in covert talks with the likes of me, the fae devil, is fraught with political risk.

I tuck the letter within my cloak, unbroken. It's a message that requires privacy, away from the prying eyes that haunt places like these.

"Tell the High King I thank him for his efforts," I respond smoothly, watching as the delegate relaxes ever so slightly.

The delegate nods, eyes darting back to the door. They rise from their stool, casting one last glance at me before slipping out into the night.

I remain seated for a moment longer, contemplating. Ironhaven, with its heart of steel and secrets, mirrors the turbulence of my own thoughts. In this city, allies and enemies blur, each choice a step through a minefield of consequences.

Rising, I leave the tavern's deceptive calm for the city's shadowed streets. The letter from Finn is a spark in the powder keg of politics and power. As I step into the night, Romarie unfolds around me, a realm caught between the iron will of its king and the hidden desires of its people.

Alone, I walk through the city, aware of the eyes that follow and the whispers that linger in my wake. The sounds of the streets carry a clamor of voices and marketplaces, but underneath it all, sits a current of fear and uncertainty, like a slow trickle of blood through the cobblestones. This is a game of power and influence, and I'm but one player among many. Yet, my motivations are not driven by the thirst for power.

Not anymore.

Morte, my fated mate, the phoenix whose fire ignites my soul, is our true endgame. For her, we will challenge fate, defy kings, and spurn gods. My path is one of shadows and fire, a journey that entwines destiny and desire.

And as I vanish into the night, Ironhaven's whispers echo behind me, a city that knows too well the dance of power and the cost of defiance. The game continues, and in it, I play for the highest stakes of all.

Approaching the portal, I feel the familiar pull of power, a resonating hum that syncs with the beat of my heart. The shadows swirl, reaching out like tendrils of night, welcoming me back to the Underworld.

I step through the threshold, the sensation of crossing realms a familiar caress. The air is warm and clammy, the churning of the vortex's energies seeping through my pores. The transition is seamless, the portal's magic enveloping me before depositing me into the heart of my domain.

As I approach my castle, the torches flare to life, and sensing my presence, their flames a silent salute to their lord. The massive doors open at my approach, the hinges whispering secrets only they know.

Inside, the corridors are silent, save for the soft whisper of my cloak trailing behind me. My chambers, a sanctuary of both solace and solitude, await at the end of a long passage. The anticipation of the letter's contents gnaws at me, a hunger that overshadows my usual composure.

Finally, within the quiet of my bedroom, I allow myself a moment of vulnerability. The room, a reflection of my essence, is adorned with artifacts of power and history. The walls are swathe with relics of conquest and war, the spoils of feuds won and battles lost. A tapestry, salvaged from a burning village, the scene of a fierce battle, sits next to a wooden box that holds the head of an elven prince, the only remnant of a conquest I had a hand in. Few elves are left in any of the realms now. There wouldn't have been any, had I not stopped the tyrant personally.

I sit at my desk, a massive structure of dark wood and worn carvings. The letter from Finn lies before me, its seal unbroken, a harbinger of news I've both longed for and dreaded.

She doesn't remember us. Why would she say yes? The torturous words are trying to prevent me from getting ahead of myself. From being let down and bereft. But love always brings hope, and hope can be a cruel thing that refuses to leave. Hope whispers reminders to me that her soul remembers; that this had been made abundantly clear in the dreamscape. It should have been enough.

With a deliberate motion, I break the seal, and the wax gives way beneath my fingers. After unfolding the parchment, my eyes devour two simple words, each letter a strike to my heart.

"Morte declines."

The words echo in my mind, a mantra of denial and despair. *Morte declines.* Declines to return to me, to us. Declines the bond we forged; the promises whispered in the dark.

A torrent of emotions crashes over me—a maelstrom of rage, betrayal, and a piercing sense of loss. The parchment crumples in my fist, the fibers protesting against the strength of my grip. My other hand slams against the desk, and the wood groans under the force, a physical manifestation of the chaos inside me.

The flames in the hearth flare, mirroring my rage, their dance a chaotic whirlwind of fire and fury. My breath comes in ragged gasps, the air thick with the tension of my wrath. Of my agony.

A REALM OF DREAMS AND SHADOWS

"Morte," I whisper into the night, the word a shard of ice in my chest. The fury of rejection—however misplaced given she doesn't yet remember us—still simmers, a storm brewing beneath the surface, but it's tempered now by a piercing ache, a void where hope once resided.

My memory drifts, unbidden, to a morning bathed in the golden hue of the sun's first light, seeping through the sheer curtains of our bedchamber. It's a rarity, this gentle waking, and I savor the moment.

There's Morte, her steady breaths a quiet serenade in the otherwise still room. She's a vision of tranquility, her crimson hair fanned out across the pillow.

My hand rests on her waist, feeling the rise and fall of her slumbering form, and I'm struck by a sudden, fierce protectiveness. I wish so desperately things could be different between us. Caius, sprawled on her other side, is still lost to sleep, the faintest hint of his grin lingering on his full, bowed lips. His translucent blue skin, luminous even in the muted light, is marked with the dance of runes that speak of ancient power.

In this moment, with Morte nestled between us, I feel a completeness I've seldom allowed myself to acknowledge. I listen to the little snores that escape her, a soft, unguarded whisper of sound that tells me she's deep in the realm of dreams.

Caius stirs, his tail twitching as he dreams, the motion almost hypnotic. I watch as he throws his head back slightly, a silent laugh shaping his features, even in sleep. He never put his wings away last night, having imbibed too much in the absinthe, and they're tucked neatly at his side, the iridescent black feathers catching the light in a display of subtle opulence.

I let out a quiet breath, feeling a surge of contentment so profound it borders on painful. Morte's presence, her very essence, fills the space around us. But then, as if summoned by the very thought, a shadow passes over my heart, a premonition of a truth I've yet to confront. It's a fleeting sensation, one that leaves a trail of ice in its wake. I push it away, unwilling to let it taint this perfect moment. So I can pretend for a little longer.

The here and now is what matters. The feel of Morte's pale skin beneath my fingertips. The sight of Caius in peaceful repose. The knowledge that in this room, under these sheets, we are more than individuals—that the three of us are meant to walk through eternity together.

The quiet of the night is shattered by the primal roar that erupts from my core, a sound that reverberates through the halls of my castle. I tear back to my office, on a warpath. My hands, instruments of both creation and destruction, move with a mind of their own, sweeping across the desk in a furious arc, sending scrolls, inkwells and quills flying.

The ancient tomes, once treasured for their knowledge and power, become casualties of my wrath. They thud against the bone-strewn walls, their pages fluttering helplessly like wounded birds. The very air seems to quiver in response to my rage, the shadows twisting and writhing in a dance of shared fury.

I turn towards the hearth, staring into its flames. With a sweep of my hand, I hurl the burning logs across the room, their embers igniting the tapestries, setting the walls ablaze. The fire spreads rapidly, a living entity that consumes everything in its path, a mirror to the destruction I feel within.

I stride to the window, my emotions a wildfire that refuses containment. With a forceful gesture, I thrust the panes wide, unleashing the tempest within me. Summoning the inferno of my bloodline, I command the flames to obey, to become one with the storm that rages in the night sky.

The rain responds, not with soothing drops, but with a cascade of fire, each ember a piece of my wrath made manifest. They descend like a furious pyre from the sky, a rare meteorological alchemy only my kind can provoke. The fiery rain paints the night with streaks of gold and crimson, a spectacular display of power that mirrors the chaos of my heart.

My legs buckle under me as I slide against the wall, burying my head in my hands.

The room, once a haven of solitude and reflection, now bears the scars of my pain. The remnants of the letter, the cause of this cataclysm, lie in tatters at my feet, a witness to the fragility of hope and the potency of despair.

The door to the bedroom bursts open, and Caius barrels in, his face a mask of shock and anguish that mirrors my own. He doesn't know the cause, but he can feel it through our bond—the heartbreak. Utter devastation. The destruction around us is a mere echo of the chaos in our hearts. He staggers at the sight, the carnage tangible in his every movement.

"Caius," I growl, my voice a mix of pain and fury, "she's gone. She's rejected us."

The words hit him like a physical blow. He stumbles, the invincible façade crumbling as the reality sinks in. A guttural sound, half-growl, half-sob, escapes his lips. He's a predator, a creature of allure and danger, yet now he stands before me, laid bare by the raw force of our shared loss.

Caius looks around the burning room, his eyes reflecting the flames that dance around us, his expression contorting with grief as his chest heaves. "No," he whispers, a denial that's as much a plea as it is a refusal to accept this cruel twist of fate. "She wouldn't. She's met us now. And even in her dreams she loved us. I know she did. If she knows we're part of her past, why wouldn't she want to return to us?"

He moves closer, his steps unsteady, as if the gravity of our situation has sucked the life out of him. His eyes, usually so full of mischievous fire, now burn with a different flame. A flame born of heartbreak and despair.

His pain is my pain, a mirror to the agony that rips through my own soul. In this moment, we are not the rulers of the Underworld, not the feared and powerful beings that command legions. We are simply two beings, united in our anguish, bound by a love that seems to have slipped through our fingers.

I stand up, my wings flaring out, a fiery display of my devastation. "We'll get Morte back. No matter what it takes."

Silence envelopes us.

"She needs to know I'm her soul bonded mate," I continue. "During the next dreamscape, I need to be in it. I'll channel the fury of an electrical storm to power it. It'll hold."

CHAPTER TWENTY-SEVEN

AGGONID

*C*aius and I barrel through the labyrinthine corridors of our dark castle, our footfalls echoing with urgency. The very air of the Underworld seems to recoil at our shared fury, the oppressive atmosphere thick with anticipation and dread.

"We find Az and Emeric. Now," I command, my words slicing through the heavy silence like a blade.

The shadows that fall across Caius's face make it seem like a mask, as if he's no more than the hollow husk of the fae who's always been ready with a joke or quick to smile. The sharp downward angle of his eyebrows and the tightness around his eyes magnifies the effect. The dangerous glint there is a reflection of our shared desperation.

The castle, usually a place of dark intrigue and whispered secrets, now feels like a prison, its walls echoing our grief. The flicker of candlelight barely meets the gloom, but the shadows that lurk beneath the flickering light are darker still.

The occasional servant scurries by with a hurried gait, as if in a race with some unseen clock. Fear is etched into their faces as water into stone. They sense the storm brewing, one that could shake the very foundations of our domain.

The taste of sorrow, thick and heavy, coats my tongue. I can feel it, the deep sense of loss that has settled within me. Morte, my mate, is lost to us. The thought is like a wound, a fresh cut that refuses to heal. I've never felt so helpless, so powerless, in all my long years. But there's no time to wallow when there's still much to do. I won't give up hope unless I hear it from her lips.

I find Az and Emeric in our usual meeting point, a secluded chamber veiled in shadows and warded with charms. A lantern hangs from the center of the room on a string of wire, its dim light illuminating the worn stone walls, pocked with holes where thick, embroidered tapestries cover openings to secret passageways. Through these hidden tunnels go supplies, spies, assassins, mercenaries, and everything else necessary to keep the Underworld from its enemies.

My gaze shifts to Az, who rises slowly to greet me. His brows are drawn together in concern as he takes in our disheveled state. Emeric, ever the perceptive one, asks, "What is it?"

"Morte has refused us," I announce. The bitter words taste like ash in my mouth.

Az's face crumples, the lines of his features etching deeper with the news. Emeric lets out a low curse, his fists clenching at his sides.

"We need to talk to her, help her to understand what we all mean to each other," Caius says, clenching his fists as a simmering cauldron of emotion brews within him. "We need to use every shred of power we have."

The silence that follows is deafening, only the sound of our labored breathing filling the void. Az hands the parchment back to Caius, and the agony of it feels realer than before. "What do we do now?" Emeric's voice is heavy with defeat.

"We pool our resources, our magic, our very essences if need be. We breach the divide between realms."

Emeric locks eyes with each of us, a silent signal that it's time. "We've tiptoed around the edges of the dreamscape, barely scratching the surface of what's possible. It's time to dive deeper, build a connection that can withstand any outside interference, especially from those like King V."

"We're ready," I state, feeling the collective strength of our group thrum with a newfound drive. "We'll weave a connection so strong it'll allow Morte to withstand the presence of all of us, to weather the storms King Valtorious might throw our way."

"Tonight, then," Emeric says, "when the realms draw close, and our powers peak, we'll reach out to her together."

"We don't just break through," Caius interjects, his voice seething with a venomous edge. "We shatter whatever barriers stand between us and Morte. Aggie and Az will channel the storm."

The room pulses with our collective energy, a maelstrom of power and emotion that threatens to tear the very air asunder.

Az steps forward, his eyes alight with an otherworldly glow. "Then let's begin. We have the might of the Underworld at our disposal."

Preparation permeates the air as demons drag more sanguimetal into the room. We're using it as a lightning conductor and attaching it to the conduit at the center of the table. The highest room in the castle, chosen for its proximity to the volatile skies, now serves as our crucible for channeling the tempest's might.

Az stands in the center of the cavernous hall, his gaze sweeping across the gathered artifacts and materials with the precision of a master at his craft. His hands, glowing faintly with the subtle sheen of metallurgy magic, move with deft assurance as he manipulates the ether to weld the intricate components into a cohesive whole. "We've got to ground this, or this much raw power is going to blow the whole castle."

"Copper," Emeric mutters, tracing a finger along an illustration of a lightning rod in a book the reapers brought us from Earth. "We need a conduit, something to channel the onslaught without succumbing to it."

Caius coughs, amusement lighting up his features. "I have copper."

"Then go get it." Az's impatient gesture sends sparks of arcane energy crackling through the air. "We need it."

"You'll need to smelt it first," Caius retorts, the amusement in his voice betraying the unconventional nature of his hoard.

Sighing, I shake my head, half in disbelief, half in anticipation. "You're not talking about..." I trail off.

Caius' wide, mischievous grin spreads across his face, radiating absolute glee. His eyes sparkle with excitement and his whole body seems to vibrate with energy as he speaks. "I am," he breathes, reveling in the audacity of his own implication.

"Whatever it is, just got get it," Az growls. "We don't have time to fuck around."

I press my lips together, a smirk threatening to break through my composure at the absurdity that's about to unfold.

A short while later, the sound of measured footsteps precedes Caius's return. A cadre of the castle's more infernal denizens enter, their muscled forms straining against the weight of a grand and lavishly decorated chest. The heavyset piece lands with a solid thud that echoes through the chamber.

"Great, I'll get to work on these now," he crouches, lifting the lid on the trunk before slamming it shut again. "What the fuck?"

Pure glee radiates from Caius, and if we weren't pressed for time, I'd revel in it a little longer. Instead, I narrow my eyes, gesturing outside. "Just how long do you think she'll stay asleep?"

"Desperate times call for ... inventive measures." Caius chuckles, a mischievous sparkle in his iced eyes. His grin is wide and unapologetic.

"What is it?" Emeric crosses to the chest with wary steps.

Az lets out a resigned sigh, lifting the lid again and gesturing to it. "Copper butt plugs. By the looks of it, hundreds of them."

"Why do you need so many?" Emeric whirls around to gape at Caius and me, his fangs glinting in the light.

"Ask him." I incline my head towards my mate. "Go on."

"I'll bite." Emeric grins. "Caius. Why do you have so many?"

Caius, with a gleam of wild amusement in his eye, sweeps a hand dramatically over the chest. "For every victory in the shadows, a celebratory indulgence," he declares. "Collecting them became a hobby of sorts, a collection for the chronicles of decadence and well, other vigorous ... exercises."

Az runs a hand through his long black hair in exasperation. "You bought one after each soul you collected?"

Caius throws his head back in a deep laugh. "No, of course not. With each competitor killed in the Wild Pursuit one year, I had these made by the metallurgist who makes the manacles. I didn't *buy* them."

"But why?" Emeric's brows furrow.

"Why not?" Caius shrugs. "Butt plugs are—"

"—enough, enough," Az growls. "Are they clean?"

I scoff, "Of course they are."

"Fine," Az lets out a resigned sigh, reaching for the copper items. "Let's just get this over with so we can see Morte." He waves his hand over the chest, the metals inside beginning to glow with heat as he readies himself to reshape their fate.

A short time later, he's turned the plugs into a giant spool of thin copper wire. Az kneels beside the intricate framework of the conduit, his hands moving with practiced ease as he affixes a thick, braided copper wire to its base. With the other end of the wire securely anchored into the earth beneath the tower, he ensures that the raw, volatile power we're about to summon will have a direct path to the ground. The copper glints against the stone. He steps back, his gaze following the line of the wire as it disappears into the soil, a grounding tether ready to bear the brunt of the tempest's fury we intend to harness.

"It's ready."

We gather in a circle, the air crackling with arcane energy as we join hands. It arcs through the room toward us, a jagged bolt of lightning that twists and turns in a writhing storm of raw power. We hold on like we're being pulled out to sea on a riptide. Our collective power is a living entity, a force of nature that bends to our will.

The room around us is alive with shimmering light, waves of prismatic colors wash across our faces, our surroundings, and our souls. The air is thick with the smell of ozone and burning skin. The metallic scent of fear hangs heavy over the room, tainting every breath until I can barely breathe.

A hum builds, low and pulsing, like the beating of some great, cosmic heart. Growing louder and louder, it almost becomes a physical thing. We're on the cusp of something monumental, a brink we're about to cross, and I can sense its immense impact bearing down on me. The world beyond the veil is calling out to us, beckoning us to join in its chaos.

My eyes snap shut as Morte's face appears, burning brightly in my mind like a flame. I reach out with my senses and feel the energy of Caius, Az, and Emeric wrap around me like an iron vice. Our energies surge together and become one, a maelstrom of power and desperation that threatens to consume me.

In the heart of the Underworld, the room transforms as we focus our collective power on conjuring a dreamscape to reach Morte. Our knowledge of Castanea is limited, pieced together from stories and whispers, but we pour every detail into our creation. We need to ensure the dream is familiar to her, to meet her on her turf.

The air shimmers, and the dramatic stone walls of the room dissolve, giving way to a lush, vibrant forest. Tall, majestic trees with bark shimmering like polished obsidian rise around us, their canopies a medley of vibrant hues. Soft, radiant moss carpets the ground, and delicate flowers bloom in abundance, their petals glowing gently in a spectrum of soft pastels.

Glowing streams meander through the dreamscape, their waters clear and sparkling, weaving through the forest like ribbons of liquid light. The streams converge into a tranquil pool at the center, mirroring the luminous sky above, a faux replica of Castanea's famed underground sanctuary.

In this dreamscape, the air pulses with the soft hum of magical energy, mimicking the vibrant life force of Castanea. Ethereal creatures, born of our imagination, flit between the trees. Their forms are blurred and indistinct, yet they emanate a sense of peace and familiarity.

We construct a clearing, encircled by the towering trees, where gentle, warm light filters through the leaves, splashing dancing patterns on the forest floor. At the clearing's center, a circle of stones forms a sacred space, reminiscent of a place for heartfelt gatherings or solemn rituals.

In this constructed sanctuary, we hope to offer Morte a sense of comfort, a reflection of her home, and a bridge across the realms that separate us.

In the quiet beauty of this otherworldly forest, we wait.

CHAPTER TWENTY-EIGHT

MORTE

The cool night whispers its secrets as I slip under my sheets, anxiety churning inside me, and the world beyond my eyelids fades swiftly. I'm anxious to get Wilder out, and frustrated over my lack of memories. Slumber claims me fast, and the next thing I know, I'm standing in a clearing. No transition, no sense of movement–just an abrupt, silent arrival. The sudden change doesn't startle me; it feels like another layer of the dream, natural as the dusk that settles around me.

The trees loom, ancient and towering, their leaves a silent rustle against the night. Faux moonlight filters through their branches, painting the moss-covered ground silver. It's peaceful here, as though I'm looking at Castanea based on a memory.

A figure emerges from the shadows, his presence commanding yet not imposing, familiar in a way that tugs at the edges of my consciousness. It's him, the fae from my earlier dreams with Az and Caius and the other male. I don't know this male's name, but his essence feels etched into the corners of my mind.

He's stunning. Where the others are built, he has a leaner build, but is still tall, and exudes so much power, it rushes to greet me, the tendrils wrapping around me. The gleam of his skin is burnished pewter, as though dipped in a star. His eyes, a deep crimson, almost match my hair. There's no fear, no flight, just a profound curiosity that anchors me to the spot.

"What's your name?" I ask as he approaches with confident steps.

"What's my name, or what do you call me?" He smirks, stopping before me.

"I guess what do I call you?"

His voice is low and full of emotion as he speaks, a deep sigh escaping his lips. "You call me Aggie," he says, the words heavy with meaning. "At first, I hated it. But now, I would give anything to hear you say it again."

My heart swells with a bittersweet ache at his words. "I can call you Aggie," I whisper gently, my fingers tracing the outline of his face. "You're one of my mates, aren't you? Is that why I don't feel afraid?"

He smiles sadly at me, leaning into my palm. "I'm your soul bonded mate."

But his words don't fill me with fear, instead they bring a sense of deep relief and comfort. It's as if the fates have deemed me worthy enough to be loved, flaws and all. His words wrap around me like a warm blanket, soothing the fluttering anxieties in my chest. And when I meet his gaze, I see an ocean of sincerity that washes over me, increasing my conviction that this man is meant for me. That and the aching in my soul. The bond between us feels tangible, pulsing with each beat of my heart.

A thought prickles at the back of my mind and I freeze. "If I call you Aggie, that means your name is ..." I trail off, a sense of hesitation creeping up in my gut. It's not because of who he is, but because of what it means.

"In the old tongue, it meant agony," he replies calmly. "Chaos and agony meet in death. Fitting isn't it?"

"And in the new?" I whisper, my voice almost lost in the gentle rustle of leaves around us.

"Aggonid," he says with a deep breath.

I inhale sharply, my heart pounding in my chest. "You're the one who's stalking me."

"What?" he takes a step towards me, but I don't back up, not even when he places a warm hand on my cheek. "I won't pretend to be a good being, Morte, I've done terrible things. But I love you, and I would stalk you to the ends of the realms and back, but only so I could keep you, not to hurt you. If someone is stalking you, I'll carve my name in their chest before I rip out their heart, feasting on it before their brain has begun to make the connection that you're mine."

My voice trembles as I break the tense silence. "So it isn't you who invades my dreams every night?"

He responds with a deep, guttural growl of frustration. "No, but I know who might be behind it."

My heart races as I eagerly wait for his answer. "Who?"

"None other than King Valtorious of Romarie."

My mind reels at this revelation. A powerful and ruthless king has been haunting my dreams? "But why would he target me?"

"Because you're mine." His arm slides around my waist, pulling me flush to him. His warmth seeps into me, and I want to bury myself in it. "He wants what he can't have."

His possessiveness should scare me. But it only feels right. So that's what makes what I have to do so difficult. The easy thing would be to ask for my memories back. To know and love these men as fiercely as they love me.

But there's an achingly beautiful male with ocean eyes who gave up his life for me, and it's my duty to give it back.

"I'm sorry I can't remember you," I whisper.

"But you can, I have your memories. If you're ready for them, you can have them."

I shake my head, taking a step back. "I can't," I choke out, my heart shredding at the absolute agony marring Aggie's face.

The declaration "I can't" is a blade severing the ethereal ties that bind me to this place of dreams and whispers. Aggie's face, a portrait of torment, blurs before my eyes as I harness every shred of will to tear away from the dream's seductive grasp.

I can almost hear the fabric of the dream tearing, a resounding snap that echoes through the chambers of my soul. I'm yanking myself back to consciousness with a force that feels like it could rend me in two. The dream shatters, an image broken on the floor of my mind, its pieces sharp with longing and regret.

Abruptly, the world of soft whispers and gentle touches is replaced by the harsh reality of my treehouse. I jolt upright, breathless, a sob trapped in my throat. My hands clutch at nothing, seeking the solidity I need to anchor me to this world, to my duty.

In the silence that follows, the absence of Aggie's presence is a chasm in the room, a hole in the world that can't be filled. My heart hammers, each beat a reminder of the life I must save, the sacrifice I must honor even as it breaks. The phantom touch of the dreamscape lingers on my skin, cruel proof of what I've just forsaken.

But the echo of my duty is louder, a clarion call that steels my resolve. I push the covers aside, the soft fabric now a mockery of the warmth I've lost. There's a weight in my chest, a heavy stone of tears and farewells only spoken in the soul.

The urgency of Wilder's plight pulls me to my feet, a marionette of responsibility. I can't afford the luxury of dreams, not when reality demands the harsh currency of action. I move, each step a deliberate march away from my mates, away from what could have been, toward what must be done.

Even as my heart shatters.

CHAPTER TWENTY-NINE

MORTE

Our bonfire next to the Castanean waterfall crackles vigorously, casting a lively dance of flames that illuminate the faces of my squadron. The night is alive with an undercurrent of tension, the kind that only comes from soldiers who've stared death in the face and laughed.

Or at least tried to.

Around the fire, the members of my squadron sit, lively and half-drunk. I lean back on my hands, watching them. Noct and Ronin are engaged in their own world, a quiet conversation, their heads close together. Noct's dimples flash in the firelight as Ronin whispers something, making her laugh—a sight that always brings a smile to my face.

Vero is recounting one of our narrow escapes, her hands animatedly mimicking our flight patterns. "And then Morte, here, swoops in like a comet, wings ablaze, and snatches that man right from the vermini's lair!"

Laughter bubbles around the circle, but my smile is half-hearted. These stories, they're our legacy, but tonight they feel like echoes from a life I can't return to.

The fire is the only light in the clearing and the flames dance like a violinist's fingers on the strings. It's roaring, but it's barely audible over the water crashing on the rocks beside us.

I take another swig from my bottle, and the liquid warmth does little to ease the chill in my bones. Wilder's face flashes in my mind, and the laughter around me dims. I can still remember the exact moment I last saw him. The sound of his scream echoes in my ears, and the image of his bloodied form haunts my dreams. I can still hear the sound of his bones snapping as his body was twisted and torn apart by the hydra fae. I close my eyes, trying to push the memory away, but it lingers.

Freya nudges me gently. "You okay, Morte? You've been quiet tonight."

I nod, forcing a smile. "Just the usual pre-mission jitters. You know how it is." They know tomorrow we're meeting for a very important mission, they just don't know what it's about.

She studies me for a moment, concern flickering in her eyes, but she doesn't press further. Instead, she turns back to the group, her laughter a bright sound in the night.

As the fire dwindles, the shadows stretch longer, and the conversations turn softer, more introspective. The reality of our existence, the fears and hopes, they all find their place in the quiet of the evening.

I stand, the fire's last warmth fading into the cool night. The sanctuary of Castanea, once a haven, now feels like a cage, holding me back from the answers I seek, from the resolution I crave. As soon as I've told them all, I'll start the next phase of my strategy to free Wilder.

As I make my way back, the dark and upcoming conversations settle on my shoulders, a familiar companion in the dance of fire and fate.

THE ATMOSPHERE in the briefing room is charged with tension as I stand before my squadron. These phoenix fae, my sisters-in-arms, are the only ones who understand the duality of our existence: the fiery rebirth that follows death, the relentless cycle we endure. They're a fierce, formidable group, each embodying the strength and resilience of our kind.

Not a hangover in sight despite our late night.

"I want to start off my saying it has been an absolute honor to fight by your sides." My voice carries across the room, and I watch as the unease ripples through my squadron. They glance at each other before they land on Noct, whose glassy eyes give away the fact that I don't come bearing good news. Her hand is cupped over her mouth as though she can physically stop a sob from tearing from her throat. "They said we were too soft, too inexperienced to fight. That our jobs should start when the battles are over, so we can record the toll of the dead. But we proved them wrong, didn't we? That though we are female, and smaller of the fae orders, we can still get the job done and still keep our hearts. Literally and figuratively." I chuckle, and their nervous laughter joins me.

"Noct is taking over as commander, and she'll be responsible for selecting a second."

Fear is a concept we understand but do not bow to, which is why none show it, only confusion. Hushed murmurs take over the room, before Freya speaks up. "Where are you going?"

"Do you all remember when they committed me two hundred years ago?" The grief I'd felt, watching my best friend take the fall for me and being sentence *vita damnationem* was too much for my fragile mind to bear. For fifteen years, they had to keep me in a cryochamber.

"Are they doing it again?" Soft-spoken Harmony asks.

I shake my head. "Two thousand years ago I fell in love with a merfae from the surface."

Shocked gasps ripple through the room.

"I'd sneak out to see him, and occasionally sneak him into Castanea. Wilder is my best friend, a man who I love with my whole soul. Two hundred years ago I was caught on the surface by a group of fae who would've discovered Castanea if I didn't fight back with all I had in me. I killed them, not realizing they were teenagers, glamored as adults."

There isn't a dry eye in the room, and the grief is so thick I could choke on it.

"Wilder found me on the beach and bound my tongue so I could never speak of it, and I had to watch as he took the fall for my crime." Tears track down my cheeks in twin streams as I lay the worst day of my life out for them all to hear. "The day he was sentenced *vita damnationem* was the day I was committed. And when I died at the prison, so did he, severing the bind on my tongue. Tomorrow, I'm confessing to the murders he was imprisoned for."

The room is suspended in a thick silence, each breath held as if in a vacuum. The truth of my words settles upon us, oppressive as the deep earth that encases our secret refuge. Noct's eyes are the first to overflow, tears spilling in silent witness to a loyalty so fierce it defies the very flames that forged us.

"There must be another way." Her voice is a fractured whisper, a plea against a fate she knows I've already embraced. "We need you."

Around the room, I see it—the cascade of realization, the dawning horror, the understanding that I'm walking willingly into the maw of the very beast fae spend their lives avoiding. Their expressions are mirrors of the same dread, the same grief that has gnawed at my insides for centuries.

Sabine's fingers tighten around her mug, her knuckles turning white, as her warrior's poise begins to fracture under the strain of the unexpected. Freya, always the calm in our storm, has a furrow pressed deep between her brows, her lips parting to voice the confusion they all feel, but no words come.

And then the anger comes, swift and hot as our namesake's flame. "You can't just give up," Bow snaps, her fierce spirit igniting the space between us. "You fight, Morte. You always fight."

Their faces blur as my vision swims with tears. "Fighting now means something different," I manage to say, my voice thick with the pain of my choice. "I'm doing this to save him. He gave up his life for me. I had so many good years, basking in your love. It's time."

My words are but ripples in a churning sea of emotion, unable to quell the whirlwind my confession has wrought. They stand, a battalion of sisters, their unity as solid as it is shaken, their shock giving way to a burgeoning, desperate understanding. This is the cost of our immortality, the price of our rebirth—the sacrifice that is sometimes demanded by honor, by love.

Their faces, etched in my memory, will be the torches that light my way through the darkness of the path I must walk alone.

CHAPTER THIRTY

MORTE

The evening in my treehouse passes in quiet reflection, a juxtaposition to the grief-marred gathering with my squadron. With the impending confession looming, I find comfort in the familiar rituals of my night routine, each action a step toward tranquility.

I wander the softly lit paths within the place I call home, the gentle glow of plants guides my way. Each step ascends me away from the word's clamor as I climb the spiral staircase to my abode nestled high in the ancient trees.

My living space blends earthly charm with magical essence. Shelves lined with ancient texts and mystical relics tell silent tales of old. I brush my fingers over the books, each a keeper of secrets and spells. With a wave of my hand, a sweet-smelling incense seeps from a small bowl, filling the room with a spicy aroma.

I turn my attention to a small altar near the window. Here rests the candle, my protective gift from Ronin, its flame guarding against intrusions with evil intent into my dreams. I whisper reinforcing incantations, watching the flame dance brightly in response.

This ritual, grounding and familiar, reminds me of the interplay between nature, magic, and life's delicate balance.

There's always a price to pay.

I pause, gazing out at the lush canopy of our sanctuary, the night embracing the treehouse in a comforting hold.

I shed my attire, each piece a symbolic unburdening. The absence of Wilder's shell bracelet at my wrist echoes a pang of loss. I touch the bare skin, a silent homage to the past and the enduring ache in my heart.

Dressed for bed, I prepare for sleep in the pallidly lit room, only the candle's glow offering solace. Despite the inviting softness of my bed, sleep proves elusive. My mind is a whirlwind of thoughts. The upcoming confession, my squadron, and the tangled paths of my past and future.

Outside, the rustling leaves and distant water's song mingle with the night, yet they fail to soothe my restless spirit. I toss in my bed, seeking comfort that remains just out of reach.

Rising, I pace my room, my steps quiet on the wooden floor. Standing by the window, I gaze into the night. Castanea rests, oblivious to the turmoil within me. My recent decision regarding the Underworld, the blank spaces in my memory, they cast long shadows over my spirit.

I return to bed, attempting various calming spells, but tonight they ring empty. My thoughts drift back to the candle, its vigilant flame a barrier against King Valtorious. Again, I reinforce its magic with a whispered spell, just in case.

The night in my treehouse deepens, drawing me into a world of dreams. My body, ensconced in the soft embrace of my bed, surrenders to sleep's call, but my mind roams free, untethered from the constraints of reality.

In my dreams, I wander through a dark forest along the edge of a river that feeds into an ocean. My steps are soft on the damp earth, and I hear whispers and sounds, as if the trees and brooks themselves are speaking to me. Motivation propels me onward, though my goal remains undefined. A part of me holds onto the hope of seeing them again.

The ache in my soul carries my feet forward. Perhaps this is part of the dream—the knowledge that it's all in my head. I take a deep breath and inhale the scents carried by the breeze: water, mud, leaves, flowers, sadness, death. Everything around me has lived and will die here under these starry skies.

Suddenly, the forest gives way to a clearing bathed in the soft glow of moonlight. Only one. The moon casts a brilliant light into the clearing, a circle of luminescent white growing larger than the surrounding forest. The shadowy forms of trees seem to bow at the edges of the glade and in the distance, evening bugs sing their night song. There, in the midst of the clearing, stands a campfire with flames dancing up towards the sky like orange streaks. Around the fire sit four figures, their faces illuminated by the flickering light. They turn towards me as I approach, their expressions a mix of hope, relief, and something akin to longing.

Aggonid stands first, his crimson gaze locking onto mine with an intensity that makes my heart skip a beat even as it breaks. I hurt him the last time I saw him.

"Morte," he says, and his voice is a deep, full-bodied melody that resonates within me.

The others rise, their movements fluid and graceful. They circle around me, their expressions earnest, filled with an emotion I can't quite place. I gaze at Caius, at his dark blue hair and skin so pale it seems to be made of moonlight. His eyes are a faint blue that remind me of frost and his lips are full and bowed, a sad smile adorning them. As though I've deeply hurt him, and he's trying not to show it.

Az stands tall and broad-shouldered with raven black hair and eyes like the Triune Sea. He exudes a sense of power and confidence that immediately draws attention. Shadows pour off of him, curling around me as though caressing me. He steps forward and takes my hand, his grip firm and warm as he pulls me into his arms. "I've missed you so much," he chokes.

My wide-eyed gaze meets the fourth male's longing stare over his shoulder. His eyes are the same as Caius', though his hair is dark, and so is his skin. Two canines greet me as he grins, his expression relieved. He oozes a raw, untamed energy that makes my pulse race at my neck.

Emeric.

I pull away from the Az's embrace, my heart constricting with confusion and grief. "You guys are all really my mates?" I ask, my voice barely above a whisper. I feel such an intense pull towards them.

The four males share a look between them before turning those eyes on me, eyes that convey a depth of love that I can't quite fathom. Aggonid steps forward, though he's hesitant this time, as though he'll scare me away.

"You are sleeping, but we crafted this," he spins around, arms in the air, "for you. This is a dreamscape. Every interaction you've had with us is real. I'm your soul bonded mate. And they," he gestures towards Caius and Az, "are also mates you acquired during a wild hunt in my realm. Emeric would've been yours, too, had I not taken over before he could."

Tears stream down my cheeks. Yes, I feel this pull between them, but I have so many questions in return. "Why would you send me away? You didn't want me?" My voice breaks, right along with my heart.

Abandoning his hesitation, Aggonid pulls me into his arms, breathing me in as the others voice their dissent. "There isn't a day that's gone by that I haven't wanted you," he whispers fiercely against my hair.

"Then why did you send me away?" I bury my head against his chest, vetiver and smoke filling my nostrils.

He cups my cheeks, forcing me to look him in the eyes. "I have always wanted you, even when I thought I shouldn't. They have always wanted you, even if it meant facing my wrath. You. Are. Wanted." He punctuates each word. "You asked me to send you back to Bedlam after winning a favor from me in a wild hunt. Before we consummated our bond. I thought I was doing the right thing by doing it, but I had no idea Luna would agree. We have spent every waking hour trying to get you back home."

I blink away the tears. "Why did you let me go?"

"We didn't," Az growls. "Luna came and snatched you from my arms."

I glance at him, witnessing the grief on his face. Never in my life have I ever felt an inkling of anything towards anyone other than Wilder. Until them. It consumes me.

"Little Bird?" Caius, with the moonlight skin takes a step forward, his expression crestfallen. "We're your mates. There isn't anything you could ever do that would make me not want you."

Even as he says it, I know there's one thing I can do that'll hurt them enough to not want me. One thing I know I'll do, and this will change things for us forever. When they can only reach me via dreamscapes, they'll tire of it, and move on.

"I don't believe that," I say, trying to suppress the tremor in my voice. "We're immortals, after all. You have eternity to find another."

A gasp parts from Caius' lips, his ice-blue eyes filling with a flurry of emotions. A myriad of pain, disbelief, and desperation. "If you think for a moment I'd rather have anyone other than you between Aggie and I, you are sorely mistaken." He glances at the others. "Should we have her head checked? Perhaps giving her back her memories isn't a good idea." He seems to think for a moment before turning his penetrating gaze back to me. "I think I'd really love to make you fall in love with me again. Should I get the manacles?"

I laugh nervously, trying to make light of what he's said. But the pain in his eyes burns me, and I hate that I'm the reason for it. Yet, I can't allow them to try and fight for something that we might never be able to have again.

But maybe I can give them something. I can't have sex with them if I don't remember them, but I can give them a little piece of me.

"Can we make this dreamscape anywhere else?" I pull back from Aggonid, still allowing him to hold me because I need his touch like I need air to breathe.

"Anywhere you desire." Emeric grins at me. His fangs aren't scary, but strangely arousing. "Where do you want to go?"

A spark of excitement ignites within me at the thought. "Do all of you have wings?" I whisper, my eyes darting between Aggonid and Emeric.

Emeric's smile widens, understanding my desire without me needing to say another word.

"Can we please fly?"

At the prison, magic is limited to only an hour each week. But for those who behave and cause no trouble, they are rewarded with daily access. Despite these allowances, I'll miss the freedom of soaring through the sky whenever I please, feeling weightless and alive with every flap of my wings.

"Fly, you say?" Aggonid's question is a low rumble, curiosity evident in his vivid red eyes. His gaze remains on mine for a moment longer before he nods and steps back, allowing me space as his wings unfurl, vast and crimson, a visual echo of my own. They spread with a breathtaking grace, a promise of flight and freedom. The air shifts with the stirring of his feathers, a gentle breeze that carries the promise of the skies.

Caius chuckles, a sound that vibrates with an infectious joy. "We're going to need a bit more room for this," he says, a playful glint in his husky-like eyes. With a casual flick of his wrist, the dreamscape shifts around us, the forest receding as the ground falls away, leaving us standing on a precipice that overlooks a sprawling, starlit vista.

Below us, a valley opens up, illuminated by the silver glow of the moon, cradling a silent lake that mirrors the night sky. The edges of the world seem to blur into the horizon, where the dark of the night meets the promise of dawn. It's a view that steals the breath, a canvas of darkness dotted with the jewels of stars, waiting for us to take flight and join them.

Az steps up beside me, his wings materializing from the shadows, grand and mysterious as the night itself. "Are you ready to soar, firefly?" he asks, his voice a blend of humor and warmth.

With a nod, I step into the embrace of my mates, their wings enveloping me in a cocoon of feathers and anticipation. Together, we leap from the edge, the cool night air rushing past us as we ascend into the skies. My heart races with the thrill of it, the sensation of being lifted higher and higher, surrounded by their strength and the boundless sky.

Aggonid leads the flight, his powerful strokes cutting through the air with a precision that speaks of centuries spent mastering the skies. Beside him, Caius moves with a wild abandon, whooping with delight as he executes a daring spiral, his tail streaming behind him like a comet's trail.

Emeric's flight is more measured, his focus on the currents and eddies that carry us effortlessly upwards. His hellhound heritage gives him an affinity for the flames, and occasionally, a spark ignites from his wings, leaving a trail of fire in our wake.

"Try to keep up, Sparky." I grin down at him, his eyes twinkling in response. He gives me a mock salute before launching himself higher, cutting through the night sky like a shooting star.

"I'm not so certain you can keep up." He grins back at me. "I'm twice the male they are." He trails off, laughing.

We climb until the world below is nothing more than a mural of shadow and silver, the stars our silent audience. Here, in this moment, the pull of my mates is undeniable, a magnetic force that draws me closer to them, even as I know the dawn will bring separation.

Caius calls to me over the rush of wind, "Let's find a place to rest, little bird. Somewhere you'll remember when you wake." His voice is filled with a playful dare, one I find myself wanting to accept, to indulge in for just a moment longer.

We glide towards an outcropping that appears as a silhouette against the moon's bright face, a plateau that rises like an island amidst the sea of clouds below us. It's an overlook that promises seclusion and serenity, an intimate stage set by the night itself for whatever may come.

As we land softly, the grass beneath our feet whispers secrets of the earth, each blade a witness to the life that thrives in the embrace of the night. The overlook grants us a vantage point over a landscape that is both wild and whispering with the kind of beauty that speaks directly to the soul.

In the distance, the horizon begins to hint at the approach of dawn, a faint blush that tinges the edge of the world with the softest pink. It's here, in this liminal space, where night meets day, that the charge between us becomes a tangible thing, an energy that hums in the air and raises the hairs on my arms.

Aggonid's hand finds mine, his touch gentle yet laden with a thousand unsaid promises. "Lay with us," he murmurs, and I can hear the plea for me to stay, to linger in this moment with them.

Caius moves behind me, his presence a heat at my back. He leans in, and I can feel the brush of his lips against the shell of my ear as he whispers, "We could show you the world from above, Morte, and still, it wouldn't compare to the world below, or what we can offer you between us."

Az stands before me, his gaze intense. "We have a lot of fun in the shadows," he says, and I see the flicker of his own fire reflected in his deep blue eyes, proof of the depth of his feelings.

"Come on." Emeric gestures to a large blanket he's splayed on the grass.

I obediently follow them to the giant comforter, and the soft fabric envelopes us in warmth. They gather round me eagerly, their hands reaching out to touch me. I rest my head in Emeric's lap, feeling his fingers gently card through my hair. Az has me sitting on his lap, his arms wrapped securely around me. Aggie settles next to him, his hand resting on my shoulder. Caius takes my feet in his lap, his strong hands massaging them gently.

The atmosphere dims, and between one blink and the next, candles are strewn all around us, gently flickering and painting long shadows on the ground. The steady flickering of the flames creates an almost hypnotic effect, drawing our gaze to their mesmerizing dance. It's as if we've been transported to another world entirely, one filled with seductive magic and intrigue. The scent of melted wax and fragrant oils fills my nose, adding to the enchantment of the moment.

Emeric's wide smile reveals a dimple on his left cheek as he looks down at me, his short curls falling into his pale blue eyes. I can't help but smile in return as I reach my fingers up to brush the loose strands out of his face. He lightly grasps my hand, intertwining our fingers and sending a jolt of electricity through me. The warmth of his touch lingers on my skin, causing small goosebumps to form.

His tongue flicks out to graze the sharp point of one of his fangs, drawing my attention. The glint of danger in his eyes is mirrored by the predatory curve of his lips.

"If you keep looking at me like you want me to eat you," Emeric drawls, "I just might."

"Morte wants us to eat her?" Caius asks, his soft tail slithering up my leg, tickling me.

Az chuckles, and the sound reverberates through his chest and into mine. His grip around me tightens for a moment before he loosens it. "That's not what he meant, Cai," he clarifies, directing a teasing wink at Emeric.

"Unless maybe it is," Caius purrs, and the sound is like velvet against my skin as he pulls me out of Az's lap and onto the blanket so he's over me. "Would my pretty little bird like that?" His strong arms bracket me as he nuzzles into my hair, the sandalwood scent of him enveloping me.

Aggie chuckles, a low and rumbly sound that sends shivers down my spine, causing me to giggle. "I think she'd rather enjoy it, Cai," he murmurs in agreement, his fingers resting on my thigh. He glances up to meet my eyes, the ghost of a smile playing on his lips as he shifts closer.

"Maybe we should find out, hmm?" he suggests, his voice a low ebony purr that causes another wave of shivers to roll down my spine. His fingers trail up my thigh, light as a feather yet carrying a heated touch that has my heart thundering in my chest, the rhythm of it echoing in my ears. "Say the word, and we're yours. What'll it be, my heart?"

I gaze at each of them in turn, the sense of standing on a precipice sharpening the moment. Emeric, with his wickedly sharp fangs and mirthful eyes; Caius, his long, dark blue hair tickling my cheeks as his tail whips behind him; Az, whose steely grip sends goosebumps through me; and Aggie, whose presence alone squeezes the air from my lungs, as though I need to hold onto and savor each breath shared in his proximity.

The silence that follows Aggie's proposition hums with anticipation, charged like the prelude to a thunderstorm. The air is thick with implication while my heart pounds out a reckless rhythm, matching the tempo set by the flicker of the candles nearby.

"Yes." The word slips from my lips, soft as a whisper yet as decisive as the roll of thunder that follows. For a moment, everything is still; the world holds its breath and even the flicker of candles seems to pause in anticipation.

"Your scent gave your answer away long before you voiced your decision," teases Emeric, his laughter rich and playful as he extends a hand to caress my cheek, his thumb brushing over my lips with an intimate familiarity that leaves me breathless. He bows his head to press a kiss against the back of my hand, the sharp point of his fang grazing my skin in an electrifying touch.

Delicious heat surges through me, swirls of desire tracing a path from Emeric's touch down to the very tips of my fingers and toes. My lips part in a silent gasp as his smile turns wicked, his nostrils flaring. "If you like what my fangs do, wait'll you find out what Az's can do to you."

My gaze swings to Az, who at that moment is looking at me with an intensity that nearly singes my skin. His dark blue eyes hold a glimmer of amusement and promise as he leans a bit closer. "Do you want to hear how my bite made you sing, or would you rather experience it?"

"Sing?"

His answer is a soft curl of his lip, the piercing in the corner glinting in the pale light. "Perhaps the better word is beg."

An involuntary whimper escapes me, and Caius' chuckle reverberates through our chests.

"Morte, recline in Az's lap so we can both feed on you," Caius whispers in my ear as he crawls off me.

My body moves of its own accord, guided by Emeric's hand on my lower back as he gently pushes me towards Az. The latter's gaze is intense, a mix of hunger and caution as I move into his space. He smoothly extends his legs, his hands gently guiding me until I'm nestled in between his strong thighs.

"Don't be frightened, firefly." Az's voice is a low rumble, a soothing balm that calms my racing heart. His arms envelop me in a warm cocoon, and I find myself relaxing against him. He strokes my hair, the simple action lulling me into a contented submission. "I promise we won't take this any further than you ask us to, okay?"

I nod my head against his chest. "Should I ... Should I undress, or—"

A gasp escapes me as my clothes disappear, baring me for them all to see. I should be shy, covering myself up from their roving eyes, but it's liberating, having these handsome males admiring my body.

Emeric positions himself next to Az, his gaze never leaving me. "Are you ready?" His voice is low and filled with anticipation. The intensity of his gaze makes my breath hitch in my throat.

A small nod is all I can manage before Caius crawls over, an air of primal dominance surrounding him as he kneels before me, his fingers trailing up my calf before stopping at my knees, giving them a little push until they fall open.

"Perfect," Aggie whispers, running a finger along my slit, the barest of touches, but enough to make me chase it.

"Eyes on me," Caius murmurs, and I find myself lost in his pale, stormy eyes. They're like swirling vortexes of power and authority, demanding obedience yet promising safety. He lowers his head, dribbling spit out of his mouth, and I suck in a breath when it hits my pussy.

Az's hand cups my cheek, tilting my head slightly to give him better access to my neck, all while I keep my gaze pinned on Caius. His warm lips graze my skin, triggering a wave of goosebumps despite the comforting warmth of his breath.

Just as Caius' tongue laps at me, a sharp prick at my neck is immediately followed by a surge of warmth, an intoxicating pleasure that floods through me like honey.

Emeric, seeing my attention being devoured by Az and Caius,

nudges my hip with his hand, and I turn to look at him. A wicked grin lights up his face as he pulls off his shirt, revealing his muscular chest and defined abs. He moves closer to me, whispering in my ear, "Enjoying yourself?"

Caught between a nod and a moan by Caius's ministrations, I manage an airy "Yes."

Emeric chuckles against me before he leans in to capture my lips with his own. The kiss is intoxicatingly slow and sensual; despite the domineering presence of the others, there is a soft tenderness in Emeric's actions that reels me further into their control. He moves to the other side of my neck, kissing along my collarbone until he reaches the stiff peak of my breast, lapping at it with his wicked tongue, his fangs dragging against my skin.

The pull of Az's fangs at my neck rolls through me, deepening my senses like a harmony flowing from a symphony, heightening every sensation, while Caius continues to taste me, a strong hand steadying my hip. I grip Emeric's bicep, the touch grounding me amidst the overwhelming sensations washing over me.

Caius takes it slow; his tongue continues its unhurried exploration. His hands, always moving, begin tracing various patterns on my inner thighs, tickling the sensitive skin there. His pale eyes, now as dark as storm clouds, never leave mine as he plunges two fingers fully into me. My back arches at the sudden intrusion and the gasp that hitches in my breath.

Aggonid chuckles, his shadows looping and curling around my splayed legs as though they were his hands, leaving the ghost of a touch in its wake. The shadows make its way to where Caius is coaxing soft mewls out of me with each come hither of his fingers.

The dark tendrils converge and mix with the warmth of Caius's touch, creating an intoxicating blend of physical and ethereal sensations. They assist him with his sweet exploration, caressing and gliding over sensitive flesh.

Caius' touch becomes rougher, but it only heightens the pleasure coursing through my veins. His fingers move with such precision, hitting that spot within me that makes my world tilt on its axis.

Emeric's mouth detaches from my breast, only to find purchase on my lips. He swallows down my cries as I near the precipice, the heat building within me threatening to burst. His kiss is all-consuming, devouring, a storm of passion in our linked lips. The sharpness of his fangs teases my lower lip, and I can taste the coppery tang of my own blood. It only adds to the sweet cocktail of sensations that envelops me. His hand snakes up my torso, a trail of fire in his wake until he captures my other breast. His thumb swipes over the peak, and my moan is swallowed by his mouth as his touch sends shockwaves of pleasure through me.

Az's grip on my hip tightens, pulling me closer. The resonating hum from his throat flows through me like a lullaby, stirring up a wild storm of emotions within me. His fangs slide from my neck leaving behind a trail of delightful sting. He presses himself against my back, his chest is a warm wall that adds to the building heat within me. I can feel every inch of him, firm and unyielding against me.

Caius' tail nudges against my clit, and it's an unfamiliar, alien sensation that sends me spiraling. My back arches into Az's solid form. My fingernails dig into Emeric's shoulders, a desperate hold for an anchor as I'm thrown into the sea.

Az's voice is a low growl in my ear, his words muttered in a language I can't understand but feel. Words of worship as I release on Caius' tongue.

The world becomes a symphony of pleasure, each of their touches a note that sends ripples through my being. Caius' teeth find the tender skin of my inner thigh, sharp and exciting. His hands are firm, leaving impressions on my waist that I'll remember in the morning light.

Emeric's tongue traces the seam of my lips, teasing his way inside in a dance as ancient as time. His hand replaces his mouth on my breast, thumb brushing over the sensitive tip with light strokes while his other slides down my body to meet Caius'. Together, they play me like the sweetest instrument, their fingers dancing on my skin as I reel from the aftershocks.

By the time I'm finished, I'm limp, sweaty, and sated with a tease of a smirk on my lips.

Aggonid chuckles, his mouth pressing to my knee as he wraps his arm around my leg. "This, for the rest of eternity. Do you want it?"

The question warms me, a primal part of me claiming it, digging its claws in to hold onto it. I smile softly, meeting his crimson eyes.

"Yes," I whisper, knowing that the difference between wanting something so desperately with all that you are, and having it, are two separate things. One forgets duty, the other embraces it.

A crushing weight settles into the depths of my bones, leaving me gasping for air. Each breath feels like a razor blade slicing through my chest as I choke out another single word, "Yes." My voice trembles with an unknown emotion that I'm not yet ready to face.

Tears pour down my face like a river as Caius' expression contorts with confusion and Aggie's features twist in agony before settling into a mask of despair.

"I'm sorry," I whimper, the words barely audible amidst my sobs. "I'm so, so sorry."

With a jolt, I wrench myself from the dreamscape, drenched in sweat and consumed by the frigid reality that awaits me outside of my dreams.

I bury my face in the soft, plush pillow, my body trembling with emotion. With a shaking hand, I quickly cast a silencing charm to muffle the raw scream building in my throat. The fabric of the pillow muffles the sound and absorbs my tears as I release all the pent-up frustration and turmoil inside me. My chest heaves with each sob, my breaths coming out jagged and uneven. It's as if the grief of the whole world is crashing down on me, and all I can do is scream into this pillow until I have no voice left.

CHAPTER THIRTY-ONE

AGGONID

The dreamscape shatters around us, a cascade of delicate fragments dissolving into the void. We stand there, in the heart of our conjured reality, the aftermath of our power lingering like a fading echo. The confusion is profound, a thick veil that envelops each of us in its suffocating grasp.

"Why?" Azazel's voice cuts through the stillness, his tone a mix of crushing disbelief and devastation. His usually composed demeanor is frayed at the edges, the revelation tearing at the fabric of his understanding.

Caius's voice is barely a whisper, filled with both frustration and satisfaction. "I made her orgasm," he says, his words tinged with pride. "I could taste it on my tongue and feel her squeeze my fingers. She loves orgasms." He looks at me anxiously, as if seeking reassurance. "My tail didn't freak her out, did it?"

"This has nothing to do with you." I grab his hand, threading my fingers through his. "Didn't you feel it through the bond? The agony? She didn't want to leave us."

Beside me, Emeric leans heavily against a giant ore of sanguimetal, his form shimmering as if struggling to maintain coherence in the wake of the dreamscape disintegrating. The exertion of holding the dreamscape has taken its toll on him, proof of the immense effort it required. "It's him again, isn't it?" he pants, his breath coming out in ragged gasps.

"Wilder," Az whispers, his mood darkening as shadows pour off him in thick waves that seem to be tied to his very being.

I pace back and forth, the remnants of the dreamscape swirling around my feet like mist. My mind races, trying to piece together the impossible puzzle before us. Morte, our Morte, with no proper recollection of who we are, but she definitely *feels* it, so she knows we're not lying. She's our fucking mate. Is she afraid if we give her memories back, she'll want to stay? The very thought sends a surge of panic through me, a fear I've never known. Will dragging Wilder down to hell change her mind?

Caius watches from the shadows, his eyes reflecting the devastation that churns within us all. His eyes are haunted, as though he's seen a thousand battles, only to sit on the sidelines with his hands tied behind his back while his loved ones were slaughtered. "This changes everything," he murmurs, more to himself than to any of us. His usual playful bravado is absent, replaced by a gravity that underscores the severity of our situation.

"We need a dreamscape every night," I declare, my voice resolute despite the uncertainty that grips my heart. I feel like I'm falling, scrambling for something to hold onto. "We can't just leave things like this. There must be a way to convince her to let us restore her memory, to make her remember us. If she remembers us, there's no way she'd leave."

"But how?" Azazel interjects, his frustration giving way to concern. "She'll never leave Wilder. She *feels* our bond, and still, she turned her back on us."

The question hangs in the air, unanswered, a challenge that looms dauntingly over us. I glance at each of them, their faces etched with the same pain that fuels my fire. I've never taken no for an answer because people don't tell me 'no.' I just need to figure out how we'll get her to say yes to giving her all of her memories from the Underworld, because then she'll want to come here, we'll just have to get Wilder here.

Not that I'm keen on adding to the little family we've made, but if it's the only way I can get her here, I'll do whatever it takes.

"Maybe she just doesn't want to be in the Underworld," Az growls. "Does anybody want to fucking be in the Underworld? No wonder she said she didn't want to come back. She doesn't even fucking remember us!"

That only eases the ache in my chest marginally. "She didn't reject *us*," I breathe, my attention now on Caius. I'm usually the strong one. But I need his reassurance right now. "We just need to make her remember and then she'll know that Wilder just needs to come here with her. Right?"

"He's at Bedlam Penitentiary. What are the protocols for getting in now?" Caius glances at Emeric, as though he should know. But how would he?

"Let me send the reapers to do some digging for me. We're not giving up on Morte."

CHAPTER THIRTY-TWO

MORTE

As my squadron and I emerge through the portal stone, a heavy silence envelops us on the northern end of Draconum. We slink forward with practiced stealth, our movements like shadows gliding over the rugged volcanic terrain. Beads of sweat cling to my skin, dampening my hair and trickling between my breasts. The air here is charged with an ancient, primal energy, thick with the pungent scent of sulfuric rock and the faint whispers of buried treasure. Everywhere we look, the land is littered with precious gems and glittering shards of gold. Endless riches that await those brave enough to venture into this untamed continent.

Either brave or foolish, if you ask me. Dragon fae love their treasure hoards as much as they love to fight and fuck. They're almost as territorial as a newly bonded fae. They're just as likely to want to seduce you as they are to fight you if you're caught trying to take their treasure.

But that's not why we've come to this peninsula. This craggy strip of land, hemmed in by the brutal churn of the ocean on either side, is but a waypoint, the threshold before the turbulent waters that separate us from our true destination. Beyond the horizon lies the formidable Penn Island, an island born of fire and brimstone, where the infamous Bedlam Penitentiary stands as a sentinel amid the smoky plumes and molten rivers that characterize this volcanic isle.

As we extend our wings, a sudden gust sweeps across the land, unearthing a strange combination of smells. A hint of ether and the tang of ozone is followed by a metallic edge that's distinctly out of place in the natural surroundings.

Freya's fingers dance over the comms device, ready to call for backup if needed, but I stay her hand as I take a few steps forward, away from the shoreline. Volcanic rock shifts under my feet, and I toe a few pieces away, noticing a silver sheen underneath, its surface shimmering under the light of Bedlam's many moons.

"What is it?" Vero crouches down to inspect it, her fiery red hair not as vibrant in the moonlight.

"Do you feel that?" Noct's hushed words break through the stillness, causing us to pause and tune in to our surroundings. We open our senses, trying to absorb every detail.

The beach beneath our feet thrums with an ancient, untamed energy, pulsing with a raw power that cannot be ignored. The air is thick with the scent of alloy and elemental, filling our lungs and electrifying our skin.

"I think it's coming from whatever this shit is." Bow picks up several small pieces of rock, unearthing a bit of metal too big to pull up.

Bow's hands are deft as she sifts through the volcanic granules, her fingers brushing against something unexpected. A metallic curvature. Together, we join in, our efforts coordinated as we excavate the beach's dark, coarse sand. Gradually, a large ring materializes from beneath the obsidian shards, its circumference expansive, about fifteen feet across.

"Is there anything in the middle?" Sabine puts her hands on her hips, and Arwen trots over to the center of the ring and starts digging.

We start chucking the rock into the sea, trying to clear the area. With each new piece unearthed, more metal deposits are revealed, creating an almost magnetic pull. It's an unnerving sensation, like walking through a field of invisible forces that tug at the very marrow of our bones.

The sheen on the metal is unmistakable.

"What is this much sanguimetal doing in Bedlam?" Arwen speaks in a hushed whisper, spinning around to take it all in.

Sanguimetal is sometimes imported from Romarie, but if there were large deposits coming in, especially one so close to the prison, someone had to know. The importation of anything from the rogue realm ran by a tyrant king is highly regulated.

Inside the circle lie thousands of pieces, as though they've been shattered off something larger. I crouch to examine a sharp fragment, its surface dull yet absorbing the scant light filtering through the dense clouds. This metal, mostly alien to both Castanea and Bedlam, raises more questions than answers.

Freya leans beside me, her gaze analytical. "This is infused with magic, but it's weak, like it's been siphoned off," she says, her voice reflecting her intrigue.

"You need to gather these pieces," I suggest. "They might provide insights into the origin and purpose of whatever the hell this is," I gesture to the circle. They lie in a deliberate arrangement, hinting at a former structure, perhaps a signaling device.

As we collect the fragments, Noct spots something near the shore. "Look at this," she calls out. We push past driftwood to find a clearing with a dense pile of metal scraps.

"This seems like a marker of some sort," Arwen observes, studying the array without touching it.

A chill runs down my spine. If this is a beacon, crafted from Romarie's distinct metal and dark magic, it could signify King Valtorious's expanding influence, a troubling notion for all of Bedlam.

"I think we should call this one in, guys," I nod to Vero. "But be vague. I don't want them disrupting what we're doing here."

"While Vero makes the call, let's thoroughly examine the area," I decide. The shore's deceptive tranquility masks deeper, darker secrets, possibly linked to Romarie's druidists and their nefarious plans.

We split up, meticulously searching the clearing and its surroundings. The beach now feels like a cryptic entity, its secrets buried under layers of rock and sand. The possibility of Romarie's druidists plotting so close to the penitentiary, potentially against Castanea or Bedlam, fills me with unease.

Harmony and Bow discover ritualistic symbols etched into a driftwood, pulsing with a sinister energy. "These are ceremonial and recently made," Harmony notes, her voice tinged with concern.

The fragments of information form a disquieting picture: sanguimetal shards, ritualistic tree carvings, a concealed beacon. Someone has been exploiting the peninsula for dark purposes.

As dawn's early light begins to pierce the shore's gloom, we reconvene. The evidence doesn't look good.

"This can't wait," I state, formulating their next steps, my last command as their leader. If I weren't so concerned, I'd probably be choked up. "Inform the Council and brace for potential repercussions."

We wade in the water, dawn's light gently breaking through the mist-crowded morning. A sense of foreboding accompanies us, the realization that we've uncovered just the tip of a larger, more menacing plot. The unease in my heart refuses to settle.

But it's no longer my path, this road where I get a say in how we dismantle our enemies.

I motion to Noct, who strides beside me with a warrior's grace. Handing her the collection of metal fragments and the dark, twisted artifacts we discovered, I say. "These need to reach the Council immediately. They need to understand the insidious nature of Romarie's influence here."

Noct's eyes, sharp and intent, meet mine. "I'll make sure they grasp the severity. Valtorious's machinations are a threat, not just to us but to all of Bedlam." She deposits them in her bag before putting her hand on my arm, her eyes taking on a glassy look. "You don't have to do this."

"I do."

And that's the last she mentions of it.

As we advance through the rugged terrain, my mind races, piecing together the fragments of the night's discoveries. The Romarie metal magic, twisted and dark, is unlike anything we've encountered. It's a clear sign that Valtorious' ambitions are growing bolder, more dangerous.

Is this why I've felt him in my dreams?

Our journey across the sea is silent, each of us lost in our thoughts as the island looms closer. The implications of our discovery are inescapable, echoing the ever-present dangers that lurk beyond our sanctuary, beyond our realm.

We stand together in the lengthening shadow of the penitentiary, a monolith of cold metal that threatens to swallow me whole. My squadron flanks me, their faces etched with sorrow so profound it's nearly tangible. It's an aching shroud that stifles our breaths and burdens our souls. Their eyes, pools of shared history and camaraderie, hold mine in a gaze brimming with the agony of parting.

"We'll be sure to inform the Council of our findings," Freya's voice cuts through the silence, a brittle sound against the hush of the encroaching tide. Her words are steady, yet the unrest in her eyes speaks volumes, echoing a turbulence within me.

I nod, and the action feels hollow and final. "Thank you," I manage, the words a heavy stone in my throat.

The sea that carried us here, once a huge expanse of freedom, now feels like a chasm between what was and what will be.

The familiar, ominous silhouette of Bedlam Penitentiary rises ahead, an imposing giant under the sky. Waves lap against the rocks below in a steady cadence, a sound that resonates with the disquiet in my heart.

A hush settles upon my squadron, the warriors with whom I've weathered countless storms. We've soared through skies ablaze with the glory of victory and waded through the aftermath of battles, our hands as much for holding as for fighting. Now, they reach out to me, clasping mine with a grip that speaks of bonds deeper than blood.

Vero scans the towering gates, the barriers that will soon separate us, with fierce eyes. "Our defenses must be fortified," she states, her words steady, but I hear the sentiment beneath—this is our final stand together.

I face them, these embodiments of courage and sacrifice. Leading them has been a privilege of a lifetime. The title 'Commander' feels like an echo from another life. "I'm no longer your commander," I say, the truth of my words slicing through me. "What we've shared ... it transcends command, transcends the battles and the blood."

A collective breath is drawn as the reality of our parting sets in. "You have been my family, my heart, my comrades in arms. In the dance of life and death, you have been the constant rhythm to which my spirit has moved." A smile breaks through the sorrow, a fleeting glimmer in the gathering darkness. "Loving each one of you and witnessing you welcome life into this world. Helping you take life out of it. And now you will all have plenty of absinthe to go around without me hogging it all."

Their laughter, a chorus of fractured harmonies, echoes around us, the sound both a balm and a blade to my soul. It's a laughter born of years of shared joys and sorrows, now a requiem for the end of an era.

I look at them, really look, engraving each beloved face into my memory. "I could have chosen no finer warriors to stand beside. No greater honor than to have lived, fought, and loved with you all." Tears break free, streaming down our faces, yet they are not a sign of weakness but a silent witness to the strength of our bond.

We linger in the shadow of parting, each second stretching into eternity, each heartbeat a drumbeat of impending solitude as we share tearful hugs. In the end, it is not the specter of confinement that chills me, but the thought of a future devoid of these remarkable souls who have been the stars in my firmament.

I turn toward the gates that will close behind me, sealing my fate. "Remember me," I whisper, not as a commander, but as a friend, a sister, a part of a legacy that will outlive the bars and chains.

As I step forward, the touch of their hands on my back is a warmth I will carry into the cold cell. It's a farewell, but not a goodbye, for within me, they will always fly free. As I stare up at the giant gates, ones I pounded on for years to let me in, the salty tang of the sea mixes with the metallic bite of rain-soaked iron. I've waited two centuries for this moment.

The sound of their wings taking flight behind me is barely heard over the crash of the waves, but it's one I'll remember for eternity. They soar onward and I step forward, my moment of reckoning finally here.

The prison's walls of metal and stone, weathered by time and torment, whisper tales of lives spent in shadows. The sentry towers, with their vigilant eyes, scrutinize every visitor, their silent judgment one I welcome now.

I pause at the entrance, the enormity of my decision anchoring me to the spot. This is it. The point of no return. The roar of the ocean crescendos, as if urging me to spill the truth that's been festering within me like a poison.

I take a deep breath, feeling the cool, briny air fill my lungs, a momentary respite from the heaviness that clings to my soul. With each step toward the prison gates, memories of Wilder flood my mind. His laughter, his touch, the depth of his eyes. The pain of our separation, the agony of his unjust imprisonment, and the secret that has bound us in silent torment.

The guards at the entrance eye me warily, their gazes a mix of curiosity and caution. They recognize me—Commander of The Great Company, a figure of authority and strength. Yet today, I stand before them not as a leader, but as a penitent soul seeking absolution.

I nod to them, recognizing a few. My voice, once a commanding presence, now trembles as I speak. "I'm here to confess a crime," I say, the words slicing through me like shards of ice.

A ripple of shock passes through the guards, their stoic expressions giving way to disbelief. They exchange glances, unsure how to proceed with such an unprecedented situation.

"Commander, are you certain?" one of them asks, his tone betraying a hint of doubt. "This is highly irregular."

There isn't any other thought in my head. I've waited two hundred years to make this right. "I am," I reply, my voice gaining strength. "I need to speak to the warden. It's time everyone knew the truth."

The guards step aside, their movements mechanical as they grapple with the reality unfolding before them. I pass through the gates, each step echoing against the cobblestone path, a somber drumbeat leading me to my fate.

The courtyard of the penitentiary is empty, save for the whispering winds and the distant cries of gulls. The sky above is a patchwork of gray and white, and the clouds are heavy with unshed tears.

I make my way to the warden's office. The building's gothic architecture is a harsh reminder of the pain and suffering contained within these walls. The heavy wooden door creaks open, its groan a lament for the souls lost to this place.

Inside, the warden awaits, his expression one of bemusement and concern. "Commander Morte, to what do I owe this unexpected visit?"

I stand before him, my heart pounding in my chest, the weight of my secret a crushing burden. "I'm here to confess," I begin, my voice a mere whisper. "I'm here to tell you about the crime I committed two hundred years ago. The crime that sent an innocent man to this prison."

The warden's eyes widen, his demeanor shifting from curiosity to solemnity. "Go on," he urges, his tone a gentle prompt in the stillness of the room.

And so, I begin my confession, the words pouring out of me like a dam breaking. I speak of Wilder, of our forbidden love, of the night that changed everything. I reveal the truth about the teenagers on the beach, the glamors that deceived me, the tragic mistake that cost them their lives.

With each word, the burden lifts, but the pain intensifies—a paradox of liberation and agony. Tears stream down my cheeks, unbidden and relentless, as I bare my soul to the warden, to the walls of this prison, to the ghosts of my past.

When I finish, a profound silence envelops the room, the atmosphere dense with the magnitude of my confession. The warden sits, his expression somber, his eyes reflecting a depth of understanding that only those who have witnessed the darkest corners of the soul can possess.

"Commander Morte," he finally says, his voice a solemn echo, "your confession. It changes everything."

I nod, my eyes still wet with tears, yet there's a certain lightness in my chest—an unburdening of a secret too heavy to carry alone any longer.

The warden stands, moving around his desk with a deliberateness that belies his earlier shock. "I must inform the High Council immediately. This ... this is unprecedented."

A sense of finality settles over me. There's no turning back now. The truth is out, hanging in the air between us like a tangible presence. "What happens now?" I ask, my words steadier than I feel.

"We'll need to verify your claims, Commander. Then we'll proceed as the law dictates." His tone is laden with responsibility, the burden of his duty evident in his furrowed brow.

I understand the gravity of his words. My confession doesn't just affect me; it impacts Wilder, the prison, the entire realm of Bedlam. "I'm ready to face whatever comes."

The warden nods, a gesture of respect that feels oddly comforting. "I'll arrange for your temporary detainment until the council can convene. This is a matter for the highest authorities."

I take a deep breath, bracing myself for what lies ahead. The path I've chosen is fraught with dubiety, but it's a path I must walk, for Wilder, for myself, for the truth.

The warden leads me down a series of corridors, and the prison's dreary walls serve as a reminder of the fate that awaits me. Guards glance at me, their expressions a mix of confusion and curiosity. The word of my arrival, of my confession, is already spreading like wildfire.

We reach a holding cell, and its bars are cold and unyielding. The warden unlocks the door, his movements methodical. "You'll stay here until we can arrange a hearing."

I step inside the cell, and the sound of the door closing behind me is a final, resounding note in the wake of my confession. The cell is sparse, a small cot and a sink the only furnishings in the otherwise spartan space.

As the warden walks away, his footsteps echoing down the hall, I sit on the cot as the reality of my situation settles around me like a shroud. I've turned myself in, confessed to a crime that will undoubtedly change the course of my life. But in doing so, I've also set in motion the possibility of justice for Wilder, a chance to right a wrong that has haunted me for two centuries.

Outside, the sky darkens, and the first drops of rain begin to fall. They tap against the barred window, a rhythmic echo of the world continuing on, indifferent to the turmoil within these walls.

I lean back, closing my eyes. For the first time in two hundred years, I feel a sense of peace. A sense of hope that, perhaps, the truth can indeed set us free.

CHAPTER THIRTY-THREE

MORTE

Crisp air greets me as I step out of the dim interior of Bedlam Penitentiary. Despite the cool weather, perspiration drips between my shoulder blades, pooling at my waistband. Each beat of my heart echoes the heaviness of what I'm about to do. The sky overhead is a canvas of twilight hues, the fading light casting long shadows across the ground.

I take a deep breath, steeling myself. Around me, the buzz of anticipation from the gathered crowd is palpable. News cameras and reporters from every major network in Bedlam have set up their equipment, their lenses trained on me. This isn't just a confession; it's a spectacle, one that will be broadcast across the continents.

With each step I take toward the makeshift podium set up just outside the gates, the magnitude of my decision presses down on me. It's a burden I've carried alone for too long, a secret that's gnawed at my conscience, shadowing every triumph with guilt.

As I approach the microphone, the clamor of the crowd hushes. Every eye is on me, waiting, watching. I clear my throat, my voice steady but laced with emotion.

"People of Bedlam," I begin, my words cutting through the silence.

"Today, I stand before you, not as Commander Morte of the Great Company, but as a fae who has lived with a heavy heart."

The crowd shifts, murmurs rising like the tide. I raise my hand, asking for their silence, and continue. "Two hundred years ago, a terrible crime was committed on our shores. A crime that led to the imprisonment of an innocent man."

A collective gasp ripples through the crowd. I can see the recognition dawning on many faces, the pieces of a puzzle falling into place.

"Wilder Ripple, a merfae of great honor and integrity, has spent two centuries in Bedlam Penitentiary for a crime he did not commit. A crime that I am responsible for."

The reaction is immediate and intense. Shockwaves of disbelief and outrage surge through the crowd. Camera flashes ignite like stars, capturing this moment of raw, unvarnished truth.

"I, Morte, Commander of the Great Company, confess to the murders that occurred on the night of the storm, two hundred years ago. It was I who took the lives of those young fae. It was I who should have faced justice."

The crowd buzzes with tension, a mix of shock, anger, and confusion. I swallow hard, my gaze steady.

"In light of this confession, I surrender myself to the authorities of Bedlam. I ask for no leniency, no mercy. I only ask for justice to be served, for the innocent to be freed, and for the truth to finally see the light."

As I finish, a heavy silence envelops the scene. The crowd is motionless, absorbing the magnitude of my words. Then, as if on cue, the prison guards approach, their steps echoing on the cobblestone.

I hold my head high as they close in, my hands trembling slightly at my sides. This is it—the moment of reckoning, the culmination of a journey that began with a single, tragic mistake.

As the guards place the magic suppressant cuffs around my wrists, a sense of relief washes over me. After two centuries, the weight of my guilt begins to lift, making way for a different kind of weight—the burden of facing the consequences of my actions.

I turn to face the crowd one last time, my eyes scanning the sea of faces. Some show anger, others confusion, but in many, there is a glimmer of understanding, a recognition of the cost of truth.

As I'm led away, the first drops of rain begin to fall, like the tears of the realm, washing away the stains of the past. Behind me, the gates of Bedlam Penitentiary loom large, a symbol of justice and retribution. But for me, they are also a gateway to redemption, a path to a peace that has eluded me for far too long.

The future is uncertain, the path ahead shrouded in darkness. But as I step through those gates, I step forward with a clear conscience, ready to face whatever fate has in store.

THE COURTHOUSE OF BEDLAM, a grand edifice of ancient stone and soaring arches, emerges before me, its very walls echoing the sobriety of the day. I walk through the grand doors, the solemnity of the moment weighing heavily upon me.

Inside, the courtroom is a cavernous space, its high ceilings adorned with frescoes that tell tales of Bedlam's rich history. The sunlight streaming through the stained-glass windows paints the room in technicolor, each hue blending with the next, creating a solemn yet awe-inspiring atmosphere.

Members of The Great Company, my loyal squadron, sit in the front rows, their expressions a mix of stoicism and concern. Their presence, a silent show of support, steadies my trembling nerves. This isn't just my trial; it's a moment that marks the end of an era for all of us.

As I take my place at the center of the courtroom, the heavy oak doors close with a resounding thud, sealing my fate within these walls. The High Judge, a figure of authority and wisdom, sits elevated above the rest, her gaze piercing yet not unkind.

"Morte, you stand before this court to answer for crimes that have long cast a shadow over your life and the realm of Bedlam," the judge begins, her voice echoing in the hallowed hall. "What say you to these charges?"

Drawing a deep breath, I find my voice amidst the whirlwind of emotions. "Your Honor, I stand here to confess my guilt. Two centuries ago, in defense of my life, I committed an act that resulted in the death of several young souls. Souls that I later learned were merely children, disguised by glamor."

A murmur ripples through the courtroom, a tangible manifestation of the shock and sorrow my words evoke. I press on, my voice unwavering despite the ache in my heart.

"Their lives were lost at my hands, and it's a burden I've carried in silence, a secret that has haunted me through the years. My actions led to the wrongful imprisonment of an innocent, Wilder, who selflessly took the blame to protect me."

I pause, my gaze sweeping over the courtroom, meeting the eyes of my squadron, the officials, and the faces of those who had come to witness this reckoning. Each look holds a different emotion, a different judgment.

"The sentence I seek is vita damnationem, the same life sentence Wilder Ripple has unjustly endured because of me. It's time I bear the consequences of my actions, to bring closure to this chapter of grief and injustice."

The judge nods solemnly, her expression reflecting the gravity of my request. "Your confession speaks of a depth of remorse and courage. However, the law of Bedlam demands a just and fair sentence, regardless of self-imposed guilt."

The prosecutor, a fae with sharp features and a keen eye, rises to present the case. "Morte's actions, while grave, were committed under the duress of self-defense. Her voluntary confession, decades of service to Bedlam, and the extenuating circumstances must be considered in her sentencing."

As the trial moves forward, every word and testimony lands with impact, bearing on me. I find myself thinking of Wilder, the long separation, the pain of all that went unsaid, and the hope that by accepting my own path, I might free him from chains he never deserved.

The High Judge eventually calls for a recess, a time to deliberate on a sentence that will not only determine my future but also redefine the past we all thought we knew. I stand alone, amidst the hushed whispers and speculative glances, bracing myself for the judgment that will seal my fate and perhaps, in some small way, atone for the lives lost because of me.

In the heart of Bedlam's courthouse, under the weight of centuries-old stone and the watchful eyes of history, I prepare to face whatever verdict awaits me.

IN THE SILENCE of the recess, the courtroom feels like a suspended world, a place where time and fate converge. I stand there, alone yet surrounded, my mind a tumult of memories and emotions. I think of Wilder, of our entwined destinies, and how this moment might finally bring some semblance of justice for the years of pain we've both endured.

The Great Company watches me with a mixture of pride and sorrow. Their eyes tell stories of battles fought together, of victories and losses, and of the unbreakable bond we share as warriors. In their gaze, I find a measure of solace, a reminder that no matter the outcome, we have faced the fires of adversity together.

The High Judge returns, her robes flowing behind her, a symbol of the justice that governs Bedlam. The courtroom falls into a hushed expectancy as she takes her seat, the impending gravity of her decision cloying the air.

"Morte, please rise," she commands, her voice resonant in the stillness.

I stand, my heart pounding in my chest, each beat a death knell. The Great Company rises with me, a silent show of solidarity.

"After careful deliberation, taking into account the nature of your crimes, your years of service to Bedlam, and the unique circumstances surrounding these events, this court has reached a decision," the judge announces, her eyes meeting mine. "Morte, for the crime of manslaughter under duress and the unintentional death of minors, you are hereby sentenced to vita damnationem, to be served in Bedlam Penitentiary."

A collective gasp fills the room, a sound that seems to echo my own shock.

"However," the judge continues, her tone shifting, "this court also recognizes the extraordinary circumstances of your confession and the actions of Wilder in your defense. Therefore, it is also decreed that Wilder shall be released immediately, his sentence for his own murders considered served."

Relief, confusion, and sorrow crash over me like a wave. Wilder is free, his name cleared, at the cost of my own freedom. But what do they mean, his own murders? I glance towards The Great Company. Their faces hold a mix of joy for Wilder and grief for me.

As I'm led away by the guards, a sense of finality settles over me. This is the end of one journey and the beginning of another, a path I must walk alone. Yet, in the depths of my heart, I know that this is not just an end. It's a redemption, a closing of a circle that began two centuries ago.

I have loved this man with all that I am, and I will continue to, even knowing I'll never see him again. I just hope that in some alternate timeline, I'm his, and he is mine. That somewhere, our love matters to some god, and they see fit to give us what we so desperately desire.

The walk to the penitentiary is a blur, the world around me both distant and acutely present. I'm aware of every step, every breath, as if I'm walking through a dream from which I cannot wake.

As the gates of Bedlam Penitentiary open before me, I step through, not as the commander of The Great Company, but as Morte Incendara, a fae seeking atonement. Behind me, the gates close with a finality that echoes in my soul, solemn proof of the price of secrets and the cost of love.

But even as the gates lock shut, a part of me holds onto a glimmer of hope. Hope that in facing my past, I've freed not just Wilder, but also a part of myself. Within these walls, I'll discover a fresh direction and a deeper grasp of the interplay between destiny and decision.

And somewhere, in the heart of Bedlam, Wilder will walk free, the chains of the past finally broken. Our paths may have diverged, but our souls remain forever entwined, bound by a love that transcends time and circumstance.

I step into the cell, a simple space marked by the passage of countless before me. The door closes with a sound that seals my fate more than any verdict could. Here, I stand encased by walls that do not care for the tales they hold. The sparse cot against one wall offers no invitation, and the high window allows just a trace of the sky, a cruel hint of the vastness beyond my reach.

The scent of stone and time fills my nostrils, proof of the years that will pass within these walls. My fingertips graze the cool, rough surface of the wall, tracing the remnants of history etched into its face.

Silence envelops me, not a comforting cloak, but proof of my solitude. This room, with its basic necessities, is both my sanctuary and my cell. The bed, a simple, stone platform meant for rest, stands as my sole companion. I perch at its edge, allowing the flood of memories to wash over me. Laughter, battle cries, the bonds of sisterhood—all now whispers that I strain to hold onto as they slip through my fingers like sand.

And tonight, I imagine I'll face another reckoning: letting my mates know I won't be able to join them.

Outside, the violent crash of the sea's waves against the shore punctuates the quiet, a rhythmic reminder that life persists beyond these barriers. The narrow glimpse of the night sky visible through the window, with stars peeking through the veil of darkness, offers a fragment of continuity with the world I've left behind.

I hope by now, Wilder is free.

Here, in this room stripped of pretenses, I'll meet myself fully. I will sit with the discomfort, the reflections, and the echoes of a life paused. I feel barren without the surge of magic through my veins and hope it won't be too many years before I get daily magic time. Until then, within these walls, I will piece together the fragments of the warrior, the friend, the leader I once was, gathering them like tinder for the rebirth that awaits.

Here, in the solitude of confinement, I will face myself, confront my demons, and perhaps, in the depths of reflection, find a peace that has long eluded me.

For now, this cell is my world, my sanctuary, and my penance. But within its walls, I will hold onto the memories of Wilder, my mates, of The Great Company, and of a life lived fiercely and with wild abandon.

In the stillness, I whisper a vow to myself. I will rise from these ashes, to learn, to grow, and to one day emerge, not just as Morte the Phoenix, but as Morte, the fae who faced her past and found her way back to the light.

CHAPTER THIRTY-FOUR

WILDER

In the depths of Bedlam Penitentiary, time moves in slow ripples, like the ocean currents I once called home. Here, in the dimness of my cell, I've learned the art of patience, the rhythm of solitude. Two centuries in confinement have not quenched the spirit of the merfae within me, but rather honed it, like a pebble smoothed by endless waves.

I pass the days in meditation, my mind drifting through the waters of the past. I remember the sun-drenched surface, the shimmering dance of light on the waves. I recall the thrill of diving deep, my body slicing through the water with the ease of a creature born to the sea. But those days are as distant as the stars above, no longer visible without a window. They moved me to suicide watch after I'd tried to kill myself, and I've been here ever since.

The unchanging rhythm of my prison life is suddenly shattered by the jarring sound of footsteps echoing through the stone corridor. Years have taught me the regular patterns of the guards, and this is an anomaly. Something is amiss. My heart, long accustomed to the slow, steady beat of solitary existence, begins to race.

Two guards appear at my cell, their expressions unreadable, but their eyes betray an unusual sense of urgency. The metallic click of the lock disengaging reverberates through the cell, a sound I've come to associate with routine, not freedom.

"Ripple." The senior guard grunts my last name, a hint of reluctance in his voice. "You're being released. Effective immediately."

Released? The word ricochets through my mind, an impossibility that grates against the reality I've known for two centuries. I rise slowly, muscles stiff from the stillness, my mind reeling.

"Released? Why? How?" My voice emerges rough, laced with disbelief and a rising tide of panic.

The guard shifts uncomfortably, glancing at his colleague before meeting my gaze. "There's been a confession. Your sentence has been revoked."

A confession? A cold shiver runs down my spine. Only one person could have confessed, the only other soul who knows the truth of that fateful night.

"Who confessed?" I demand, my voice hardening. The walls of the cell seem to close in on me, the air thickening. "Tell me!"

"It was the Commander of The Great Company, Morte Incendara." The guard's voice holds a mix of pity and respect. "She's taken full responsibility for the incident. Your release is part of the legal process following her confession."

Morte. Her name, spoken aloud by the guard, is a blade to my heart. Within seconds, I'm pulled back 2,000 years.

∼

2,000 Years Ago

THE COVERT THRILL of the night still simmers within me as I stand in Morte's treehouse, shedding the last of my makeshift camouflage. The leaves and branches that served as my cloak fall away, leaving trails of forest on her floor.

"You could have chosen something less ... leafy," I grumble, even as a grin tugs at the corners of my mouth.

Morte's laughter rings clear, a melody that resonates more sweetly than any song of the sea. "But where would be the fun in that?" Her eyes dance with mischief, reflecting the golden glow of the candles lit around her home.

In the sparse light, the room takes on a hushed sanctity, a private alcove carved out from the world. But I haven't had time to take in the space yet. Instead, I watch Morte, my gaze following the smooth lines of her form, feeling a kinship that goes beyond words.

"Come here," she says, her tone soft, pulling me toward her like the moon pulls the tide.

I move closer, drawn by the gentle command of her voice. The space between us disappears, and we stand in silent acknowledgement, as though we are but two souls cut from the same cloth of night.

Her fingers trace a path down my cheek, leaving a trail of fire in their wake. "Come to bed with me?" she whispers.

And I know what she's asking.

I let her eager grip pull me towards the bed, and I look down to see a small mattress waiting for us. It's quaint and cozy, with crisp white sheets pulled taut over the corners. The pillows are plump and inviting, but all I can imagine is Morte's hair fanned across them as I lose myself in her. Worship her. Give her all of me and take all of her.

A faint scent of lavender lingers in the air, adding to the peaceful atmosphere. This bed was clearly made for just one person.

Fitting ourselves onto the narrow mattress requires a delicate negotiation of space. I curve my body around hers, an imperfect fit of angles and edges. There's a clumsy tangle of limbs, a quiet laugh shared at our predicament.

But in this moment, with her by my side, it's all the space we need. As the night deepens, the simple bed in the corner of the room becomes the center of our universe.

Morte's grin is pressed into the fabric of my shirt, her voice playful as she quips, "It seemed bigger when it was just me." The vibration of her mirth sends a warmth through me that's at odds with the tightness constricting my throat.

Words jostle within, each vying for escape. I yearn to release them into the wild, let them echo across the expanse of treetops, to the very depths of the ocean, so every fae, beast, and creature, big or small, know how I feel.

Yet, when I finally speak, the torrent of my emotions is funneled into a whisper, words tethered by the gravity of what they mean.

"I love you," I confess, the sentiment a fierce whisper, as if saying it louder might fracture the precious bubble of serenity enveloping us in her small treehouse bed.

She stills, her eyes searching mine, and time condenses into this very moment, as though balanced on a needle.

Her voice reverberates through my very soul. "And I love you," she breathes out, her words stitching themselves into the very fabric of my being, each word a delicate brushstroke painting a future I dare to hope for.

She doesn't know it, but those three little words are a vow, to love and protect her.

"She's lying!" I grab the guard by his shoulder, desperation seeping through my voice. "She's protecting me. You have to keep me here. I won't let her take the blame for what I did."

He flinches at my touch, but his expression remains resolute. "The confession is valid. Your little girlfriend had her trial. You're a free man." He grabs my hands, using a device to unlock the magic suppressant manacles around my wrist.

As the magic suppressant manacles release their hold, a sensation long forgotten surges within me. An overwhelming tide of energy, returning with the force of a long-withheld storm breaking free. My magic, dormant for the most part of two centuries aside from a few hours a week, awakens with a vigor that courses through my veins like a wild, untamed river.

The sensation is exhilarating, a flood of power and freedom that fills every fiber of my being. It's like feeling the sun's warmth after an endless night. The pulse of the ocean, a rhythmic, enduring presence, reverberates through me, rekindling a connection to the sea that had been muted and distant.

Yet, this resurgence carries with it a poignant reminder of its cost. The vitality of my magic is now inextricably linked with Morte's sacrifice. I was happy to take the blame so she could be free, even if it meant we couldn't be together.

As the energy flows, it does more than revive my connection to the ocean; it awakens a flood of memories and emotions. The sea's call, once a source of unending joy, now murmurs with the truth of Morte's confession, a revelation that reshapes the echoes of my past. The tides speak not just of freedom, but of the heavy price of love and devotion.

"Can I see her?" I turn around, grief coating every word. "I need to see her."

The guard just shakes his head. "I'm to escort you to the gates at once."

"No, this can't be happening," I murmur, my voice a hoarse whisper. The realization that Morte is now facing the consequences I've endured for centuries is a torment far greater than any physical confinement.

"I need a moment," I manage to say, my mind racing. The notion of leaving this cell, which has been both a prison and a refuge, suddenly feels daunting, overwhelming. I glance around the sparse room that has been my world, the stone walls, the simple cot, the small pond that offered a sliver of the sea, an ocean I'm now free to see, but at what cost?

The guards nod, stepping back. I can see the unease in their eyes, the discomfort at being the bearers of such news. They understand the shift in the tides of my fate.

I gather the few possessions I have—a tattered book of merfae lore, the shell necklace left behind when Morte died, her letter, a small stone carved with the image of the sea, a piece of cloth imbued with the scent of salt and freedom. Each item is a fragment of the life I left behind, of the days spent dreaming of the ocean's embrace.

With each step towards the exit, my heart grows heavier. The light of the outside world beckons, but it's a bitter freedom, tainted by the knowledge of Morte's imprisonment. How can I embrace this liberty knowing she is now bound by the chains I've just shed?

As I emerge from the bowels of the prison, the brightness of the day is blinding. I pause, taking a deep breath of the fresh, open air, yet it offers no solace. My mind is consumed with thoughts of Morte, her selfless act a mirror of the love that has bound us across time and circumstance.

Freedom; a word that once held the promise of life renewed now echoes with the hollow ring of sacrifice and loss. I step into the world, a free merfae, but my spirit remains ensnared in a prison of guilt and concern. Wherever this path leads, it's one I must walk with the weight of a love both liberating and confining, as deep and fathomless as the sea itself.

CHAPTER THIRTY-FIVE

MORTE

The concept of time blurs into an unending loop of silence and shadows. My cell, an undecorated enclosure of cold stone and iron, offers little in the way of comfort or distraction. The only variation in my monotonous existence is the narrow beam of sunlight that creeps across the floor, marking the slow passage of the days.

My connection to the outside world is limited to the occasional clatter of a tray slid under the door, bearing meals as tasteless as the grey walls that surround me. I eat because I must, not because I want to. The food is a dull reminder of the vibrant life I once led, now reduced to a memory.

The isolation weighs heavily on me. As a phoenix fae, confinement is antithetical to my very nature. I crave the sky, the feel of the wind beneath my wings, the exhilaration of flight. Here, in this cell, I am grounded, caged, my essence dimmed. I pace the small space like a caged animal, my footsteps echoing against the walls.

Exercise is my only respite from the creeping despair. I engage in rigorous physical training, using the limited space to its fullest. Push-ups, sit-ups, and stretches become my routine, a desperate attempt to maintain my physical strength. Each movement is a small act of defiance, a refusal to let the prison break me.

But it's the absence of magic that gnaws at me the most. Once a week, for a mere hour, I'm allowed to access my powers. Over the years, I'll earn more time. It's a cruel tease, a fleeting taste of freedom that only serves to underscore my captivity. During these brief moments, I unleash my magic, letting it surge through me, a torrent of pent-up energy and frustration. I transform into my phoenix form, feeling the rush of fire coursing through my veins, a brief reminder of who I am, of the power I wield.

Yet, as quickly as it comes, it's taken away, leaving me feeling more confined than ever. The rest of the time, I'm left with only my thoughts for company, a dangerous thing. Memories of my squadron, of missions and camaraderie, fill my mind, each recollection a sharp stab of longing.

In the solitude of my cell, I'm forced to confront the ghosts of my past. The weight of my secret, the one I carried for centuries, now feels like a chain around my neck. I replay the events over and over in my mind, wondering if there was another way, a path I could have taken that wouldn't have led me here.

At night, the darkness of the cell is all-encompassing. I lie on the hard mattress, staring into the void, my mind a whirlwind of regret and sorrow. Sleep, when it comes, is fitful and haunted. Dreams of flying free, of feeling the sun on my wings, are cruel reminders of what I've lost.

Lately, I haven't seen my mates when I close my eyes, not since I've been incarcerated. Perhaps they've already grown tired of me, or maybe I scared them off when I pulled away from the dream.

And yet, in these moments of despair, a flicker of hope remains. The knowledge that my sacrifice has freed Wilder, that he no longer bears the burden of my actions, offers a small measure of solace. It's this thought that I cling to in the darkest hours, a fluoresce in the endless night of my confinement.

Despite everything, a part of me refuses to give in to despair. I am

Morte Incendara, a warrior, a phoenix fae. This prison may hold my body, but it cannot quench the fire that burns within my soul. In the depths of the night, I cling to this thought, this flickering flame.

CHAPTER THIRTY-SIX

WILDER

The water around me is a serene shade of blue, shimmering with the sunlight that filters through the surface. Submerged in the depths near Convectus, I propel myself through the water, my merfae form gliding effortlessly through its element. Schools of colorful fish dart past me, their scales reflecting the light in a rainbow of hues. Ahead of me, I see the familiar shape of my parents' home, nestled among the swaying sea kelp.

I can taste the saltiness of the water on my lips as I swim, each droplet echoing the essence of my origins. There's a gentle pull from the ocean's current.

As I dive deeper, the water turns from crystal clear to a dark, murky blue.

In the ocean's cool embrace, I draw nearer to my destination, long-awaited. Two hundred years-time since my last swim in these waters, and since then my parents' faces have been just memories. As I Approach their home, a teal coral cave teeming with life beneath the waves, recollections flood my consciousness, each a vivid echo of the past.

I mentally prepare myself for the emotions that will surely come with our reunion. Joy, relief, sadness, and guilt all churn within me like a complex whirlpool, threatening to pull me under.

In all likelihood, my parents will be equally devastated and angry with me once I tell them what I did. But I'd do it all over again. For two thousand years, I've been obsessed with Morte.

The dark shadows of the cave give way to a burst of light as my parents emerge from its depths. Their powerful merfae bodies command attention, exuding an air of regality and strength. My mother is the first to reach me with open arms and a desperate yearning for reunion in her expression. Her piercing oceanic eyes search mine as we meet in a flurry of bubbles.

But it's my father's intense gaze that cuts through the water like a sharp knife. Years of suppressed worry and questions are etched on his face, demanding answers. Our merfae forms intertwine in a confluence of relief and sorrow as we cling to each other, communicating our emotions through the currents of the ocean.

Our reunion radiates with joy, every moment brimming with love and a feeling of belonging, though one of us is missing.

I miss her so fucking much.

Beneath the surface of this familial warmth, I carry a deep secret about Morte, a revelation that will inevitably cast a shadow over our happiness. I savor the comfort of being with my family, but the truth of what I must share looms over me.

In the secluded cavity beneath the sea, where the pulsating rhythm of the ocean gives way to an enveloping calm, we return to our fae forms. The transformation unfolds amidst the tranquil sway of aquatic flora, setting a scene of otherworldly serenity.

As I gather my thoughts, preparing to unburden my heart, my father places a reassuring hand on my shoulder. "Morte has already been here," he utters, his tone tinged with sorrow. "She told us everything." The words, laden with years of pain and sacrifice, hang in the water around us.

Shock ripples through me like waves crashing against a rocky shore. "She did?" I whisper, too grieved to speak louder.

Mom's delicate hand rests against her mouth, tears mixing with the salty sea spray as she nods. "We must do something," Mom says, grief lining her features. "She's our daughter in all but blood. We can't leave her to this fate."

Dad paces, his strategic mind already turning. "She didn't know they were children. If I'd known the truth of what happened that day ... Gods. Two hundred years, Wilder." He pauses, turning to face me. "I might've been able to get you out. But now that we know this, it changes everything."

Our reunion turns into a war council, discussing potential allies, legal loopholes, and even daring plans of rescue. Whatever it takes, I'll get her out of there. She saved the lives of thousands, and didn't know the fae she'd slain were children. It shouldn't have been vita damnationem. It was self-defense.

CHAPTER THIRTY-SEVEN

AZAZEL

The Underworld's oppressive gloom feels heavier tonight, a shadowed weight that presses against my chest with every breath. We gather, the four of us, in the cavernous hall that has witnessed countless strategies and battles. But this meeting is unlike any before.

Aggonid, the embodiment of darkness and power, looms over us all, a figure of brooding intensity. He wants to rip a portal open and snatch Morte back from Bedlam, but we've convinced him it's best if she doesn't hate us when she gets here, which she would if we took her from Wilder again.

"We must convince her to take her memories back," Emeric growls, his voice echoing off the arched ceiling. "Tell her we'll do everything we can to bring Wilder here."

Caius pivots away from the window, his gaze radiating a predatory gleam. "I should be the one to do it. I had no trouble charming her before, and it'll be just as effortless this time. I'm easy to love." He grins. "I really don't mind sharing."

I clench my fists at my sides, because I *do* mind. Would things have been different if I were honest at the beginning? Could she be mine now, just the two of us? "We're wasting time with this bickering," I snarl, though I know my vitriol shouldn't be directed at them. "Morte is out there, alone and without memories of us. We need to act, not stand here debating like predatory assholes, eager to get our dicks wet." I step forward, feeling the heat of their gazes upon me. "I'll go," I declare, my voice steady, trying to make them see reason. "My connection with her may not be as deep as yours, Aggonid, or as complex as yours, Caius. But it's strong. And maybe, just maybe, that's what she needs right now. She knows she loves me, because she can feel it."

Emeric nods, a grudging respect in his eyes. "Az has a point. They had a really strong connection before the mating bond, and her mind is a patchwork now. She has one goal; the same one it's always been: free Wilder. If we solve that problem, she's ours."

Aggonid's glare is a physical force, but he gives a curt nod. "Fine. But if there's any sign of trouble, if she's in any distress, you pull back. We can't risk further damage."

The four of us make our way to the highest point of the castle and arrange the conduit how we need it. Aggonid works to drum up a storm and the atmosphere crackles with electricity, charged by the potent combination of our shared magic as we embark on the elaborate task of crafting the dreamscape again. Thunder rattles the windows as lightning arcs across the sky. Our movements are precise, intricate, like skilled weavers working in tandem to create a patchwork of thought and power.

As the dreamscape takes shape, a reflection of Castanea's fertile beauty and serene ambiance, I prepare for what I'll say to her. I step into the swirling vortex of light and shadow, the doorway to Morte's subconscious. The last thing I see is the hopeful faces of my newfound allies, their silent nod of approval and hesitant hope, because failure isn't an option.

The world shifts, reality blurs, and I find myself in the center of the dreamscape. We've crafted it with a gentle brook murmuring beside a path lined with silver-barked trees, hanging stalagmites, and luminescent plant life that pulses with each step I take.

And as I venture deeper, calling softly for Morte, the only sound is the whisper of phantom winds through ethereal trees and the gentle bubbling of the brook beside me. The dreamscape is a realm of beauty and shadows, and I am its solitary wanderer, seeking the lost heart of our story.

The forest unfolds around me, its trees bathed in twilight.

As I trudge ahead, my boots sinking into the soft mud of the stream bank, a figure emerges from the shadows. Morte stands motionless, her slender frame outlined by the glimmering water behind her. As I draw near, she slowly turns to face me, and a sad smile adorns her face at seeing me.

"Hi," she whispers as she allows me to pull her into my arms.

Her body sinks into mine, and she nestles there perfectly, her head resting against my chest as I flare my wings, further cocooning us.

A small gasp escapes her lips as she looks up, seeing the serrated edges of each feather, their edges tipped in white. "They're beautiful." She reaches between us to stroke them.

A full-body shudder runs through me, a thrill racing through my body with her touch.

"Fuck," I breathe as she snatches her hand back, muttering an apology. "Don't do that unless you want to either give me a heart attack or want me to bury myself so deep in you that you forget everyone else's name but mine."

She opens her mouth to say something, but she seems lost for words, so I fill her in.

"Stroke my fangs or my wings, and you're propositioning me, firefly." My words come out husky, and her pupils blow wide at my insinuation. "Unless that's what you were looking to achieve, then by all means, continue." I grin down at her.

The scent of her arousal perfumes the air, and it takes everything in me to hold her to me, rather than lower her to the ground and take her like I want to.

I release her, allowing her some space. It'd be so easy to get lost in her, but that's not why I'm here.

She lowers herself to sit on a boulder at the edge of the stream and sticks her bare feet in it, letting the water sluice around her ankles.

I study her intently. Her piercing eyes mirror the pale glow of the moon above us, searching for any signs of discomfort before taking a seat next to her. Tension eases off my shoulders when I see that she doesn't even flinch as I join her.

"My wings don't do that," she starts, breaking the silence. "At least I don't think so."

"It does if your mate does it," I say cautiously, not wanting to overwhelm her, but I can't fight the temptation. "Unfurl yours so I can show you." I grin.

Morte's hand inches closer to mine, a tentative bridge across the gap of forgotten memories. "Maybe another time," she sighs, melancholy strong in her voice. Something is bothering her, but before I can ask her what it is, she speaks again. "I want to remember," she whispers. "I feel like we had something special, and I want to know you."

"You do?" Shock ripples through me.

Her fingers brush against mine, a featherlight touch that sends waves through the dreamscape. I want to prepare her for what she'll see, because not all of it's pretty.

"Let's start at the beginning then," I suggest, offering a smile. "Let me tell you about the Underworld, about how I saved your life the first night we met."

"You did?" she gasps. "How?"

I chuckle, shaking my head. "You ate poisonous berries." I take her hand in mine, and she lets me. "And I helped stave off the worst of it."

"Wow," she whispers. "And this was in the Underworld? I figured everyone there would be ruthless, looking to hurt others. But you saved me?"

As I nod, her hand lingering in mine, I start weaving our story, a tale of realms beyond, of a love that defied the odds. With each word, I hope to reignite the spark of memory, to bring back the Morte who knew me, who knew us. Maybe the power of our love can help her remember, all without my having to give them back physically.

The stream's gentle murmur accompanies my words as I recount our past, a narrative punctuated by Morte's focused gaze and occasional nods. Her hand remains in mine, a physical link to the hope that kindles inside me, that maybe things aren't as bleak as they seem. That maybe, maybe she'll come back to us.

"My memories," she muses after a while, her voice tinged with a mix of curiosity and skepticism. "You say they're stored somewhere?"

"Yes," I confirm. "But it's not as simple as retrieving a lost item. They're delicate, intertwined with your very essence. We can return them to you, right within the dreamscape."

Her brow furrows. "How is it even possible that you can communicate with me while I'm in Bedlam? You guys are dead, right?" Her last word comes out barely a wisp of a sound, as though the idea pains her.

I take a deep breath. "Our souls are still here. Aggonid keeps them when we die. It's what he uses for the favors he grants, which is why the winner of the hunt always gets a favor for killing other participants. He'd have no favors without it."

She seems to ponder this, her eyes reflecting the flickering gemstones in the cavern above. "Is it dangerous to give them back?"

"It is. But you're the strongest person I know." I pause, watching the play of emotions across her face. "I can't promise it'll be easy, or that everything will make sense immediately. But I can promise you're not alone in this. I'm here, and so are the others."

"The others," she echoes softly, a hint of a frown creasing her features. "They didn't want to see me?" Her big eyes meet mine, and I swear I see a reflection of pain, or rejection in them.

"Hey." I turn to face her fully. "They do. We have the strongest emotional connection, so that's why I got to come in while they keep the dreamscape open. Emeric has been working day and night in the castle, looking through every book he can get his hands on to find a way to do this safely, so you aren't hurt."

Her hand squeezes mine, a sign of growing trust or perhaps a need for reassurance. "And you believe that together, you can restore what I've lost?"

"I do," I assert with conviction. "We have them in a chest, hidden safely from prying eyes."

Her eyes study the water, a thousand questions behind them. "It's strange," she says quietly. "I feel a connection, a pull towards you, but it's like grasping at smoke. It's there, but elusive."

"That's a start," I reply, heartened by her admission. "The heart remembers what the mind has forgotten. We just need to give it time. And as soon as we're one-hundred percent positive we won't harm you by giving your memories back, we'll do it."

"Do you love me?" Her question is guarded, unsure, as though she's afraid I'll take it all away.

As she looks at me, uncertainty in her gaze, I hold her face gently. "Even if the stars forgot to shine and the universe fell into silence, my soul would recognize yours. My love for you transcends lifetimes and realms. You may have forgotten, but I'm here to remind you of that love, to guide you back home to us. However long it takes, Morte. I'll never give up on you."

Tears well in her eyes, spilling down her cheeks as I use my thumbs to brush them away. "I want to believe you, to remember this ... this connection we have." She considers her words, and I see the moment she pulls back. "But I don't understand how it's possible, Az. I'm in love with someone else."

I nod, murmuring, "I know, baby." I give her a sad smile. "You told me all about Wilder. We didn't replace him. Could never replace him. He will always hold a special place in your heart. But love can be a multifaceted thing. It's possible to love more than one person, to have different forms of love for different people, or to have the same love for multiple people. I know this, because you do. Love isn't a finite resource. It expands and adapts, allowing us to forge connections with more than one person."

"I told you about Wilder?" she whispers, blinking away her tears.

"Late one night you told me all about him, how you two couldn't be together, but he took the fall for the accident on the beach—"

"It wasn't an accident. I murdered those children." Her eyes squeeze shut, face crumpling with tears as though she's in physical agony.

"Did you know they were children?"

"No, but—"

I can see the torment in her eyes, the weight of guilt and regret she carries. My heart aches for her, for the burden she has shouldered alone all this time. Leaning closer, I lift her chin gently, forcing her to meet my gaze.

"Morte," I say softly. "You didn't murder those children. It was a tragic accident, driven by self-defense and the instinct to protect your own kind. You were backed into a corner, forced to make a split-second decision."

Her tears continue to flow, but there's a glimmer of hope amidst the pain. "But I killed them," she whispers brokenly.

"Yes," I acknowledge quietly as I pull her into my arms. "And it's something you will carry with you forever, but you don't need to do it alone. You have mates who will be here to remind you of who you are, especially when you've forgotten. You are not defined by your mistakes. You are defined by how you choose to move forward from them."

She shakes her head against my chest, her voice muffled by her tears. "But I still took their lives. How can I live with that?"

I stroke her hair soothingly, trying to find the right words to offer comfort in this moment of anguish. "We all have darkness within us. We've all done things we regret, things that haunt us. Let me carry this for you, you've had it by yourself long enough."

She clings to me, her tears soaking into my shirt as she tries to steady her breathing. "I don't know how to live with this guilt," she whispers brokenly.

As the dreamscape quivers, its edges fraying like torn fabric, Morte's expression shifts to one of alarm. The serene landscape around us wobbles, the gems in the sky blinking erratically.

"We're losing this place," I say, urgency sharpening my voice. "The connection is weakening."

Panic flickers in her eyes. "What's happening? Why does it keep falling apart?"

"It's difficult to maintain," I explain hurriedly. "We're stretching our powers to their limits to reach you."

She looks around, witnessing the disintegration of the world we've built. "Can't you fix it? Make it stable?"

I shake my head, regret etching into my features. "It's not easy to conjure storms to hold this open. Aggonid is doing it by himself while the others harness the power using the conduit. We're not strong enough to hold it much longer, not like this. While we have the best emotional connection, I'm powerful, so without my help, it's weaker."

Understanding dawns on her face, a mix of disappointment and grief. "Then what do we do?"

"Remember what I said," I urge her, as the ground beneath us starts to dissolve into nothingness. "We have your memories. They're safe, but we need to find a way to bring them to you safely."

Her hand grips mine tighter, a lifeline in the chaos. "How? How will you do that?"

"I don't know yet," I admit, the honesty heavy on my tongue. "But we'll find a way. I promise you, we won't stop until you remember, until you're whole again."

The dreamscape shudders violently, a final tremor before it begins to fade away. Her image blurs, becoming translucent.

"Az," she says, my name a whisper on her lips. "Please don't leave me."

But the force pulling me back is relentless. "I'll come back for you, Morte. Hold on to that."

The world around us collapses completely, disintegrating into the void. The last thing I see is her eyes, wide with fear and grief, before I'm thrust back into the darkness of the Underworld.

The air sucks from my lungs as I crash to my knees, the grief in my chest a hollow, devouring feeling.

In the cold, echoing silence, I clench my fists. This isn't the end. I'll rally Emeric, Aggonid, and Caius. We'll rebuild the dreamscape, stronger this time. We'll return to her, over and over, until we bridge this chasm that separates us. Our bond, our shared history, it's not lost. Just hidden. And I will do everything in my power to reclaim it, for her, for us.

As the last tendrils of the dreamscape dissolve, the harsh reality of the Underworld closes in around me. The scent of brimstone and ash fills my nostrils.

Emeric, Aggonid, and Caius are still here, their postures tense.

"She's agreed," I report, my voice barely more than a growl. "Before I even said anything. Something has changed, but she didn't say what. Just that she wants her memories."

Emeric steps closer, his face etched with lines of concern. "That's good news, though, isn't it?"

"I suppose," I shake my head, feeling a surge of frustration. "But she agreed too easily. I think maybe she's feeling our absence just as bad as we feel hers. She seems depressed."

Aggonid paces, his steps echoing through the hall. "Emeric, you can have whatever resources you need. If you need reapers to fetch something from any realm, near or far, whatever it takes. You've got it. We need this now."

"Give me an hour and I'll let you know what I need to test this on." He slips out the door.

"She cried." I card my hand through my long, dark hair. "He's definitely the reason she didn't want her memories back initially, though I don't know what's changed."

Caius grumbles, "It's always about that fucking fish."

His words hang in the air, a challenge we're all too aware of. I sigh.

I lean against one of the pillars, feeling the cool stone against my back. "Her mind is so fragile right now, and not just because her memories are missing. The ache in her chest she's feeling isn't because of Wilder's rejection of what they have, but at our absence, so everything feels like brittle glass. Any reckless move could fracture what little trust she's shown. We can't forget the impact this is having on her, mentally and emotionally. Things weren't always great for her here, either. It'll be a lot for her to process."

The room falls silent, each of us lost in our thoughts, the burden of our quest weighing heavily. Surrendering to a life without her isn't an option.

Aggonid finally breaks the silence. "Let's reconvene after some rest and careful thought. I'll let you know when Emeric comes back.

You're welcome to take any of the guest rooms," he offers me, and I give him a nod.

A bath will do me some good. I can't remember the last time I had one, because every waking hour is spent researching and strategizing.

Our group disperses, each member absorbed in their own thoughts and concerns. I remain, staring into the flickering shadows, Morte's face from the dreamscape haunting my thoughts. Her grief is the size of an ocean. I don't like her tears, not because they hurt me, but because they hurt her. I do like the way she allowed me to hold her while she fell apart, though.

As long as she'll let me, I will.

I won't rest until I see the light of recognition in her eyes, until her smile dispels the shadows that have grown around my heart.

I fucking vow it.

CHAPTER THIRTY-EIGHT

MORTE

The sharp clank of heavy, iron doors reverberates through the metal corridor, like a warning bell tolling for my impending encounter with the other inmates at Bedlam Penitentiary. My heart thuds against my ribcage, not out of fear, but a deep-rooted instinct honed over years as a warrior. Each step I take is calculated and deliberate, concealing the unrest brewing beneath my stoic exterior. The cold, damp air smells of mildew and despair, as though the very walls have absorbed our grief, leaching us of all we are.

I'm escorted into a common area, an open space surrounded by towering walls. The only source of natural light is the mesh of iron that allows thin slices of daylight to pierce through. The atmosphere is dense and thick, carrying with it a mix of scents–the pungent tang of sweat, the sharp bite of metal, and something primal and untamed that cannot be named. It's an assault on my senses, a jarring contrast to the loneliness and solitude of my cell.

I don't know how long it's been since I've been outside my cell. I've been too lost in my head.

The inmates here are a motley crew, each bearing the marks of their transgressions and their time in this place. All genders, orders, and walks of life converge here, with one thing in common: we're all monsters.

There are those with eyes too sharp, gazes calculating; others wear their brutality openly, muscles coiled like springs, ready to unleash violence at the slightest provocation. Then there are the quiet ones, their danger hidden behind placid masks, perhaps the most perilous of all.

As I step into their midst, conversations falter. Eyes turn toward me, assessing, weighing. I am an unknown, a new element in their confined world, and like predators sensing a new prey, they watch with keen interest.

I keep my posture relaxed yet alert, a delicate balance of non-threatening and not-to-be-trifled-with. My time as a commander taught me well—show no weakness but incite no unnecessary battles.

A tall, burly figure approaches me, her movements betraying a feral grace. Scars adorn her face like badges of honor, her eyes a deep shade of amber that seem to glow with an inner fire. They don't usually heal injuries here unless they're severe, which allows time for scars to set in.

"You're the phoenix commander," she says, her voice a low rumble, deeper than I expected. "Heard you let some lovesick fool take the fall for some high-profile crime you committed."

Ignoring the way my heart splinters at the mention of it, I keep a bored, unemotional expression on my face.

Her tone is curious, probing.

I meet her gaze squarely. "I'm here to serve my sentence, same as anyone else."

She studies me for a moment longer, then nods, a gesture of what seems like respect. "Name's Kiera. Watch your back in here, especially as there's a huge target on it. You didn't hear it from me."

As she walks away, a sense of foreboding settles in my stomach. Kiera's warning, though cryptic, rings with sincerity. In this place, danger lurks in every shadow, behind every seemingly benign smile.

I find a small alcove against the rough, stone wall, my back pressed firmly against it. It offers me protection and a clear view of the outdoor courtyard, where the inmates gather like animals in a cage. I observe their interactions with detached interest—alliances whispered in hushed tones, power dynamics playing out in silent exchanges.

I knew going in here it'd be a possibility that others would wish to enact revenge upon me due to my station and my part to play in putting so many others in here.

But nothing can hurt me any more than I've hurt myself by walking away from my mates who only want to love me.

The inmates can kill me, but I'll just come back, as long as Wilder is alive. I'll regenerate.

In one corner, a group of prisoners gather, their laughter ringing too loud, their movements too animated. But there's an underlying tension to their mirth, a hint of madness or perhaps desperation. Across the courtyard, another inmate sits alone on a bench, her eyes fixed on a distant point as if lost in a world far removed from the grim reality of Bedlam Penitentiary. Her stillness is haunting amidst the chaos and noise surrounding her.

The heaviness of my isolation weighs on me, a constant reminder of what I no longer have and what I gave up. But I push those thoughts aside, concentrating on the present moment. This is my truth, a result of my choices, and the consequences that have shaped my entire life. I look forward to sleep, where I find a pocket of peace, where I'm transported to a version of Castanea in my dreams. Maybe my mates will have found a way to give me back my memories.

As the hour passes, the tension intensifies, as whispers reach ears about who I am. Every moment is a test, every interaction a potential challenge.

But as daunting as it is, there's a part of me that thrives in this environment. The warrior within me is alert, alive, ready to face whatever this prison throws my way. In the heart of darkness, I find a flicker of the fire that has always driven me. The will to survive, to adapt, and ultimately, to find redemption.

I welcome the pain they'll throw my way. It's the least I deserve.

When the bell sounds for us to disperse, its metallic chime reverberates through the common area, signaling an end to this period of wary observation and tense interactions. The inmates begin to move, a slow, reluctant shuffle towards various exits, each disappearing back into their own corners of this grim existence.

I linger for a moment, taking a final survey of the yard. It's a chessboard of motives and hidden agendas, and I'm still learning the rules. As I turn to leave, a shadow detaches itself from the corner of the yard and moves towards me with a predatory grace.

The figure is tall and slender, cloaked in an aura of danger, as though he still has his magic and the giant cuffs around his wrists do little to quell it. His eyes, a piercing silver, lock onto mine with an intensity that's unsettling. His hair is cropped short to his head and he sports mating tattoos up and down his bare arms. He moves with a confidence that speaks of someone well-acquainted with power, and possibly, cruelty.

"Morte Incendara," he says, his voice silky and cold. "The phoenix who fell from grace. Best tread carefully, there are those who haven't forgotten they ended up here because of you."

His words carry an unspoken threat, a challenge that sets my nerves on edge.

I straighten, meeting his gaze without flinching. "Hazards of the job," I mutter.

He smiles, but there's no warmth in it. It's the smile of a predator sizing up its prey. "Let's just say, your reputation precedes you. And here, reputations are all we have. You'll find that the prison has its own kind of hierarchy, and you, birdie, are an interesting addition."

His cryptic words do little to ease the knot of tension in my gut. I'm no stranger to navigating dangerous waters, but this is a different kind of battlefield. One where the rules are obscure, and alliances are as fickle as the wind.

"I'm not here to play games," I reply, keeping my voice even. "I'm just serving my time."

He steps closer, his presence invasive. "Everyone serves their time, Incendara. But how they serve it ... that's where the game lies." He circles me, a shark assessing its prey. "You'd do well to remember that."

I just level him with a blank stare. If he thinks to scare me, it won't work. I've lost everything I've ever cared about.

I enter my cell, the door closing with a definitive clang as the magical bolt slides into place. Here, in this small, cold space, I'm left alone with my thoughts, my regrets, and the haunting memories of what I've lost.

But even in the depths of despair, a part of me refuses to surrender. I am Morte Incendara, a phoenix fae, and though I've fallen, I've risen from the ashes before. And I will rise again. In the solitude of my cell, I make a silent vow. I will endure. I will survive.

And somehow, I'll find redemption.

CHAPTER THIRTY-NINE

WILDER

I push my feet forward, their soles burning against the desolate ground of The Wastelands, as if I'm walking through embers. The sun pierces my skin like a thousand needles, and its fiery breath envelopes me from every angle. At night, the cold creeps in like an icy fog, sapping away any remaining warmth from my body. Yet, none of this deters me; my mission is ironclad, driven by a purpose that transcends physical discomfort.

I've got to speak to Morte's closest friend in Castanea. I've heard she's taken over as commander, and I believe with her help, I might be able to see my Little Bird.

I trudge through the barren wasteland, guided by the vivid and painful memories of Morte. We used to walk this desert together, more times than I can count. I can almost feel her vibrant spirit beside me, a bright light in this desert of death. But now her presence is but a ghostly echo in my mind, a void that swallows my every step and holds me in its icy grip.

After days, I finally reach my destination. A hidden pond serves as a gateway to Castanea, so I plunge into its depths without hesitation. The transition is swift, a rush of water enveloping me, transporting me from the barren surface to the hidden world below.

The shift is jarring. From the dry, scorching surface to the humid, cool underbelly of the earth. The air here teems with life, an echo of sounds and scents that invigorates my senses, and I haven't even made my way through the labyrinthian tunnels leading out of this cavern and into the living spaces. Here, water trickles from unseen sources and pools together in small ponds deep enough to swim in. It feels like I've stepped into another dimension entirely, an untouched paradise buried beneath desolation.

Pausing at the edge of a clear pool, I catch my reflection. It's just me now, without her by my side. The water's surface ripples with my touch, distorting the image.

Gods, it's been centuries since I've been here.

I tread familiar paths, pathways once walked in secrecy and laughter with Morte. The silence now is a grim token of her absence, each turn a memory of times past. Where laughter and conversation once filled these spaces, there's now just the sound of my own movements. The air, normally fragrant with earth and growth, seems dull without her presence.

As I walk, the cool dampness of the underground is a comfort against the heat of emotion rising within me. I'm haunted by memories, each one sharp and clear like the crystals embedded in the cave walls. They are beautiful, precious, but just out of reach.

"Shhh, we have to be quiet," Morte whispers. "They're doing rounds at the other end of this tunnel, but they'll come running if they hear us."

My arms bracket her head where she's pressed against the cave wall. "I can sense if anyone is coming. They're patrolling far from here," I say against her ear. We've learned how to do cloaking spells, so I don't have to wear a disguise anymore, but that won't stop someone from investigating a noise. "The scent of your arousal makes it very difficult for me to concentrate on keeping this cloak up."

She gives me a wicked grin as goosebumps line her skin. "Then keep your hands to yourself."

"I tried. I can't," I groan. "Come on, let's hurry back."

Grief stirs inside me at the memory. The paths are empty, the vibrant life of this place muted by the void she left. I can almost hear the echo of her footsteps beside mine, a ghost rhythm syncing with my own. It's a silent duet we perform; her absence the most profound note in our song. It's a quiet that's too loud, a stillness that's too active.

I was too caught in my mind to notice the disturbance in the air. Rounding a bend, I'm suddenly confronted by a blond Tolden in a silver guard's uniform. His posture is alert, his green eyes quickly assessing me as a potential intruder in their sanctuary.

"State your business," he commands, his baritone cautious yet firm as he keeps a hand on his sword at his waist.

"I'm here to see Noct Fuego. Morte Incendra's friend?" I reply, my voice steady. "My name is Wilder Ripple."

Recognition flickers in his eyes, and his stance relaxes slightly. "You're the one she ... the one who confessed to her crime."

"Yes," I acknowledge.

He sighs, understanding softening his features. "Why did you do it?"

I meet his eyes, squaring my shoulders. "Because for over two thousand years, I've been in love with her, and I'd do it all over again."

His hand drops from his sword, his posture resigned as he turns around. "Follow me. I'll guide you to Morte's treehouse where you can wait for Noct."

I don't tell him I already know the way.

He speaks into a communications device before gesturing for me to follow him. We move silently through the multileveled tunnels, each twist and turn a step deeper into the heart of this hidden world.

"Here we are," the guard announces, pausing at the entrance of the treehouse. His gaze lingers on the structure before he turns to me. "You can go inside. I'll wait here."

The old door groans as I pull on it, swinging open to reveal a world that's unmistakably Morte's. The carved wood of the banister welcomes my touch, and the dusty books resting pristinely on their shelves whisper tales of her life, a life I've been absent from for far too long.

I drift through the rooms, fingers trailing across surfaces, lingering on objects that feel particularly intimate. Photographs, small pieces of jewelry, and handwritten notes—they all seem to pulse with her energy. It's as if her spirit lingers here, a ghostly presence that fills the air with quiet whispers of the past.

Suddenly, the peaceful reverie is broken by a rush of movement at the door. A woman with maroon hair cascading wildly around her face bursts in, her silver eyes shimmering with unshed tears. She lunges forward, wrapping her arms around me in a tight embrace as she almost knocks me off-center, but thanks to my merfae order, I have a strong core to keep me upright.

"Wilder," she murmurs, her voice thick with emotion. Pulling back, she clasps my shoulders, her gaze intense. "I wish she hadn't kept you hidden from us. We would've found a way to make sure you two didn't have to hide your friendship."

Her sudden familiarity catches me off guard. "Are you Noct?"

She steps back, a laugh escaping her lips. "Sorry." Extending her hand, she introduces herself. "Noct Fuego, Morte's best friend."

"Noct," I echo, a bittersweet smile touching my lips as I shake her hand. "She spoke of you often. Thank you for being there for her, especially when I couldn't."

Her expression softens with sympathy, a shared understanding of our mutual loss evident in her eyes. "I'm just glad you're here now," she says, peeking outside to address the guard. "I've got it from here."

His gaze flicks between us, his protective instincts palpable as he considers it before he turns and continues down the footbridge.

"Sorry." She closes the door and props herself against it.

Noct's demeanor shifts as she turns serious, gesturing around the room. "Morte left instructions for her belongings. The treehouse is yours, if you'll have it."

The news hits me like a wave, overwhelming and poignant. "She left this for me?" My voice breaks slightly, choked with emotion. The treehouse, our haven of dreams and shared moments, now a legacy of her love.

"She thought you might need a direct path to the water," Noct explains, moving to a panel on the wall. With a graceful wave of her hand, a hidden compartment in the floor slides open, revealing a slide leading down. "She built this for you, a swift route to the stream."

The sight of the slide, proof of Morte's thoughtfulness, stirs a tumult of emotions within me. "Thank you," I whisper, my voice thick with gratitude and sorrow.

Noct's eyes meet mine, empathy radiating from them. "She loves you deeply, Wilder. You know that, right?"

Running a hand through my hair, I struggle to maintain composure. "I know," I reply, my words barely above a whisper. "And I need your help."

"Anything. Tell me what you need."

Her willingness to assist brings a small measure of relief. "I need to visit her at the prison."

A frown creases her brow. "Visitors aren't allowed. Only mates can have visits."

I nod, understanding her confusion. "I'm aware."

"But merfae ... they only mate with their anchors."

A heavy sigh escapes me as I meet her questioning gaze.

"I'm aware."

CHAPTER FORTY

EMERIC

In the crafted dreamscape, a moonlit terrace overlooking an endless sea, I wait for Morte. My heart beats a rhythm of anticipation; this is my stage, and I'm ready to play my part. The air is tinged with magic, the night alive with possibilities. Nerves, like butterflies, take flight in my stomach.

I'm not as close with her as the others. We haven't mated, and I'm not even sure she would if given the opportunity.

But gods, do I want to.

For days now, we've been testing memory retrieval and restoration on several demons, and several aviary fae orders with a lot of success. Memory restoration works much better if we familiarize the subject with the feel of the memory before giving it back.

As the moon bathes the veranda in a soft, dreamlike glow, her figure materializes at the far end. She moves with an ethereal grace, her long hair billowing behind her like wings. I quickly straighten my jacket and smooth down my hair, trying to exude confidence as I make my way towards her. My heart races with anticipation. It's time to charm the phoenix who has forgotten her way.

"Welcome," I say, sweeping my arm in a grand gesture. "It's beautiful, isn't it?"

She regards me with a mix of curiosity, amusement, and caution, taking in the dreamscape. "Emeric," she echoes, her voice laced with a hint of skepticism as she glances around. "This is your doing?"

"Guilty as charged," I admit with a playful bow. "Thought you could use a change of scenery."

Her lips twitch, a reluctant smile as her eyes dart to the fireworks going off in the distance. "It's beautiful, but why this?"

"Mmm," I muse as I stride closer, closing the distance but respecting her space. "You're here because there's a whole chunk of your life you don't remember. And I'm here to help you find it. The first time we met, we were in a restaurant."

"A restaurant?" Surprise colors her features.

"Well, a bar. A bar that serves food." I wince. "You were pawing at Az, nearly climbing into his lap."

She folds her arms, her stance guarded yet humored. "Now, that I don't believe." She chuckles.

"Oh, but it's true!"

I lead her along the balcony, where twinkling fae lights shimmer, and shadows and moonlight play at our feet. I catch a glint of curiosity in her eyes, a spark that tells me she's both wary and intrigued.

"Ever wonder what kind of mischief we got up to in the Underworld?" I ask, throwing her a roguish grin.

She arches an eyebrow. "Mischief? In the Underworld?"

"Absolutely. It's not all fire and brimstone, you know." I wink. "You stood me up."

A laugh escapes her, sudden and bright. "I did what?"

"When I left you and Az at the bar, I slid my address across the table to you, but you never showed." I frown as I lean on the railing overlooking a small pond. Giant, colorful explosions reflect on its surface. "I'd been so smitten the moment I laid eyes on you."

"Smitten, huh?" she says, as though she's testing the taste of it on her tongue. Glancing at her, her brow is raised in skepticism. "So, you're telling me I was on a date with Az, and was supposed to meet you at your house afterward?"

"Well, maybe it was wishful thinking." I grin at her, and she cracks a smile. "In the note I passed you, I said, 'He might have a big cock, but I've got two.'"

"I was a virgin, so if you told me that, no wonder I didn't show. I wouldn't have any idea what to do with one, let alone two!"

I level her with an amused smirk. "Well, that's a thing of the past. You, Morte Incendara, are not a virgin anymore."

"Obviously." She rolls her eyes. "I do believe that's how mating works."

"You lost it the night of the Wild Pursuit."

"The what?"

"It's one of the wild hunts in the Underworld. Fuck or fight if you're caught. And you," I say with a smirk, fully turning to face her. "Did not fight."

A soft, delicate pink blooms on her cheeks, like a rose in full bloom. As she opens her mouth to speak, her lips part slightly and the color deepens, accentuating her natural beauty. She opens her mouth to object, to say something, but can't find the words. I rescue her, gesturing to the table and chairs, pulling one out for her.

"I can see why I'd fall for you," she whispers. "You're—"

The dreamscape seems to quiver and tremble, its edges blurring and melting into one another. Time seems to stretch, thinning and fading like mist in the morning light. The world around us shimmers like a mirage, a fleeting illusion that dances on the edge of our reality.

Her smile fades, replaced by a dawning realization. "This is slipping away, isn't it?"

"I don't want you to go," I hold her gaze, earnest now. "We're always getting interrupted, always—"

The world around us crumbles into stardust, the dream dissolving. The dreamscape collapses, leaving a lingering echo of laughter and tacit promises in the void of our parting.

I wake in the hidden space at the top of the castle, and the guys are huddled around me.

"Well, how did it go?" Az helps me up.

I growl, "It ends too quickly. I barely have time for a conversation, let alone getting her in the right headspace to give her back a memory."

"What if Aggonid and I start the dreamscape again together? She loved watching us together in the past, we can use that to our advantage." Caius's voice is husky with anticipation. "These are some of my favorite memories, so she should get those back first."

"So you're just going to go in there, dicks swinging?" Az growls. "If we're going to seduce her, it might as well be me. She loves my magic. If I feed from her, it'll give her the best orgasm of her life."

I roll my eyes at their antics, but I can't deny the truth in their words. Morte is strong-willed, loyal to a fault, and it's going to take a lot to break through the walls she's built around herself. Seduction might just be the key to easing her into those specific memories.

"Okay, so we seduce her," I say, trying to keep a straight face. "We need to be careful. We don't want to push her too far, too fast. Perhaps seeing the two of you together," I gesture to the mated pair, "will be enough of an introduction to intimacy before Az shows her what she's really missing out on."

Aggonid smirks, his eyes glinting with anticipation. "I like this plan. We'll start slowly, give her time to adjust to the idea of being with us before we go all in."

Caius nods in agreement. "We'll make sure she's comfortable every step of the way."

Az smirks, his eyes darkening with lust. "And when she's ready, I'll give her the best orgasm of her life."

I chuckle at their eagerness, but I know this won't be easy. Morte is a powerful fae, and her loyalty to Wilder runs deep, so these memories are the ones she'll resist the most. "Don't forget, this isn't just about satisfying our own desires. We're doing this to gain her trust enough to make the transfer of each memory easier."

The others all nod in agreement, a silent understanding passing between them. We all know what's at stake, and none of us plan to let her slip away from us again. We will make her ours, no matter what. We've got a plan, now all that's left to do is execute it.

"So we'll start tomorrow night. You should probably be having sex, or whatever it is you plan to do, when the dream begins, as you will have little time." I look around the room, my gaze settling on each of the three men in turn. "Are we all in agreement?"

They all nod, though Az does so begrudgingly, and I give a brief nod in return. "Good. Then let's get to work."

∽

Aggonid

A THUNDEROUS CRACK splits the silence as Morte appears beside us in her dream. My hips drive hard against Caius, grinding and writhing with each powerful thrust as my gaze never wavers from Morte's form. Her eyes are wide with surprise and a flush blooms on her cheeks, but I can sense something else hidden beneath the surface.

Using my shadows, I coil them around her ankles, and a quaking shudder passes through her body. Even if she doesn't remember me, her body still remembers my touch. We've dressed her in a nightgown of fine silks that cling to every curve and allow slits to peek up the thighs. Her nipples pucker as I call forth a cool breeze to curl around her frame, and I can see an unquenchable hunger building in her heavy stare.

My shadows climb higher, until they caress her inner thigh, and she lets out a soft moan. She trembles at my touch, her breaths growing shallow as I reach the apex of her thighs. "What are you doing to me?" she whispers into the night, but there is no denying the pleasure written in her eyes.

"Something we've done many times before," I smirk at her as I pick up my pace against Caius, electricity arcing between us. "Something you loved to watch."

Her grip on the footboard tightens, her knuckles turning an ashen white, desperately trying to resist what her body longs for. I grasp Caius' cock firmly, my fingers tracing the intricate patterns of piercings that decorate it. His soft moan fills the room, and her gaze shifts between us, widening with a newfound hunger and curiosity at the decorations our mate wears on his flesh.

Caius moans beneath my grip, his body bucking as he begs for more. His eyes flash with pleasure, and Morte's gaze follows suit. I can see her struggle between desire and caution, and I move my shadows against her, wrapping my dark energy around her like a protective embrace.

"The last time you were between us," Caius groans as I tighten my fist around him, "you came so hard you passed out right after. Why don't you come join us?"

Morte's face burns red, but I can see the temptation in her gaze. She knows what she'd be getting into, and her body is craving it.

"Come, love," I whisper, my shadows wrapping around her. "Let us show you how beautiful pleasure can be."

Just as her hand leaves the wood, the dreamscape shudders. She glances up at us, a hint of fear marring her features. "You're leaving already?"

"The dream's collapsing." My voice echoes through the room, and suddenly I'm aware of the walls crumbling around us. "It's harder to sustain two of us in here, and we've been here too long. It's not safe anymore."

She reaches for us just as she dematerializes. We wake up in our separate realities, and I'm still buried in Caius as Az and Emeric curse, retreating from the room.

"Should we ask them to stay?" Caius grins up at me, igniting a flare of jealousy within me as I quirk a brow at him, struggling to maintain composure.

"I've got your cock in my hand," I growl. "Would you like it to stay attached?"

He huffs a laugh and pulls me in for a deep kiss. "Mmm, I should think so." He grips my hips, holding me to him as he bucks up. "But I do enjoy them watching, don't you?"

"They can look," I groan as the heat builds in me, "but they'll lose their hands if they touch."

"Fuck, I love when you talk about maiming people while you're drilling into me," Caius groans, and I smirk as I thrust harder.

My thumb toys with the ring on his cock, using his precum to circle it. The sensations make him shudder, and his eyes close with pleasure. I see the way his body responds to me, and I know he won't last much longer.

My own release builds, threatening to overtake me, and I lean forward to press my forehead to his. "I want you to come so hard, Morte can feel it in Bedlam," I whisper against his lips, and he grunts in agreement.

Caius shivers and grips my hips hard enough to bruise, and with a few more thrusts he comes with a guttural cry. I follow him over the edge as we collapse against each other, breathing heavily.

CHAPTER FORTY-ONE

MORTE

The iron door grinds open, and a metallic echo resonates through the dismal corridor of Bedlam Penitentiary. Each step I take, accompanied by the clank of my shackles, serves as a harsh reality check of how at risk I am without magic flowing through my veins. But today, for a brief moment, I'll be free. The guards, their faces etched with indifference, lead me towards the one place within these walls where I can briefly taste the freedom I once took for granted.

The caged dome looms above, a vast expanse of interwoven metal bars under the open sky. It's here, in this confined sky, that they'll allow the solace of flight, a chance to stretch my wings and remember who I am beyond these walls.

As we approach, the anticipation builds within me. My heart races, not with fear, but with a longing that has become all too familiar. The guards unlock my shackles, the sound of metal clinking against stone a prelude to my temporary liberation.

A moment of pure, unbridled joy floods through me, igniting every nerve with a raw, primal energy. It feels like the first burst of flame in a phoenix's rebirth, wild and untamed, a vibrant force rekindling the embers of my essence.

I stand taller, my senses sharpening as the magic infuses my body, the gloom of the prison now a mere backdrop to the vivid sensation of my own power. It's a silent explosion of vitality, a rush that paints my world with a spectrum of sensations so intense that I almost feel I could weave the very fabric of reality with my fingertips.

My pulse quickens, aligning with the latent energy that surrounds us all, a rhythm I had almost forgotten in the dampening silence of captivity. Now, every breath is an affirmation of my strength, every heartbeat a drum echoing the deep, resonant song of my soul.

"I feel like I could demolish a whole mountain," I chuckle out loud, testing flames in my hands.

As the guards step back, their wary eyes on me, I revel in the sheer potential that courses through my being. Magic, once stifled and suppressed, now sings within me, a melody of power and possibility that promises I am no longer bound by chains, but only by the breadth of my own will.

I step into the dome, my bare feet touching the cool grass. Above me, the sky stretches out, a canvas of blue streaked with wisps of white. The sun beams down, its rays piercing through the metal lattice, casting shadows that dance at my feet.

I close my eyes, inhaling deeply. The scent of fresh air mingles with the earthy aroma of the grass, and I could just roll in it. For a moment, I allow myself to forget that I'm in prison. That I'm a monster.

With a deep, steadying breath, I shed my fae form, the transformation as familiar as it is liberating. My body elongates, feathers sprouting, wings unfurling. The phoenix within, a creature of fire and rebirth, takes over. My plumage, a vibrant mix of iridescent crimson, shimmers under the sunlight.

I launch myself into the air, my powerful wings beating against the wind. The sensation of flight, the rush of air beneath my wings, fills me with an exhilarating mix of joy and sorrow. Here, in this caged sky, I am both free and imprisoned, soaring yet bound.

My beast cries out, a haunting sound, as though calling to her mates. A pang of agony lances through me.

I climb higher, each beat of my wings a defiance against my fate. The sky above beckons, a realm without bars, without constraints. I circle the dome, the world below reduced to a blur of colors and shapes. The wind whispers secrets, tales of the world beyond these bars, of the life I left behind.

As I glide, my thoughts drift to Wilder, to the love that endures despite the miles and oceans between us. My heart aches with the longing to see him, to feel his embrace. But it is this very love that has led me here, to this prison of my own making.

For an hour, I'm allowed this semblance of liberty, to remember the skies I once roamed with impunity. But as the minutes tick by, the inevitable return to my cell looms closer. I savor each second, each stroke of my wings, knowing that soon, I will be confined once more.

Below, the guards watch, their eyes following my every move. I'm a spectacle, a fallen phoenix, a reminder of the consequences of unchecked power and passion.

But in this moment, I'm more than my crimes, more than the prisoner they see. I am Morte Incendara, a creature of fire and rebirth, soaring within the boundaries of my caged sky.

As the hour draws to a close, I descend as the bell tolls, my wings folding as I land softly on the grass. The transformation back to my fae form is a reluctant one, each feather retracting, each inch of my wings shrinking, until I stand there, a mere shadow of the phoenix I truly am.

My beast whimpers inside me, reluctant to let go, but she must.

The guards approach, their steps methodical, their expressions unreadable. The shackles return, cold metal encircling my wrists, the sound of my freedom ending with a definitive click. Magic leaves me, snuffed out like a candle.

As I'm led back to my cell, the memory of flight lingers, a bittersweet reminder of the sky I can no longer call my own.

Hours pass. The walls, barren and cold, close in around me. I sit on the edge of my cot, my fingers tracing the patterns of the blanket, a futile attempt to find comfort in its threadbare texture.

Suddenly, the sound of boots echoes down the corridor, the

rhythmic clank of metal against stone growing louder with each step. I rise, my heart pounding in my chest, a mix of anticipation and dread filling me. The guards rarely come at this hour unless something unusual is afoot.

The door to my cell swings open, the metal hinges groaning in protest. Two guards stand there, their expressions impassive.

"Morte Incendara," one of them says, his voice devoid of emotion. "You're needed on the other side of the prison. Follow us."

Confusion swirls within me. "Can I ask what this is about?" I inquire, trying to mask the tremor in my voice.

"No information is given," the guard replies curtly. "You'll find out when we get there."

I nod, a sense of unease settling in my stomach. I step out of my cell, the guards flanking me as we begin the journey through the labyrinthine corridors of Bedlam Penitentiary.

The walk is interminable, each step echoing like a steady drumbeat against the metal bones of the prison. We pass by row after row of cells, some eerily silent, their inhabitants too broken to even make a sound, while others are filled with the hushed murmurs of inmates lost in their own worlds of regrets and dreams. Shouts pierce through the cacophony, threatening and vulgar, taunts about my appearance or perverse desires to see me dissected or skewered on their cock. These words only add to the already suffocating atmosphere, thick with despair and desperation.

At last, we come upon a formidable sanguimetal door. Its surface is etched with deep scratches and dents. It's seen many battles, and will likely see many more, as uprisings come and go. One of the guards retrieves a large key from his pocket, its metallic gleam catching the faint light as he inserts it into the lock, turning it with a resounding click.

A loud creak echoes through the room as the heavy door swings open, revealing a bedroom flooded with bright artificial light. Blinking to adjust my eyes, I take in the stark and functional space before me. There is no sense of comfort or coziness here, only efficiency. A basic bed with plain linens sits off to the side, while a simple table surrounded by a few chairs occupies the center of the room. The walls are bare, save for a single clock ticking away the seconds and minutes. It feels sterile, like a hospital room rather than a place to call home.

My mind struggles to process what I'm seeing as my gaze sweeps to the other side of the table. A figure is seated, their back to me, but I feel their presence as if it were my own. My breath catches in my throat as the figure turns, and our eyes meet.

"Wilder?"

CHAPTER FORTY-TWO

WILDER

As soon as her eyes meet mine, everything else fades into insignificance. Morte stands before me, a vision of perfection and longing that I have dreamed of during the endless days and nights of my incarceration. Her presence fills the room, radiating warmth and light that eclipse the cold, sterile environment of the prison meeting area. The sound of her soft breaths and the gentle rustle of her clothing are the only things I can focus on in this moment. My heart beats wildly in my chest as I take in every detail of her, from the curve of her lips to the disbelief in her eyes. It's like time has stopped just for us, and I never want it to end.

Her eyes, wide with a mixture of shock and recognition, lock onto mine. The deep-sea color of her irises reflects the tumultuous emotions churning within her. I can see the questions, the confusion, and the longing in that single glance.

Without a word, she takes a step forward, her movements hurried, desperate. The distance between us diminishes with each step, the air charged with the intensity of the moment.

As she stands before me, her gaze never leaving mine, a sob escapes her lips. The sound pierces my heart, a poignant reminder of the pain and separation we've endured. Tears spill down her cheeks, each one evidence of the love and sorrow that has defined our relationship.

I reach out, my arms open, a quiet invitation. She doesn't hesitate, collapsing into my embrace. I hold her tightly, feeling her body tremble against mine. Her tears soak into my shirt, each drop precious proof of her presence, her reality.

Her scent, a blend of the familiar and the bittersweet, envelops me. The smell of spun sugar and briny seas, intertwined with the sterile air of the prison, creates a paradoxical harmony. It's a scent I've dreamt of, longed for, during the endless nights and decades in my cell.

Her hands clutch at the fabric of my shirt, gripping me as if I might disappear at any moment. I bury my face in her hair, the soft strands caressing my skin. I want to say so much, to tell her everything that's in my heart, but words seem inadequate in the face of our reunion.

Her body fits perfectly against mine, as if we were two pieces of a puzzle long separated, now finally reunited. The feel of her in my arms, the warmth of her skin against mine, is a balm to the wounds of my soul.

"I didn't think I'd ever see you again," she whispers, her broken voice muffled against my chest.

Her words resonate deep within me, a mixture of joy and sorrow. "I'm here now, Morte. I'm here," I murmur.

We stand there, holding each other, the world around us forgotten. In this moment, nothing else matters but the fact that we're together again. After years of separation, of longing and despair, we're reunited in a place that symbolizes our greatest challenges and our deepest love.

As she lifts her head to look at me, our eyes meet again, and I see the reflection of my own emotions in hers. Love, relief, and a shared understanding of the journey that still lies ahead of us. In this embrace, in the heart of the prison that once held me captive, we find a moment of peace, a haven amid chaos.

"I never stopped loving you, Wilder," she says, her voice barely above a whisper.

"And I never will stop loving you, Morte," I reply, the words a vow, a promise that transcends the barriers of time and circumstance.

In the boundaries of Bedlam Penitentiary, we stand together, two souls bound by an unbreakable bond, ready to face whatever the future holds.

"How are you here? They don't allow visitors, only mates—."

I take a deep breath, the weight of two centuries worth of untold truths pressing against my chest. "I've known for a long time, Morte. At my sentencing ... I realized you were my anchor."

CHAPTER FORTY-THREE

MORTE

Betrayal, hot and sharp, sears my chest. His words hang in the air, echoing between us like a church bell tolling midnight. He knew. For two hundred years, he knew. And he kept it from me.

My heart beats like a war drum, echoing the profound shock of his revelation. His words resonate in my mind, each syllable an echo of the truth he'd withheld. Two centuries of silence, two centuries of longing, and he had known all along.

Every breath feels like a struggle, as if I'm drowning in a sea of emotions I can't fully comprehend. Relief washes over me, followed swiftly by grief. A purging rain that leaves my soul raw and exposed.

"Your anchor?" The words lurch from my throat, stripped bare and rasping as I race to grapple with my emotions. "Two hundred years you knew, and you said nothing?"

"Wait," he breathes.

His touch, seconds ago a comfort, now feels like molten iron against my skin. I pull back, breaking our contact but unable to break free from the magnetic pull of his gaze. His eyes mirror my turmoil—the surprise there is genuine, shadowed with a grief that seems to mirror my own.

Piercing pain ripples through me, a wave of bitter agony strengthened by two centuries of longing. My breathing becomes labored and ragged as I begin to spiral. He knew.

He knew and he didn't want me.

The realization is a punch in the gut, leaving me winded and shattered. I can see it in his eyes—the regret, the remorse. But it does nothing to muffle the deafening truth.

He knew and he didn't want me! My heart breaks.

"Stop," he breathes, reaching out to me. His hands hover over my skin, apprehensive, unsure of their welcome.

But I don't want his touch right now—not when I'm raw and aching—so I step back, putting distance between us. I've pined for this man for two thousand years.

"You had two hundred years," I hiss, my voice trembling with barely suppressed emotion. "Two hundred years to tell me—to choose me, and you didn't. You chose silence, Wilder. You chose isolation. Anything other than being fated to me." My words end on a shriek as my knees give way.

He captures me, drawing me against his chest. "Stop and let me speak," he urges. "I have always wanted you. Every day, every hour, every cell in my body for two thousand years, has wanted you. It was never a lack of desire. It was because I love you with every fiber of my being that I refused to tell you. I didn't want you wasting your love on someone who couldn't give their all to you!"

My heart stammers, stuttering in its rhythm, as his words fall around me like rain. They're refreshing but painful, too; a cloudburst that leaves me soaked to the bone, chilled to the core. "Is that what you thought?" I whisper, my voice choked and broken. "That because I couldn't have you full time, that I shouldn't want you at all?"

He nods, face gravely serious, and his gaze searches mine. "I was imprisoned, Morte. Physically and emotionally bound by my own decisions. I didn't want you to share that cell."

My tears, bitter and hot, soak into the rough fabric of my prison clothes. His words are raw and uncompromisingly honest. They scrape at my insides like a thorny rose, both beautiful and painful. It hurts.

"But it was my crime," I sob. "My mistake that put you in that cell, Wilder. I would have chosen you," I choke. "I would have chosen you over freedom, over sunshine, over *air*. I would have chosen to share your cell if it meant being with you. Do you have any idea what I went through after you were sentenced?"

The courtroom's sterile air suffocates me as they clamp the suppression cuffs onto Wilder, each click a chisel chipping away at my soul. My gaze locks with his, a silent scream etched in my eyes, my heart thrashing against my ribs like a caged bird desperate for escape. The verdict echoes, a life sentence—a cruel and unending eternity—resounds in my skull, a relentless drumbeat signaling the end of everything we never had the chance to begin.

I lunge forward, a feral cry clawing its way up my throat, muffled by the magic that seals my lips—his doing, his sacrifice. My hands outstretch, reaching for him, craving to shred the verdict into a thousand pieces with my bare fingers. But before I can touch him, before I can unleash the storm brewing within, strong arms encircle me, pinning me down, a sharp prick at my neck, and the world begins to blur.

His face, etched with a sorrow that mirrors my internal devastation, starts to fade as the sedative drags me under. I fight it, every fiber of my being rebelling against the imposed calm. Wilder's name is a mantra in my mind, a plea, a prayer, a curse. The guards' grip is unyielding, their faces masks of detached duty as they haul me away, my cries suffocated, my magic nullified, my spirit shattered.

The last thing I see before darkness claims me is Wilder's retreating form, being dragged away to a fate worse than death, his head turned back, eyes searching for mine in a silent vow that screams across the void between us. It's a promise of enduring love, of indomitable spirit, even as the doors of Bedlam Penitentiary swing closed, severing our gaze, cleaving my world in two.

He guides me over to the bed, pulling me into his lap. "Tell me. Tell me everything."

"After you were sentenced, I lost my mind, Wilder," I whisper, the tears of my broken confession laid bare. "For fifteen years, they had to sedate me in a cryochamber."

Shock flickers in his ocean eyes, followed quickly by regret—a bottomless pit of sorrow that echoes my own. "I didn't know," he whispers brokenly. "Gods, Morte... I didn't know."

"When I got out, I'd spend every night outside the prison, sleeping on the rocky shore just so I could feel close to you."

"That's why I planned to tell you when you came here," he tucks me under his arm as he lays us back. "I didn't know how bad it was for you. You were hurting just as much as I was. If I'd known, I swear it, I would have told you right away. I thought keeping this from you would spare you the pain. But then you died and didn't come back."

My sobs turn into soft wails as I press my face against his chest, my arms wrapping tightly around him, as though he'll disappear if I don't clutch him with all my might. "I'm sorry," I cry, my voice muffled by his shirt. "I'm sorry for leaving you like that. I didn't mean to hurt you."

"Don't cry, Little Bird," he coos, cupping my cheek and wiping at the tears with his thumb. "I didn't get a chance to tell you then. But it's always been you, Morte. You're the one constant in my life, my guiding light through all these dark years. I clung to that hope that you'd be out there, happy, and free. I assumed you'd regenerated and had to leave by the time I came back to life. It wasn't until I got your letter that I learned where you'd been."

"My letter?" I pull back, tears sticking to my lashes as my brows pull in confusion.

"High King Finian delivered it himself," he chuckles. "Had the entire prison staff terrified they were in trouble when he showed."

"I didn't write any letter," I shake my head. "I know they wouldn't deliver them. I tried for over a hundred years."

He tilts his head at me, eyes darting between mine. "What do you mean? It was your handwriting, talking about the Underworld."

I gasp, mouth dropping open. "I have no memories of my time there. Do you still have it?"

"They wouldn't let me bring anything in," he frowns. "But I've read it probably thirty thousand times since. Do you want to know what it says?" When I nod, he recites it, line by line.

I search his face as if trying to piece together a puzzle that's been missing for ages. "I wrote that?" My voice is a tremor of disbelief and wonder. "But I don't remember any of it. The Underworld, the Forsaken Hunt ... none of it."

Only fragments of what my mates have told me.

"It's true, every word. I'd lost it when I found out where you were." His voice breaks slightly.

A stream of tears scorches my cheeks as I tremble in his arms, knowing I'm about to break his heart, and he does his best to caress them away. His skin is burning hot against my fingertips when I slip them under his shirt, needing to feel him, to be closer. To know this is real and I haven't lost my mind.

"Wilder," I whisper, the heartache painting every choked word, "I wish you had told me."

"I wanted to protect you," he confesses.

"I'm mated."

CHAPTER FORTY-FOUR

WILDER

"Mated?" Agony cleaves my chest, like a hot poker. Her words bludgeon my heart, hitting me like ice-cold waves crashing over my head. I'm drowning in a sea of disbelief and torment. My throat locks, my lungs ache, and I can't breathe. I can't ... Gods, I can't breathe.

"I have a soul bond," she whispers, so low it's nearly drowned by the rush of the blood roaring in my veins.

"M-Morte," I stammer, her name a ragged plea torn from a wound so deep that even the immortality coursing through me can't hope to heal it. "To whom.? I can't finish the question.

"Aggonid," she says softly, and the sound tilts my world on its axis.

When her eyes lift to mine, they're clear and filled with such profound sorrow, I know it to be true.

The word echoes in my head like a death knell. A blow that stabs deeper than any blade, burning hotter than any fire magic she could level at me. My anchor, my flame, my little bird, is mated to another. Not just another, but the devil.

"And I'm mated to two others. Azazel and Caius." She winces, and I'm waiting for her to crack a smile, to tell me it's a cruel joke, payback for the agony I've put her through.

But it never comes.

I should let her go, put distance between us, but I can't. So I remain still, thoughts running rampant in my head. A chill works its way through me.

"Why are you here?" I ask, afraid to know the truth, but needing to hear it anyway.

"Because of you," she whispers. "A plea with the gods to return me to the fae realm so I could set you free."

"But your mates, yo—"

She puts her hand over my mouth, stopping me. "There isn't a person in this realm or the next that could've kept me from getting you out. I may have not known I was your anchor, but gods did I feel it," she hisses. "I would peel the skin from my bones before I'd let you rot in here another day."

I blink back my own tears, swallowing hard as I attempt to digest her words. She's anchored to me, tethered in a way she can't be to anyone else. Yet she's chosen ... No, she's been *forced* into a union with others. My heart aches for her, for us.

I take her hand away from my mouth and kiss the open palm, tasting the salty remnants of her tears. "Your mates ..." I begin again, only to have her hiss in frustration.

"They're not you," she interjects, her gaze as fierce as I've ever seen it. "And they never will be. I love you all."

"But where does this leave us?" I breathe, shaking my head and fighting the urge to scream to the heavens. To curse the fates and all those who set us on this path.

"Here!" she shouts, throwing her hands out to gesture to the room. "I am here, and you are there! Now you can go be happy with someone because I've been taken and tainted and loved and I turn my back on everyone I love."

I flinch as her voice echoes off the cold, stone walls of the prison. A stunned silence hangs between us, thick as brine. The only sound in the room is her labored breathing and the raw emotion in her voice that lingers, sharp as a cut from a broken glass.

"Morte," I start softly, reaching out to her. My fingers comb through her crimson hair, catching on its silky strands. She looks up at me with those radiant turquoise eyes that have always felt like home. But now there's a storm raging within them, as though she's alone in a sea of despair.

It's a good thing I call the ocean my home.

CHAPTER FORTY-FIVE

MORTE

"If you think for one moment I believe that, then you're wrong. If you turned your back on the people you loved, you wouldn't be in this prison. You protected all of Castanea, and you're paying for it now. I gave you an opportunity at a better life, one without bars, but you took it back because you couldn't turn your back on me. I think you've done enough of this self-sacrificing bullshit to last another few hundred lifetimes. Enough," I growl. "I love every part of you, have always loved every part of you. You are mine just as I've always been yours."

The agony in my chest eases at his words. "What are you saying?"

He grips my cheeks, his eyes blazing as he holds me. "I'm saying that we're in this, Morte. For the long haul, for the impossible, for the heart-wrenching. I'm not going anywhere," he murmurs, his voice breaking on the last few words. "I can share you with all the gods in every realm if I must, but I cannot bear to lose you." His thumbs stroke my wet cheeks gently, and his voice softens further. "Not again. Never again."

A sob wracks my body as his words soothe an old ache within me. A prisoner's life is notorious for its loneliness, but here and now, despite everything, I feel anything but alone.

I press my forehead against his, the echoes of his promise wrapping around me like a comforting shroud. "You'll share me?" I ask in disbelief, even as I lean into his touch. "Even after everything? You'll still—"

"I told you, Little Bird," Wilder interrupts, threading his fingers through mine. "I would pluck the stars from the skies for you. Burn down the heavens. Smite every god in existence and all of those to come. If sharing you is what it takes to keep you in my life, then yes." His voice is like a caress, soft and gentle against the tender wound of my heart.

We sit in silence for a moment, the enormity of our situation sinking in. The walls of the prison seem to close in around us.

"I still can't believe I'm your anchor," I breathe, a whirlwind of nerves and exhilaration swirling within me. He gently draws my chin to look at him. "I'd spent two thousand years cursing the gods for not giving you me."

Wilder chuckles, a low rumble that vibrates through his chest and into mine. "I'd say they finally got it right," he grins, his fingers tracing soothing patterns along my back. "I'll never let them take you away from me again. I've belonged to you for thousands of years, and will continue to belong to you for thousands more, beyond the time all the realms in all the universes release their last breaths. I am yours." He lowers himself to his knees, pressing between my legs, his arms splayed wide. "They can flay me open, carve out my heart, and still, it will beat for only you."

"Have me, all of me," I whisper.

His hand, large and reassuring, finds mine, his fingers intertwining with mine in a silent promise of solidarity and strength. The sensation of his skin against mine, warm and alive, sends a current of electricity through me, reigniting long-dormant desires and awakening a hunger that had been stifled during his confinement.

Wilder's eyes search mine, a question lingering in their depths. I know what he's asking, what he's offering. A chance to reclaim a piece of ourselves that had been lost in the abyss of our separation. My heart races at the thought, a mix of anticipation and fear swirling within me.

But it's the love I see in his gaze, deep and as vast as the ocean, that makes my decision. I nod, a quiet acquiescence to his silent query. In response, his lips find mine in a kiss that ignites a fire within me, a blaze of passion and longing that consumes us both.

The kiss deepens, our emotions spilling over, unchecked and raw as he climbs back onto the bed. There's a desperation in the way he holds me, a fervor in the way our bodies mold together, as if trying to make up for lost time, for all the moments stolen from us.

His scent, a blend of mint and the faraway seas, fills my senses, transporting me to memories of a life once lived freely, of days spent in his arms without fear of separation or loss. His touch, gentle yet insistent, stirs something within me, a desire that's as much a part of me as the fire that courses through my veins.

We break apart, breathless, our foreheads resting against each other. His voice, when he speaks, is a low, throaty purr that sends shivers down my spine. "You've always been my anchor. Even when I didn't realize it, you were the one thing keeping me grounded, keeping me sane."

I lean into his touch, the warmth of his hands on my back soothing the raw edges of my soul. "And you've always been my home. No matter where I am, as long as I'm with you, I'm where I belong."

In the embrace of the man I've loved for two millennia, I find a peace I thought I'd lost forever. A peace that comes not just from being in his arms, but from knowing that, in this vast and often cruel world, our love remains a constant.

"Tell me you want this." He tilts my chin up so I'm looking at him.

His fingers trace lazy patterns on my skin as I press my lips to his neck, savoring the salty tang of his skin. My hands roam over his chest, exploring every inch of him as if touching him for the first time, and my lips follow. His heartbeat thunders in my ears, a steady rhythm that matches the ebb and flow of waves.

"Tell me you want this. That you want me," he whispers again.

I answer by throwing a leg around his waist and pulling him close, my mouth finding his in a desperate kiss. This is what I want, what I need—to be here, with him, in this moment, forever. His hands find mine, our fingers intertwined, and I give myself over to the beauty of it all, of us. I grind my core against his, a silent plea, my need for him growing with each passing second. He responds in kind, his hips moving against mine, but it's not enough.

"More," I beg.

He chuckles, a deep rumble that travels through me like thunder.

His hands slide down to the hem of my shirt, pulling it up and over my head in one smooth motion. Just as quickly, his arms are under me, and he's flipped us so he's on top. Air rushes out of my lungs as I land on my back, grinning up at him.

His eyes roam hungrily over my body, and I can feel the heat radiating off of him. I arch into him, my breath hitching in anticipation as his lips brush against mine. Our kiss deepens, a slow, languid exploration that speaks of a love that runs as deep as the ocean.

He helps me pull off the prison-issue sports bra I'm wearing, and heat flushes my cheeks as his eyes take in my exposed body. He kisses my neck, my collarbone, working his way down my body until his tongue finds my breast. I gasp, and my fingers tangle in his hair as he swirls his tongue around my nipple. His warm, rough hands travel down my sides, tracing a trail of fire that leaves me trembling.

My chest rises and falls with every ragged breath as he moves down my body, his lips trailing sweet kisses. He pauses at the sensitive skin of my stomach, exploring it with a tenderness that sends shivers up my spine.

He undoes the button of my pants, and my eyes follow his fingers to the zipper. After sliding them off, he quickly discards them on the floor before focusing his attention on my panties. His eyes stay locked on mine as he slides them down my hips, and I'm left exposed and vulnerable. He takes his time admiring me, and my heart thunders in my chest.

"I want to see what's mine," he groans.

He runs a finger over the fine curls before he spreads me with his thumbs. Heat creeps up my cheeks, and I'm embarrassed by the wanton display of my body. But it's quickly forgotten as he slides his fingers inside me. I gasp, my hips bucking against his hand as he expertly strokes me, as though every cell of his is attuned to my body and what it needs. He moves his fingers in and out, slowly increasing the speed until I'm panting. He lays a kiss to my stomach, rubbing his cheek against my skin as though marveling at the softness of me.

His mouth moves lower still, until his breath is hot against the apex of my thighs. I can feel the anticipation emanating off him as he looks up at me with hunger in his eyes. He presses his nose to my core, inhaling deeply. I'd be mortified if it weren't for his eyes shuttering as though it were the sweetest scent he'd ever encountered.

"I won't stop until you've soaked my face."

"I—"

He spreads me wider, and I moan as his tongue finds its mark, sending shockwaves of pleasure throughout my body. Un-fae-like sounds fill the room, my fingers balling into fists as he swirls his tongue around me, like a man on a mission to annihilate me. I can't control the movements of my body, my hips rolling against him as he works me into a frenzy.

I'm trembling, my fingers fisting the sheets as he licks and sucks. His teeth scrape against me, and I cry out. I'm so close. The pressure builds until it reaches critical mass, crashing over me like a million stars exploding behind my eyelids.

I ride wave after wave of pleasure, my entire body alight with sensations. I'm vaguely aware of his hands on my hips, anchoring me to him as I come undone.

When I finally come down from my high, I'm left breathless and spent in his arms.

He grins up at me, still parked between my spread thighs, and his face is absolutely drenched. Before I can comment on it, or hide in mortification, his lips find mine in a tender kiss, and I melt into him, finally feeling the peace I'd been searching for all this time.

"I love you," he whispers against my lips, and I find I don't mind that I can taste myself on them. "We don't have to—"

"Are you kidding me?" I interrupt, my brows pinched, fingers threading through his long hair. "I've waited two thousand years for this moment with you."

He smiles, a beautiful, heartbreakingly tender smile that sets my heart aflame. "What's another thousand more?"

"Wilder Ripple, so help me—"

His chuckle drowns out my words, and I can't help but laugh, too. "Fuck, I've missed that fire, Little Bird."

"Then come get it." I nip at his bottom lip, and he growls, pinning me to the bed.

"Greedy little thing, aren't you?" He rests his full weight on me, and it's not insubstantial. I'm a pretty standard six foot six inches, and he's got mass and height on me. I find that I really, really like the feel of his bulk pressing me into the mattress.

I'm tiny compared to him, and I freaking love it.

With my magic suppressant cuff on, I can't feel my phoenix as much as I normally would, but she's pacing my mind, impatient, demanding I get on with it. "You have no idea," I whisper. I yank my hands free, and use them to tear his shirt off him, exposing his strong, muscular chest as my fingers trace the lines of his body, memorizing every hollow and peak.

His muscles twitch beneath my fingertips, as though the tattooed waves undulate under my touch, and I can feel his desire rising with every caress. He pulls away, his eyes smoldering as he looks down at me. He grins that mischievous, boyish grin I fell in love with as he rises to his knees, his abs contracting causing a distraction until he moves his hand to his belt. Slowly, he undoes it, and I'm momentarily lost in the sound of it sliding through the little hoops. He slides them over his ass, taking his black boxer briefs with them.

My breath catches as I take in the sight of him. His cock, long and thick, is bioluminescent, glowing with a beautiful, deep blue light that matches the color of his magic. He fists it, tugging it slowly. "This is how I know you're my anchor, Morte." His words startle me, and my attention meets his eyes. "It glows only for you."

"I didn't know it did that." I marvel as I reach out, tracing a gentle line down his length, and he groans, his eyes fluttering shut as I lean forward and press a gentle kiss to the tip. "This isn't going to fit inside of me."

He chuckles. "Little Bird," he takes my hand, showing me how to stroke it, and it's so smooth and warm beneath my touch. "I was fucking *made* for you."

As though possessed, he leans down and tosses me onto my back. He moves over me, his skin pressing against mine, and his heart thunders against my chest. His mouth finds my neck, his hands exploring my body in a way that leaves me trembling. His lips move lower, and I gasp as he takes my nipple into his mouth. I arch my back, my fingers digging into his shoulders as he works me over, his mouth and hands finding every sensitive spot.

He positions himself between my legs, and I can feel the head of his cock pressing against me. His eyes meet mine, and it's like coming home. He slides inside, and I gasp as he lets out a low groan. The sensation is unlike anything I've ever experienced before. He moves slowly, and each thrust feels like the first. We move together, our bodies in perfect harmony as we reach for something that neither of us can put into words.

"So fucking wet for me. I told you I'd fit. And if I didn't, I'd make it."

Fuck. "That filthy mouth of yours—"

I don't get to finish my sentence before he's interrupting me. "Yours is next."

His hips rock against mine as I wrap my legs around his waist, riding each wave of pleasure as he thrusts into me. My body trembles as he picks up the pace, a hot tension building between us. Each piston of his body against mine propels the bed across the floor.

He grips my ass with his hands, bringing me into his lap as he rises to his knees. His grunts come out as little curses, and I can do nothing but wrap my arms around his neck to hold on as though I'm a rag doll, as he works to bring us closer and closer to our release.

Wilder lifts me so we can both watch where he splits me in two, slowing down, watching as he glides in and out of me. "Look how pink your little cunt turns as it milks my cock," he groans.

He's always had a dirty mouth but hearing it in this context just about sends me over.

My hands tangle in his hair as I pull his face to mine, using his shoulders to push me up, meeting each of his thrusts with my own. My body tightens around him, and I can feel him swell within me as he latches onto my neck, his fangs puncturing me. I cry out as I come, his thrusts becoming more powerful as his growls mingle with mine, following me over the edge.

His breathing becomes shallow, and his movements become erratic as he slams into me for one final time, calling out my name as his orgasm overtakes him.

We collapse onto the bed, our sweat-slicked bodies still tangled together. Wilder wraps his arms around me, pulling me closer as he kisses the top of my head. We lay there, in the afterglow of our lovemaking, until we both drift off into a peaceful sleep.

Wilder

THE MUTED ECHO of morning stirs me from slumber. Beneath the dim light seeping through the high windows, Morte's presence is a soothing balm against the harsh reality of Bedlam Penitentiary. Her head rests on my chest, a peaceful contrast to the turmoil that has defined our lives. Her rhythmic breathing, coupled with the soft rise and fall of her chest, anchors me to this moment, a rare respite in our fragmented existence.

A clatter at the cell door disrupts the stillness of dawn. The familiar sound of a tray sliding through the slot jolts us back to reality. I feel Morte shift beside me, her movements fluid and graceful even tucked against me.

"Morning," she murmurs, her voice laced with a hint of sleep and a depth of emotion that resonates within me.

"Good morning." I grin down at her, my tone infused with the warmth and contentment that her proximity brings. I watch as she stretches, her movements unveiling the sublime contours of her form, a reminder of the physical connection we've just shared, one that has irrevocably altered the dynamics of our relationship. My mating bites pepper her skin, and it brings a deep sense of contentment seeing it.

I lost count how many times we woke, only to go again.

As she collects the breakfast tray, her fingers brush against mine, sending a cascade of sensations that linger far longer than the fleeting touch. We eat in a comfortable quiet, the simple act of sharing a meal in this cell morphing into something intimate, something profoundly ours.

Her presence is a vivid splash of color in the monochrome world of incarceration. Her laughter, light and genuine, fills the space, turning the cell into something bearable, even for a fleeting moment. She's a living, breathing contradiction to the cold, unyielding reality of our surroundings.

Her hand finds mine under the table, a silent communion that speaks volumes. We've become a credo to resilience, to a love that endures the bleakest of circumstances. "I can't say I've ever been more grateful for prison food." A half-smile plays on my lips.

She chuckles, a sound that radiates warmth and life, transforming the cell into a semblance of normalcy. "Suddenly, everything pales in comparison to last night." Her gaze conveys a myriad of promises.

Propped with our backs against the wall as we sit on the mattress, legs and arms intertwined, our voices blend with the clanging of metal doors and shouts from the guards. We reminisce about some of the adventures we went on, laughing until tears stream down our faces. Our eyes meet in a silent understanding that goes beyond our words, and for a moment, the prison walls disappear.

"How did you manage to get to the prison every night?" You can't sift from The Wastelands, so it always takes several days to traverse.

She grins at me. "I stole Crucey's portal stone."

I chuckle, picturing it now. I've never met Crucey but have heard plenty of stories—the real ones—which have been all good. The rest of Bedlam knew about Crucey, just not who she really was. They thought her the most ruthless monster in all the realms, but that's just the story she weaved to keep the Tolden safe.

My thoughts quickly sober at the thought Morte had to risk getting caught every night, just to ease the ache in her soul at being apart from me. It hits me like a dam breaking.

Morte's embrace is my sanctuary, her arms a haven in the storm of my despair. Her touch, tender and unwavering, anchors me in the present, a balm to the wounds of our past. She whispers words of solace, each syllable a melody that weaves through the cracks of my fractured spirit. "We were caught in fate's cruel net, yet here we are, together at last. Our love, our bond, transcending the chains of circumstance."

Her admission intertwines with mine, a shared truth laid bare. "I felt it, too, Morte. In every tide, in every breath of the sea breeze. You were the pulse of my world, the essence of my being." My voice steadies, strengthened by the depth of our connection. "In the moment of my deepest despair, when the sentence fell upon me like a death knell, it was your name that echoed in my heart. You are the rhythm that guides my ocean, the soul that lights my path. My heart, my life, my very existence—it's forever entwined with yours. I have loved you for two thousand years, and I will love you for twenty million more."

I look up at her with watery eyes, my gaze searching for any sign of doubt or regret. Instead, I find only love and understanding reflected back at me. My past mistakes seem less burdensome, replaced by a glimmer of hope for our future together.

Morte's fingers gently brush away the tears that stain my cheeks, her touch a soothing balm against the ache in my chest.

"No apologies and no regrets," she whispers, her thumb wiping away a stray tear cascading down my cheek. "We can't change the past, but we can shape our future, and it might not be ideal, but at least I'm yours and you are mine. We have the power to create a love story they'll talk about for eons."

"They'll hear it, too," I chuckle, and she gives me a playful shove. "Who knew Little Bird could sing so sweetly for me?"

As we embrace, the world around us fades away, leaving only the warmth of each other's presence as she smiles into my chest. The clanging of metal doors and the shouts of guards become distant echoes as time itself seems to bend to accommodate our love. We're no longer prisoners confined by walls and circumstances. Instead, we're warriors, fighting against a world that seeks to consume us.

I'd burn it all to the ground for her.

The hours trickle by, each second a bittersweet drop in the finite ocean of our time together. As shadows dance upon the cell walls, marking the march of time, I cling to each moment with my anchor. Each laugh, each touch, each shared glance is a gem I tuck into the vaults of my heart, bracing for the looming emptiness that awaits my return to a world without her.

We sit together, hands entwined, as the day stretches into evening. The reality of our situation, the countdown to our separation, stalks us. Yet, for now, she's here, in my arms, and that's all that truly matters.

CHAPTER FORTY-SIX

MORTE

"I need you," I whisper, the chill of the room settling into my bones.

We're both naked, having spent most of the early evening lost in each other.

Wilder's eyes search mine, filled with a fervor that matches my own. His hands tighten around mine, as though he's afraid to let go, as though he knows that these moments together are all we have. And they're not enough. They'll never be enough.

"You've always had me." He cups my cheeks. "For as long as I live and an eternity after that, I'm yours. Every part of me." His hips press against me, his erection trapped between us.

My lips descend upon his, hungry and possessive, a silent declaration of my feelings for him. He kisses me back with equal fervor, his hands gripping my hips, pulling me closer until there's no space left between us.

Desire ignites like a wildfire, consuming me. Every touch is filled with an intensity born from millennia of longing, years of being denied the one person who completes me, who was made for me. I moan into his mouth as his fingers find their way to the apex of my thighs, aching to be filled by him.

Without breaking our kiss, he guides himself inside me, filling me completely with a single, desperate thrust. He groans against my mouth before flipping us and resting his forehead against the crook of my shoulder, driving me into the mattress. "Do you know how many nights I pictured this? Sinking into you, our bodies becoming one?" His voice is a low growl, raw with need.

I thread my fingers through his hair, my nails grazing gently against his scalp. "Every night," I breathe. "Let's make up for lost time."

"Tell me what you need," he begs. "I need to feel your pussy squeezing my cock. Milking it."

"This," I groan as he angles himself just right. "Faster."

Wilder's movements become frenzied, fueled by a primal hunger that matches my own. With each thrust, we merge deeper and deeper, our bodies entwined in a dance of passion and desperation. The room is suffused with the scent of our desire, mingling with the musky air of confinement.

"You were made for me, Morte. This tiny pussy. Your pale skin. Your wicked tongue. Your dirty mind." His thumb settles between us, stroking my clit with each thrust of his hips. "I want to tie you up, have you at my mercy."

"I dreamt you did that," I breathe. "Months ago."

"As soon as I get you out, I will," he promises. "Legs splayed wide, and me on my knees so you can soak my face."

I whimper, and he responds with a grin. "You like the idea of me on my knees for you? Worshipping your body? Praying at your temple?"

"Yes," I cry out as he drags his cock against my back wall.

"Every day, and every night, for 2,000 years, I've stroked my cock to the thought of you under me." He sighs. "I should've been picturing you on a throne, and me at your feet. You are my god."

Tears spill down my cheeks as moans and gasps fill the space, harmonizing with the occasional creak of the bed frame as it bears witness to our ardor. Time collapses around us, the prison walls fading into insignificance as we lose ourselves in the ecstasy of our reunion. Our bodies move in perfect synchrony, every touch and caress igniting a fire that engulfs us both.

I arch my back, offering myself fully to him, as he uses every ounce of strength to please me. Pleasure courses through my veins like liquid fire, pooling in the pit of my stomach before spreading outwards, consuming every fiber of my being. Our cries intertwine, an opus of ecstasy that echoes through the small prison cell.

I've spent my entire life wanting this, working for this.

In this moment, time bends to our will. There is only Wilder and me, two souls desperate to reclaim what was taken from us. Our bodies move in perfect rhythm, a dance of unrestrained passion and longing. Each thrust brings us closer to the precipice of release, but it's so much more than physical pleasure.

It's a declaration of defiance against a world that seeks to tear us apart. In this act of love, we reclaim our power, transcending the boundaries imposed on us by society and circumstance.

"Break for me, Little Bird," he breathes against my ear. "Let me hear you sing."

As our bodies reach their crescendo, I cling to Wilder, my fingernails digging into his back as waves of pleasure crash over us. We shatter together, our cries merging into one as we find solace in each other's arms. In this fleeting moment of bliss and release, we are free. Free from the shackles of our past, free from the prison bars that confine us.

As our bodies come down from the heights of ecstasy, we remain intertwined, our breaths mingling in the aftermath of our love's storm. Our reality settles upon us once more, reminding us of the impending separation that awaits us.

But for now, in this fragile sliver of time, we bask in the afterglow of our reunion. Our bodies may be confined within these walls, but our hearts and souls roam boundlessly in a realm where only love exists.

In the quiet intimacy of our embrace, our whispered dreams paint a world untouched by sorrow. "I'll find a way to free you," Wilder whispers against my lips, his voice brimming with millennia of grief.

"Whatever it takes, I will tear down these walls and bring you back to me."

Tears pour in earnest down my cheeks as I hold him tighter, wishing desperately that his words could be true. We both know the odds are stacked against us—they always have been—but in this moment, with his arms around me, I dare to dream. To believe, against all odds, that he will find a way. That love will find a way.

Because relegating our love to twice-monthly conjugal visits is a prospect too bleak to bear. "I'm tired of fate dictating our paths. I'm tired of stolen moments. I want to choose you, Wilder. In every lifetime, in every realm, it's you I would choose. Without hesitation. Without regret."

His grip on me tightens, his eyes brimming with love, tears, and entire lifetimes and oceans of grief. "I will fight for us, for our freedom, until my last breath. I'll bring the full might of the oceans. The lakes. The rivers. The streams. The very blood in their veins until they heed my call. You will be free, Morte, because I'm yours, just as you are mine."

The sound of heavy boots interrupts our tender moment, and we freeze, heartache gripping my chest as Wilder quickly tucks the sheets around us. The cell door creaks open, revealing the stern face of the prison guard. His eyes graze over us, lingering on our bodies entwined on the bed. Disgust fills his gaze, but I refuse to apologize or let it break me.

This is my mate.

"Time's up," he gruffly announces, his tone laced with disdain. "Separate."

Wilder's jaw clenches, anger simmering beneath the surface as he reluctantly pulls away from me. I reach out for him, my fingers desperately grazing his as a silent promise that we'll find a way back to each other.

He pulls me in again for a bone-crushing hug, burying his head in my hair. "I love you," he chokes.

"I love you," I sob, clinging to his shoulders as the guard's voice interrupts us.

"It's time to go, Ripple, lest you want to find yourself locked back up again."

He pulls back, speaking to the guard. "Is that an option?"

"Out. Now." The guard steps into the room

Agony sears my chest as Wilder's eyes lock with mine as he releases me. "This isn't goodbye. I'll see you soon, okay?"

I'm trembling so bad, I can do nothing but nod my head, lips caught between my teeth to keep my wracking sobs in. It's not supposed to be like this. I knew what I had, the entire time I had him, and now they're taking him away from me again. It's not fair.

The desperate plea of, "Baby, don't cry," falls from his lips like sharp icicles, piercing the air with bitter misery. Slowly, he rises to his feet and retrieves his scattered clothes, pulling them on in a haphazard manner. He brings mine to me, holding up the sheet to shield me from the guard's eyes so I can dress.

The room is filled with an unbearable heaviness, and the air crackles with unspoken words and unsaid goodbyes. Wilder's hand lingers on my cheek, his touch gentle yet burning with an intensity that matches the ache in my heart. I can see the anguish etched into every line of his face, the load of our separation bearing down on him.

"Stay strong," he whispers, his voice trembling with emotion. "We'll find our way back to each other. Feel me in the rain. The water pouring down your throat. In the blood that surges through your veins. I'm here." His fingers trace a path along the inside of my arm, along the rivers beneath my skin.

"Please don't leave me," I whimper, sucking in deep gasps of air. There isn't enough.

I try to protest, but I'm silenced as he presses his lips against mine. My heart breaks as I taste the agony in his kiss and feel his pain seeping into me. I nod, tears streaming down my face, knowing that this is our saddest goodbye. That each time will feel like the most heart-wrenching farewell, etching itself into my soul.

He steps away from me, towards the impatient guard with arms crossed and a cruel smirk etched on his face, leaving me to face a fate worse than death alone.

The guard's gaze flickers between us, a sneer curling his lips as if reveling in our pain. I despise him in this moment, unable to comprehend how someone could be so callous.

As the guard escorts Wilder away, his absence slices through me, leaving a void where warmth once lingered. The cell, still echoing with the whispers of our fleeting union, turns into a barren landscape of what-ifs and could-have-beens.

A vision of a different life breaks through the sorrow—a life where joy might have sprung from the love we share. I imagine us, not divided by these merciless circumstances, but united, holding a child of our own. The gentle sound of our child's giggles fills the void, painting the barren room with hues of what might have been. Ten little fingers, ten little toes, with hair as dark as night, and my pale skin. Wilder's eyes, and my fire. This image, vivid and poignant, lingers for a breath before it fades, leaving a profound ache in its wake as the reality of the present engulfs me once more. Watching Wilder being led away, the future we yearned for recedes, leaving me in the grip of a cold present.

A female guard steps in, her eyes an unreadable mask. She motions for me to raise my hands. Before I can grasp the gravity of her intent, she murmurs an incantation. A spell lashes out, a crushing force that seizes my abdomen like a vice of iron, extinguishing the nascent spark of life that might have kindled from our love.

In her gaze sits a flicker of pity. A silent acknowledgement of the hope she's snuffing out. "I'm sorry," she murmurs, her words a hollow echo in the void she's created.

Her apology is a feeble balm to the raw wound in my heart. A guttural cry escapes my lips, a sound torn from the depths of my being. I collapse to the cold floor, concrete tearing into my knees, my body wracked with sobs. Each tear is a mourning for the life that will never be, a dream extinguished before it could ever take flight.

In the aftermath of her spell, the cell feels colder, emptier–a tomb for the future Wilder and I might have shared. The walls seem to absorb my cries, my grief a mere whisper in the vast expanse of loss and desolation.

In this moment, stripped of illusions, I'm nothing but a vessel of shattered dreams and longings. The echo of his touch still lingers on my skin, his seed still dripping out of me, both a haunting reminder of a love that defies the bars of my prison yet cannot transcend the cruel dictates of fate.

And so, I weep. Not just for the child that will never be, but for the fragments of my heart that lie scattered in the wake of their departure, each shard a witness to the love and loss that define my existence.

CHAPTER FORTY-SEVEN

WILDER

The heavy traipse through the Wastelands has taken a toll on my weary soul. Only my all-consuming thoughts of Morte and our time together had been enough to keep me moving forward. I'm on a mission, one born of undying love and a resolve forged in desolation. With each step towards Castanea, the reunion with Morte's friends and allies looms in the distance, a pivotal moment that will set the course for what comes next. In the expanse of this barren desert, I find clarity in my solitude. Now, as I approach the world she calls home, I'm ready—to plan, to fight, to do whatever it takes to bring her back to me.

I'm fucking wrecked.

I dive into the clear water of the small pond that leads to the underground oasis, surrendering to the pull of magic that longs to drag me down. In seconds, I'm spit out below the surface, landing in a hidden grotto adorned with massive stalagmites. Shifting into my merfae form for a bit, I glide through the currents, wetting my gills. I can sense Morte's essence lingering in the very molecules of the water, and it eases the ache in my chest.

Gracefully gliding through the water, my merfae form slices through the shadowy depths like a predator in pursuit. As I ascend, my body transitions into my fae form, emerging from the water's embrace. Droplets shimmer on my skin, catching the subtle glow of bioluminescent light that dances across the cavern walls, casting a serene, otherworldly radiance in this hidden underwater realm.

I'm jogging through the winding tunnels, my feet splashing through puddles and water sloshing in my boots with each step. My grief sharpens as fury fills me, my emotions all over the place at being apart from my anchor so soon after mating.

I let two hundred years go by, when I could've been loving her. Giving her all of me, in any form she could have it. And now she's trapped behind thick walls and metal bars I must find a way to breach.

With a roar that echoes through the depths of the earth, I summon the full fury of the ocean to my side. Every sea, river, lake, and spring rises up in a tumultuous wave, crashing against each other with a deafening force. The power surging within me is unstoppable, fueled by the might of every drop of water in this realm. I'm an unstoppable force, fueled by the endless depths of the ocean.

Few can rival the power of a merfae. Our magic works in tandem with the sea and the moons. I take some deep breaths, centering myself before pushing off the wall, jogging back down the corridor. I've got to keep it together, or her friends will never want to help me.

Stepping into Morte's home brings bone-deep longing. The familiar scent of her fills my senses, intertwining with the perfumed aroma of her belongings. A smirk adorns my face, unbidden. Did she spray it, knowing I'd be here, amongst her things?

As I make my way through each room, taking in the remnants of her life before imprisonment, a mixture of anger and sorrow churns within me. Anger at the world that unjustly took her away from me, and sorrow for the pain she has endured while trapped behind cold, unforgiving bars.

She doesn't even have her magic to warm her.

At least when I was in prison, I was used to the cold. She can't feel the heat of her beast, nor my touch to chase away the chill.

I find myself standing in front of her bedroom door, my hand hovering above the handle. The silence hangs heavy in the air, broken only by the sound of my own breaths. With a deep inhale, I push open the door, and cross to her bed, burying myself in her pillow.

Closing my eyes, I inhale deeply, letting the intoxicating scent of Morte envelop me. It's a heady mix of her essence—spun sugar and salty seas—and the lingering memories we've shared in this very room.

Nostalgia floods my mind, each story a precious gem. The nights we spent tangled in each other's arms, whispering secrets and dreams into the darkness. The stolen kisses that ignited flames deep within our souls. The way her laughter echoed through the room, filling it with joy and light.

But now, all that remains are echoes and shadows.

Shucking my clothes, I stumble into the shower, bracing my arms against the tile as the water thunders against my back. I allow it to wash away the dirt and sand from my journey across the Wastelands. Grabbing a loofa on a string, I pump Morte's body wash into it, lathering my body with her scent.

I close my eyes, letting the warm water and the intoxicating aroma of her body wash transport me back to the nights we shared in this very house. When I'd sit on her bed, and she left the bathroom door open. The steam fills the bathroom, transforming it into our own little sanctuary where I was free to explore her body with my eyes, yearning to feel her smooth skin under my hands.

As I lather the soap over my skin, memories of her touch from when I finally had her pinned beneath me flood my mind. The way her fingers traced delicate patterns across my chest, igniting a fire that consumed us both. The gentle press of her lips against my neck, each kiss leaving a trail of sparks in its wake. The way she moaned my name like a prayer on her lips, her voice carrying the weight of our love millennia in the making.

The water cascades down my body, cleansing away the grime of the outside world while simultaneously reminding me of our separation. How I long to have Morte standing here with me, to feel the softness of her body pressed against mine as we make love.

I let out a deep sigh, a mixture of frustration and desire, as I lean against the shower wall. The water pounds against my back, mimicking the rhythm of my racing heart. Thoughts of Morte fill every corner of my mind, consuming me like a voracious flame.

My hand travels down my chest, tracing the ridges and valleys of my muscles, as if trying to recreate the touch of her fingertips. The steam in the shower swirls around me, creating a haze that mirrors the fog of my desire. I close my eyes, imagining her delicate hands against my skin, her nails leaving trails of delicious pain in their wake.

In my mind, I can see her—her body flushed with desire, her eyes filled with an untamed passion that matches my own. Imagining her beneath me, her legs wrapped around my waist, fuels the fire within me. My hand moves faster, matching the rhythm of my racing heart.

The steam-filled bathroom becomes a sanctuary of desire as I succumb to the intoxication of my own touch. Each stroke sends ripples of pleasure through my body, mirroring the waves crashing against the shore. I imagine Morte's soft moans mingling with the sound of the water, her voice carrying the melody of our shared ecstasy.

In my mind, I can feel her thighs tighten around me, her nails digging into my back as I invade her depths. The image becomes so vivid that it feels as if she's truly here with me, our bodies locked in a dance of passion and desperation. The fantasy unfolds before me like a scene from a forbidden dream, and I lose myself in the intoxicating rhythm we once shared.

The steam clouds my vision, amplifying the sensations coursing through me as I approach the precipice of release. My breath quickens, and heavy panting that echoes in my ears. Imagining her hands tangled in my hair, the sting of her grip on it a delicious pain I cling to.

With each stroke, her moans mingle with the sound of the water raining down on us. Her soft lips press against mine, fueling my desire, pushing me closer to the edge. As I call out her name into the steam-filled air, my body tenses and shudders with release.

I need to fill her, to pump her full until my seed is all spent, dripping down the inside of her thighs, only so I can shove it back where it belongs.

Breathing heavily, I lean my forearm against the shower wall, the water now lukewarm against my flushed skin. My heart still gallops, but a sense of emptiness settles within me. The physical release brings momentary relief, but it cannot compare to the connection I long for with my anchor.

I step out of the shower and wrap a towel around my waist, my mind already shifting back to tomorrow's task:

Do whatever it takes to plead her case with the powers that be. Morte worked too long, too hard, to be thrown away and forgotten about by the realm that took so much but gave her so little in return.

Pausing in front of the window, a growl builds deep inside of me. Each one of these Tolden would be dead if it weren't for Morte's sacrifice.

I stalk through the dimly lit living room, my bare feet making soft thuds against the hardwood floor. I reach the kitchen and open a cabinet to retrieve a tall glass for water. As I turn to leave, something catches my eye on the table. A small shrine is arranged meticulously, with candles and offerings laid out in perfect symmetry. The faint scent of pyrolysis lingers in the air. In the center of it all sits a snuffed candle, still smoking and casting a ghostly haze over the sacred space.

A feeling of unease washes over me like a cold, damp fog as I stare at the object in front of me. A nagging thought tugs at my consciousness, urging me to pay closer attention. I turn to the counter and reach for the small piece of paper with Morte's detailed instructions scrawled on it in flowing script. My eyes scan down to number six, dread crawling up my spine, taking residence in my heart.

6. Don't let the candle go out.

The inky darkness of the night wraps around me, a suffocating cloak that seems to thicken with my every breath. Panic claws at my chest.

The protective candle—the one thing between Morte and unspeakable darkness—has been extinguished.

Barefoot, I stumble from the warmth of Morte's treehouse, the urgent need to find Noct consuming me. The delicate fae flies flit around the treetops, but they feel like obstacles in my path. As I sprint, I conjure clothes so I can drop my towel. The usually serene pathways of the underground now feel like a maze designed to entrap, each shadow a lurking menace.

"Noct!" My voice shatters the nocturnal symphony of chirping insects and rustling leaves. It's a shout laced with a terror that is foreign to my nature. A terror for her, not of her.

I race across the swaying bridges, the hollow thud of my footsteps a drumbeat in the hushed world. Noct's home, somewhere north of here, seems like a distant refuge, and every second lost a betrayal to Morte's safety.

The sense of foreboding grows with every passing moment, a dark cloud that threatens the very essence of my being. It's not just fear; it's a premonition. Something terrible is on the horizon, something that the extinguished candle has heralded.

I feel it in my blood. Taste it on the back of my tongue.

I round another platform, my shouts growing more desperate. Lights flicker on in the wake of my passage, faces peeking from behind curtains and doors, a mix of concern and curiosity etched on sleepy features. They all know me now—the man who had himself imprisoned on behalf of their hero—now a harbinger of chaos in their tranquil world.

"Help me." My voice cracks as I plead with passing shadows. "I need to find Noct!"

A figure steps forward from a doorway, a neighbor, concern etched on his face, a child clinging to his leg. His outstretched arm points me towards Noct's house, standing like a lighthouse in the storm of my panic. For a moment, the chaos around me blurs into the background as I latch onto this lifeline.

I don't stop to offer thanks; I can't. Gratitude is a currency I'll repay later, should the fates allow it.

Finally, Noct's house looms before me, its sturdy wooden door a barrier to the answers I seek. I hammer against it with the side of my fist, the sound echoing like a war drum through the night.

The door swings open, revealing Noct, her silver eyes wide with alarm. I pause at the threshold, the urgency I feel surely etched on my face in stark, desperate lines.

"Noct," I start, my voice urgent but respectful of the space between us. "It's about Morte. Something's wrong. We need to act quickly."

She ushers me in, but I shake my head as I turn to head back in the direction of Morte's treehouse.

"It's the candle," I manage to gasp, my words stumbling over each other in a mix of fear and haste. "It went out. There's something wrong with Morte. I can feel it." A tightness grips my chest, a sensation beyond physical discomfort. It's a deep, unmistakable fear that resonates through the invisible, yet unbreakable tether of our mating bond. This isn't just my emotion; it's a shared distress, a signal of danger from the connection that binds me to Morte.

Noct's expression morphs from surprise to a primal fear that spread across her features like wildfire. She's a warrior, quick to respond to any threat, especially one involving her closest friend.

"Show me," she commands, already moving to follow me.

We race back to Morte's house, my heart a drumbeat out of sync with the world, my thoughts a maelstrom centered on her. The sense of foreboding settles over me like a shroud, a dark omen that this night is the herald of a change neither of us may be prepared for.

As we approach Morte's treehouse, the air feels thicker, charged with a tension that's almost palpable, a lingering malice that threads itself through the treetops. I lead Noct to the small shrine where the candle had been burning—a space now marred by the extinguished wick, still perfuming the air.

Noct examines the shrine with a practiced eye, her movements methodical, the mark of a warrior who remains calm despite her own fear. She's silent, but her furrowed brow speaks volumes. After a moment, she steps back, her gaze meeting mine with a resolution that's as comforting as it is alarming.

My hand flies to my chest, trying to grip onto my racing heart as the overwhelming fear and panic from the mating bond threatens to consume me. I stumble backwards, grasping for anything to steady myself against the onslaught of emotions until my back collides with the sturdy table. My fingers dig into the wood, leaving deep grooves as I fight to stay upright in the face of such intense sensations.

"We need to get to Convectus Castle immediately," Noct says decisively. "The High King and Queen might be able to help. They have resources we don't to get into the prison immediately."

My mind races. Convectus Castle, the seat of power, is days away. "But that would take time, days we don't have," I protest. The thought of being so far from Morte while she's in danger is unbearable.

Noct reaches into the small pouch at her belt, pulling out a small, luminescent stone. "Not with this," she says, holding up a portal stone, and I curse in relief. I've never seen one before, but its sheen and enormous power is unmistakable. "It can take us to the castle in moments. From there, we can reach out to the High King and Queen. They have the means to check on Morte at Bedlam Penitentiary."

We can't sift to the island, nor can we sift from The Wastelands, even if we're on the surface. This is our only option, and the idea of using a portal stone hadn't even crossed my mind—they're as rare as merfae. It's risky, unpredictable at times, but the urgency of the situation leaves no room for hesitation.

"Let's go," I whisper.

Noct nods, her expression steely. "Prepare yourself. Portaling is not a gentle journey."

As she begins the incantation to activate the portal stone, I brace myself, both for the journey ahead and for the unknown fate awaiting Morte. The air around us starts to shimmer, the boundaries of reality blurring as the power of the stone comes to life.

The portal's maw opens with a deafening silence, a swirling vortex of shimmering blues and greens, beckoning us through to the surface. As we pass through, the air feels electric against our skin, and the scenery shifts before our eyes. We traverse over a desolate land, the ground below us barren and cracked, before soaring over a small stretch of jagged mountains. The landscape changes once again as we descend into a quaint town, its cobblestone streets illuminated by the soft glow of lanterns. Finally, we arrive just outside the gates where the king and queen hold court.

They're not likely here in the middle of the night, but the guards will be able to get them for us.

Stepping through the portal is a visceral experience, and the sensation of being pulled and stretched envelopes us until we emerge under the vastness of the open sky. In the silence that follows the portal's closing, the night seems to inhale deeply, the sudden stillness almost ringing in our ears. The moons, hanging like celestial guardians, bathe the landscape in a silver luminescence that feels both alien and familiar. Grass blades, tipped with dew, shimmer under the night's kiss, their whispers soft as they sway in a gentle breeze. Fae flies dance atop their greenery, as though drunken and merry.

I can smell the brine of the ocean in the distance, hear the roar of its call that sings in my veins, begging me to join it. Giant, vegetation-covered mountains loom in the distance, their might a natural fortress around the castle.

The castle isn't far from the gates we pass through, and as we race across the fields, the portal stone's residual magic fuels our speed. We dodge between the night blooms and over the silver streams that crisscross the landscape like threads of moonlight.

Upon reaching the towering fortress that encases the heart of Convectus Castle, the guards startle at our sudden emergence—barefoot and in sleepwear. Their initial shock quickly gives way to recognition as they notice Noct. Known realm-wide as a member of The Great Company, her presence commands respect and immediate attention.

She steps forward, embodying both authority and a profound sense of urgency. Her voice, firm and resolute, cuts through the midnight air, leaving no room for doubt or delay. "We must speak with High King Finian and High Queen Lana immediately," she asserts. "It's a matter of life and death."

Her words, heavy with demand, hang in the air, compelling the guards into swift action.

We're ushered into the gleaming hall, where magic hangs thick in the air, an ever-present guard against the unknown. The vastness of the hall, with its high arched ceilings and intricate tapestries depicting battles and myths of old, is overwhelming. The dim light of moonbeams filters through stained glass windows, painting kaleidoscopic patterns on the polished marble floor.

Noct and I, still clad in our night attire, stand in stark contrast to the grandeur around us. Our bare feet are cold against the stone, proof of the urgency that brought us here. The guards, having relayed our message, leave us in this chamber of echoes and whispers.

While waiting, Noct paces the length of the hall, her footsteps silent but her presence as commanding as the statues of past rulers lining the walls. Her brow is furrowed, her eyes distant, undoubtedly strategizing our next move.

I find myself drawn to one of the large windows, gazing out into the night, feeling the grief in every cell in my body. The moons, silent observers in the sky, seem to hold secrets too profound for our understanding. I can't help but wonder about the countless others who have stood here before us, seeking aid or solace in times of crisis.

Noct stops pacing and joins me at the window. Her silver eyes reflect the moonlight, giving her an ethereal appearance. "They will come," she says, more to herself than to me. "They must."

We stand side by side in silence, each lost in our thoughts. The tension between us is a living thing, a shared anxiety for Morte's fate. Despite the grandeur and the magic that permeates the air, there's a fragility to this moment, a sense of being on the cusp of something irreversible.

The wait stretches on, the silence punctuated only by the occasional whisper of fabric as Noct shifts her stance.

Eventually, the sound of footsteps announces the approach of someone. We turn, expecting the arrival of the royals, hoping that with them comes the aid we so desperately need for Morte. The door to the great hall creaks open, and High King Finian and High Queen

Lana enter, their faces grave and concerned. The significance of their titles is immediately evident, the seriousness of their roles mirrored in their eyes.

Lana's thick brown curls dance wildly across her face, proof to her having just been pulled out of bed. Finian's ash blond hair is tied up out of his face, lending him a harsher appearance.

The High King startles at seeing me, recognition from his visit to me at the prison apparent. They greet us formally, their voices low and measured, though not unkind. They listen intently as Noct explains the situation, her voice cracking with emotion as she speaks of Morte's predicament.

"Wait." Lana ushers us to a side room, away from prying eyes and ears as she shuts the door behind us after we're all inside. She gestures to a small table with several high-backed chairs around it. "Please, sit." Once we're all seated, she reaches a hand out to lay on Noct's. "What do you mean, Morte is in prison?" She glances at her soul bonded mate, confusion evident in the furrow of her brows.

Finian's shoulders shrug as he turns his attention back to us. "I didn't know that, either." He glances at me. "And the last place I saw you was in prison." He states the obvious.

"She's in danger." I lean forward, trying, but failing to keep the anger out of my voice. "We can get to why later—please send someone to check on her right away."

Lana stands, pushing back from the table as she rushes to the door and pokes her head out of it, whispering to a guard on the other side of the door. Footsteps echo with their retreat, and my shoulders relax marginally.

When she returns to the table, she takes a seat and nods her head at me to continue.

I explain what happened two hundred years ago, and how I took the blame and bound Morte's tongue to prevent her from telling the truth. Lana's eyes water as she clings to her mate's hand, and the heartache lining her features is a small comfort.

"She's my anchor," I whisper. "And someone is after her."

"Anchor?" Lana asks.

"Like a soul bonded mate, but for merfae," Finian supplies, his features softening as he glances at his own soul bonded mate.

She cocks her head at him. "I thought mermaids weren't real. You told Hannah they weren't."

I cough, clearing my throat. "No, not mermaids. Merfae. Much more powerful than the fabled creatures of the sea." I offer her a small smile.

Finian leans back in his chair, a calculated look on his face. "It's probably Aggonid searching for her," he says, and Lana's head whips his way. "He wanted her to come back to the Underworld."

"Aggonid?" Fear spikes in my chest at the mention of the fae devil. They're soul bonded. This can't be good.

Grief mars Lana's features, no doubt reliving the agony of losing her mate, Gideon, who Finn had to drag back from hell, and came back haunted. It's whispered amongst the guards at the prison, a tale meant to keep us inmates in line, so we stay out of the devil's clutches.

Finian hesitates. "She'd been in the Underworld under his tutelage and my mother brought her back to Bedlam per her request. He asked for her back, stating the realm was unstable without her, and she declined. I wouldn't be surprised if he tried to collect her himself."

I grip the table, splintering it, the words getting caught in my throat. I agreed I'd share her, but if he takes her from Bedlam, how will I ever see her again?

"Can he do that?" Noct whispers.

Fuck, I haven't told her yet.

Finian winces. "Not without consequence, but he's a god, and I wouldn't put it past him to try."

"Could he get into the prison?" Lana turns to her mate. "I thought it was impenetrable?"

His fingers flex around hers. "There isn't a place in all the realms beyond his reach. It might take him some time, but he can get anyone, anywhere. It's his role as leader of the Underworld."

Lana's face falls upon hearing this.

As the king and queen speak in hushed tones amongst themselves, I find myself lost in my thoughts. If Aggonid is truly the one after her, and he drags her back to the Underworld, I'll follow her anywhere. I look at my hands, still gripping the table. The power within me surges, threatening to break free, and I will it back under control.

My attention snaps to Lana when I hear the next words she utters.

"We must pardon her." Her brows are pinched, her hand squeezing her king's.

"What?" I sit up in the chair, not breathing in case I misheard her.

Lana seems to gather her thoughts, weighing each word with the gravity of the situation. "On Earth, where I'm from," she continues, her voice steady but imbued with a deep conviction, "Morte's actions would be viewed through a different lens. There, in a similar situation, someone might face charges of involuntary manslaughter or be considered to have acted in self-defense."

She locks eyes with Finian, her gaze unwavering. "Morte was in an impossible position. She faced an immediate threat to her life and the safety of her people. The law must consider the context of her actions. She was defending herself against those who would exploit and harm her, and her response, though tragic, was a result of that threat."

With a hint of emotion in her tone, Lana continues. "On Earth, justice isn't just about punishment; it's about understanding the circumstances, the intent behind actions. Morte's case requires that understanding. It's not black and white. She was pushed into a corner, fighting for her life and her people's secrecy. You and I know better than anyone how important it is to protect the ones you love."

She pauses, letting her words sink in. "Given these extraordinary circumstances, I believe a full pardon is not only just but necessary. It recognizes the complexity of her situation and the fact that her actions, though regrettable, stemmed from a need to protect and survive. We've both done worse for each other," she whispers, allowing a single tear to streak down her cheek.

The room falls silent as Lana's words echo off the ancient walls, her argument hanging in the air, a plea for mercy and understanding in a world where such things are often scarce. The king and queen exchange a look, a silent conversation in their shared gaze as they weigh the decision before them. All royal fae can read minds, and no doubt they're conversing now.

Meanwhile, I sit there, clinging to every incline of head, every minute gesture, the hope inside me flickering like a fragile flame in the dark.

Finian's eyes, filled with a depth of understanding only a soul-bonded mate could possess, meet mine. "We know the agony of separation all too well," he says softly. "And we recognize the turmoil in your heart. But know this, Wilder: by dawn, we will officially pardon Morte."

All the air leaves my lungs, and I can barely feel Noct's sudden, reassuring grip on my arm as she lets out a quiet expiration.

Lana nods in solemn agreement. "Tonight, though, you must find rest. It's not just a command, but counsel from those who have weathered similar storms. Strength, both of heart and body, will be crucial in the days and weeks to come." She gestures to our outfits. "I'll have clothes brought for you."

Her words, though meant to soothe, do little to quell the tempest inside me. But I recognize the wisdom in them. Morte's safety, the prospect of her pardon, hinges on our ability to face what comes next with clear minds and rested bodies.

"We'll do our best," Noct says, her voice steady despite the shadows of worry in her eyes. We exchange a glance, an agreement to lean on each other for support.

"As soon as we receive word about Morte, we'll have someone come collect you," the king offers.

As we're escorted to a guest room, the castle's silent halls seem to echo with the significance of pending decisions and the passage of time. In the privacy of the room, Noct and I sit in a thick silence, each absorbed in our thoughts, yet drawing a quiet strength from each other's presence.

I should be relieved, but fear has me wound so tight.

The night stretches on, an interminable canvas of shadows and moonlight. Despite the comfort of the bedroom, sleep is a reluctant visitor. My thoughts keep drifting to Morte, imagining her in a place far from here, alone and afraid. The bond between us, a usually comforting presence, now feels like a tightrope stretched taut with alarm.

Dawn, with its promise of a new beginning and Morte's pardon, can't come soon enough. In this room, amidst the soft rustle of fabric and the distant sound of the castle settling, I find myself unnerved.

Noct shoves a cookie in her mouth, nervously pacing about the room as her other hand clutches a cup. "I feel like I'm going to be sick," she whispers.

I'm used to quietly stewing in my own grief, with no one to talk to, so her words startle me for a moment before they register.

"Morte has mates." I lean back on the couch, staring at the ceiling.

"What?" Noct's mug of tea tumbles out of her hand.

"Aggonid is her soul bond. Azazel and Caius are her other mates." Fear grips my chest. "What if he's going to take her from me?"

She comes to the other side of the couch, staring down at me. "He might be the devil, but if you think anyone can take her away from *you*, soul bond or not, you don't know her well enough."

"But he could take her to the Underworld!" I sit up so that I can face her properly instead of upside down.

"She clawed her way back to get you before." She puts another cookie in her mouth, and I'd chuckle at it if I didn't feel like my world was falling apart.

"I just got her back," I breathe, feeling haunted.

She rounds the couch to sit next to me. "I know the feeling well."

"What do you mean?" I take a cookie when she offers it to me, but I can't find the will to eat.

"You might've been best friends for centuries, but she was always mine. Aside from Ronin." She winces. "I thought she was dead for two years. I grieved her with every bit of my soul, so much so that it caused me to miscarry twice in her absence."

I blink, feeling choked up. "I—I'm sorry."

What do you say to someone who has lost their whole world? I'm out of practice speaking to people, and them speaking to me as though I matter. That my opinion matters. I glance at the cookie in her hand, wanting to ask, but knowing that'd be the dumbest thing to ever come out of my mouth. You don't ask grieving mothers if they're expecting another.

She glances down at the half-eaten piece, chuckling nervously to herself. "No, no, we're not expecting now." She sighs. "She'd never get over it if she knew."

I suppose not.

Before long, we retire to our rooms, and I try to sleep in a bed that feels too big without my anchor by my side.

The night stretches on, endless and heavy, as I find myself restless within the margins of my own private bedroom. Each tick of the clock seems to echo the pounding of my fears, amplifying the dread that lurks in the silence of my secluded room.

The early morning light begins to seep through the heavy curtains, splashing a pale glow across the floor that offers no comfort. It's at this liminal hour, when the world hovers between night and day, that a soft knock on the door jolts me from my vigil.

I answer the door to find a royal emissary, clad in an elaborate uniform of gold and purple. His face is marked with lines of worry as he stands in the hallway, his chest rising and falling rapidly as if he's just run a great distance. His eyes, wide and filled with fear, betray the gravity of his message even before he speaks.

"Mr. Ripple," he begins, his voice quivering, "the guards have returned with news from Bedlam Penitentiary. Morte Incendara's cell ... it was found empty."

The words slash through me like a jagged knife, shredding any semblance of hope I had left. My body trembles with the effort to stay composed, my fists clenching so tightly that my nails cut into my palms. "Empty," I choke out, the word bitter and metallic on my tongue. "How can you be so certain?" My voice cracks with desperation as I search for any glimmer of reassurance.

The guard nods, his eyes downcast. "The High King and Queen request your presence in the council chamber immediately."

In a flash of swift movement, Noct is at my side, her warrior's instincts honed and ready for action. We race after the page, our feet echoing through the grand hallways of the awakening castle. The air crackles with electricity, the tension palpable that builds like a brewing storm. The looming walls and towering spires seem to watch us as we hurry along, their ancient stone seeming to pulse with a foreboding sense of danger.

The Council chamber is abuzz with hushed voices and the rustle of maps and missives as we enter. King Finian and High Queen Lana preside over a table strewn with intelligence reports, their faces etched with concern.

"Report," Finian commands, his gaze settling on a grim-faced guard who steps forward.

"Your Majesties," the man begins, maintaining a crisp salute despite the weight of his news. "At 0400 hours, we completed our inspection of Bedlam Penitentiary. Interestingly, the magical wards remained intact, and inmate Incendara's cell was found empty."

The emissary's words slice through the fog of my waking mind, a cruel blade of reality that shreds the last vestiges of my denial. My vision narrows, the ornate edges of the room blurring into irrelevance as a singular, piercing thought impales my consciousness.

Morte is gone.

A strangled gasp escapes my lips, the sound of it foreign and ragged in the solemnity of the council chamber. The room spins, the faces of the assembled a blur of colors and shapes, indistinct and unimportant against the backdrop of my dread.

Noct's hand finds my arm, a grounding force, but it's distant, a lifeline thrown across an abyss that has already claimed me.

"There were no signs of struggle or the usual traces of portal magic. However, we did detect unusual fluctuations in the ambient magic, particularly around the metal structure of the cell, which is quite uncommon. It's almost as if the metal itself interacted with some external force. It's perplexing; she seems to have vanished into thin air."

The room falls silent, the guard's report hanging in the air like a specter.

"Vanished," Lana whispers, her expression one of disbelief. "How is that possible?"

The man shakes his head. "We're investigating all possibilities, but it's as though she was plucked from her cell by unseen forces."

"Were ashes present?" I cup the back of my neck, fear nearly choking me.

"No, sir," the guard replies.

Noct's hand grips mine, her touch both comforting and steadying.

"We have to find her," I say, my voice hoarse. "Please." I turn towards the royals. "I just got her back."

Finian's jaw sets, his kingly poise unwavering. "We will move heaven and earth to find her," he vows. "Our best trackers, our most skilled teams—they'll be tasked with this search." He turns his attention to Noct. "I want The Great Company on this immediately."

"And the Underworld?" Noct asks, her voice sharp. "Could Aggonid be behind this?"

"It's within his power," Finian admits, "but he risks much by such an act. A direct violation of our sovereignty. And why manipulate the metal when he can simply rip open a portal in her cell?"

Lana steps forward, her queenly composure giving way to a more personal concern. "We can't rule out any possibilities. This abduction, if it is such, bears the mark of considerable power."

The room erupts into a flurry of activity, orders given, strategies debated. Through it all, I stand beside Noct, my mind reeling with the implications of my anchor's disappearance.

"We'll start with the closest realms," Finian decides, his command cutting through the chaos. "Alert our allies, secure their borders. If Morte has been taken, the culprit may still be near. I'll organize a meeting with Aggonid immediately."

"Wait," I breathe, and when they don't, I yell, "WAIT!"

Everyone's attention turns towards me. "It has to be Aggonid. He's her soul bonded mate."

Gasps ring out around us, fear and dread in equal measure across their faces.

Lana nods in agreement, her gaze meeting mine with a silent promise. "We'll find her, Wilder. You have our word."

As the royal couple turns to coordinate the search with the queen's other mates filing in, Noct and I step back, our own silent conversation strangled by fear. Morte is out there, somewhere, and I can feel the pull of our bond, a beacon guiding me through the dark. Only it feels much weaker than before. As though she's in another realm or weakened in some way.

"We won't stop until we bring her home." Noct puts her arms around me, giving me the strength of her support as my knees threaten to buckle.

"If he took her ... then I need to go with." I interrupt the royals speaking in hushed voices over the scattered maps on the table. "I'd like to come to this meeting you set up with Aggonid."

They exchange nervous glances with each other. "I'm not so certain that's a good idea," Gideon, Lana's mate who returned from hell interjects. "I've spent more time than I'd like with him. He's just as likely to strike you dead as he is to listen to your reasoning. And if he brings his mate, Caius? He's even more unhinged than he is."

"I understand the risk," I reason, my gaze drowning in the ocean of his vast blues. He's the more poetic, unabashed mates of the queen's, and speaking to his true nature will sway him to my side. Despite his power and his wrath, if I can appeal to anyone, it's Gideon.

"We don't have time for cautious decisions. Every sinew, every shard of my being screams that this decision, dangerous though it may be, is the one I must make. Please." I drop to my knees, hands splayed on my thighs, willing him to understand as I bare my soul. "She is more than my anchor; she is the very essence of my existence. You know how this feels, Gideon. You, who tore through the gates of hell, who kindled war's fierce flames for Lana's love, you know the depths of this grief." My voice falters, a broken whisper amidst our shared understanding of the heavy price of love. "Grant me permission to chase my dawn, to wrest my entire world from the jaws of despair. She's everything to me."

Gideon's eyes soften, and Lana grips his shoulder, her eyes shimmering with tears. He nods, slowly. "Very well." He gives me a sad smile before glancing at Finn. "If the rest are okay with it, I am, too."

I nod, rising slowly to my feet. With that agreement made, Lana sends out a realm-wide missive to all their forces about Morte's official pardon and subsequent kidnapping before we make our way to a secret passageway hidden within the castle walls that'll lead us to the small portal to Romarie.

It's time to call for Aggonid.

CHAPTER FORTY-EIGHT

MORTE

Consciousness greets me not with the familiar, harsh clang of prison bars, but with the softness of linen and the cushion of a mattress beneath me. My eyes flutter open to opulence I've never known—a room grand in size, adorned with rich tapestries, metal adornments, and gilded furniture that glimmers in the slanting light of dawn. The disparity between this place and the stark cell of my recent memories is jarring, disorienting.

My limbs, heavy with an unknown lethargy, resist movement as I attempt to rise. The clink of metal alerts me to the suppression cuffs binding my wrists—cuffs that hold my magic at bay, rendering me as vulnerable as a fledgling. A shiver crawls up my spine, not from the chill of the unfamiliar room, but from the realization of my predicament.

I'm not alone.

Across the room, seated in a high-backed chair that seems more a throne than a piece of furniture, is a figure shrouded in shadows. The morning light spills into the room, yet cautiously avoids the space where he sits, as if the sun itself is wary of this man.

"You're awake." His voice resonates, a timbre both deep and chillingly familiar. "I trust you find your accommodations satisfactory?"

I don't need to see his face to recognize the veiled threat in his words, nor the power that laces each syllable. I draw in a steady breath, willing my voice to be calm and even. "Where am I?"

His chuckle is a dark melody that fills the space between us. "Somewhere safe, Lady Morte. Somewhere your ... talents can be appreciated. Happy to have you back."

Back?

This doesn't look like the Underworld to me. Or at least, what I imagine the Underworld looks like.

I take stock of my surroundings, noting the strategic placement of artifacts and weapons—decorative yet undoubtedly lethal—along the walls. So whoever this is, he doesn't see me as a threat, or he doesn't know who I really am, as I have easy access to things I can maim him with. The windows, tall and imposing, offer a view of skies I don't recognize, clouds that paint a picture of a world beyond my reach.

"You haven't answered my question," I press, my gaze steady, though my heart hammers a frantic rhythm against my ribs.

"You're in my castle," he reveals at last, stepping into the light. A handsome man, though harsh lines, not of age, but of a subtle brutality, mar his face, and in his regal bearing, emerges as a figure both elegant and ominous.

His presence commands the room, and his attire is a tapis of wealth and might. The morning sun that dances upon the golden threads of his cloak does little to soften the hard lines of his expression. He watches me with eyes that hold centuries of secrets, eyes that have witnessed the turning of ages and the fall of empires.

I remain silent, my mind racing as I search for the undercurrents beneath his words. His mention of 'talents' is no casual compliment; it's an acknowledgment of my power, a power he seeks to harness for purposes I've yet to fathom.

He moves with predatory grace, each step measured, a testament to the control he wields over not just his domain, but the very air we breathe. "You have a role to play in the events to come," he continues, stopping just out of arm's reach. "Your ... cooperation is expected."

The iron grip of the cuffs feels suddenly tighter. Yet, within me, a fire ignites—a refusal to bend, to break under his gaze.

"My cooperation," I echo, the edge in my voice belying the calm I project. "And if I refuse?"

A smile plays upon his lips, not of amusement but of a challenge anticipated. "You won't," he says with certainty. "The stakes are far greater than you know."

Questions swarm in my mind, each more urgent than the last. The stakes, my role, the reason for my abduction from the supposed safety of the prison—all threads in a larger weave I cannot yet see. But one thing is clear: despair will not claim me. Not while breath still fills my lungs and resolve courses through my veins.

I meet his gaze squarely, my chin lifted in defiance. "Then enlighten me. What game do we play?"

The fae regards me for a moment, as if measuring my worth, then nods as if to himself. "In time, Lady Morte. For now, rest. Gather your strength." He gestures to the room, to the splendor that serves as my gilded cage. "You will need it. I love breaking them in hard and fast."

With that, he turns and exits, leaving me to the silence and my thoughts. The door closes with a whisper, the click of the lock a soft declaration of my captivity.

Breaking them in? What the fuck does that mean?

I push against the suppression cuffs, testing their strength. The metal bites into my skin, and that's when I notice dried blood on the inside of my elbow. What would he need to draw my blood for?

I refuse to succumb to fear. If this man believes he can break me, bend me to his will, he is sorely mistaken.

In this opulent prison, I'm determined to find a way out. The gilded furniture may shimmer under the light of the false dawn, but it holds no appeal for me. It represents a life of luxury and submission that I reject with every fiber of my being.

With measured steps, I begin to explore the room. Conscious of hidden eyes and ears, I speak softly to myself, strategizing my next move. My fingers brush against the cool surface of a golden vase, letting it catch my reflection. I scrutinize my disheveled appearance—my wild red hair framing defiant eyes that flicker with obstinacy.

There is power in knowledge, and if I'm to defeat this enigmatic captor, I need to know the game. After spending the entire day mentally cataloging every inch of this room, I can't find anything that'll help me. The weapons on the wall are bolted down with magic of some sort.

As the last rays of sunlight fade from the sky, a soft knock echoes through the quiet room. The door swings open and a woman enters with a tray of food in her hands. Her long, pale hair falls in tight curls down her back, but she doesn't meet my gaze. My eyes are drawn to the shackles on her ankles, pulling tight against her skin with each shuffle she takes. Anger courses through me at the sight of such cruelty. The slip she has on is but a scrap of fabric that barely covers her. It's as if they're trying to strip away any shred of dignity or freedom this woman may have left.

"Hey." I approach her with caution, my hands out so as to not spook her. Fear fills her eyes as they flicker to mine. "I'm not going to hurt you."

A gasp escapes me when I notice the fresh gash across her cheek. She turns her cheek to her shoulder, as to hide from me.

"Did he do this to you?" My voice breaks for her.

She bites her lip, shaking her head as she shuffles back.

The woman's terror gives me pause. I soften my voice, holding my hands up in a placating gesture.

"It's okay," I say gently. "You don't have to tell me anything you're not comfortable with." I gesture to the tray of food she carries. "Is that for me?"

She gives a small nod and shuffles forward to place it on the table near the window. I note the simple fare—bread, a chunk of cheese, water in a paper cup. Nothing that could be used as a potential weapon.

My captor is thorough.

"Thank you," I say. "It was kind of you to bring it."

The woman risks a swift glance at me, perhaps surprised by my civil tone. In that brief look, I see a glimmer of something in her eyes. Not fear, but hope. Maybe even a small spark of defiance not yet extinguished despite her circumstances.

"My name is Morte. What's yours?"

She hesitates, eyes darting around as if expecting punishment for speaking. "He calls me Willow," she finally whispers.

Willow. I repeat the name in my mind, determined not to forget her or her plight.

As I observe her, I take in her rail-thin appearance. The darkness under her eyes is prominent, evidence of sleepless nights and exhaustion. Her cheeks are hollowed out, the bones of her face protruding against her pale skin. Her suppressant cuffs are noticeably larger than mine, a clear indication that she possesses a great deal of power, perhaps too much for standard restraints to contain. It's as if her very presence exudes an intense energy that needs to be restrained at all times.

This fucking monster.

Willow, like the tiny, thin branches of the tree.

"Do you want me to use your real name?" I whisper back, and it takes everything in me to keep the absolute rage out of my tone.

"Marina." The word barely reaches my ears.

Marina. The name lingers in the air, a fragile thread connecting us. I can see the flicker of recognition in her eyes at the sound of her true name, a spark of defiance that fuels my fire to free us both from this gilded prison.

"Marina," I repeat softly, letting the syllables roll off my tongue. I commit it to memory, vowing to remember her true identity and not allow her to be consumed by the dehumanizing anonymity imposed upon her. "We're going to get out of here, Marina. Together."

Her eyes widen with a mixture of fear and hope, as if daring to believe that escape may be within reach. But a shadow passes across them, reminding us both of the ever-present danger lurking beyond these walls.

"He watches us," Marina whispers, her voice trembling. "Every move we make. Every word we speak."

I nod, understanding the gravity of our situation. We're captives in a twisted game, pieces on a macabre chessboard manipulated by a sadistic puppeteer.

"Who is he?" I don't think this is the Underworld, unless the dreams I've conjured were all figments of my imagination.

Hell has a certain macabre beauty to it. This place is too grandiose, with its opulence and false light, as though all its extravagance is an illusion. Darkness lurks behind this façade, and that's more terrifying than a realm that doesn't pretend to be anything other than what it is.

Her mouth opens to speak, but noise in the hallway has her scurrying towards the door as fast as her manacles can take her. She spares a last glance at me before slipping out of the room, the only sound the soft snick of the door closing and the lock engaging.

Well, fuck.

CHAPTER FORTY-NINE

CAIUS

"Are we certain this will do it?" Aggonid's unease is evident in the way he keeps himself back from the sanguimetal, eyeing it from afar. The metal, known for its ability to amplify magic—but at a cost—gleams under the faint light, its surface a canvas of deep crimson and obsidian swirls.

Az, ever the charming little jerk, gives a curt nod. "It's our best shot at sustaining the dreamscape longer," he says, his hands deftly assembling the necessary components. "You won't find anyone in the Underworld better at manipulating its magic than me, though. I wouldn't risk her if I weren't one-hundred-percent confident in this."

I've never seen my big scary devil so nervous. But I know the real reason he worries about us transferring her memories.

His aren't all good.

So when the guard barges into the room, trembling and bumbling about an urgent summons from the High King of the Fae, Aggonid happily excuses himself. "Duty calls," he says as he kisses me on the lips and departs.

This type of summons has only happened one other time—when they needed to drag the little vampire back to Bedlam. Whatever is so important must be of that magnitude to warrant such a request.

"He left quick." Az studies the door. "You'd think he'd want to be here for this."

"We don't need his magic if we've got this." Emeric peeks out from under the table, grunting as though he's really struggling to connect something.

We had the reapers bring several items from the Earth realm. EMF generator, bioluminescent algae, and charged ley line soil. Four of the nine reapers we sent to Romarie didn't return when we'd sent them for more sanguimetal.

It's as if they'd simply vanished.

"This should do it." Emeric fiddles with the components while Az works to fuse pieces of sanguimetal to it. "I don't think the dreamscape will close unless we want it to now."

I might've had some of the demons spend all evening dragging giant hunks of metal to the castle using their powers. The clanking and scraping of metal against stone echoed through the corridors, accompanied by the occasional roar or scream as a demon gave up. I only had to kill six of them to keep them going, their blood staining the ground like dark ink.

"Let's get started then," I urge, my voice a low growl of impatience.

We form a tight triangle, our bodies tense. Az reaches into the box and takes out a sharp shard of refined sanguimetal. We're supposed to drip our life's essence over the ley line sand. It allegedly gives the little ghosties an incentive to help us.

Az runs it over his palm, leaving thin crimson lines. Emeric follows suit, grimacing as he presses the metal against his skin. I take the last piece, wincing as it cuts my palm. We hover our bloody hands over the largest plot of sand in the center of our circle.

With focused breaths and closed eyes, we each channel our inner magic into the sand and metal. The air around us crackles with electricity as our energy combines and infuses with the sanguimetal.

"Focus on her," Azazel instructs. "Remember the goal."

I allow Morte's image to fill my mind. Her laughter, her defiance, her spirit—all fueling the magic that flows from my core. The sanguimetal responds, a pulsing heart of darkness and blood, absorbing our magic and amplifying it back twentyfold.

Emeric's voice breaks the concentration, a whisper that sounds almost reverent. "It's working."

My eyes fly open when I sense a shift in the temperature. A slight breeze rustles my hair, tickling my nose.

The dreamscape begins to materialize around us, a realm of our collective creation, more vivid and stable than any we've conjured before. The air shimmers with the magic we've unleashed, the new component's power making the impossible seem trivial.

Power thrums in every cell, bleeding out of my pores, coalescing around us like little droplets of blood. And it just might be.

In this dreamscape, our thoughts and desires take shape. The landscape forms—a dense forest bathed in twilight, the air rich with the scent of pine and earth. It's a place from my memories with Morte, a secret haven where our conversations had stretched into the early hours of morning.

"The effects won't last forever." Az grins, spinning around as he takes in the place. "But we should have several hours with her."

Emeric crouches by the chest of memories at our feet. "We should use this time to give her some of her memories back. If she tolerates it well, maybe even all of them in the time we have."

I tap a finger on my chin. "Aggonid would be pleased if the next time he sees her, she's requesting to come home where she belongs."

Azazel nods, his expression eager. "Then let's make the most of it. Bring her here."

We focus, calling out to Morte across realms and barriers, our invitation a lighthouse in the vastness of her subconscious. The forest around us seems to hold its breath, waiting for her arrival.

Moments stretch, each one laden with anxious anticipation, until finally, a figure emerges from the enveloping shadows between the trees. It's Morte, but her presence is tinged with an aura of distress that's almost palpable. She steps into the clearing, her usual poise replaced by paranoia that's shadowed with an undercurrent of fear.

Her eyes, typically bright with curiosity or defiance, now flicker with something I don't recognize. As she stands before us, a heaviness fills the space, evidence of something deeply wrong.

As her gaze locks with mine, time itself seems to fracture, leaving just Morte and me adrift in a realm where the usual anchors of existence have no hold. The vulnerability in her eyes, is a quiet plea that slices through the facade of our surreal dreamscape.

"Is everything alright?" The question escapes me, even as I observe her closely, searching for clues in her demeanor.

Her response is a silent shake of her head, a subtle yet profound gesture in this world built on thoughts and magic. She moves towards us, her steps hesitant yet purposeful. The sight of her seeking comfort is both intriguing and unsettling, stirring a cocktail of emotions within me.

She reaches Azazel, bypassing me, and it's like a cold wave crashing over my senses. She wraps her arms around his waist, seeking refuge in his embrace. Part of me aches to be the one she turns to, to be her solace. Yet, there's a twisted satisfaction in witnessing this display of vulnerability, this crack in her usually rigid armor. If she can seek comfort with us, then she's ready to know all of us.

Azazel, ever the puzzling shadow, seems momentarily stunned, and a rare glimpse of unguarded emotion flashes across his face. But then, like a cloak being drawn, he envelops her in his arms, his posture shifting into one of protection. His embrace is a fortress, a sanctuary he offers without a word. The way he cradles her, with a tenderness that belies the dark aura he often radiates, speaks volumes of the depth of his feelings towards her.

Emeric watches from a short distance, his expression a careful mask of neutrality, but I can sense the undercurrent of his own complex feelings. He's always been a storm beneath a calm surface, and I wonder how this tableau affects him.

As for me, I stand there, part observer, part participant, the sensation of being both inside and outside this moment.

Using magic, I haul the chest of memories closer to us, propping my leg on top of it and resting my elbow on my leg. "Happy to see you again, love. How about you tell us what's wrong while we prepare a memory?"

She gasps, pulling back from Az's hold. "You have my memories?! You figured out how to give them to me safely?'

"I do." I straighten, spreading my arms wide, waiting for her to let me hold her, too. But she just looks at me expectantly, missing her cue that it's my turn now.

That's alright. I'll help her remember.

"It was this give-and-take that made you fall for me." I chuckle. "You give me something I want, and I give you something you want. And because you don't remember me yet, I won't even make you bargain for it. This is how we build trust."

My grin is wide as she catches on to the part about her needing to tell us what's wrong first.

"I've been kidnapped," she whispers.

My smile falls as a snarl rips from my throat. "You what?!"

"I'm okay, for now." She flails her arms as I scoop her up, holding her tight to my chest. "Though I'm not sure where I'm at yet, nor do I know who has me. I've met him, a fae whose order I don't know, but he hasn't said his name."

"What does he look like?" Emeric asks.

She gestures towards Azazel, who shifts uncomfortably. "A bit like Az, though not as handsome. He's a real asshole. I'm going to kill him, then you can torture him when he comes to the Underworld. He mutilates his servants."

Az pales, his chest heaving as she continues.

"I'm locked in a room. A castle, I think."

Emeric, rubs his chin, pacing. "Any windows? Can you see outside? Maybe if you describe it—"

"I have a window, but I think he's spelled what I'm viewing. I see the same exact clouds pass by every ten minutes or so. And the shift from day to night doesn't feel right."

"Why would he do that?" Emeric speaks as though he's only voicing a thought and isn't looking for an answer.

I exhale sharply as I watch Az's reaction, the tension palpable in the way his shoulders tense up. "To whittle her mental state," he mutters, his voice barely more than a whisper. It's unsettling to see him like this—shaken, his usual cool façade cracked by the gravity of Morte's situation.

I glance at Emeric, who's stopped his pacing, now eyeing Az with concern. The realization that Morte's captor is manipulating her perception, probably to break her spirit, hits me like a punch to the gut. It's a sick game, and it stirs a cold fury within me.

Though I do this on a daily basis to denizens of hell, they've earned it. She hasn't.

"But why?" I ask, more to myself than anyone else. The cruelty of it is baffling, even to someone as accustomed to the madness of the Underworld as me.

Az's eyes flicker to mine, haunted. "Control," he says, and the word hangs between us, heavy and ominous.

Emeric massages his forehead, glancing back and forth between us. "We have to find a way to free her," he declares, his tone filled with desperation. "No matter what it takes."

"Memories first. I feel like a huge part of me is missing." Morte wiggles out of my arms, and I pout in disappointment, but let her down. I don't let her out of my grasp. though. Now I've got her where I want her, I'm keeping her.

I watch Az's eyes dilate as they scan the intricate carvings and symbols on the trunk before him.

"How does this work?" she asks, a note of curiosity in her voice as she gestures towards it.

Emeric, standing close to Morte, places a reassuring hand on her forearm. "I think you should be the one to open them," he suggests, his voice tinged with excitement.

Morte hesitates, her gaze fixed on the trunk. She takes a deep breath and crouches down in front of it. After a moment, she changes her mind, opting to sit on the soft grass. She looks up at the trunk, a mix of apprehension and curiosity in her eyes, clearly wondering what secrets her memories hold within its ornate exterior.

I remain silent, observing the scene. But inside, I'm buzzing, doing whatever I can to hold myself back from ripping the chest open and giving her all her memories in one fell swoop. This trunk will change everything. Anticipation builds in the air, a silent charge that holds us all in its grip.

CHAPTER FIFTY

MORTE

Anxiety churns within me as I ease onto the soft grass, shrouded in a deep sense of dread. The chest's carvings stand imposing, each symbol buzzing with an alien force that resonates in my bones. The air thickens, suffused with forgotten memories pressing in, desperate to break free. Their intensity feels like an encroaching presence, poised to engulf me.

I reach out hesitantly, my fingers tracing the cool, embossed wood before finding the latch. It clicks open with a sound that burrows deep within me, as if unlocking something more than just a trunk. I lift the lid slowly, the hinges creaking softly, revealing its contents.

Inside, the memories are not as I expected. They take shape as a collection of gleaming orbs, each one pulsating with its own distinct rhythm and suspended effortlessly above the trunk. The orbs radiate a gentle, otherworldly glow that illuminates everything in the vicinity. I find myself unable to look away, entranced by their beauty and complexity. Some orbs shine with a brilliant intensity while others barely flicker, their light on the verge of fading away completely.

Along the edge of the trunk, I notice inscriptions, akin to dates or markers in time. They provide a chronological order to these memories. With a hesitant breath, I decide to start at the beginning, at the earliest date marked.

Reaching out, my hand hovers over the first orb. It's a small, dim sphere, pulsating weakly. The moment my fingers make contact, a jolt of energy surges through me, and I'm transported.

I find myself in a memory so vivid, it's as if I'm reliving it. I'm in a place that's oppressively hot, the air thick with the scent of sulfur and scorched earth. Chains bind my wrists, their cold metal biting into my skin. The heat is unbearable, searing the metal that imprisons me. I look around, disoriented, my heart pounding in my ears.

For a moment, I believe I'm still in Bedlam Penitentiary, but something feels fundamentally different. The atmosphere is charged with a power that Bedlam never held. As I struggle against my bonds, the realization dawns on me with a sinking feeling of dread.

Something is really wrong.

Why do the guards have me chained when I'm the one who's supposed to help them?

The surroundings are cavernous, the walls glowing with an eerie, fiery light. Shadows dance along the rugged surfaces, creating a nightmarish tableau. The heat is relentless, searing my skin, making it difficult to breathe. The pain from the chains and the oppressive environment is excruciating.

In the distance, I hear the faint echoes of agonized screams, a chorus of despair that chills me to the bone. I yell out for Wilder, but it isn't his voice that responds.

It's Caius, telling me to shut up?

As the memory unfolds, I remain a prisoner of my own past, forced to endure the sensations and emotions of those initial moments after my death at the prison. The sense of confusion, fear, and utter helplessness consumes me, but I force myself to continue, to witness what I've forgotten.

The memory shifts, and I see a figure approaching through the heat haze. The details are hazy at first, but as it draws closer, I see his imposing form. Caius is—

Caius is naked.

I avert my eyes from the memory, briefly registering a glint of light between his legs. I can't take my eyes off his piercing.

Despite the terror that grips me in this memory, a part of me feels a strange sense of relief at his arrival. At least I'm not alone in this infernal landscape.

But the memory fades before I can interact with him, leaving me back in the present, my hand still touching the orb. I withdraw it quickly, the sensation of the chains and the heat lingering on my skin like a ghostly imprint.

I sit back, my breath ragged, trying to process the onslaught of emotions and sensations. The experience was overwhelming, and the horrors I endured, the horrors that were taken from me, are now resurfacing with a vengeance.

Around me, the other orbs hover patiently, each one a gateway to another fragment of my past. I steel myself, knowing that this journey through my memories is only just beginning. There's so much more to uncover, so many more truths to face. But for now, I need a moment to gather my strength, to brace myself for the next plunge into the depths of my forgotten life in the Underworld.

But not before I scowl at the sheepish-looking asshole in front of me. "You chained me?"

"Hey!" He puts his hands up. "I chain everyone. It's my job."

"You kept calling me bird names." I narrow my eyes at him.

"But you're such a pretty bird," he coos, tucking a stray piece of hair behind my ear. "And you love being chained. You even chained Aggonid to you for weeks!"

"I'm not so sure that counts," Az mutters, disgruntled.

After the initial shock of the first memory, I gather my wits to continue through my past. Each orb in the trunk represents a fragment of my life in the Underworld—a life I'm only now beginning to piece back together.

I reach out hesitantly for the next orb, its glow dimmer than the others. As my fingers make contact, a rush of sensations envelop me. I'm back in the Underworld, feeling the oppressive heat and the constant sense of danger. This memory is less intense but just as poignant—a moment of quiet reflection in a world that seldom sleeps. I see myself sitting alone, pondering my fate, the sense of isolation palpable. It's here I meet Irid, Caius' sister, and she tells me about the wild hunts. She also gifts me a tiny shack and a necklace that'll keep me safe. The memory fades, leaving a residue of loneliness.

I move to the next orb, a little more confidently this time. The scene that unfolds is one of resilience—I'm learning to navigate the treacherous terrain of the Underworld, adapting to its cruel rules. There's fear, but also a growing sense of self-reliance. I watch as I cautiously move about the little hut Irid gifted me.

With each memory, I feel a little more whole, a little more connected to the person I'd become during my lost years. The gaps in my identity are slowly being filled, painting a picture of a life lived in the shadows of a forgotten realm.

Finally, I spot an orb that shines brighter than the rest. As it's next in line, I pluck it eagerly, having paid attention to the orb's luminescence to determine how profound the memory is. My heart races in anticipation as I gently cradle the orb, preparing myself to relive that pivotal moment.

The memory engulfs me, transporting me back to a night just outside my little home. I'm in a forest, the air thick with the scent of unknown flora, and I'm eating berries found along the perimeter.

Then he appears—Azazel, emerging from the darkness like a phantom. His presence is both intimidating and mesmerizing, his wings a dark canvas against the night sky, and with each swish of them, they flutter like silk. I remember the fear that coursed through me, quickly replaced by a sense of relief as he offered help instead of harm.

In this memory, I see the kindness in his actions, the genuine concern in his eyes as he treats my wounds. He's a protector in a realm where protection is a rare commodity. His words are cautious, but his actions speak of empathy and understanding—a lifeline I didn't expect to find in the ruthless environment around us.

The memory is vivid, each detail etched in my mind with startling clarity. I can almost feel his hands on my skin, the gentle touch that eased my pain, the shame of liking his touch. It's a moment of vulnerability, of unexpected connection in a place where connections are fraught with danger.

As the memory fades, I'm left with a renewed sense of who I was in the Underworld.

I sit back, the orbs still floating around me, each one a doorway to another piece of my past.

Az is in my peripheral, and I meet his eyes, relaxing my features. "I just met you." I smile at him. "You saved me."

He shuffles his feet as he clears his throat. "I did." His expression is different now than in the memory—it's shy, less confident, hesitant.

Without thinking, I reach out to take his hand, feeling the warmth of his skin against mine. He allows me to pull him down to sit next to me on the grassy knoll.

"Thank you." I say quietly, resting my head on his shoulder. The scent of freshly cut grass and a hint of cologne surrounds us.

"You're welcome," he replies softly, guiding my hand to pick another orb.

Memory after memory absorbs into me, and each one a piece of a puzzle. The Underworld unfolds in my mind, a world of fire and ash, desperation and hope. While not always happy memories, they're not all terrible ones my mind conjured up when I didn't have real ones to lean on.

I take a deep breath, bracing myself for the next memory. My hand hovers over a particularly vivid orb, pulsing with an intense energy that beckons me. I grasp it, and immediately I'm transported to a moment of desperation and audacity—the night I chained myself to Aggonid.

The heat of the Underworld wraps around me, a suffocating embrace as the memory unfolds. Aggonid's face looms before me, a terrifying beast of fury and power. I feel the fear that gripped me then, the terror of his wrath, yet beneath it, a spark of defiance.

The clash of our wills is palpable. His fingers encircle my throat, pinning me against the wall, his anger a physical force. I gasp for air, panic surging, but in that chaos, a plan forms—a desperate, wild plan to bind us together, to gain some measure of control. Because if he won't send me back to where I belong, I'll make him wish he did.

I see myself lashing out, the clink of the manacle as it secures around his wrist, the sudden shock in his eyes. I relive the tumultuous emotions—the adrenaline, the triumph, the dawning realization of what I've done.

The memory fades, and I'm left sitting in the dreamscape, the orb now dim in my hand. Empty. My heart pounds in my chest, a mix of residual fear and newfound resolve. That night, I had taken a stand, however reckless. I had fought against the overwhelming power of the Underworld and its rulers.

I look up at Azazel, my eyes meeting his. There's understanding there, a recognition of the lengths to which I've gone to survive. He squeezes my hand gently, offering silent support.

Furrowing my brow, I glance at the dates on the inscriptions. "Emeric isn't in these," I say, looking to the male in question.

He grins down at me, his eyes twinkling with mischief. "I didn't meet you until later on."

"I was gone two years," I protest, "why are there so few dates listed?"

He shrugs casually before stretching out in the grass beside me. "Time moves differently here. It expands and contracts." He leans in closer, his voice dropping to a diabolical tone. "It's one way to punish denizens of hell."

I take a moment, collecting myself, before reaching for the next orb.

Each one is a story, each one resonating with a different emotion, and many all at once. It takes hours to pour through these. There's a sense of camaraderie in one memory, betrayal in another, and of resilience in yet another. And throughout it all, these guys' presence are a constant, steady hand guiding me, helping me through the sorrow, although some of them are the source of it.

As I near the end of the journey, I feel so much heartache at having forgotten all of this. With all three men settled around me now, I glance at each one, feeling the love they have for me.

There's one noticeable absence from my Underworld men.

The brutal sting of rejection ripples through my entire being, a physical ache that twists and turns in my gut. The abandonment of the one who has both loved and hurt me consumes me, leaving a gaping hole in my chest. As I realize once again that he doesn't want me, I'm struck with the harsh reality that he never truly did. It's a truth that cuts deep, reopening old wounds and crushing any flicker of hope that may have remained.

"Hey, what's wrong?" Emeric reaches out to take my hand, but I don't look up.

Shame heats my cheeks as I scrub at the tears marring them. "I'm okay, just sad." I chuckle, but it's bordering on hysteria. "Just figures he wouldn't be here."

"Who?" Caius leans in so he's in my direct line of sight.

"Aggonid."

Caius huffs, pulling me into his lap as he cradles me to his chest, and that just makes me cry harder. "My sweet baby birdie," he coos as he grabs hold of my chin and tilts it so I'm looking into iced irises, that despite their color, hold so much warmth for me. The runes on his skin flash at me as his pupils dilate. "If you think for a second that he hasn't been tearing the world apart in your absence, you just haven't gone far enough in your memories yet. He set fire to the rain, leveled our bedroom, and threatened to murder Luna and all her descendants since you've been gone."

A gasp escapes me. "Why would he do that? The Drake family are good, kind people."

"We've all grown more than a little unhinged without you." He smooths his thumb across my cheek.

"Then why isn't he here?" I sniffle, blinking away the tears.

Az interjects, "He's been called to Romarie. No doubt because you'd been kidnapped."

"Whoever has me, I'm going to kill him."

Caius grins at me. "I'd tell you to be careful, but I'd be lying if I said I wasn't looking forward to you dying again. I miss seeing you in person—"

"If I die, I'll just regenerate. I'm tethered to Wilder. I'm his anchor."

"Then we send Aggonid up there to kill him, and then he's down here. It shouldn't be hard for him to get into the prison." Caius shrugs.

"He's not in prison anymore. I am. Well, I was, anyway. I confessed, and he was released."

"Why did you do that?"

I narrow my eyes at him. "Because I've loved this merfae for two thousand years, Caius, and he wasn't the one who killed children. I did. I'm not letting him spend another second in that prison, wasting away, when he can be free, as he's deserved to be this entire time!"

"Hey," Emeric offers. "This dreamscape probably won't hold much longer. Let's get you the rest of your memories, and we can figure out how we're getting you home, okay?"

"I can't leave Wilder," I whisper.

"We know you love him, but you love us, too. You'll see it soon." Caius frowns at me before wrapping his arms tighter around me. "It hurts. Every second without you is torture."

"I refuse to choose between you. I told you he's my anchor. That might not mean anything to you, but it means everything to me."

"So get him a new one?" Caius smooths my hair.

"You idiot," Az scoffs. "It means they're mates. Think soul bonded, but it happens exclusively when one of them is merfae."

"Oh. I was wondering how a bird could be an anchor," Caius muses. "Aggonid is your soul bonded mate."

"Apparently, you can have both." Emeric sighs, gesturing to the orbs as to tell me to get on with it.

I pull a few small ones into my lap, allowing the memories of the Underworld to rush into me like a tidal wave. The next bright orb is the Forsaken Hunt, and that's when tears flow freely as I try to stem Azazel's bleeding.

It was then, losing him, that I realized I was in love with him.

But Emeric and I were able to save him, and I freed him from his servitude to Aggonid.

I draw in a deep breath, steadying myself for the next plunge into my forgotten history. The guys' presence beside me is a tangible comfort, someone's hand on my knee, grounding me to the present as I navigate the treacherous waters of my past.

"Thank you," I murmur, my voice barely above a whisper. His response is a gentle squeeze of my leg, a silent acknowledgment.

I reach for another orb, this one pulsating with a bright energy that speaks of pivotal moments. The orb shimmers as I touch it, and the memory engulfs me.

I'm back in the Underworld, the heat oppressive, the air thick with tension. Aggonid and I are preparing to take a portal to Romarie, but there's an undercurrent of unease that I can't shake off. The memory is vivid, each emotion raw and unfiltered. Aggonid's grip on my hand is both protective and possessive, a complex mix of emotions I'm only now beginning to understand.

Then, we're in Romarie, stalking the castle grounds before we run into who we've come to see.

As the man in the memory turns around, I nearly drop the orb. King Valtorious stands before us, his presence as commanding and unsettling as it was the first time. A surge of anger blows through me, the unfairness of it all, the manipulation and deceit. I've been a pawn in a larger game, one that I am only now beginning to comprehend.

My grip tightens on the orb, the memories flooding back with an intensity that's almost overwhelming. The time in Romarie, the deceptive calm before the storm, and the slow realization of Valtorious's true intentions—it all comes rushing back.

I blink back the tears that threaten to fall, my heart pounding in my chest. The memories are a mix of pain and revelation, each one shedding light on the complex web of politics and power plays I had been entangled in.

"Are you okay?" Emeric's voice breaks through my thoughts, his concern evident.

I nod, swallowing hard. " I know who kidnapped me."

Caius's grip around my waist tightens, his growl warm against my ear. "Who did this to you?" His snarl shouldn't sound so hot. "I'll rip their spine from their corpse and spend the rest of eternity torturing them until they beg me to end them again and again, but I won't. Their purgatory will be my personal playground."

Gods, that shouldn't be so hot, either.

"I need to understand it all," I whisper, more to myself than to him. "Every piece of the puzzle." Slipping out of his hold, I get to my feet, needing to move. I feel as though I'm crawling out of my skin as I calculate ways I can use this information to get me out of the king's clutches.

As I watch the scenes of history unfolding before me, the memories blur and swirl around my mind. I blink rapidly, trying to focus on what is happening in front of me. Once the scene concludes, I rub at my eyes, feeling the exhaustion creeping in. Gazing down at my palms, I see what's left of my orbs—shattered fragments that resemble a broken mosaic. Carefully, I gather the remaining pieces into my arms, cradling them protectively. The containers are empty, but I don't know what happens when you break them. Maybe nothing.

Suddenly, a wave of dizziness washes over me and I collapse into someone's arms, grateful for their support.

"Easy there," Emeric coos in my ear. "Can't say I'm upset you're here, though."

"I need to know more." I scramble towards the chest, pulling the rest into my lap.

"It's too much for her," Az rasps, his voice barely restrained.

But I don't hear what's said after that, because I'm plunged into a memory of the Wild Pursuit, a primal hunt where my animalistic tendencies took over, and it's the most intense and debaucherous display unlike anything I've ever experienced in my life.

My insatiable craving for more, more, more, only intensifies as each mating bond snaps into place, claiming the males for myself. My entire being is consumed with pleasure as I relive every moment until the memory shifts violently and I'm thrust into the throne room.

The sight of Irid brutally beheading Aggonid sends the bile from my stomach to my throat.

"No," I breathe, unable to control the overwhelming surge of pain coursing through me.

"You're reliving it, aren't you?" Caius stares at me, his big, glassy eyes shredding me. "I wish I could forget that one," he whispers, his runes doing an almost mournful shimmer against his skin. "It still haunts my dreams every night. Maybe I can ask Aggie to take that memory from me."

I want to hold him, to grieve with him, but I'm retching into the grass. The vision of my soul bond being so callously cleaved from existence will haunt me the rest of eternity

Az crouches before me, his eyes a mixture of pain and empathy, reflecting the unrest within me. Emeric joins us, his presence a silent support. "You brought him back," Az whispers, his voice a soothing balm amidst the chaos of my emotions. "I swear, take this last memory. You'll see for yourself."

Reconciling the memory with the fragments of agony I have, I believe I do need to see the rest of it to have some semblance of closure, just so I can put my mind at ease. Hope, fragile and fleeting, sparks within me. I lunge for the offered orb, clutching it to my chest. The memory floods into me, a torrent of emotions and images.

The memory engulfs me in its intensity. Days of walking through the Underworld, a shell of the fae I once was, my heart an empty chasm echoing with loss.

And then, laughter—smooth, familiar, a sound I thought was lost forever. Aggonid stands before us, alive, his eyes sparkling with mischief and life. The relief that washes over me in the memory is overwhelming. Caius and I stumble forward, our hands reaching out to touch, to confirm that this is real, that he is indeed standing before us.

The memory shifts abruptly, jarring in its suddenness. The moon goddess's intervention rips me away from the Underworld, from the reunion that was our salvation. I'm torn from the warmth and safety of my mates, propelled into an unknown future by forces beyond my control.

As the memory fades and I return to the present, the impact of those events settles heavily upon me. Being taken just when everything was falling into place is a cruel twist of fate. He has so much more groveling to do, but gods, do I miss him.

My body sinks to the ground, my knees pressing into the soft earth below. I'm surrounded by empty globules, each void of light. Indecision wars inside of me, pulling me in different directions as I try to make sense of where I should go from here, and what my future looks like.

The noise in my head is deafening, drowning out all other thoughts and sounds. But I push through the chaos, my next steps already mapped out in my mind. As I lift my gaze, I meet the nervous expressions of my mates and Emeric, their eyes darting between each other and me.

They aren't prepared when I lunge.

CHAPTER FIFTY-ONE

EMERIC

The dreamscape around us quivers, a subtle tremor that only I seem to notice at first. The air shimmers, the edges of our created world blurring, signaling its imminent collapse. But it's Morte's next move that captures my attention.

She's on her feet, a whirlwind of emotion and speed. I watch, almost holding my breath, as she locks eyes with Azazel. There's a depth of understanding, a connection that transcends the physical space between them. Then, with a fluidity born of raw emotion, she lunges forward.

Azazel, caught off guard, stumbles back a step as Morte throws her arms around him. His initial shock swiftly gives way to relief, his arms enveloping her in an embrace that speaks volumes. I can't help but smile at the sight, a warmth spreading through me, despite the fraying edges of our dreamscape.

Morte's kiss is a promise, a reaffirmation of something profound and enduring. Azazel responds with equal fervor, his hands cradling her face gently. When they finally part, there's a silent communication, a shared understanding that needs no words.

She then turns to Caius, her movements fluid and full of purpose. Caius, always the jealous one, softens under her touch, his usual bravado melting away to reveal the genuine affection he harbors for her. Their kiss is tender, a contrast to the fiery passion she shared with Azazel, but no less significant.

Finally, Morte's gaze falls on me. My heart skips a beat, a mix of anticipation and something akin to fear. I've been in love with her for a while, but I don't know if she reciprocates it. She steps closer, her eyes searching mine for a moment that feels like an eternity. Then, she wraps her arms around me, pulling me into a hug that is both comforting and filled with a promise of more.

I return her embrace, feeling a surge of emotions I can't quite name. As we part, our eyes lock, and there's a tacit acknowledgment of the bond we share, one that might evolve into something deeper, given time.

Seeming to let go of pretenses, she slams her mouth against mine, her lips demanding, hungry, desperate for the same connection I've been longing for.

My hands grip her waist, pulling her closer, feeling the heat of her body against mine. As our lips part, we both gasp for air, her eyes reflecting a mix of astonishment and longing.

"I remember everything," she breathes.

CHAPTER FIFTY-TWO

MORTE

"Thank fuck," Caius collapses into the grass next to me.

The echoes of Emeric's lips linger on mine, awakening memories, igniting flames. I draw back, my breaths coming in short, sharp gasps as weeks of longing and suppressed yearning flood through me like a dam broken.

"I remember everything," I whisper again, the revelation rocking me to my core. The memories cascade through my mind—vivid, intense, sweet, and scorching. Each touch, each kiss we've shared through what feels like lifetimes, and each reunion is a piece of a mosaic that is my heart, now nearly whole once more.

Just two pieces missing. Aggonid and Wilder.

My gaze drifts over my mates. Their expressions are a tableau of desire, concern, and love—so much love it's nearly overwhelming. The heat in Azazel's eyes, the tender promise in Caius's smirk, the open vulnerability in Emeric's gaze—it's all for me, about me, within me.

This is the moment of reckoning, of absolute truth, where the past and present collide, where the paths of fate that have woven around us tighten and pull us irrevocably together. It's time to reclaim the passion, the love, the unity that was always meant to be ours.

Without a word, I reach for them, my hands finding theirs, our fingers intertwining. The warmth from their skin seeps into mine, a pulsing rhythm that syncs with my heartbeat. I pull them closer, the energy between us igniting like a spark to tinder, flaring into an inferno that promises to consume and yet resurrect.

Caius climbs to his feet and leans in close, his warm breath tickling my ear as he whispers, "Please tell me you want me now, Birdie." His voice is hoarse with longing, and tension radiates from his body.

In response, I grab his head and pull him down into a passionate kiss. Our lips meet with an urgent hunger, our bodies pressing together in a fierce embrace. When we finally break apart for air, I gasp out, "Yes, I want you." The words hang between us like a promise, heavy and sweet.

The sky paints a soft glow over us, its silvery light illuminating every contour of his beautiful face.

I run my thumbs over the runes pulsing on his skin. "I love these." I kiss each one I can see.

"I have them here, too." He grabs my hand, holding it to his erection.

I laugh. "No, you don't." I grin at him. "You forget, I have all my memories now."

"Mmm, I think you should have a better look, just to be sure," he groans.

"Cheeky," I retort, the laughter in my eyes matching his. I playfully slap his chest, my heart fluttering at the gruff chuckle that escapes him.

"You have to admit," Emeric says, and I turn my head towards him, still laughing. "He's one smooth fucker."

"Stop distracting her, she was going to say yes," Caius growls, pulling me into his orbit.

With a wicked grin, I comply, my hands exploring the chiseled plane of his body, which is now suddenly naked. His muscles flex and his skin smolders beneath my touch with each press of my lips to the runes decorating him.

His pulse quickens under my fingertips, each throb bringing a sweet relief that my mates are here with me, even when I'm a realm away.

"Yes, yes. I was," I breathe against his skin, my lips brushing past his rune-marked collarbone, down his chest. "And I still am."

His sharp intake of breath adds to the sense of anticipation hanging thick in the air around us. His hands weave into my hair, the grip a delicious bite as he guides me with purpose.

"Fuck," Emeric curses, as someone—probably Caius—uses his magic to make me naked. A cool breeze grazes my backside.

The setting transforms, the dreamscape revealing a lavish bedroom adorned with golden sheets and opulent furnishings. I've spent a lot of time in this room.

With a sigh of relief, Caius lets his body fall onto the plush bed, sinking into its softness as he pulls me down between his strong thighs. Our bodies mold together in a perfect fit, every inch of skin pressed against each other's. The piercings on his erection lay against my stomach, and I'd forgotten how intimidating they were.

His breath tickles my ear as he whispers, "I've changed my mind." I hold my breath, waiting to hear what he desires now.

"I know I want your mouth on me," he confesses, "but right now, I need this pretty little pussy more."

My cheeks flush with heat at his words as I glance back at Emeric and Az, now crawling onto the mattress.

Emeric smirks, sliding a hand up the back of my thigh. "Well, if you've changed your mind," he teases, his fingers ghosting over the curve of my behind. "Maybe I'll take your place."

"No chance in hell," Caius grunts, wrapping an arm around me and pulling me flush against him. His lips find mine, devouring them in a searing kiss. When we finally pull apart for air, our breaths mingle between us, hot and heady.

Satisfaction ignites in Emeric's gaze, his eyes twinkling with anticipation. Az, on the other hand, wears a smirk that holds more than a hint of tease. His fingers trail down my spine, eliciting a shiver that makes Caius growl beneath me.

"Join in or watch, pet," he purrs. "But quit distracting her. I've waited too long to have her."

Az chuckles, the sound dark and rich like the finest chocolate. "To be fair," he coos, the promise in his voice sending a delicious thrill through me, "I've waited longer than you have. I mated her first."

"And I've never mated her," Emeric grumbles.

Caius sits up suddenly, and I nearly tumble off him before he has the foresight to grab me. "Two cocks."

"And?" I sit up, straddling his lap as I cling to his neck in case he gets any other ideas.

"I want to see them," Caius remarks, pinning me to his chest so he can see over my shoulder.

I turn my gaze back to Az and Emeric. "Well, you heard the man."

Az chuckles, and the sound vibrates through my spine as his fingers continue to trace patterns on my back. "What say you, Emeric?"

The smirk on Emeric's face widens as he repositions himself, sliding down the bed to sit at Caius' feet. He shrugs off his clothes with a nonchalance that somehow ratchets up the tension in the room. "Why not?"

Caius' grip tightens as he watches Emeric undress. I can feel the anticipation radiating off him, can hear the hitch in his throat as he takes in the sight, and I pull free so I can face the room and see, too.

And oh, what a sight it is. Emeric, comfortable in his skin, the lines of his body lean and hard, pulling at the air in the room like a deep breath before a plunge. His smirk is still there, playful yet devilish, promising things that make my insides flutter in anticipation. Two penises stand proudly, one sitting right atop the other with a small gap between them. Veins run along their length like rivers on a map.

A curse tumbles from my lips, communicating my excitement and fear about how I'll handle those.

I glance at Az expectantly, as if to say, *your turn.*

Az' teasing smirk finally gives way to a more serious expression as he undresses, a predator's grace pouring into every move he makes as shadows slink off him. The scant bedroom light dances over his body, highlighting the ridges of his muscles and the coiling tattoos. His piercings glint in the soft light, a wicked tease that sends my pulse racing. As his last piece of clothing falls away to reveal him in all his glory, I let my gaze linger over him, drinking in the sight before me.

"Lucky you," Caius purrs in my ear, his breath warm. "Which cock will you take first? Or will you take them all, like a good little birdie?"

My heart thunders in my chest, but I raise my head high, meeting Caius's gaze behind me. His eyes are radiant and heavy with desire, a mirror of my own. "I'm your birdie," I breathe. "But don't think for a moment that makes me little."

He throws his head back and laughs, the sound full and bright as it echoes through the room. "No, but your pussy is so tight," he playfully teases, his hand confidently sliding around my waist and coming to rest between my thighs.

"Yes, it is," Az groans. "Enough fucking talking."

Emeric moves closer, and the bed shifts beneath his weight. The sight of him, so formidable and virile, sends a hot flush through me. His gaze is locked on mine, but his smirk is all for Caius. "Do you wish to watch your birdie fly?"

Caius' hand tightens against me, thumb brushing against my sensitive skin. "Fly, Morte," he murmurs low in his throat. "Show us how you soar."

And so, I do.

Pushing off from Caius's lap, I land softly between Emeric and Az– my two dream mates in the flesh. My heart is a drum echoing loudly in the silent room, matched only by the thunderous rhythm of their own.

Emeric is the first to move, his hand reaching up to gently cup my cheek as he tilts my face towards him. His dual cocks twitch with anticipation as he leans in to claim a kiss. His lips are warm and soft, his tongue teasing mine with slow, languid strokes as if we have all the time in the world.

Breaking away, Emeric's eyes twinkle with a mischievous light. "Are you ready to dance on the stars, Morte?" he whispers huskily, his voice laced with a dark promise that sends shivers down my spine.

As if in response, Az's warm hand lands on my thigh, his fingers squeezing lightly as he pulls me towards him. His piercing gaze is locked onto mine, an unspoken command hanging in the air between us. With a smirk playing at his lips, he lowers his head to my chest. His hot mouth closes around one of my nipples, his tongue teasing me with feather-like flicks. His actions draw a gasp from my lips, my body arching toward the sensation.

"Fly, Morte." He echoes Caius's words, but it's not a command but an invitation. An invitation to lose myself in these men, in their hands and mouths and cocks that promise pleasure beyond what I've ever known.

Eager to take up their invitation, I reach out to both of them at once—my hand finding purchase on Az's broad shoulder while the other ventures towards the hellhound's twin members. My fingers brush against the smooth skin, feeling the pulsing heat beneath my touch. A low groan echoes in the room as I wrap my fingers around them, and a shuddering breath is dragged from Emeric's lips. I wrap my hands around the impressive girth of his twin cocks, sliding my hand slowly up and down the length of him, squeezing gently, and his breath hitches. His cocks vibrate against my palm, and I hear Caius gasp at the reaction.

"How the fuck is that fair?" He pouts, moving in closer to inspect Emeric. "Did they mean to do that?"

Emeric laughs, a deep rumble in his chest. "For her, always."

I chuckle, the sound light and breathy in the charged room. "Life's not fair, Caius," I tease, my eyes still locked on Emeric.

His gaze is heavy with desire, a smirk playing at his lips as he watches me stroke him. There's a heady satisfaction in holding such power over a man like Emeric, a godlike creature of myth now reduced to soft groans and trembling hands in my grasp.

"But," I add, my voice dropping an octave lower and a wicked glint sparking in my eyes as I turn to face Caius, "you're welcome to watch and see if I can take them."

Caius's gaze is scorching, the desire evident in his eyes. "I like watching you, birdie," he murmurs, his voice deep and thick with need. "Especially when you're taking what's yours."

Those words send a jolt of arousal through me, making me grip Emeric tighter and eliciting a low growl from him. His fingers dig into my hips, pulling me closer to him.

"Enough teasing," he grumbles, his tone impatient yet full of anticipation. "Take us, Morte." His command leaves no room for argument, and I don't have the slightest intention to start one.

With a coy smile, I slide onto Emeric, wrapping my arms around his broad shoulders, the vibration soothing any ache. The groan that tears from his lips is almost enough to push me over the edge, but I keep my control. For now. I let out a shuddering breath, feeling him inside me as he stretches me deliciously.

I don't think I can handle two cocks at once, so his upper cock nudges against my clit, the buzzing nearly combusting me.

Beside us, Az begins to move, his hand sliding up and down my thigh before reaching between my legs. His fingers glide over my slick skin, dipping inside along with Emeric, and it's all I can do not to cry out from the double sensation.

Emeric grins, his fangs glinting in the light, and I can't take my eyes off them. "Is this what you want." He licks one. "Want me sinking these into your neck while I bury myself in your flesh?"

A shuddering moan escapes my lips at his words, and my body coils tighter with anticipation. "Yes," I breathe out, my voice barely a whisper against the electric tension in the room. His sharpened fangs send a thrill of fear rippling through me, but it's quickly drowned by the wave of tantalizing pleasure coursing through my veins.

Emeric's grin widens, his canines gleaming ominously, and a dark promise etched into his gaze. "As you wish," he purrs, nipping at my neck with teeth that are alarmingly sharp.

From the corner of my eye, I catch sight of Caius watching intensely, his expression one of unadulterated desire and something else. Something deeper and rawer.

Emeric's canines sink into me, and there's no spark of pain, only pure, unfiltered pleasure. A moan slips past my lips, almost drowned out by Emeric's low growl vibrating against my throat. The room spins, my vision blurs, and the sensations ravishing my body is overwhelming. All I can focus on are the two men inside me; Emeric with his fangs buried deep in my neck, his hips thrusting in perfect rhythm with Az whose fingers are curled inside me.

His fangs retract, leaving a tingling sensation in their wake, and he buries himself deeper inside me. The room is filled with the sounds of our connection–ragged breaths, soft gasps and the wet slide of skin against skin.

Caius moves closer, his eyes riveted on the sight before him. There's an envy in his gaze, but it's not a bitter one; it's laced with intrigue, anticipation, and unmistakable desire. He reaches out to touch me, fingertips brushing down along my spine, an added sensation that grounds me.

"You can take them both, pretty bird," he coos before glancing behind me to Az. "Do you want to take her ass, or do you want me to?"

Azazel's voice is thick with desire when he answers, "She'll need lubrication."

Caius chuckles darkly as he flashes his fangs before ripping into his own wrist. Blood pours from his wound. "Got it right here."

"That's—" Az hesitates, glancing at me. "The most fucked up and unhinged thing I've ever seen you do."

"Says the fae who happily drinks from her vein." Blood-stained teeth grin back at him. "If you won't do it, I will!"

"Morte?" Az whispers in my ear.

"Go on," I breathe, getting closer to detonating with Emeric inside me. Having Caius' blood involved so intimately is surprisingly hot.

Az huffs, grabbing Caius' bleeding arm, though I can't see what he does with it. From the sound of it, he's slicking himself up.

When I feel a gentle probing at my back entrance, I gasp at the strange sensation. It's offset somewhat by Emeric's continued thrusting, but nonetheless it's new and foreign—and not unwelcome.

"Az, Emeric," I manage to gasp out, my voice strained. "Don't stop."

And they don't.

As Az pushes in slowly, the pressure mounting within me is both intoxicating and daunting. Caius hovers near, murmuring soft encouragements, his strong hand sliding up and down my back in a soothing rhythm while his other hand holds me steady.

Emeric growls at the sensation of my body accommodating both men.

"Fuck," Emeric snarls, hips jerking a little too hard, forcing a gasp from my lips. "You feel so damn good."

I can only manage a weak nod, my mind ablaze with pleasure and sensation. Az pushes in deeper, careful not to hurt me. The fullness is something I've never experienced before. It takes a few seconds for my body to adjust to the intrusion before I give them an approving nod.

"Move," I command breathlessly, my knuckles whitening on Emeric's shoulders as my hold on him tightens.

"You take them so well," Caius purrs, his voice filled with a primal satisfaction, the beast inside of me preening under his attention. "Such a good little birdie, taking two cocks at once."

Emeric's eyes gleam with satisfaction as his movements begin again, his thrusts hitting that sweet spot inside me while Az matches his pace from the other end. Caius' fingers ghost over my skin, adding onto the mounting pleasure.

I close my eyes and let myself get lost in them—in the rhythm they set, in the heat that radiates from them, in the raw pleasure that they elicit from me. My heartbeat is a wild rhythm, matching the rhythm of our bodies as we move as one.

"More," I gasp out, my voice hoarse with need. "I need more."

Emeric's grin turns positively predatory as he buries himself deeper inside me, his hands gripping my hips tightly to control the pace. I glance behind me, Az's gaze is intense, a thin sheen of sweat on his forehead as he pushes into me.

"Yes," I cry out, my head tossed back as the pleasure intensifying within me as I rest against Az's chest. "Just like that."

Explosions of light dance behind my eyelids as I tumble over the edge, crying out, their names mingling together in a strangled sigh that echoes around the spheres of the dreamscape. The intensity of my orgasm triggers theirs, and I can feel them pulsating within me as they ride out their own release.

Az's grip tightens on my hips as he drives into me, his rhythm faltering as he fills me. Emeric's strong hands are holding me steady, his thrusts becoming ragged and desperate, his fangs sinking back into my neck. The taste of my blood on his tongue pushes him over the edge, his growl vibrating through my skin as he spills inside me.

It takes me a moment to register Emeric came twice. First against my clit from his top cock, and the second time, inside me.

Caius stares, wild-eyed awe blazing in his pale blues.

As they slowly dismantle the connection between us, they carefully remove themselves, stroking my sides to help me down from the high. Emeric's rough thumb traces circles on my thigh while Az's hands run through my hair. I can feel Caius' fingers dancing across my back, soothing the heated skin there.

"Stay," I murmur, my voice a mere whisper against the silence of the dreamscape. "Don't let me wake up from this, please," I beg.

"Oh, sweet Little Bird." Caius pulls me into his arms, and I flail my limbs as I untangle from my other mates. "We'll always be here when you shut your eyes. And when you wake, we'll work on storming Valtorious' castle and punting his head once we sever it."

"You say the sweetest things," I sigh, grinning up at him.

But our moment is short-lived. The dreamscape around us shivers violently, a sinister force encroaching upon our sanctuary. The curtains on the windows sway unnaturally, the room darkens, and a sense of impending doom fills the air.

"We're losing the dreamscape," Az announces, urgency lacing his voice. "I love you, Morte. Know that no matter what happens, I love you. What we have is real. Cling to that."

The fabric of our created world unravels rapidly, the edges fraying into nonexistence.

My eyes widen with realization and a touch of fear. "But I can't go back with you," I whisper, my voice trembling.

"We know," Emeric says softly, and my chest tightens at the

thought of separating from them so soon. "But we'll find a way to get you out of Romarie, I promise."

Azazel leans forward, his expression pained. "We'll do everything to keep you safe, even from afar." His hand reaches out, touching mine for a fleeting moment before the dreamscape pulls us apart.

Caius roars to the sky as they disintegrate before my eyes.

Then, the dreamscape shatters like glass, sending each of us spiraling back to our respective realities.

∼

Emeric

I LAND HEAVILY in the Underworld, the familiar yet unwelcoming aura of the realm enveloping me. Beside me, Azazel and Caius materialize, both wearing expressions of deep concern and frustration.

"We need a plan," Caius growls, pushing himself up. "We can't let her face Valtorious alone."

Azazel paces, his jaw set. "He'll torture her."

I stand, brushing off the remnants of the dreamscape. "Boys, I think it's time to prepare for war."

The three of us exchange a look, an agreement solidifying among us.

As we initiate our plan, the seriousness of our task hits me. Thinking of Morte alone in Romarie, subject to King Valtorious' rule, chills me. We're up against the clock and hidden enemies. But one thing's certain: we won't stop until we've brought her back, safe and sound. First, though, we've got to figure out how to get all of us into Romarie together.

CHAPTER FIFTY-THREE

WILDER

The heavy door of The Gilded Anvil groans on its hinges as I push it open, stepping into the dark entry of the tavern. The atmosphere is thick with the scents of ale and tobacco, mingling with the subtle undercurrents of tension and apprehension. I scan the room, my gaze cutting through the dimness, keeping each of my steps measured and deliberate.

My eyes lock onto a solitary figure in the back, unmistakably Aggonid. He looks like a god on his throne the way he lounges casually in his chair.

His presence fills the space around him, a silent assertion of power. His hair, a cascade of silver, is swept back, revealing the angular contours of his face. The harsh lighting plays across his skin, throwing the sharp angles of his cheekbones and jaw into relief. Even seated, he exudes an aura of authority, his posture effortlessly commanding.

If he's taken Morte from me ...

I stride towards him, my boots thudding softly on the worn floorboards. Each step feels laden with fury. As I approach, Aggonid's eyes flicker up to meet mine, a glint of silver in the dim room before he turns to High King Finian at my side.

"I wasn't expecting guests." The devil smirks, tapping his fingers on the tabletop.

I slide into the seat across from him. "Where's my anchor?" I clip.

He gives a bored look to Finian. "Really? Another one you want to trade for?" he says before turning his attention back to me, calculating.

"Have you taken Morte?" The High King asks.

This causes him to sit up, back straight as his head snaps back Finn. "What the fuck did you just say?" The revelation hits Aggonid like a physical blow, his devil-may-care façade shattering in an instant. His silver eyes blaze with a fury that sends a shiver down my spine. "You're telling me my soul bonded mate is missing?" he growls, the edge in his voice cutting through the hushed murmurs of the tavern.

I lean back, instinctively bracing myself against the raw power emanating from him. This isn't just the fae devil in a rage; this is a man consumed by the fear of losing his soul-bonded mate.

A large part of me is relieved we're both on the same team, but another huge part of me is shocked at his words.

She's not with him?

High King Finian maintains his composure but there's a flicker of concern in his eyes. "If you don't have her, we believe King Valtorious might have taken her," he says, his voice steady despite the tension crackling in the air.

Aggonid's fist slams down on the table, making the glasses rattle. "Valtorious?" he spits out the name like a curse. "If he has laid a finger on her ..."

His threat hangs in the air, unfinished but unmistakable in its intent. If he wanted to maintain the illusion he isn't the ruler of the Underworld, he's blown his cover now. He's unguarded and seething with a wrath that strangles the room with his power.

"We need to form a plan, Aggonid," Finian interjects, trying to steer his fury into action. "We can't just barge into Valtorious's stronghold without a strategy."

He glares at me, his anger momentarily redirected. "Who the fuck is this?" he snarls.

"Wilder." I narrow my eyes at him. "But you already knew that."

"That fish prick?"

I shove back from the table, getting into his face, feeling the oceans rise at my fury.

A deafening roar fills the room as every molecule of liquid surges and boils in a frenzy. Patrons scream and scramble for the exits, their instincts screeching at them to flee before they become part of the violent chaos unfolding before their eyes, as they feel the heat in their very blood. The air thickens with steam and fear as the room becomes a tsunami, ready to crash at any moment.

Finian intervenes, his tone calm but firm. "The fight belongs to both of you. Morte is as much connected to Wilder as she is to you. We need to work together. Now both of you sit the fuck down before all of Romarie's guards blow our cover."

The tension at our table is a live wire, but Aggonid's anger shifts, becoming something more focused. "Fine," he grinds out through clenched teeth. "Let's go get this fucker. It's about time I feel his heart in my hand and his blood staining my teeth."

We all know he means every word; the threat of his wrath a dark promise hanging in the air.

Before we can respond, Aggonid stands so abruptly his chair scrapes against the floor. "I'll start gathering intel from my contacts, and I've got to get her other mates from the Underworld. They need to be here for this. We'll meet back here at midnight." He strides out of the tavern, leaving a trail of uneasy whispers behind him.

I exchange a look with Finian as the enormity of our task settles heavily on us. Morte is out there, possibly in danger, and every moment we waste increases the risk to her. We need to act fast, and we need to be smart about it.

As I follow Finian out into the night, the streets of Romarie feel more ominous than ever. The city, a warren of metal and shadows, now holds the key to finding Morte. And I'll tear through every inch of it if that's what it takes to bring her back.

CHAPTER FIFTY-FOUR

MORTE

Trapped within the gilded cage of King Valtorious's castle, I pace the length of my luxurious prison. The room, though opulent, feels more like a beautifully adorned cell. Every inch of it screams wealth and power, from the plush velvet curtains to the intricately carved furniture. But none of it matters. I'm a prisoner, the knowledge of my captor's identity burning in my mind like a festering wound.

King Valtorious, my captor, the man whose twisted games now ensnare me, remains a shadow just beyond my reach. His presence looms over the castle like a malevolent specter, his eyes watching me from every corner, every whispering servant a potential spy.

I stop by the window, gazing out at the city of Romarie. The view, even though I know it's fabricated, is breathtaking, a sprawling landscape of metal and stone stretching out beneath a star-filled sky. But even this beauty can't mask the sense of dread that clings to the air like a thick fog.

My thoughts turn to my squadron in Bedlam. They have no idea where I am, and the frustration of being unable to reach out to them gnaws at me, because we've faced worse than this. I need to find a way to communicate, to let them know I'm here, in the belly of the beast.

Is this somehow connected to the sanguimetal we found on the beach on Draconum? What is his end game? Valtorious' threat against the realms have always been dismissed as the machinations of a mad king, but how much merit does it hold now?

He underestimates my resolve. I've faced darkness before, danced with the devil, made him claim me despite his reservations, and managed to survive in the end. This is just another test, another battle to fight.

We've beat him before.

If only I can just figure out how to get these damned cuffs off me. I turn away from the window, my mind racing with plans and possibilities. I sit at the desk, and the smooth surface is cold under my fingertips. There's an elegance to the room, a deceptive tranquility that belies the danger lurking just outside its walls. But I'm not fooled by the luxury. This room is a reminder of Valtorious's power, a symbol of his dominance. But it's also a place of solitude, a place where I can think, plan, and prepare for what's to come.

In the silence of the room, I close my eyes, centering myself, drawing on the strength that's always been my salvation. I think of my mates, and their love is a beacon in the darkness, guiding me, giving me the courage to face whatever lies ahead.

When the door finally opens, and Valtorious steps in, his smile all charm and deceit, I'm ready for him. I rise to meet him, my expression calm, my heart steady. I know the game he's playing, and I'm prepared to play it better.

He thinks he's captured a bird, but he's forgotten one thing. Phoenixes rise from the ashes. And I'm about to set his world on fire.

CHAPTER FIFTY-FIVE

MORTE

King Valtorious is dressed in finery befitting a monarch, his dark eyes gleaming with an unsettling mix of amusement and calculation. Despite the dread that courses through me, I stand tall, meeting his gaze with a composure born of necessity.

"Good evening, Morte." His voice is smooth, dripping with a charm that doesn't reach his eyes. "I trust your accommodations are to your liking?"

I mask my contempt with a neutral expression. "They're lavish, as expected from a king."

Valtorious smiles, a predator basking in the satisfaction of his catch. "I'm glad to hear it. Tonight, there's a celebration in the castle, and you'll be my honored guest."

The invitation is a thinly veiled command. I'm no guest here; I'm a prisoner, a pawn in whatever twisted game he's playing. But I can't afford to show weakness or fear. "A celebration?" I ask, feigning curiosity.

"Yes, a ball to commemorate our recent victories." His grin widens. "It will be an excellent opportunity for you to see the splendor of my realm."

I nod, understanding the unspoken message. This ball is a display of power, a show meant to intimidate and impress. Considering the last time Aggonid and I slain half his guard, I'm surprised he's keeping up the pretense of camaraderie. I've been to my fair share of balls in both Castanea and Bedlam proper, but I prefer to be soaring under open skies.

But for me, tonight is an opportunity to gather information, to find any weakness in Valtorious's armor.

As he turns to leave, he pauses at the door. "Wear something fitting for the occasion," he says, his eyes lingering on me for a moment longer before he departs.

The moment the door closes behind him, I let out the breath I've been holding. Tonight's ball isn't just a social event; it's a battlefield, and I need to be prepared.

I approach the wardrobe, opening it to reveal an array of dresses. Each one is more scandalous than the last, designed to ensnare and impress. I choose a gown that's a deep shade of midnight blue, its fabric shimmering like stars in the Bedlam sky. It's beautiful, yet functional, allowing for movement, should the need arise. It shows far too much skin for my liking, but at least I'll be agile in it.

After dressing quickly, I study my reflection in the mirror. The gown transforms me, but beneath the surface, I'm still the warrior, still the phoenix ready to rise. I add a few touches to ensure I'm not defenseless, concealing a small shiv I'd crafted by yanking apart the metal on the fireplace within the folds of my dress. It wasn't until I got my memories back that I'd even thought to do that. The last time I was here, Aggonid and I had stripped the room of all its metal.

I grasp the brass doorknob, eager to leave the room, but it's locked tight. With a sigh, I sink onto the small couch against the wall, my legs bouncing with nervous energy as I wait to be collected. Finally, a sharp knock echoes through the room and I follow the guard's brisk pace through winding corridors. My heart races as we approach the grand ballroom, knowing that tonight is not just a simple dance. It's a battle of wits and wills.

As I step into the opulent room, the scent of flowers and candle wax fills my nostrils, and a hush falls over the crowd. This isn't just a social event; it's a strategic game where every move counts.

Nobles and dignitaries from across Romarie mingle, their laughter and conversation a discordant melody against the backdrop of my own mission. I blend in, my demeanor poised and graceful, while my mind works overtime, analyzing every detail, every interaction.

I keep to the edges of the room, watching Valtorious as he moves among his guests, a king in his court, all while I'm flanked by guards. But I'm not deceived by the opulence and the façade of merriment. The tension in the air permeates the festivities. Valtorious is a master at masking his true intentions, but I can sense the undercurrents of fear and ambition that drive him.

As the evening progresses, I gather snippets of conversation, piecing together the politics and alliances within Valtorious's court. But the most critical piece of information remains elusive: how to escape this place and reunite with my mates.

And who the hell are the surprise guests people keep talking about?

While I'm busy hiding forks from the food table between the folds of my gown, a hand lands on my shoulder. I startle, fearing I've been caught, but when I turn around, it's just a guard jutting his chin towards the dais. He ushers me to the front to stand with King Valtorious.

It takes just seconds to work out why.

CHAPTER FIFTY-SIX

WILDER

The Romarie grand ballroom doors burst open with a resounding slam that echoes through the grand hall. I step into the opulent room, flanked by Aggonid, Caius, Emeric, High King Finian, High Queen Lana, and our formidable entourage. The scent of metal, perfume, floral arrangements, and candle wax is almost overpowering, but it's the sharp undercurrent of tension that truly fills the air.

The rhythmic thud of our march echoes through the grand hall, a deafening beat silencing even the most boisterous conversations. In an instant, all eyes are on us—the unexpected visitors from afar. The nobles and dignitaries from across Romarie stand frozen, their mouths agape as they take in our unexpected arrival. The once lively atmosphere, filled with peals of laughter and animated chatter, is now heavy with tension and unease. It's as if a storm has rolled in, casting a dark shadow over the room.

I survey the room, my gaze immediately locking onto Morte. She stands tall and regal near the raised platform, flanked by a pair of fierce guards who emanate an aura of unwavering loyalty. Despite the chaos erupting around her, her posture remains resolute and sure. Our eyes meet for a brief moment, a silent exchange of grief and understanding passing between us. We'd give anything to run into each other's arms.

She's a warrior now. She understands us running to save her is exactly what Valtorious wants.

But I see a sense of relief in her eyes, and I feel her express all the love she has for me through our bond.

∽

Aggonid

AMIDST THE SEA of shocked faces, my eyes seek the one who anchors my tumultuous soul to a semblance of peace. There she stands.

Morte.

My warrior, my fire, my heart's solid pulse.

Her posture is rigid, strong, but it's her eyes that betray the tumult within. A storm of emotions flows through our bond; the agony of separation, the joy of our reunion, the undying embers of our love. There are so many words I want to say to her.

I'm sorry, I love you, forgive me. Have me. Don't leave me.

The restraint it takes not to rush to her, to close the gap with a few desperate strides, is a battle as fierce as any I've fought. But in her eyes, I find my command. She signals to me to stay the course, her slight nod barely perceptible to others, yet to me, it roars louder than any command ever given.

In the fleeting exchange, a single tear betrays my stoic façade, a silent drop that I will away before it can fall. It's not the time for tears, not when every eye is upon us, gauging our every move for weakness. Yet, in the depths of me, where only she can see, my soul weeps with a relief so profound it borders on pain.

Her eyes barely scan the army we've brought, and in them, I find a flicker of pain when she realizes who is missing.

CHAPTER FIFTY-SEVEN

WILDER

King Valtorious, atop his dais, turns to face us, a smug smile playing on his lips. His confidence is infuriating, yet unsurprising. "Ah, the royal contingent of Bedlam," he announces, his voice booming across the hall. "What an unexpected honor. The fish is a surprise, too."

His tone drips with sarcasm, but it's his next words that send a chill down my spine. "I'm glad you're here, for I have a formal request. A peaceful takeover of the Underworld." His eyes flicker to Aggonid with a disdainful sneer. "Your current ruler is unstable, a monster who seizes power with no regard for consequences."

As King Valtorious declares his intention, the grand ballroom transforms into a theater of shocked reactions. Gasps echo through the room, a chorus of disbelief and alarm, as the crowd recoils from the audacity of his words.

The air crackles with a mixture of fear and intrigue, resonating with the raw power of his statement. Whispers spread like wildfire, each murmur a blend of speculation and concern. The faces of the gathered nobles and dignitaries mirror a canvas of emotions—from shock to sly calculations—as they digest the implications of his proposal.

A subtle shift occurs among the attendees, as if an unseen wave has passed through them, realigning the room's dynamics. Eyes dart from face to face, seeking allies or gauging adversaries in this new paradigm that Valtorious has boldly proposed.

The king's sneer towards Aggonid seems to ignite a silent battle of wills, a clash of loyalties and power.

Aggonid's jaw clenches, but he stays quiet, keeping his composure despite the fury I'm sure he's experiencing. The only giveaway are the shadows pouring off him, spilling onto the floor and curling around table legs and chairs as it infiltrates the room.

Valtorious continues, reveling in his moment. "Support the formal request I'll be making to the god's council for ascension. Aggonid is weak. His mate's sister decapitated him, for god's sake. And the worst of his failings? He doesn't even recognize when his realm is being infiltrated."

I stand firm, my focus on Morte. She's the key, the reason we're all here. As Valtorious' gaze sweeps over us, I can feel his scrutiny, his mind calculating the threat we pose.

Finian steps forward, his tenor calm but authoritative. "King Valtorious, this is a serious allegation. You speak of peace, yet you hold our ally against her will."

Valtorious laughs, a cold, humorless sound. "She's here as my guest. Morte is quite safe. Far better than where you had her," he sneers. "Prison? For your esteemed leader of the phoenix warriors?" He tsks.

The lie about her being a guest hangs heavy in the air, a blatant falsehood that none of us are buying. I exchange a glance with Aggonid; it's clear we need to tread carefully. Valtorious believes he holds all the cards, but he doesn't know our collective power.

Lana, her expression steely, adds, "Your definition of a guest seems to be at odds with reality, Valtorious. And Morte has been given a full pardon for her ... accident."

Morte's eyes turn towards mine, as if to gauge the truth of that statement. I give her a minute affirmation in the incline of my head. A surge of deep-seated relief flows through our bond, as though if she weren't in warrior mode, she'd crash to her knees and weep.

Nothing will keep us apart.

The Romarie king shrugs, unfazed by her words. "Semantics. The point is, I offer a solution to the chaos Aggonid has brought upon us all. Under my rule, the Underworld will know order and stability." He lifts his hands, motioning towards the crowd, as though to say, look at them. They all pay homage to me.

His words are met with nods from some of the nobles, but there's an underlying current of fear in their agreement. Valtorious has them under his thumb, their loyalty born of intimidation rather than respect.

A surge of anger builds inside me, but I keep it in check, knowing the stakes. This is not the time for rash actions. We need a plan, a way to turn the tables on Valtorious without endangering Morte or igniting a full-scale conflict.

The standoff continues, a silent battle of wills. Valtorious stands confident on his dais, believing he's in control. But he's underestimated the bond between us, the strength that comes from unity.

It's then that I realize the weight of this moment. We're not just here to rescue Morte. We're here to dismantle the tyranny that Valtorious represents, to free not only her but also the people of Romarie from his grasp.

As the tension in the room builds, I know that this is just the beginning. And as I glance once more at Morte, I see the fire in her eyes, the implicit promise that we'll rise from this challenge stronger than ever. Together, we'll bring an end to Valtorious's reign of terror, freeing the people under his oppressive rule, and in its ashes, we will allow them to build a future of their choosing.

And I'll have her back by my side where she belongs.

CHAPTER FIFTY-EIGHT

AZAZEL

Dread.

It crawls up my spine, rooting me to the spot from across the room where I watch King Valtorious wrap his arm around my mate, tugging her into his side. Revulsion colors her features. She doesn't speak, but I can feel the calculation through the bond, eyes cataloguing the room as she seeks all avenues to put an end to this.

I know she can feel the absolute horror from me, but she can't see me, not yet. But soon, she'll know everything.

"Come on out," he declares.

In the charged silence of the ballroom, King Valtorious' voice booms with a declaration that roots me to the spot, a proclamation heavy with implication.

The command slices through the façade I've maintained for millennia. A shudder ripples through me, a mix of dread and anger, as the murmurs of the crowd swell into a crescendo of whispers and gasps. Their eyes, wide with speculation, fixate on me, dissecting my every reaction.

I take a step forward, feeling the weight of every gaze. The sea of faces parts, creating a path that leads to an inevitable truth I've fought to keep from Morte. Each step is heavier than the last, a march towards the unraveling of a carefully woven web of lies. I can't tear my eyes away from her, from my mate, whose expression is a mirror of the horror clawing its way up my throat. Her eyes, those deep wells of strength I've drawn from, now reflect a betrayal that cuts deeper than any weapon.

I want to reach out, tell her this changes nothing about who I am nor who we are to each other, but the words are shackles I cannot break. As I draw closer to the dais, to the man who claims me as his blood, the air thickens with the weight of a thousand words. My chest tightens, a silent plea for understanding, for forgiveness I dare not voice aloud.

My father's voice booms, resonating with a sense of triumph. "Glad you could make it. Your journey among the dead ends tonight. Welcome home, son."

CHAPTER FIFTY-NINE

MORTE

My carefully constructed façade of indifference crumbles, and I crash to my knees, my heart shattering at the figure stalking forward through the parted crowd. A keening wail claws up my throat, the slice of betrayal too much to bear.

He's my mate.

My mate.

My fucking mate!

A well of grief surges through my bond, along with anger, rage, and betrayal—all coming from my other mates.

Azazel's wings, immense and ethereal, ripple behind him, radiating with an otherworldly glow. The tips of his feathers, glowing like molten silver, trail behind him as he walks. His hair, black as the night, falls in perfect waves around his fierce, beautiful face. His eyes, deep blue flames, meet mine, and in them, I see a storm of emotions. Conflict, sorrow, love.

He steps forward, his presence commanding the room. Azazel, who whispered to me once in the darkness of the Underworld, *"You can't trust anyone here. Least of all me."*

The revelation hits me like a physical blow. He was a spy. Valtorious's son. All this time, the man I loved, the man who I thought was my only ally in the darkness, had been playing a role. My world shatters around me, the pieces of my heart breaking with it.

As he approaches the dais, I go weak, my palms hitting the cold, hard floor with a thud. The impact is nothing compared to the agony that rips through my soul.

Around me, the room fades into a blur, the voices and faces melting into insignificance. All I can see is Azazel, his figure now standing beside Valtorious, his father.

The words he once said echo in my mind, a haunting reminder of the truth I refused to see. *"Least of all me."* The irony of it all is a bitter pill to swallow. The man who saved me, who loved me, was the very embodiment of the deceit and treachery I'd been fighting against.

As I raise my gaze to meet his, betrayal rips through me like a knife, leaving behind a gaping wound that will never heal. How could he? How could he crush my heart so callously?

In this moment, as I kneel on all fours on the floor of Valtorious's dais, my heart breaking into a thousand pieces, I realize the true extent of the web of lies and deception that have ensnared me, and it fractures the very essence of what I thought was love. The pieces of a sinister puzzle fall into place. Each tender moment, every secret shared in the sanctity of darkness, was it all a ruse? A calculated step by Azazel to serve his father's vile ambitions? The thought is a venom seeping into my veins, poisoning every memory with suspicion.

The agony of this thought constricts around my heart, squeezing until it feels like it might burst. I gaze upon Az, the majestic and powerful figure he cuts, and a bitter laugh escapes me, mirthless and sharp. He's promised me eternity, but was it all a façade? My love, my confidant, my mate. Is he the architect of my undoing? Of *all* our undoing? His role in this twisted plot to weaken Aggonid by binding me to him, by sharing a mate's mark, unveils the darkest betrayal.

Could it be that the intensity of his gaze, which once spoke volumes of a love that defied the ages, was but the glare of a master manipulator? Did his lips, which claimed mine with such fervor, whisper lies as sweet as the kisses he bestowed? The questions claw at me, each one a spike driving deeper into my soul.

I struggle for breath as sobs rack my frame. Had my devotion been a pawn in his game all along? His proximity to the king, the man who claims him as a son, feels like a mockery of the bond we shared. The room is charged with the musk of deceit, and the chill of isolation wraps around me, a cold shroud for the warmth that once was.

I seek out his gaze, imploring, searching for a sliver of truth in the chaos of my thoughts. But the connection that once was a beacon now is a mirage, leaving me to drown in the sea of duplicity. As the crowd's murmurs rise like a distant storm, I'm adrift, alone, betrayed not just by my lover, but by my own heart that refuses to let go of the love that may have never been mine to hold.

As the world around me fades to black, the last thing I see is his tormented face, filled with a sorrow as deep as my own.

TBC

Morte's entire world has been shattered. The first man she'd fallen in love with in the Underworld is the architect of her greatest betrayal. As she grapples with the truth of his deception, the stakes have never been higher. With war knocking on the door of the castle she's held captive in, can she fight back against the forces that seek to control both her destiny and the fates of all the realms?

FIND out in A Realm of Grief and Sorrow (Aggonid's Realm Book 3).

ACKNOWLEDGMENTS

Dearest Reader,

I know you're really mad at me right now. But Az did warn you, didn't he? *Least of all me.*

Now there are two mates who need to do a whole lot of groveling to make up for the absolute clusterfuck they've made of Morte's heart. In time, my dears, in time. I don't think I made y'all cry as much in this one, unfortunately. I do try, though.

As always, you and I are in this weird little codependent relationship. I write because the stories demand it, but I continue to write because your words of affirmation literally breathe life into them. Your breaths become gales, and these stories would be nothing if it weren't for your love. Am I exposing my praise kink?

Maybe a little.

So thank you, **reader**. I'll mend your wounded little heart in the conclusion of this story, which I hope to have published by August. I can't make those promises, though, because I'm finding it causes me a lot of stress. I prefer to deliver a great story versus one hobbled together while a pre-order deadline breathes down my neck.

I haven't been shy about my history of struggles with mental health, and I got really burnt out last year, which is why I didn't move this preorder date sooner like I had planned. Burn out can take literal years to recover from. Coupled with my health (hey, fellow zebras and spoonies, I see you!), I need to be mindful of my own limitations.

I need to thank my **family**, who've endured eighteen hour days of me in my writing cocoon because the words just couldn't stop flowing. AD/HD is like that, so I've got to wrangle that flow when I can.

In particular, Leo has yet again helped me out of a tight spot. You might've noticed a difference in the cover between the first and second book. My original cover artist couldn't continue the series because of her health, and so I defaulted back to my trusty teen, who's now in college for graphic design. They absolutely blew it out of the water, yet again. I gave them my very meticulously planned-out cover that I made in Canva, to which they promptly responded, "Ma, you suck at color composition." Sigh. I know. But look how beautiful they made it in the end?

And Jess, my editor, who probably is questioning my sanity after reading chapter fifty-two. The comment she made in the margins of the document said, "That's … niche." Ah. Yes, dark romance readers are a bit of a different breed, yeah? She also found Caius' copper butt plugs "interesting." :) *insert chuckle* Thanks a million for my tight deadlines, you're really a wizard.

I have a bajillion and one people to thank, who've helped make me a better writer, or a better marketer, or who held my hand when I was knee-deep in the trenches, stressed about the direction I wanted to take things in my manuscript. Maggie Stiefvater, Bobby Kim, Britt Andrews, Becca Syme, Quell, PJ, and about a hundred others I'm probably forgetting.

Until next time, friends.

XOXO

Kathy Haan

ABOUT THE AUTHOR

As a blood descendant of literary greats like Jane Austen and Emily Dickinson, and from a long line of artists and creators, #1 bestselling author Kathy Haan believes that the secret to telling a great story is living one. The second youngest, in a massive horde of children between her parents, she did her best to gain attention and kept everyone entertained with jokes and wild stories.

She lives a life of adventure with her hunky husband, three children, and Great Pyrenees in the Midwest, United States. While this is her eighth book, you might've seen her work in Forbes or Fortune, where she's a regular contributor. Or, in Notoriety Network's 12x international award-winning documentary, #SHEROproject.

ALSO BY KATHY HAAN

Bedlam Moon Trilogy (Complete)

Lana sets out to find the truth about her past, and when a hot vampire begins to unravel it for her, she's caught up in the web of an evil cult, prophecies, and curses. All while falling for the King of Vampires and his royal court. This is a why choose romance.

Bedlam Moon (Book One)

Tales of Bedlam (Book Two)

Wicked Bedlam (Book Three)

Fae Academia Series (Incomplete, 8 planned)

A spin-off of the Bedlam Moon Trilogy, we follow Lana's daughter, Rose, while she attends a magical university. The summer before college is perfect until the family begins to receive threats, and Rose ends up getting into a different college from her twin brother and her boyfriend. A male roommate, his hot friends, and a sexy professor all find themselves eager to win her affection. This is a why choose romance.

Bedlam Academy (Book One)

Arcane Scholar (Book Two, May 2023)

Forbidden Rose (Book Three, ETA Q2 2024)

Aggonid's Realm Series (Incomplete)

A Realm of Fire and Ash (Book One)

A Realm of Dreams and Shadows (Book Two)

A Realm of Grief and Sorrow (Book Three, TBA Q3 2024)

When the commander of an elite group of phoenixes ends up dead for real, she tries to convince the fae devil there's been a huge mistake. Can she convince him to let her go before he snags her heart? This is an enemies to lovers why choose romance.

Fae Gods (Incomplete)

Fae Gods (April 2023)

Fae Guardians (TBA)

They watched their charge her entire life, completely invisible to her and only intervening when necessary. When they get fed up with her miserable marriage, Jocelyn's fae god watchers decide to help. After all, no fae of royal lineage deserves to be left to wilt away on Earth. They devise a plan to reveal their true selves to her, calling themselves the Marriage Doctors. But what happens when, during the course of their live-in lessons, the infallible gods fall for their off-limits charge? This is a why choose romance.

Bedlam Penitentiary (Incomplete)

Bedlam Penitentiary (ETA end of Q4 2024)

At the most ruthless prison in the fae realm, you're either at the top of the magical food chain, or you've got to form alliances with those with the most power. Because at a prison where you must expend your magic or you'll die, it's a no man's land full of dangerous criminals. This is a why choose romance.

PREVIEW OF BEDLAM MOON

CHAPTER ONE

Time is a funny thing. The worst moment of my life is so fresh in my memory, but twenty-six years is an entire lifetime to be away from her. I was eight years old when she vanished. Long enough to remember her, but not long enough to hang on to the details.

There's a sign outside the entrance to the long, overgrown driveway that leads to the cabin. It reads, *NO TRE3PA33ING* with inverted S's. Below the sign is a little alien ship attacking Earth, although I'm not sure how ominous any would-be trespassers think it is.

I turn my Jeep off of the main logging road and drive down the gravel entrance, which snakes around giant pine trees and wildflowers. Weeds grow amongst the rocks, cracking them apart and taking their place. After the last set of evergreens, the vegetation grows thin and the driveway opens up into a clearing in front of the cabin. The old place sits on a hill overlooking a small pond that ripples in the early summer breeze.

My hands shake involuntarily as I pull the Jeep next to the cedar log cabin. The old beams of sunlight stream through the branches of the pines and oaks, creating an oasis of light in a patchwork of darkness. I place the vehicle in park and shut off the engine. *So many years.* I slide my trembling hands under my thighs in an attempt to steady them and lean against the headrest before closing my eyes.

I thought I'd never come back here again, let alone find the place, but somehow my heart knew the way. The police tape around the weather-warped porch has faded to a warm, soft yellow color reminiscent of a baby chick.

This is where I last saw Mom.

She went out to catch breakfast at the little bluegill-stocked pond on our property. She hadn't returned by the time I woke up, so I went to look for her. The fish was good that time of year, and she wanted to fry up a batch of fresh fish cakes for dinner that night. Her fishing pole and tackle box sat next to her chair, but she wasn't there. They never found my mom, and with no dad around, they sent me to foster care.

Now I'm back at the place where my entire world fell apart.

But there's a bud of hope blooming in my chest when I open my eyes and turn my gaze to the small brown package, still untouched, sitting on my front passenger seat.

Whenever I'm traveling the world, my best friend Hannah receives mail for me and lets me know what bills I have. When she got this package, she forwarded it to the concierge at the Minneapolis airport so I could fly back from the Amazon and see if this leads me to more clues at the cabin.

When I relax my hands and slow my breathing, I reach for the box and place the parcel on my lap. After taking a few deep breaths—like my former therapist taught me—I use the Jeep key to pierce the packing tape Hannah placed around it. I pull out the white slip of paper and worry my lip while reading the scrawling print.

Lana,

I'm sorry I didn't send this to you sooner. This was

in your mother's things, and Annabelle would want you to have it now.
Love,
D

The handwriting is unfamiliar. I set the mysterious letter on my seat and unfold the cream-colored tissue paper at the bottom of the box. Nestled within it is the key that Hannah told me about. The new key in my hand is strange; its handle a deep, dark metal with a pattern of blue and red gemstones embedded in the surface, too many to count. It almost seems to vibrate with energy, ricocheting through my limbs.

Not an ordinary key, indeed.

I turn it over in my hand and trace the intricate details with my finger. Tilting my head back against the headrest, I vaguely remember my mom having a similar key, but this isn't hers.

I remember little about hers, other than its weight and the pearly sheen that glimmered in the light. When I had friends over, we'd spark our imaginations, dreaming up stories of how her key could open any door in any house. Mom wasn't too keen on my fascination with it and would insist I be gentle with it.

Now, I have a similar key of my own, but who sent it? An array of small, vibrant blue and red gems adorns the entire handle. There are far too many to count, and I have a strange suspicion these might not be ordinary gems.

Palming the key in my hand, I grab my backpack from the floor of the passenger seat and toss the letter, box, and tissue paper inside. Stepping out of the Jeep, my gaze lands on the aged humble abode I spent every summer in during my youth. After twenty-six years of neglect, the wood is weathering, and a pang of guilt hits my stomach that I haven't been back to look after the place.

I grip the police tape and ball it up before shoving it into my jacket pocket, cursing as thunder cracks in the distance. I look up. The sky is blue, but along the horizon, storm clouds threaten to drop a lot of rain.

I cup my hand over my eyes as I peer into the glass on the wooden door. Inside the cabin everything is just as it was when I left it; in the kitchen is an oak table where my mom and I would roll out dough for biscuits. One of the legs is a little shorter than the others and makes a wobbling sound when you rest your elbows on it. Part of me thought Mom did that on purpose so I wouldn't.

Standing back from the door again, I eye the keyhole, slightly larger than a dime. The door is a dark green, with a large brass knob in the center. I've come too far not to try it.

I position the key against the hole, not sure if it will fit. The key feels warm and tingles in my hand. What is happening?

A black barrel sprouts from the bottom of the keyhole and darts around like an insect. It starts to spin faster and faster, like a drill bit, the sound of metal sliding against metal. Just as quickly as it began, it stops, exhaling a puff of smoke and leaving a hole large enough for me to fit my pinky finger through. I glance around the property in disbelief, wondering how someone pulled such an elaborate prank on me. And *why*?

At first, the key doesn't look like it will fit. I push on it anyway, and the bit shrinks and slides into the keyhole perfectly. I turn the key, and it rotates smoothly in my hand as the door unlocks. I push the door open, and it creaks with almost thirty years of disuse.

No ordinary key, indeed, I think again before placing it in my jacket pocket.

With my hand on the doorknob, I step over the threshold and close the rustic, wooden door behind me as I take in my familiar surroundings. It's like stepping into a time capsule: the worn pine floorboards, the fieldstone fireplace with lopsided cinder blocks for hearthstones, and the red and purple oval rug made from old t-shirts draped in front of it. On particularly chilly nights, I'd fall asleep on the rug while playing with my dolls. By morning, my mom had scooped me up and placed me in bed.

I glance over at the kitchen. The old oak table that had been covered in so much spilled food and craft projects as a child is still here, and the cabinet with glass doors is still above it. Inside there are all my old school photos, ribbons, and medals.

I step over to my rocking chair and stare at the ashes in the hearth, long cold, as a melancholic ache crushes my chest. In front of the fireplace is my white stuffed gorilla I named Kongo after watching it in theaters. Thinking back on it, I was far too young to see it, but Mom let me anyway. She'd given this to me when I got my tonsils and adenoids taken out. It kept me company through many late-night bedtime stories, where she'd read me R.L. Stine books until I was old enough to read them myself. All of my Barbie dolls are still stacked next to it in an unceremonious heap.

The cabin isn't huge but it's big enough for two people; a tiny kitchen, a Queen-sized bed, a twin-sized bed, and a couple of rocking chairs placed in front of the fireplace along the opposite wall.

The entire property is off-grid, and there are still a few logs in the holder next to the fireplace, but I will need to gather some more firewood if I plan on being comfortable tonight. This far North, thunderstorms can often welcome evenings just on this side of cold. After bringing in the rest of my bags and the supplies, I look for the ax we kept here for chopping wood and I find it in our tall cabinet in the kitchen.

Walking outside, a dark gray rain jacket on, and new hiking boots squeaking on the soggy overgrown path that wraps around the cabin, I make a mental note to clean the leaves off it in the morning.

In the shed I find protective glasses and a splitting wedge, which will make my job a lot easier. With the storm headed this way, I don't have much time to get the job done. I'm happy to find a felled black walnut tree nearby. Mom always hated them, and not because they dropped huge green husks that fell from them and clogged up our push mower.

I spend forty-five minutes chopping wood, resting on my knees every thirty seconds. It's the same thing I do when I travel so people don't see me huffing and puffing while climbing the hills of Riomaggiore. Only then, I turn around and snap pictures so it looks like I'm meaning to stop, and not just out of breath.

So, I might be a little more than out of shape.

The sky darkens until it's difficult to tell when one log splits into two, and that's when I give myself permission to stop. The first of the raindrops hit my cheeks, helping cool my overheated skin. Exhaustion takes over me after the back-breaking labor and carrying the split logs into the cabin to nestle in the wood holder next to the fireplace. I contemplate heading straight to bed, but a rumble in my stomach warns me otherwise.

I didn't know how hungry I was until I smell the smoky, spiced scent that now tickles my nostrils. I follow the odor around the side of the cabin, straining to find the source of the smell. And then I whip my head up when I hear the crunch of gravel out front.

As I approach the front of the cabin, I spy a tall, shadowy figure stalking up the driveway, and I freeze mid-stride. Ice bubbling to the surface of my blood, I stand still, like a deer caught in the sights of a predator, more afraid than I've ever been. I'm in the middle of nowhere, and the fading light of day, coupled with the storm right near us, gives the area an ominous feel.

Who on Earth is here?

"I'm sorry for frightening you, *Sahira*." He has an accent that I can't quite place, and his voice is like liquid honey.

"Who … who are you?" I fumble to turn on the flashlight on my phone.

I point the beam of light at the figure, slowly closing the gap between us. In front of me is a man built like a granite mountain, and I glance around for any sign of another person.

The second I determine he's alone, my eyes lock onto him, drinking in every detail as if my life depended on it—and it might—his jet-black hair resting across his forehead, terra cotta skin, and dark eyelashes that frame striking blue eyes, like gemstones caught in the light of the setting sun.

He appears to be in his early thirties, his complexion flawless enough to pass for a professional model on any magazine cover. Paired with his tailored suit, so at odds with the Northern woods, he appears as though someone plucked him from the pages and deposited him in my path.

My heart thrashes in my chest at the intensity radiating from his gaze. Raw emotion flashes across his face, as though I were the answer to every question, prayer, and hope he's ever had. I feel undressed in front of him, like my soul is laid bare before him and he cradles it carefully in his hands. I'm overpowered by a flood of emotions so powerful I can barely breathe.

I should be afraid and curse myself for leaving my ax by the chopping block. Instead, I continue to freeze where I'm at, staring far longer than is acceptable for a first encounter.

The man standing before me is more than just beautiful. He's exquisite. My mouth hangs open slightly as I take in his well-defined arms hidden underneath his tight two-piece suit, his lean waist, and the way his strong legs take root in the ground below him. He must be well over six feet, and his broad shoulders hold a confidence I don't feel right now.

My eyes travel to his face. He has a dark, sun-drenched look to him that makes me think he's from the Middle East, although his blue eyes suggest I might not understand what the hell I'm talking about.

Is he an investigator? Did Hannah let them know about the box I received?

The corners of his mouth curl up, revealing a brilliant straight set of teeth, radiating kindness. Like a warm embrace, I'm overcome with a feeling of peace, one I don't fully understand. How could his smile be so captivating and comforting? Was it the soft twinkle in his eye or the slight curve of his lips? I'm aware I should be afraid, but instead, I feel a strange sense of safety, especially as the intensity in his eyes fades.

I angle my body toward the man on the driveway, giving a little wave as I push my long, tangled hair behind my ears. My rain jacket hangs open, and that's when I notice my oversized t-shirt and black leggings are covered in dust and small bits of wood. I desperately need a shower and my muscles ache from chopping wood. I should run for the ax, not get lost in this stranger's eyes.

"I'm Osgood Finlandian, but you can call me Oz. I own a cabin down the road and thought I'd check out the place after I drove by and saw tire tracks leading here. No one's been here in a good twenty-five years, so I wanted to make sure people weren't breaking in."

Twenty-five years? While true, the man in front of me can't be over thirty-five or forty. I don't recall any other kids living nearby when I was little. Unless you count the occasional family staying at the campgrounds between here and the entrance to the forest.

"Thanks for looking in on the place. I'm Lana Chapman-Sawyer. This is my cabin, but I haven't been here since I was a kid." I'm still wary of the stranger in front of me.

"Ah, okay." He runs a hand through his thick, jaw-length hair. "You're the woman whose mom disappeared here ... I'm sorry."

And there it is—the inevitable moment when people remember the scared little girl whose mom vanished. My stomach flip-flops at the idea that this beautiful stranger knows about the absolute worst event of my entire life. It broke me, and I've spent the rest of my life trying to find the pieces again.

"Yeah," I absentmindedly toe gravel at my feet. "I was eight when she disappeared. I'm back to piece together what might have happened to her." No sense in hiding the story; he already knows it.

Everyone did.

"Would you like some help? My family has owned a lot of this forest for several centuries, and I don't think there's another person alive who can navigate these woods better than I do."

I think about that for a moment, digesting Oz's offer, and consider the odds. Investigators spent years trying to figure out what happened to Mom, to no avail, so I could use the help. Besides, despite being startled when Oz first arrived, I believe I can trust this man. My intuition has never steered me wrong before.

"Actually, that would be great. Thank you. Uh ... I'd invite you in, but I haven't settled in yet, and I'm still trying to find my bearings." Glancing at the storm, I wince. The nice thing would be to invite him in, especially as the rain picks up, but I'm still hesitant.

While I don't have a lot of belongings, my stuff litters the table and both of the beds. I'm also very certain that the bra I'd taken off and flung across the room as soon as I got in the cabin is on full display somewhere on the floor. With that realization, I throw my arms over my chest and zip my jacket.

Oz averts his eyes. "Not a problem, Lana. Would you like to come over to my place, and we can map out a game plan? I've got a hot shower. You can freshen up while I make us something to eat. You've had a long day from the looks of it."

Ouch. Was he admitting I look like shit? Despite my embarrassment over my disheveled state, the idea of being close to him stirs up something inside me.

"I'd kill for a hot shower, thank you. Let me grab a few things really quick." I start walking away but hesitate, turning back to meet his gaze. "Just wait here, okay?"

He inclines his head, and I pivot on one leg before bolting up the creaking porch steps to the cabin, taking them two at a time. Adrenaline courses through me as I slip on the top step, and in a horrifying second, I stumble. My arms stretch outward, desperate for something to grab onto, but instead of the unforgiving ground, my hands meet those of a stranger. He catches me as I trip, his muscled arms holding me steady. His skin is cold, but his touch sears through me like fire, blazing a path through my chest before pooling low in my belly.

Oz helps right me, and I dust myself off. He saves my dignity and doesn't say a word. Mortified, I run into the cabin to grab my stuff, and after shutting the door, I shrink down against it.

Well, that was freaking embarrassing.

I collect myself against the door, but then I remember Oz is still waiting outside for me, so I dart across the room, grabbing clean clothes and some toiletries. I pause my hand over my makeup bag and consider whether I should bother putting on makeup after I shower.

He's seen me at my worst, and it is late in the evening. I don't want him thinking that I'm trying to impress him.

I mean, I *am* trying to impress him, but I don't want him actually *knowing* that.

Who am I kidding? Of course I'm going to put makeup on. Sure, he's probably not interested, but I can always bring my best self, right? Maybe this man likes thick chicks, and we'll spend the evening rutting in the woods.

A wicked grin crosses my face, and I grab the makeup bag and toss it in my backpack. *Careful, Oz; I'm a man-eater when I have my hair and makeup done.* With that thought still on my mind, I exit the cabin, locking the door behind me.

A grin spreads across Oz's face, and his two eyebrows rise in unison. "All set?"

The air between us is perfumed sweet with a hint of spice and vanilla, so I take a deep breath through my nose before I respond. Perhaps it's the wildflowers at the side of the house.

I give him a nod, and we start down the long driveway. Now that I'm side-by-side with Oz, a breeze sends another aroma up my nose of Earth and elemental, which is likely the storm that seems to be holding out on us. I can't help but take a deep breath to inhale more.

As the leaves and gravel crunch beneath our feet, I gaze down at Oz's leather shoes. Why is he dressed so nicely out here? They're huge and had to have cost more than my entire outfit combined.

"Size fifteen." Oz quirks an eyebrow at me.

I glance down at my boots. "I thought I had big feet."

He smirks. "Where were you before you came back to the cabin?"

Do I explain that after my adoptive parents died, I had an early mid-life crisis and sold everything I owned so I could escape and travel the world? That, since then, I've traveled through much of Europe, Central, and South America, hitching rides on boats and buses and clinging to the sides of trucks? I'm not sure if he's ready for that level of crazy yet. Instead, I tell him about South America.

"I was traveling in Colombia for a bit, and I stayed near Leticia in the Amazon Rainforest, right off the Amazon River."

"I spent a lot of time in that area, so I'm familiar with the Amazon. ¿Habla Español?"

"No. I took Spanish, but I remember little. Are you fluent?"

"I speak a few languages, and I've done a lot of traveling. I have business dealings all over the world."

As a free-spirited person, I feel even more inadequate learning those things about Oz, and I can only imagine what he thinks of me now. The gal who got an MBA only to give up a lucrative corporate job in pursuit of adventure.

The rain starts, and I pull my hood up. Oz plucks a black umbrella out of the inside pocket of his coat. We continue small talk and walk another half mile, wedged together under his umbrella until we reach the entrance to his cabin's driveway. He starts up the pavement, and I follow suit, but there's no cabin in view at all, although I spy light through the trees. My nerves stir a little.

"It's about a quarter-mile walk. Are you going to be alright?" He eyes my obviously brand-new, never-been-scuffed-before hiking boots.

I tell him to press on, although my heels are chafing.

Eventually, the "cabin" comes into view. The only word that comes close to describing this place is "compound." His definition of cabin and my definition of cabin differ wildly. His definition is grand, mine simple; he focuses on what you can see, I on what you cannot but feel.

The jack pine trees standing between me and the lodge-like building are so tall that I can't see their canopy in the dark. Each window of the place is at least twenty feet high, and a single door—just as big—sits at the front.

It's beautiful, and it fits him. Though, the idea of Oz living here, alone, in this seclusion doesn't make sense to me. Where are his friends? His family? If anything, it stirs a deep sadness in my chest.

Is he alone, too?

Embarrassed, Oz admits he got a little carried away when designing the place.

His cabin is resplendent in forest green with warm wooden beams. I step back and crane my neck to take it all in. The wood is stained a deep oak color, and the roof is made of cedar, which softens the security lights that filter through the trees. Scents of dirt and moss tickle my nose.

I can't breathe, can't think of anything but the big, lonely home in front of me. Yes, it's warm and inviting, but are the halls hollow and free of the pitter patter of little feet? Do the walls hold a lifetime of memories, or secrets of sorrow, too?

The wooden front door and the window frames, even the roof beams look as if they've been whittled by hand. Understanding dawns on me now. Each and every square inch of this place is meticulously crafted, with a heart and an artisan's soul. Details I'd been too naïve to notice now come alive. From the driveway, this place is foreboding and a little cold. But up close? At the heart of it?

This is Oz.

My feet carry me up the stairs, and my heart places me somewhere I never thought I'd be again—home.

Wait, *home*? I shake my head. What the hell is wrong with me? I don't know this man, nor have I ever been inside his home. And I definitely didn't know this place sat right next door until today.

He holds the door open. "After you."

As I step inside, a cool gust of wind rushes through the side of my hair, billowing it back. Oz steps around me and takes my jacket from me, and places it in a closet near the front door. A glow of firelight warms the cold moisture off the marble floor as I step in.

I am at his *house*. This is a *big* house, but I can feel the warmth from the decor, which echoes sentiments of an old world gone by. A vintage chandelier, its beaded chain dripping with crystals, hangs from the vaulted ceiling and casts light upon the entry. All around the walls hang artwork, its curator one with a unique eye for the past and how it could inform the present.

My eye catches a painting across the foyer, and I step closer to capture a better look at the artwork. The painting is of a curvy woman, dressed in nothing but a sheer blanket draped around her ample bosom and tiny waist. My face heats at the signature in the bottom right corner of the canvas—*O. Finlandian,* painted in big loopy swoops.

He painted this woman, stroke by stroke, with such passion she seems to come alive under his brush.

Lucky girl. I pull at my filthy shirt, feeling like an intruder in my dirty clothes, and ask Oz to show me to the bathroom so I can shower.

He walks me past the expansive kitchen, where I inhale the smells of baking bread, up the wooden stairs, and down to the bathroom at the end of the hallway. It has a standalone, deep jetted tub along one wall and a marble-tiled walk-in shower along the other.

Oz flicks on the towel warmer and sets a very fluffy bath sheet along the top bar. "Do you want a towel for your hair, too?"

He must spend a lot of time around long-haired women, but probably not enough time around curly-haired ones. "No thanks. Because I have curly hair, I usually wrap it in a t-shirt to dry."

At that, he inclines his head, leaves the room, and returns with one of his t-shirts.

"Oh, you don't have to … "

"I insist." He extends his arm towards me, the t-shirt clutched in his hand.

I reluctantly take his shirt from him and set it on top of the towel, giving my thanks. He leaves the room, and I lock the door.

Foolish to be here, in a stranger's house using their shower, but let's not push it by leaving the door unlocked. I won't make it easier for him to murder me.

After undressing, I pick up his shirt, hold it up to my face, and inhale deeply. *It was him earlier;* that intoxicating aroma of earth, vanilla, spice, and an elemental sort of scent reminding me of thunderstorms.

My mind races with a million questions. What kind of crazy am I, drawn to a stranger like this? I want to trust him, but at the same time, he has that irresistible charm that all the women in true crime documentaries fall for. Still, he has a lovely Burberry-scented body and a face that could make even an angel cry.

Or sin.

Those pants of his hug his sculpted thighs so tightly, and I'd be a fool to not be attracted to him. I wonder if he's as into me as I am him?

Gods help me.

Get Bedlam Moon here.

Printed in Poland
by Amazon Fulfillment
Poland Sp. z o.o., Wrocław